KU-272-283

SIMON TOYNE

Dark Objects

HarperCollins*Publishers*

HarperCollins*Publishers*
1 London Bridge Street,
London SE1 9GF

HarperCollins*Publishers*
Macken House, 39/40 Mayor Street Upper,
Dublin 1, D01 C9W8, Ireland

www.harpercollins.co.uk

This paperback edition 2023
1
First published by HarperCollins*Publishers* 2022

A catalogue record for this book is available from the British Library

ISBN: 978-0-00-755170-5

Typeset in Sabon LT Std by Palimpsest Book Production Limited,
Falkirk, Stirlingshire

Printed and Bound in the UK using 100% Renewable
Electricity at CPI Group (UK) Ltd

This book is produced from independently certified FSC™ paper
to ensure responsible

For more information visit: www.harpercollins.co.uk/green

For my mother and father,
For bringing me up in a house full of books

SIMON TOYNE

Dark Objects

I

THE MILLER HOUSE

1

Monday morning. Seven thirty.

Celia Barnes unlocks the door to the Miller house for what will be her last time.

She does not know, as she fits the stubby security key into the lock, that in a few short hours it will be bagged and logged along with several other items from the house as pieces of evidence in a murder investigation.

But he knows.

He watches her in his rear-view mirror, watches her turn the key, watches her lean against the heavy door to open it. He is parked down the hill, as close as he can get without parking illegally but far enough away to avoid the steady gaze of the two security cameras fixed high on the front of the house.

The Miller house lies hidden behind a double-height section of brick that blends in with the soot-blackened wall running the length of Swain's Lane and separating it from Highgate Cemetery beyond. The only indication that anything other than trees, and tombs, and dead Londoners lie on the other side of this higher section of brick is a large square of opaque glass set into the top left corner, and the solid door fitted flush to the wall and painted dark grey to match the sooty brickwork.

Celia Barnes steps through the door now, disappearing into the wall like it's a trick, and she's part of a performance, which – in a sense – she is.

He watches the door close behind her, slow and heavy on its automatic closers, like the door to an old-fashioned bank vault where treasures and secrets are kept.

He checks the time then slips a surgical mask over his face. It was not so long ago that anyone wearing a mask in public, especially a medical one, would have drawn attention. Now they were commonplace, a fact that had been extremely useful over the last few months.

He steps out of the car, fastening his coat against the morning damp as he heads away from the Miller house and down the hill towards one of the gates leading into the cemetery. Official opening hours are ten to four, but he picked the lock earlier and will lock it again when he leaves – the gate that leads to the cemetery, the cemetery that leads to the back of the Miller house.

His heart beats faster as he walks, but he forces himself to go slowly, to take his time. Afterwards, when blue-and-white police tape ribbons the house, questions will be asked and someone might remember a man in a hurry. And he has plenty of time. He knows Celia's routine, knows which rooms she will clean first and how long she will spend in each. At this moment he knows as much about Celia Barnes as she does herself, more even, because he can also see her future – he knows what will happen to her next, though this knowledge brings him no pleasure.

Celia Barnes is an innocent in all of this and yet what she is about to experience will be horrifying and cruel. But it is also necessary.

Inside the Miller house a soft beeping sound echoes across the dark, polished wood that lines the empty hallway and up

4

the steel and teak staircase that rises through the centre of the building like the spine of the house.

Celia Barnes glances up at the security camera pointing down at the door, waits a second for the face-recognition software to verify who she is, then opens a small teak hatch set into the concrete wall by the door. A keypad lights up inside next to a square sensor and she squints at the sequence she wrote on her hand. The code is long and complex, a mixture of symbols, numbers and letters that gets changed regularly and texted to her by Mike, the owner of the house. She only has thirty seconds before the alarm goes off so writes the code on her hand before leaving her flat in big, biro letters so she doesn't have to fumble for her phone or her glasses and waste precious time. On her second day cleaning for the Millers she had got the code wrong, or possibly taken too long, or maybe both and had set the damn thing off. The noise was unbelievable, an ear-splitting siren shriek that ripped through the house and brought the police hammering on the door in under two minutes. *Two minutes!*

When her own flat had been burgled just before Christmas it had taken more than two hours for anyone to show up, and even then it had only been a PCSO, one of those Police Community Support Officers her Derek called 'plastic coppers'. But then she lived in a two-bed, ex-council flat in Archway, not some architect-designed Highgate mansion worth three or four million quid or whatever it was.

When she first got the job here Celia had tried to find out. She does it with all the houses she cleans, takes a guess at how much the house is worth then pops the address into Rightmove to check the sold prices on the street. She's actually got pretty good at it, so much so that her Derek says she should jack in the cleaning and go work for one of those upmarket estate agents doing valuations and driving around in one of those fancy little electric BMW jobs. Celia loves that he thinks she could do a job like that, loves what it reveals about the way he sees her, but she knows she could never do it. They'd never hire her for a job like that, she's not enough – not young enough, confident enough, or posh enough. She's also only good at guessing the prices of houses that are similar to others, she never has a clue how much the quirky one-offs are worth, the modern mansions that look more like offices than homes. There is no record of how much the Miller house sold for, for example, not on Rightmove, or Zoopla, or any of the property sites she regularly uses. There is no other house like the Miller house on this street, or in the whole of Highgate come to that, so she has no idea how much it's worth other than 'a lot', and that's not going to get her a job in a swanky estate agent now, is it?

Celia's hand trembles slightly as she taps in the last few digits of the code, her anxiety levels closer to those of someone deactivating a bomb than switching off a house alarm. This is another reason she could never work for a posh estate agent, all those different alarms to deal with, all the different codes, all the people, all the stress. Give her a good audio-book, an empty house, a hoover and a bucket of bleach any day of the week; she's perfectly happy with her little lot. Her Derek's got his bit of disability pension from the railways, they paid their mortgage off on the flat last year, and her cleaning brings in enough each week to keep them nice and comfy. She's more than happy.

She enters the code then presses her thumb to the square sensor. The beeping falls mercifully silent.

Celia Barnes lets out a long breath she didn't know she'd been holding and shrugs off her coat as she makes her way across the white resin floor to the twisted staircase, listening out for any signs of life. Just because the alarm was on doesn't mean there's no one at home; she'd found this out the hard way once when she'd burst in on Mike one morning, working out in the mini-gym off the master bedroom. He'd had his earphones in so hadn't heard her, and was wearing gym shorts and nothing else and, my, but what a sight that had been. Celia had stood there, frozen to the spot, mesmerized by the way his muscles moved beneath his smooth, tanned skin as he lifted the weights and studied himself in the floor-to-ceiling mirror. He'd looked like one of those men in the celebrity magazines she flicked through at the hairdressers, those cartoonish men with perfect, tanned skin and knots of muscles in their stomachs that looked like they'd been painted on. Except Mike Miller was real, there he'd been, right in front of her, in the flesh.

She had traced the outline of him with her eyes, up his legs, over the firm curve of his bum and his back. That was when she'd realized he'd stopped lifting the weights and was now looking right back at her in the mirror. She'd blushed and felt flustered and faint, but Mike had just smiled and then *he* had apologized to *her*, and wasn't that just like Mike? So laid-back, so confident that even an awkward moment like that could be smiled away as if it was nothing at all.

It was unfair really how some people seemed to have everything – money, health, beauty, charm. Kate Miller was the same. The Millers were a different breed, a golden couple, like an evolutionary step up had given them all the gifts and lifted them above the level of ordinary folk. It would have been the easiest thing in the world to hate them – if only they hadn't been so nice.

Celia reaches the stairwell and pauses, looking through the wall of glass across the overgrown cemetery to the distant marvel of London. A few of the other houses she cleans have views over the city too, but nothing like this. Because the Miller house backs on to the cemetery there are no other buildings to block the view and even the security fence has been specially designed so that what you can see when you look out through the floor-to-ceiling windows are the trees, their green leaves fading now to autumn amber, and London shimmering in the far distance.

He watches her from the shadow of a sycamore tree.

He is standing a few metres off the main pathway and tucked out of sight behind the tomb of some long-forgotten Victorian milliner. Celia Barnes does not look his way. She does not look down at the cemetery at all. She looks at the distant view, like she always does.

Almost the entire back wall of the Miller house is glass, three floors of perfectly aligned, highly polished panels that mirror the sky and make the house appear almost invisible. Celia Barnes is framed in the dead centre of it, a tiny, semi-transparent figure, floating among grey, reflected clouds. He watches her in her stillness, a moment of calm before the coming storm, then she turns and heads downstairs to the utility room where the cleaning equipment is kept.

She walks slowly, placing each foot deliberately and softly on the hardwood steps as she descends, keeping her footfalls soft so as not to wake anyone who may still be sleeping somewhere in the vast house. It is thoughtful of her, but there is no need. She could make as much noise as she likes and no one would hear, not in the house, and not out here in the cemetery. The wall of sky-reflecting glass – triple-glazed and imported from Norway where it was designed to keep out the worst of the Norwegian winter – also blocks out sound. The people inside the house are insulated from the constant hum of the city. No sound gets in. And no sound gets out either.

He watches until she slips from sight then moves forward, keeping to the shadows as he moves through rows of crooked tombstones and laurel bushes, heading closer to the cleverly designed security fence and the house that lies beyond.

Celia hangs her coat on the hook behind the utility room door, takes a mop bucket from beneath the stainless-steel sink and starts filling it. She fits her earbuds into place and restarts the audiobook on her phone, the latest Donna Leon. She may spend the next few hours cleaning someone else's toilets and floors in a house in Highgate but in her head she will be in Venice with Commissario Brunetti, zipping around the canals on a Vaporetto, eating deliciously described Venetian food and grumbling about the tourists as he tracks down another devious killer.

She tips bleach into the bucket and watches the water rise and froth until it is half full, then turns off the tap and heads into the house.

The first room she cleans is the downstairs toilet because it hardly gets used and is an easy one to tick off her list. It is also furthest from the master bedroom so any noise she makes here is less likely to disturb the Millers – if they're in. Celia opens the garage door as she passes by to check. Neon lights flicker on revealing that both Kate and Mike's cars are there, so she closes the door softly and continues to the downstairs toilet, closing the door behind her before starting to clean. If Kate and Mike are sleeping let them sleep a little longer.

It takes Celia less than five minutes to wipe down the already spotless marble surfaces and sweep and mop the floor, an American-accented voice describing Brunetti inspecting a body in the Campo Santo Stefano as she works. Then she refills her bucket in the utility room and heads upstairs to the ground floor, pausing her audiobook at the top of the stairs to listen again for any sign that the Millers are stirring. She hears nothing, restarts her audiobook and returns to Venice in her head as she steps into the main living room.

The Millers' living room, like the rest of the house, is white: white walls, white floors, white furniture, the only visible colour the orangey green of the autumn graveyard seen through the wall of glass on her left.

But now there is another colour.

Now there is also red, vivid stripes of red that slash across the walls and ceiling, across the white leather sofa and the large photograph of Kate and Mike Miller that hangs above the white marble fireplace. In the picture they are wearing matching white shirts, hugging and smiling, their teeth as white and perfect as the house. Only Kate's smile is now broken by something black, and green, and ugly sticking into the centre of her face.

Celia takes a step forward, trying to process what she's seeing. It looks like a pot of red nail polish has been thrown around the room and she automatically starts thinking about how she might clean it up and get the stains out. Then she takes another step, sees something on the floor, something hidden by the sofa when she first came in, and realizes what the red is.

He watches the bucket fall from Celia's hands, the distance and thickness of the glass rendering the action silent. Her hands fly to her mouth and she staggers backwards, eyes wide and fixed on the floor.

From where he is standing he cannot see what Celia is looking at, but he can see the horror of it reflected in her face and it saddens him. Her anguish was not his desire but it was unavoidable and he had to be here to make sure her strong and natural instinct to clean would not compel her to disturb the careful scene he has left behind.

Up in the Miller house Celia Barnes continues to stagger away from the horror in the centre of the room until her back hits the wall and she dislodges another photograph showing the whiter-than-white Millers, smiling in their happy perfection. The jolt seems to break Celia from her trance and her hands fall from her mouth and she fumbles her phone from her pocket, breaking her gaze for a moment to stab a number into it before resuming her wide-eyed stare at the floor as she lifts the phone to her ear.

He takes a small handheld radio from his pocket, his eyes flicking away from Celia Barnes just long enough to activate it before looking back at her. She continues to stare down, eyes wide, hand visibly shaking as it holds the phone to her ear. She starts to talk, her free hand fluttering as she speaks, gesturing at the floor as if the person on the other end of the line can see what she is describing. After a few moments she stops talking and starts nodding instead.

His Tetra radio cannot intercept mobile phone signals but it can pick up the radio traffic of the emergency services that should follow. The police dispatcher on the other end of the line will be calming her now, reassuring her, telling her to hold on for a moment while they call for assistance. He listens to the whisper of the wind through the branches above his head then a soft digital squawk pops in his ear.

'Urgent assistant required,' a female voice says. 'Report of a serious knife assault at . . . number three Swain's Lane, NW8.'

There is a pause then a different voice answers, a police squad car, acknowledging the call and confirming it is inbound.

Up in the Miller house Celia Barnes continues to nod and stare at the floor. The dispatcher will now be telling her that officers are coming, that she should stay where she is and – most important of all – that she should not touch anything.

He watches for a few moments more, making sure that Celia Barnes does what she is told and does not move closer to the body or disturb any of the things he has so carefully left to be found.

Somewhere in the distance the dim wail of a siren starts up, rising and falling, and getting louder. He waits until there is no doubt where it's heading then walks slowly backwards, his eyes locked on Celia Barnes for as long as he can still see her, framed in the centre of the wall of glass, floating in the reflected sky like a ghost above the graveyard.

2

Tannahill Khan, halfway down four flights of stairs with three heavy boxes pulling his arms from his sockets, feels the phone buzz in his pocket.

'Shit,' he mutters, knowing what a call to that phone means.

He traps the stack of boxes against the wall with his body, pulls the phone from his jacket and checks the caller ID – Special Ops Dispatch.

'Shit,' he murmurs again before answering. 'DCI Khan.'

'We have a report of a serious assault,' the dispatcher says, 'knife attack.' She lists the details – home intrusion, female victim, private address in Highgate.

Tannahill does a rough calculation in his head of how much extra pain this is going to add to his already painful day. 'OK,' he says. 'Could you tell the other DCs to pick me up outside the NoLMS offices in the HAT car.'

'Roger.' The dispatcher hangs up.

NoLMS – North London Murder Squad – Tannahill had stressed the L but everyone who wasn't in the unit pronounced it 'gnomes', largely to take the piss out of anyone who *was* in it.

Tannahill tucks the phone back in his pocket, adjusts his grip on the stack of boxes and continues his journey down.

13

His plan had been to spend the morning going over the data gleaned from the documents in these boxes before the lunchtime press conference where the latest crime stats are due to be released. A few weeks back his boss had given him the heads-up on how bad they were and told him to try to find something in previous figures that made the current ones seem less alarming, particularly in relation to his area of expertise, knife crime. *You think these figures are bad, it's nothing compared to 2004* – that kind of thing. Spin basically.

Unfortunately the only thing Tannahill had found was evidence that highlighted just how terrible the latest figures really were. He had planned to spend the morning massaging the historical data by lumping other crimes under the general headline of 'street crime' to make the old figures seem higher, but now this new case had popped up and totally torpedoed his day. Maybe if people stopped stabbing each other for five minutes he might have a fighting chance of figuring out why people kept stabbing each other every five minutes.

He pushes through the front door of the building and spots a black Mercedes MPV parked across the road on double-yellow lines, hazard-lights blinking, a black-jacketed driver standing by the open front door smoking a cigarette. Tannahill hefts the boxes to secure his slipping grip and makes his way over. 'You the courier?' he asks.

The driver blows smoke out with his reply. 'Do I look like a facking courier, mate?'

He is clean-shaven, short black hair, black T-shirt under a black jacket, wireless buds in his ears, probably Bluetoothed to the phone charging in the cradle visible through the open door of the Mercedes. 'Yes,' Tannahill says.

The driver drops his cigarette and steps on it as he moves closer until his chest bumps against the stack of evidence boxes, knocking Tannahill back on his heels slightly. 'You being funny, mate?' He is short and has to look up at Tannahill, though the height difference doesn't seem to bother him.

14

Tannahill can smell the sour smoke and coffee fog of his breath. He is about to reply when another car appears down the street, a black Volkswagen people carrier, practically identical to the parked Mercedes. It moves slowly, the driver leaning forward in his seat as he checks the numbers of the buildings. The current offices of NoLMS are spread over a couple of rented floors of an ugly anonymous building in Holloway which is almost impossible to find, even with GPS.

'My mistake,' Tannahill says, stepping past the angry driver and into the road so the real courier can see him.

'Oi, ISIS, where you think you're going?' the driver says, following him into the road. 'What's in them boxes anyway, a bomb?'

Tannahill feels a familiar anger rise inside him but the duty phone buzzes in his pocket again, reminding him he has much bigger fish to fry as the Volkswagen pulls to a halt in front of him and the tailgate starts to rise. He moves to the back of the car, the boxes feeling ten times heavier now than when he started, and the courier gets out to help.

'Oi, ISIS, don't you ignore me,' the other driver shouts.

The courier looks shocked. 'Don't worry about him,' Tannahill says, lowering the boxes gratefully into the back of the Volkswagen, 'you got the transfer documents?'

'You two a couple of benders?' the driver continues, refusing to let it drop. 'Them boxes full of dildos or summink?'

Tannahill flexes the stiffness from his hands, scribbles his signature on the paperwork then pulls his buzzing phone from his pocket, silencing it with a jab of his finger.

'I'm on the street out front,' Tannahill says, 'how close are you?' He nods at the answer then hangs up. He waits for the courier to drive away then finally turns to the angry driver. 'What was that you said I looked like?'

The driver sneers. 'A poof,' he says, 'you look like a poof and a terrorist.'

Tannahill nods. 'It's the brown skin, isn't it? Brown skin,

15

must be a terrorist. When I was growing up I was called all sorts – Paki, camel jockey, raghead. My dad was Pakistani, you see. Irish mum, but I got his skin and hair, so . . .'

A siren starts up somewhere nearby, the sound bouncing off the buildings, making it impossible to tell where it's coming from.

'When I went to big school I pretended to be Italian for a while, thought it might silence the twats. Didn't really think it through. Ended up being called a dago and a spic instead, until someone found out the truth and all the old names came flooding back – or they did until 9-11.'

The sound of the siren doubles as a dark grey Vauxhall Insignia appears round the corner, blue lights flashing behind the grille. Tannahill holds his hand up to the driver.

'Since 9-11 and 7-7 I mostly get called things like Osama, or Taliban, or – what was the one you called me? ISIS.'

The car pulls to a halt, the ear-splitting siren shredding the air. Tannahill draws his hand across his throat in a cutting motion and the siren goes silent. He pulls a small leather wallet from his pocket, lets it fall open and watches the driver's expression change as he sees the warrant card and reads the words printed on it:

POLICE OFFICER
TANNAHILL KHAN
Detective Chief Inspector

'So let me ask you again,' Tannahill says, slipping the wallet back in his pocket. 'What do I look like?'

The driver swallows. 'A copper,' he says, all the piss and vinegar now drained from his voice.

Tannahill nods slowly then looks over at the parked Mercedes MPV. 'This your vehicle, sir?'

The driver nods.

16

'Nice.' Tannahill moves round to the front and looks at the registration plate. 'This year's reg too. Let me ask you something, do you know what an ANPR camera is?'

The driver shakes his head.

'It stands for Automatic Number Plate Recognition. It's everywhere now – traffic lights, junctions, roundabouts, car parks – we only have to tap in the registration of a car we're interested in and the moment it drives by a camera on the network, it pings up on a central computer, which sends an alert to the nearest squad car, which then pulls it over faster than you can say *I didn't do anything officer, someone must've put my registration on the system because I was a bit racist.*' Tannahill takes a step closer and lowers his voice. 'Look at me.' The driver looks up but his chin is down, like a dog who knows he's chewed the wrong shoe.

'We all make mistakes. The most important thing is to own them and learn from them, do you understand what I'm saying?'

The driver nods. Swallows. 'Sorry,' he murmurs.

'What was that?'

'Sorry,' he says, a little louder this time.

Tannahill pauses for just long enough for it to become uncomfortable then smiles. 'Good lad.' He steps away from him and gets into the passenger seat of the waiting HAT car. 'Oh, and just for the record,' he says, before closing the door. 'You really do look like a courier.'

Then he slams the door and the HAT car takes off down the street, lights flashing, siren screaming.

3

The morning settles over London, grey and wet like an old duvet left out by the bins. Laughton Rees – big hair, small face, bushbaby eyes – stands in her bathrobe in her tiny kitchen and stares out at the rain-glossed rooftops, her own faint reflection making her appear ghostly and formless.

Somewhere in the distance a siren starts up and she automatically reaches for the police scanner by the kettle, a hand-built gift from a Sepura engineer she'd met through work and then disastrously attempted to date. The only good thing about the whole experience was that she got this scanner out of it.

She checks behind to make sure she is alone before switching it on. She nudges the volume right down until the chatter is almost inaudible then leans in and listens with a detached, professional interest. None of the cases she eavesdrops on like this will cross her desk, not for a long while at least, and she finds it comforting, like listening to the shipping forecast from the cosy comfort of a warm, land-locked bed, knowing the storms being described are a long, long way away. She finds comfort in the gently ambiguous language too: a *disturbance* reported; a *suspected* assault. They never use words like 'murder' or 'rape', but Laughton can tell the serious ones by the nature of the responses. This is a bad one, judging by the number of units inbound; a serious knife assault at an address in Highgate. Murder, most likely. Another one.

Laughton feels the side of the teapot – still warm but probably no longer drinkable – and checks the time on the microwave: 7.58.

She's been up for almost four hours now.

She tips the stewed, black liquid into the sink, still listening to the low burble of the police scanner, and pulls her phone from the bathrobe pocket. One more pot then she'll engage with the day and the daily battle of getting her daughter up and ready for school.

'HAT car inbound,' a message crackles on the scanner. 'ETA five minutes.'

HAT car – *Homicide Assessment Team*.

Definitely a murder investigation then.

Laughton turns on the cold tap, adjusts the flow so it's slow and steady then sets the timer on her phone for sixty seconds, the default amount for most of her rituals, and sets it going. The kettle ritual dictates that she must start filling it the exact moment sixty seconds are up, one second either way and she'll have to start over. She moves the kettle closer to the tap, her eyes fixed on the countdown.

Three. Two. One.

Kettle under the water.

Aaaand relax.

She fills it to the three-cup mark and sets it to boil. Three is another number that crops up a lot in the various rituals that weave through her life and when she realizes this will be her third pot of tea that morning the thought calms her a little.

'A three-pot problem,' she murmurs, though she knows this isn't true. The thing that has kept her awake half the night is barely a one-cup problem, yet here she is, still going over the things she wants to say to her daughter's headmaster, practising her arguments, sharpening and tweaking them with the same diligence she would take before appearing as an expert witness in court. She spoons loose-leaf tea into the pot and fires up her argument again, saying the words out loud so she can get used to the way they feel in her mouth.

'Mr Day, thank you for seeing me, I know you're very busy so I'll get to the point. I feel my daughter is being let down by your school and its well-meaning but ineffective policy on bullying.'

Too strong? She has tried softer lead-ins but only has five minutes with the man and two hours' worth of things she wants to say. The kettle boils and Laughton pours water into the teapot while it's still bubbling – maximum heat, maximum flavour, like her mother taught her – and the sudden and unexpected memory of her makes her wonder if her mother ever stood, like she now stands, worrying about her like she now worries about her own daughter? Probably not, not about something like this at any rate. Her mother would have just marched into school without an appointment the moment she heard the word 'bullying' and confronted Mr Day with a broadside of eloquent and furious anger until he did something about it. She had always been fearless like that, never avoided confrontation if it was required. It was one of the things that had made her so magnificent. It was also one of the things that had killed her.

Laughton stirs the tea – three times clockwise, three times anti-clockwise – then puts the lid on the pot.

She is not like her mother. Like most children of trauma she hates confrontation of any kind – even a five-minute, scheduled meeting with a headmaster. So she swirls the tea in the pot and runs through what she wants to say to Mr Day for what feels like the thousandth time, even as a detached and sensible part of her brain knows it's all pointless because real people never behave like their imagined versions and never stick to the script, no matter how well rehearsed it is.

The scanner crackles with a new message.

The HAT car has reached the scene now and Laughton imagines the forensics team bursting from the car, clustering round the open boot as they shimmy into their paper suits, grabbing their crime scene kits, setting up the murder log and a perimeter.

More radio chatter. An ambulance this time.

The paramedic sounds unhurried and businesslike. Definitely a homicide. Ambulance drivers only sound this relaxed when there are no lives to save.

Laughton takes a fresh white mug from a cupboard of identical ones, their handles all turned forty-five degrees to the right and tries to refocus.

'Mr Day, I can tell from what you have achieved in this school that you are not afraid of changing things that aren't working.' That's good. Flatter the bastard then hit him with the hard stuff. 'And your policy on bullying isn't working. As a matter of fact it's a huge pile of ineffective liberal bullshit.'

OK, not that obviously – right sentiment, wrong words.

'Don't go to the meeting.' The voice makes her jump. She turns to find Gracie leaning on the living-room door-frame, her messy, nut brown, pre-Raphaelite hair tumbling over the shoulders of her black dressing gown. '*Please* don't go,' she says, her huge eyes pleading.

'I didn't see you there,' Laughton says, switching off the police scanner and opening the cupboard where the Cheerios are kept.

'I know. If you had you wouldn't have done the weird timing thing with the kettle and started talking to yourself.'

Laughton flushes, embarrassed her daughter has been standing there long enough to witness the rituals she tries so hard to hide from her.

'I don't want you to go to my school,' Gracie repeats. 'If you go in and say any of those things you were saying it's only going to make things worse. And don't call him Mr Day, he likes everyone to call him Jonathan. In fact don't call him anything because . . . just . . . don't go.'

'I'm not going to say any of *those* things.' Laughton takes a bowl from another cupboard and pours cereal into it. 'I was just sharpening my argument.'

'But I don't want you to have an argument with my headmaster.'

'That's not . . . I'm not going to *argue* with him.'

'You just said you were sharpening your argument.'

'Figure of speech,' Laughton pours milk into the bowl and slides it along the work surface towards Gracie. 'Lawyers call their opinions arguments, doesn't mean they spend all day shouting at each other.'

Gracie moves forward, her black dressing gown like her mood made manifest. 'You're not a lawyer though.'

'No, I'm your mother and I am going to go into your school this morning to *discuss* with your headteacher why he's letting the bitches and the bullies make your life miserable.'

'Please don't call them that.'

'What do you want me to call them?'

'I don't want you to call them anything because I don't want you to go. I can sort this out myself.'

'Can you though?'

'Yes. I'll sort it, I promise. Please don't go to the meeting. Tell them something came up and you need to reschedule or something.'

'No way. It took me ages to even get this meeting. It's probably easier to see the pope than your headmaster. Eat your breakfast and be ready to leave in ten minutes. I'm going to sort it out, all right? I am actually quite good at this kind of thing.'

'No you're not,' Gracie takes a spoon from the drawer and stabs it into the bowl. 'You're going to lose your temper, start counting to three or tapping your fingers on the side of your head and he's going to think you're nuts and it's only going to make things worse. I wish I hadn't told you any of this now. I'm not a kid. I can look after myself.'

Laughton watches her daughter angrily devour her cereal. At fifteen Gracie is now the age Laughton was when she lost her mother. Maybe that's why she feels extra protective towards her. And yet lately, the more she tries to put her arms around her, the more Gracie seems to push her away. She can feel her drifting, becoming more secretive, more distant – unreachable. And the situation at school isn't helping but at least that's something she can focus on and try and fix.

'Ten minutes,' she says, then walks out of the room before Gracie can notice the shine of tears in her eyes.

Outside in the far distance a siren starts up again.

4

Tannahill stands outside the living room of the Miller house waiting for the Crime Scene Manager to remove the EyeSpy360 camera and move on to record the rest of the rooms in the house. Later these 360-degree images will be stitched together, allowing anyone on the team to walk virtually through the house and see everything just as it was with hotlinks on specific items that can be opened up to reveal the more detailed images and footage he is about to capture. He sets his own camera to record, double-checks it's running, then takes a deep breath and steps into the room, his white paper body suit whispering as he moves.

He stops inside the door and pans the camera slowly around the entire room, starting at the furthest point left and working right, forcing himself not to rush as a memorized mantra runs through his mind:

Nothing is unimportant at a murder scene.
  You must train yourself to notice things that seem unremarkable.
    You must never be distracted by the obvious.

The single most obvious thing at this scene – at any murder scene – is the body, so Tannahill ignores it for now, though the unusual way it has been arranged makes this difficult. He catches a glimpse of it at the bottom of the frame as the camera passes the mid-point of the room – the woman lying on her back, arms outstretched like in a crucifixion, and the four strange objects positioned around her.

He forces himself to focus on the room and continues his slow pan, capturing every vivid red stripe that dribbles and drips across the walls, the ceiling, the furniture, the floor. Usually the blood evidence has to be teased from a crime scene using Luminol and black-light techniques to lift it from the background grime, but here the stark whiteness of everything provides a perfect backdrop. He follows the patterns of blood with his camera, recording the specific shapes they make, angling the camera upward to the thin slashes of red on the ceiling, cast-off patterns made by the murder weapon as it stabbed, then arced up, then stabbed back down into the body of the woman Tannahill is currently doing his level best to ignore. Even after five years working on the murder squad it still amazes him how much blood is contained in a human body.

He completes the first pass and begins a second, more detailed one, focusing first on the large photograph hanging above the fireplace that shows a man and a woman dressed in all white. The cleaner who found the body identified her as Kate Miller and the man as her husband Mike, current whereabouts unknown. They look happy in the picture, happy and perfect: good hair expensively cut, flawless skin that might be from Photoshop, or expensive skin treatments, or both. It's hard to pin an age on them. They look youthful but also like they might have had work done. You can see it around the eyes, and on the wrinkle-free foreheads, and in the porcelain whiteness of their perfectly even teeth.

Tannahill zooms in on Kate Miller's image, more specifically on the object driven into the centre of her smile. It's a knife, the blood from its blade staining the pierced canvas so it looks like smudged lipstick. He holds the camera steady, recording the neon green of the grip and the black of the blade, straight cutting edge on one side, serrated on the other. It's a zombie knife, weapon of choice for the London street gangs, ugly, vicious and wholly out of place here in this room and in this house.

Another memorized mantra runs through Tannahill's mind: *Every murder scene has its own personality.*

In his time in Homicide Tannahill has found this to be particularly true. Some crime scenes are chaotic, some are violent, most are quite low-key and unremarkable, just like most killers, but the one thing they all have in common is consistency. If the killer had been chaotic and frenzied then the whole crime scene would be the same – furniture knocked over, items broken, doors splintered and left hanging on hinges, the body often a shattered mess left slumped in a corner where they retreated to try and escape the attack that ultimately killed them. Generally you could see the mindset of the killer imprinted on the scene they left behind and it was coherent.

But that was not the case here.

Here there was evidence of two distinct and opposing personalities. One, chaotic and frenzied, a violent individual who had stabbed the victim multiple times, their arm flying back with each blow, the force and speed sending arcs of blood spraying across the clean white surfaces of the room. Then there was a second, calmer, much more ordered person-ality, one that had managed to gain access to this seemingly super secure house, and had taken time to arrange the body after the vicious killing, meticulously placing specific objects around it before exiting the house again. Maybe it was two people. Or maybe it was just one person who didn't need to gain access to the house because he was already here.

Tannahill glances back at the photograph above the fire-place.

Mike Miller, whereabouts unknown.

It wouldn't be the first time a loving husband had brutally murdered his wife. Fifty-five per cent of all homicides were classified as 'intimate partner violence-related' – he learned that little titbit from the boxes of data he's been ploughing through for the past few weeks. And in this case husband-turned-killer would certainly explain a lot, such as the alarm not going off and the clear violence of the attack; nothing fuels rage and violence quite like love gone bad. But that didn't explain everything, like why the murder weapon was a street knife and not a kitchen knife grabbed in the heat of an angry moment. It didn't explain the presence or purpose of the strange objects around the body either, the ones that didn't seem to belong in a house like this at all.

Tannahill moves further into the room, heading away from the window and keeping to the edge of the floor, the mantra of his training still running through his mind:

You should always endeavour to tread where the killer did not.

He reaches the far end of the room and turns, his heart hammering against his ribs as he catches his own dim reflection in the wall of glass, ghostly in his white paper suit. He holds the wide shot for a moment, capturing the room from this different perspective, the chaos and violence of the blood, the calm order of everything else. Once they start dismantling the crime scene, this video and the photos he takes will be the only way to see it exactly as the killer left it, possibly the only way to prove or disprove theories as yet unformed. He holds the shot until he's sure he's got it then takes a step forward, tilts the camera down, and finally allows himself to focus on the body.

Since transferring to the North London Murder Squad

Tannahill has attended and processed dozens of homicides and studied archive evidence of hundreds more. But he has never seen anything like this.

Kate Miller is lying on her back, legs out straight, arms outstretched, her blonde hair framing her head like a halo, the defensive wounds on her hands like stigmata. The white rug she is lying on is almost black with blood, suggesting that this is where she died, bleeding out from her numerous injuries, a mixture of slashes and teardrop-shaped stab wounds in keeping with the blade on the knife driven through her photograph. Around her body are four objects:

A small stuffed unicorn.

Two tarnished medals on faded ribbons.

A set of keys.

A slim book.

They are arranged in a diamond shape – unicorn above her head, book at her feet, medals hanging from a small metal bar balanced on the index finger of her left hand, keys on the ground to her right.

There is also a fifth item: an eye mask draped loosely across the victim's face. Tannahill zooms in on it. It looks cheap, shiny black material with a thin strip of elastic zig-zagging across its surface, the folds still sharp from the packaging. It appears to be clean and dry, no evidence of blood, suggesting it was placed on the body post-mortem, after the bleeding had stopped. Tannahill crouches lower to get a better angle and sees something that makes ice slide down his spine. Kate Miller's eyes are open. They stare out, glassy and sightless, from beneath the mask. He takes a series of stills then switches back to video and turns his attention to the other four objects, his mind reaching for explanations as to what they might mean, and why they are here.

The keys, a Chubb and a Yale on a simple metal ring, might be the keys to this house, though Tannahill doubts it somehow. They seem way too ordinary for a house like this, though the Yale key is bright blue and shiny, so it might be unusual enough to be traceable.

The unicorn toy is a mass-produced, factory item with the label still pinned to one ear. It has been placed sideways to the body, its face pointing right and staring with black, glassy eyes reminiscent of the ones beneath the eye mask. It strikes Tannahill as odd to find a toy in a house otherwise devoid of any traces of children – no bikes or trikes or skateboards in the hall, no tiny shoes by the door, no pictures of children or by them. He holds the unicorn for the count of ten then moves on to the next object.

The medals seem as out of place as the toy, two six-pointed stars the colour of old pennies on faded ribbons – one purple, one blue, green and white – that have been threaded on to a thin, metal bar and carefully balanced on the outstretched index finger of the victim's left hand. He snaps a series of stills, the coppery medals blending in with their bloody background, then turns the camera to the final object, the one placed at the victim's feet.

He has left this until last for the same reason he initially ignored the body, because there is something about it that tugs at his attention, something even familiar about it. The book is face down, the front cover and title hidden, and the back is almost blank – no blurb about the contents, no biography of the author. The only visible writing is the name of the publisher – Crown Hill Publications – which also seems familiar.

Tannahill steps closer, carefully picking his way through the blood, his blue plastic shoe-covers whispering over the white resin floor. He takes a series of photographs to record exactly how the book has been placed in relation to the body, then crouches lower and peers at the title on the spine. The moment he reads it he realizes why it snagged his attention. He has not only read the book, he has memorized whole passages from it, the same phrases that have been running through his head the whole time he's been processing this crime scene. He raises the camera, his body working on autopilot, running on instructions he has learned from the book lying on the floor in front of him. The digital focus hunts for a second before sharpening on the title and the name of the author:

How to Process a Murder
Laughton Rees

It feels like a taunt, a clear message from the killer saying – *don't waste your time looking for clues because I've read the same books as you, I know what you're looking for and I know how you look for them.*

But it isn't just this that could have a seismic effect on the investigation going forward – it is also the person who wrote it.

II
THE BOOK

Extract from *How to Process a Murder*
by Laughton Rees

A real murder scene is not like the ones you see on TV and in films.

There are no wise-cracking detectives drinking coffee and trading gallows humour as they step over a bloodied corpse. There will be humour, and there will certainly be coffee, but that will come later.

In the beginning there is only silence and reverence, the same type and tone you would find at a funeral. Also, like a funeral, there will be a steady procession of people filing past the body, witnesses to what has happened, both civilian and professional, casual and key. And though the testimony of these people will help form an understanding of what has taken place here, there are other witnesses whose contribution to the investigation can be just as valuable. For everything that was disturbed by the killer or their victim, everything that was touched, no matter how lightly, can also tell you something about what took place here and why. For there is a peculiar alchemy that occurs in the white heat of violence that turns the basest of things into something more valuable than gold. And it is these unremarkable objects, the overturned and sometimes overlooked, that can help tell the story of what happened here.

These are the dark objects that will help you catch your killer.

5

The first message buzzes at 8.27 on the Highgate Ladies Book Club WhatsApp group.

– *Something's happening at the Miller house – police cars outside.*

– *I saw thm 2 on way 2 yoga* – someone immediately confirms – *2 policemen stndng by the door.*

A member of the group who lives close to Swain's Lane grabs a lead and drags her bewildered old spaniel out for a second walk, hoping a stroll through the cemetery behind the Miller house might yield fresh gossip, which it does, though not of the calibre she was hoping for.

– *They've cloned the cemetery* – she types, eager fingers hitting 'send' before she notices autocorrect has made a nonsense of her message.

– *CLOSED* – she types quickly to head off the swarms of corrections from the Olympic-standard pedants of the Book Club – *They've sealed off the pavement outside the house. I asked what was going on but was told to move on.*

And as nothing on the suburban landscape inflames interest more than a wall, so the barrier to information hastily erected around the Miller house only serves to galvanize the resourceful, well-connected, and perennially bored neighbours to greater feats of industry and espionage. 'Miller house', 'Highgate incident', and 'Police' are tapped into Google along with the Millers' names, just as they were a year earlier when the couple first moved in, and with similarly frustrating results. Nothing comes back – not a photograph, not an article, not even a Facebook page. In the modern age where everyone of any substance can always be stalked through a Google search, Mike and Kate Miller are ghosts.

– *I bet he hit her and she called the police* – a new message says.

– *OMG I was thinking that* – buzzes an immediate response – *I met them at the cemetery Trust summer party and they seemed way too happy. No one is THAT happy.*

– *Exactly. They're too perfect to be THAT perfect.*

– *I met them at the summer party too.*

Another message cuts in:

– *I found them both to be utterly charming, and so, so glamorous.*

– *Bit up themselves though, aren't they?*

– *That's what I thought, I'm so glad you said that.*

– *Well I think they're lovely* – Heather Robinson, lady captain of the golf club and nearest neighbour to the Millers, chimes in – *last Xmas I knocked on their door selling tickets for the raffle and Kate Miller bought all ten books on the spot. Gave me a Company Coutts cheque. She also won two prizes, decent prizes too, but told me to put them back into the next raffle. I hope nothing terrible has happened to them.*

There is a brief, chastened pause where everyone sheepishly considers their meanness for a moment, then—

– *2 prizes!?* – a new message exclaims – *Some ppl R born lucky. Bn doing the rffle 10 yrs and nvr won.*

– *Me either. And it's easy to be generous when you're rolling in cash.*

– *But who are they? Does anyone know where they came from or how they made their money?*

– *I heard it's all her money.*

– *A friend of my husband said it's all him, that he inherited a fortune and that she's some kind of Swedish aristo, or Danish maybe, one of the Scandi countries anyway. Did you see that police drama on BBC Four btw, the one with the autistic detective who shags everyone? Me and Rog binged it last week.*

– *I think they were dodgy* – another says, ignoring the group's usual diversion of TV chatter – *No one that young has that much money without something shady going on.*

– *I saw people in paper suits going into the house* – a new message says, elevating things to a whole new level because everybody's binge-watched the police dramas and knows what paper suits and policemen mean.

– *There was an ambulance at the house* – another message buzzes immediately afterwards – *I think I saw Kate Miller getting into it.*

The author of this message, Jane Farrow, new to the book group and eager to work her way into favour, did not see Kate Miller getting into anything but thought she *might* have done, and so this tiny lie, born of insecurity and a burning desire to be of use, sets everyone hurtling down the wrong track. Contact lists are hastily consulted, keen eyes searching for anyone they know in the medical field who might be able to find out where Kate Miller has been taken and, by extension, what has happened to her.

In the days to come when what has actually happened in the Miller house becomes global news, Jane Farrow will look back at this moment and re-read her message to the WhatsApp group she never gets messages from any more. And though no one will ever tell her to her face why she's been ghosted, she will know in her heart that this was the moment it all went wrong. Because she had *not* seen Kate Miller getting into an ambulance, and the information they have all been collectively and aggressively chasing down all morning is about to come to them and prove it.

– *THE POLICE ARE HERE* – a new message declares in caps.

It comes from Heather Robinson, lady captain and nearest neighbour of the Millers.

– *I'm in the kitchen making tea. Bob's in the living room talking to them now.*

Heather arranges four bone china cups and saucers on a tray and considers biscuits as the replies come buzzing like flies, sending her phone skittering across the granite countertop.

> – *Plain-clothes or uniforms?*
>> – *What have they said?*
>>> – *What happened?*
>>>> – *What happened?*
>>>>> – *What happened?*

Heather decides against biscuits, swaps the fine china for the mugs she keeps for plumbers, builders and other trade, then sweeps her buzzing phone off the granite.

– *Kettle's boiled* – she types with fumbling fingers – *I'll let you know what they say once they've gone.*

6

Laughton Rees sits in a high-ceilinged corridor outside the headmaster's office of St Mark's C of E school in Holloway, feeling like she's twelve and in trouble again. She taps her fingers on the sides of her chair in patterns of three and runs through what she wants to say for the thousandth time, her eyes darting around and taking in the details of the old building, cracked paint peeling from cast-iron radiators, tall windows designed to let in maximum light before electric lighting existed. It reminds her of the school she went to when her mother was still around, back when everything had been relatively normal.

'Mrs Rees?' She looks up at Mr Day, headmaster of St Mark's, standing framed in his office doorway. He is lean and tanned, sandy, wavy hair brushed forward like a Roman emperor. 'Sorry to keep you,' his bright blue eyes twinkle amid laughter lines deepened by a deep tan. 'Please, come in.'

Laughton follows him into a surprisingly large office and he gestures towards a row of soft seating arranged around a low coffee table covered with copies of the school manifesto, 'Learning to Learn Differently'. There's also a slim file folder with Gracie's name on it, the same type old police files are kept in, and the sight of her daughter's name on one makes Laughton's heart race and her mouth go dry.

'Thank you for seeing me, Mr Day,' she says, sitting in one of the low chairs and sinking uncomfortably low in it.

'Jonathan,' he sits opposite and smiles benevolently, 'call me Jonathan, we're not big on formality here at St Mark's. So,' he leans forward and lowers his voice like he's about to share a secret, 'I understand you're a crime writer?'

'No, I'm . . . not exactly.' Laughton shuffles forward in her seat to un-sink herself and balances on the front edge. 'I write about crime, but not fiction.'

Jonathan nods. 'Still, I imagine you must see some pretty toe-curling sights in your line of work, crime scenes, murders, that kind of thing?'

'Er . . . sometimes, yes, but only in pictures. I'm an academic so I study solved cases, not live ones. I don't attend crime scenes.'

'Right.' He looks disappointed.

'So, Gracie,' Laughton says, anxious to steer the conversation back in a more rehearsed direction.

'Yes. How's she getting on?'

'Well, not great actually.'

'Right.' Jonathan sits back and folds his arms in a classic defensive, closed-down display. Laughton looks away, breaking eye contact to make him feel more comfortable, instinctively using techniques she has studied and written about in relation to interviewing criminals. She focuses instead on the racing bike hanging on a special bracket on the far wall, surrounded by twenty or so student portraits of Mr Day, which gives her an idea.

'Mr Day,' she says, looking him in the eye again but making sure her head is angled down and her eyeline below his.

'Jonathan,' he corrects.

'Yes, sorry – Jonathan. You have clearly done some amazing things at this school.'

40

He smiles and his arms relax a little. 'Thank you.'

Laughton takes a copy of 'Learning to Learn Differently' from the table. 'You also wrote something in here that I thought was very wise . . .' She flicks through the pages of smiling children and inspirational quotes. 'You wrote about the importance of failure as a learning tool.'

Jonathan unfolds his arms to receive the full force of her compliments and in this one gesture Laughton realizes she wasted half the night worrying. Appealing to a man with pictures of himself all over his office walls is easy. All you have to do is flatter him.

'Here it is: *At St Mark's we allow children to "fail" because we believe that through this "failure" they will gain a deeper and more sustained understanding of an idea.*'

Jonathan nods. 'I firmly believe you learn more from your own mistakes than from someone else's successes, so failing is essential.'

'Good, well then I think this meeting could prove to be a useful learning opportunity.'

'How so?'

'Because your current policy on bullying is failing.'

Jonathan shoots her a half-smiling, half-quizzical look. 'Well, we don't tolerate bullying in any form, so I'm not sure how that can be viewed as a failure.'

'No, I agree, a zero-tolerance policy on bullying is essential in any school. What I'm not really clear about is *how* you don't tolerate bullying here. Take my daughter's experience, for example. Gracie has, unfortunately, had a truly miserable time since moving to this school. From day one she has been systematically excluded, both in class and out, in person and through social media. When I first spoke to her teacher about it months ago she told me it was a particularly cliquey year group and advised me to give it time to sort itself out. Well it's been almost a year now and far from getting better it's got progressively worse, to the point where she has now been threatened with a knife – all of which I have reported in detail to Gracie's class rep, her teacher, and also to Mrs Rowe, who I believe is head of overall pastoral care in the school, but nothing has been done, nothing has changed. So the evidence suggests that bullying is not only being tolerated at this school, it is being allowed to thrive.'

Jonathan shifts uncomfortably in his chair. 'Well, firstly, I'm sure Lois – Mrs Rowe, who indeed is in charge of pastoral care – will have looked into everything thoroughly. She sends her apologies, by the way, she's on a training course this week, but everything will be here in your daughter's file.'

He picks up Gracie's file and opens it just as the door swings open behind him. He turns and smiles at the messy-haired, eleven-year-old boy who shuffles into the office clutching a piece of paper.

'Morning, Carter. What's that you've got?'

The boy shyly hands him the piece of paper and shoots Laughton a cold look.

'Well look at this!' Jonathan turns the page so Laughton can see the drawing of a man with scribbly reddish-brown hair and blue eyes. 'This is so good it will just have to go in the gallery, won't it?'

He rises, takes a pinch of Blu-Tack from a lump clearly left on the wall for magic moments like these, and adds the picture to the others.

'Can we do reading now?' the boy says, shooting another unfriendly glance at Laughton.

Jonathan looks at her, his eyebrows raised in query as if expecting her to say, *Hey, you go right ahead*. When she does not, he turns back to the boy.

'I'm in the middle of something right now, Carter,' he says, and the boy's shoulders drop. 'But when I've finished we'll read for a bit, OK?'

The boy glances back at Laughton like she just stole his ice cream, then sulks out of the room.

'One of our SEN students,' Jonathan explains, sitting back down and picking up the file. 'Special Educational Needs. We allow them to be a bit free range so they don't feel stressed; and my open-door policy means I tend to get little visits all day long.'

He holds the file at arm's length and peers at it like he needs glasses but is too vain to use them. 'You say your daughter has been threatened with physical violence . . .' He reads for a moment then glances up. 'Has she experienced any?'

Laughton feels annoyance flare inside her.

'Well, as I'm sure you're aware,' she says, as calmly as she can, 'physical violence is only one element of bullying behaviour and is predominantly displayed by boys. Girls are much subtler in their bullying strategies, which doesn't make them any less mean or the suffering they cause any less painful. Being excluded from your peer group *is* bullying, being targeted on social media *is* bullying, and being threatened with violence is a violent act in itself, so yes, she has experienced violence, and quite frankly I'm a little dismayed that, after all the things that *have* happened to my daughter, your first response is to try and shift the focus on to things that have *not*.'

'Mrs Rees, I can assure you I'm simply trying to form a—'

'It's Miss, and if I have to call you Jonathan please feel free to call me Laughton.'

'Laughton?' He frowns. 'That's an interesting name.'

'Yes, long story, can we stick to the subject please, I know your time is precious – your secretary made that *very* clear on the numerous occasions I tried to schedule this meeting.'

Jonathan nods slowly and looks back down at the file. '*Miss* Laughton Rees. Gracie is your only child I see, and' – he turns the page over – 'there's no father listed. Can I take this to mean you are a single parent?'

'Yes,' she says, forcing herself to remain calm, 'I am a single parent, though I'm not sure how my marital status has any bearing on my daughter being bullied.'

'Well, if you don't mind me talking frankly, in my twenty-plus years' experience in education, the children of lone parents sometimes grow up with a, how can I put this? A slightly unrealistic expectation of how much attention they are entitled to receive. As a result, they often end up feeling left out or ignored, particularly in the school environment, when in fact they are simply having to adjust to a normal level of attention. It's actually a very healthy adjustment in the long term, but in the short term we often see various attention-grabbing strategies playing out.'

'So you're saying my daughter isn't really being bullied, she's just . . . attention-seeking?'

'Not at all. I'm saying we need to look at the bigger picture before we start drawing any conclusions.' He holds up Gracie's file. 'Looking at your daughter's grades, she appears to be flying. That's not normally the sign of an unhappy child.'

'Maybe not normally, but I know my own daughter and, believe me, her improved grades are not necessarily a good sign. She's like me; when things get stressful she buries herself in work, it's a control thing.'

'Well that may be so, but I'm afraid most people are not going to view improved grades as evidence that she is suffering at this school – quite the opposite in fact. It's very difficult for us to justify any kind of intervention without solid evidence. As far as I can see, we only have your daughter's word that any of this has happened, and she won't even name the person who has allegedly threatened her. I'm sure in your books your detective characters have to collect hard evidence before they go around kicking in doors and arresting people.'

'Well, as I said, I don't write crime novels, and the fact you've already forgotten that is, I believe, *evidence* of the fundamental problem you have at your school.'

Jonathan flinched. 'And what problem is that?'

'You don't listen, or rather you only hear what you want to hear. I think you don't want to admit you have a bullying problem here because, if you did, you'd have to *do* something about it. So rather than taking any steps to find out who's bullying Grace, you doubt her instead because it's easier, which quite frankly is fucking outrageous.'

Jonathan stares at her, the shock evident on his face. Laughton hadn't meant to swear but emotion got the better of her and she's actually glad. He needed to be verbally slapped for all the slippery shit he was saying. She feels good that it happened, like a proper mother for once, like how she imagines her own mother must have felt all the time. Then a small voice brings everything tumbling down.

'You said the f-word.'

Laughton turns and sees the kid from earlier, standing by the door, eyes wide and staring right at her. The boy turns to Jonathan, already out of his seat and heading over to him. 'Hey, Carter, we didn't see you there. Why don't you pop outside for just one second, then we'll definitely do some reading, OK? Miss Rees was just leaving.'

'Was I?'

Jonathan shoots her a cold look. 'Yes. I'll talk to Lois about your daughter when she's back and then we'll come up with a plan of action.'

Laughton rises uncertainly from her seat. 'How soon will that happen?'

'Next week when she's back from her course.'

Laughton shakes her head. 'That's not good enough. I'm not going to let Gracie go through another week of this. If you're not prepared to treat this with the urgency it deserves then I'm going to take it up with the governors.'

Jonathan nods. 'Of course, you have every right to do that, though the governors are fully on-board with current school policy and the way the school is run, so I imagine they'll only reiterate what I've already said. Also, if you do choose to go above my head, I will obviously have to give my side of things and report what was said at this meeting, including your unfortunate outburst in front of a child, which may not make them warm to either you or your cause.'

Laughton stares up into his vaguely patronizing face. She'd so like to punch it right now or give him a full roundhouse kick to the side of the head.

'I'm sorry I used strong language,' she says. 'Clearly this is a subject I feel passionately about and, in my defence, I did think it was just us two having an adult discussion and didn't realize a child was present. Maybe if the door had been closed . . .'

Jonathan stiffens and Laughton lets the sentence trail off, deciding that taking a swipe at his open-door policy is probably not a wise move right now. She nods instead then steps past him out of the office and into the corridor where the boy is waiting.

'Come on in, Carter,' Jonathan says, all smiles and twinkly eyes again as he ushers the boy into the safety of the office before closing the door behind him with a solid *thunk*.

'Oh so *now* you close your door,' Laughton mutters under her breath.

The bell rings, harsh and metallic, and the corridor instantly swarms with noise and children. Laughton – feeling suddenly conspicuous, and deflated, and angry, and definitely not in control – drifts away on the current of kids, tapping her thumbs against each finger in turn, in steady patterns of three.

7

– *KATE MILLER HAS BEEN MURDERED!!!*

The message pops up on the Highgate Book Club WhatsApp group at 10.18.

The initial response is a shocked quietness. The phones that have been buzzing non-stop since the police cars were first spotted outside the Miller house go quiet, as if a minute's silence is being observed.

Then the reactions come . . .

– *OMG. That's awful!*
  – *I can't believe it.*
    – *I only saw her yesterday.*
      – *Who would do such a thing?*
        – *Do the police know who did it?*
          – *What about Mike, is he OK?*
            – *Yes, what about Mike? Poor Mike.*

The questions are aimed at Heather Robinson, author of the shocking five-word message, current lady captain, and also the Millers' nearest neighbour, which meant her door was knocked on first so she now possesses the information they've been collectively hunting down all morning.

But as the questions continue to buzz, Heather Robinson remains frustratingly silent, as if hoarding the valuable thing that has fallen in her lap. And during this silence a cold wind blows through the comfortable streets of Highgate, penetrating the double-glazed sash windows and banishing the comforting glow of the under-floor heating. And the name of this chill wind is 'fear', because if the Millers aren't safe then who is? If violence and tragedy can reach out and touch the richest, most glamorous, youngest, and – on the surface at least – happiest of them all, where does that leave the rest of them?

Then Heather Robinson finally replies and the cold breeze becomes a hurricane.

- *Mike Miller is missing* – her message says.
- *The police asked lots of questions about him.*
- *I'm pretty sure they think he killed Kate!!*

8

Tannahill steps out of the living room and hands the camera to the officer in charge of exhibits so she can upload the contents to the central crime report, commonly referred to as the Murder Book. In the time it has taken him to process the crime scene the hallway has also been processed and cleared, and a large room opposite that looks like a study has been turned into a makeshift field office. Detective Constable Baker is over by the front door, talking on his phone and pacing. He sees Tannahill, waves a greeting and ambles over, phone still clamped to his ear.

Tannahill has worked with Baker for almost a year now and can't quite figure him out. Given his experience, he could easily have risen higher in the ranks but seems perfectly happy sticking at his current level and pay grade. He also has a wife, two daughters, and an enviable family life in a career legendary for its ability to wreck them. Maybe his lack of ambition and the happiness that came with it was the key to his success.

Baker hangs up as he reaches him. 'How's it looking?' he says, nodding at the living room.

'Messy. What about you?'

'Well, we've established the man of the house isn't hiding upstairs, and kicked the first officer on scene up the arse for not checking the property properly. We bagged a couple of toothbrushes and hairbrushes to harvest DNA samples of the owners, and started a house-to-house to see what we can find out, but so far nobody seems to know very much about the Millers.'

'Anything on the CCTV?'

Baker shakes his head. 'It was switched off. I've arranged for the hard drive to be cloned in case there's anything useful on it, but I doubt there'll be anything from last night. It all seems pretty calm and well planned. No sign of a break-in, nothing was tripped, nothing was broken, so whoever got in either had keys and codes or they were known to the victim and she let him in. We've contacted the company who installed the security system to get a list of who had access, but my guess is it was just the owners, and seeing as one of them's dead and the other one's missing, it isn't hard to figure out what happened.'

'You think he killed her?'

Baker shrugs. 'Nine times out of ten it's the husband.'

Tannahill glances back into the living room where the chief exhibits officer and an assistant are standing over the still form of Kate Miller, her arms outstretched and sightless eyes staring upward now the mask has been taken away and carefully placed in an evidence bag by the assistant. 'I don't know,' he says. 'It doesn't make sense.'

'Does it ever?'

'No, but if you wanted to murder your wife or a domestic spiralled out of control and you ended up killing her, what's the most obvious thing to do to try and cover it up?'

'Make it look like a burglary gone wrong.'

'Exactly. You smash a window, turn some furniture over, then you call the police and tell them you came in and found your missus in a pool of blood, and do your best to act like you're now losing your mind with shock and grief.

50

What you don't do is stage an elaborate scene by placing a bunch of weird objects around the body, then vanish.'

'Yeah, those objects are pretty extra. You ever see anything like that before?'

Tannahill shakes his head. 'Only in books. I'm hoping forensics might be able to pull something useful off them.'

Baker sucks air through his teeth. 'Yeah, well don't hold your breath on that score. Apart from the bloodbath in there, the rest of the house is squeaky clean: no prints, no blood traces on any of the access routes, nothing on the front or back door handles, nothing on or around any of the baths, sinks or showers – of which there are many.' He nods at the living room. 'I reckon they must have cleaned themselves up in there, changed their clothes, shoes, everything, then taken the whole lot away in a plastic bag or something. Like I said: calm and well planned. Whoever our killer is, they'd obviously done their homework.'

'Unfortunately, they did.' Tannahill nods at the junior exhibits officer emerging from the room holding an evidence bag in each hand. 'Hold that book up a second, would you.'

The paper-suited officer holds up the bag containing the book and Baker reads the title and the name of the author through the plastic.

'Laughton Rees. Oh shit!'

The exhibits officer peers at the book too and frowns, his eyes the only thing visible between his mask and the hood of the paper suit. 'Who's Laughton Rees?'

'Trouble,' Baker replies, 'a massive potential headache.'

'Laughton Rees is Commissioner Rees's daughter,' Tannahill explains. 'And in less than two hours her dad is going to be standing in a room full of journalists telling them knife crime in the capital is at an all-time high, so if the press catch wind that another knife-related murder happened this morning, and that the crime scene appears to have been forensically cleaned using a book his daughter wrote as a kind of guide, then it's not going to look very good for him, is it?'

'Ooooh,' the exhibits officer says, nodding slowly. 'Yeah, that is bad, isn't it?'

9

Laughton stalks away from her meeting with the headmaster through corridors clogged with children. She feels like kicking the wall or breaking something. Laughton is fluent in anger and familiar with this particular brand, one born of the frustration of not being listened to. It's the same kind she feels when reading through old murder files, where victims had detailed their fears in statements that were then ignored about the person who would eventually kill them. She feels like marching straight into Gracie's classroom and yanking her out of school.

But even as she mentally indulges in this scorched earth fantasy, her more practical, pragmatic side starts a debate in her head.

Pulling Gracie out of St Mark's might feel great in the moment but how long would that feeling last? A day? Two? Then what? On paper this was still the best school in the area, or the best state school at least, and the last OFSTED report had deemed it 'Outstanding' in all areas, which was why I sent Gracie here in the first place.

YEAH, WELL THERE'S BEEN NOTHING OUT-STANDING ABOUT GRACIE'S EXPERIENCE HERE, her angry side shouts back.

Not strictly true, her practical self replies. *Gracie's academic performance has been outstanding.*

YES, BUT YOU ALSO HAVE TO MAKE IT TO GRADUATION WITHOUT BEING STABBED.

Oh come on, you know for a fact the incidence of serious violent crime in schools is negligible.

STILL HAPPENS, THOUGH.

And look at this place. You can see the school is struggling. It's not the school's fault it's been chronically underfunded. It's just like the police force, and you know how that works out.

Yes, she knows how that works. It doesn't, basically. Too few people stretched way too thinly.

There are thirty-six pupils in Gracie's class when there should be a maximum of thirty. For the last two terms her teacher has been intermittently off work with stress, most likely due to the strain of dealing with an overstuffed and unmanageable classroom. As a result, Gracie has had a procession of supply teachers who have all tried their best but, in a school as overpopulated as this, that amounts to little more than crowd-control. And yet somehow Gracie is still acing her subjects and Laughton feels huge pride at this. Because using work as a distraction is one thing, doing it really well under pressure takes strength.

Laughton rounds the corner of the building, head tilted down to avoid the possible embarrassment of encountering Gracie, and collides with a girl hurrying in the other direction. Books and loose pages explode into the air and scatter across the ground.

'Oh God, I'm so sorry.' Laughton scurries about, chasing down pages before the breeze snatches them away. She shuffles the sheets into some vague order and hands them back to the girl. 'Oh hi,' she says, recognizing her. 'Maya, isn't it?' The girl nods and takes the pages back.

'I'm Gracie's mum,' Laughton says, unsure if the girl remembers her.

'Yeah, hi.' Maya's eyes flit up to hers then down at the floor again.

Maya had been one of Gracie's friends when she first started at St Mark's, had even come to the flat after school a few times, though not for a while. She picks another sheet of paper off the floor and hands it over. 'Haven't seen you for a while,' she says, 'have you and Gracie fallen out?'

Maya shrugs. 'Not really, she just . . . we just don't really hang out any more.'

'Who does she hang out with?'

'No one much.'

Laughton feels the tight knot of anxiety in her gut twist a little tighter. She can tell Maya is itching to get away, but she isn't going to pass up a chance of getting a different perspective on her daughter's school life.

'Gracie's having a pretty tough time at the moment,' she says. 'She's being picked on by some girls.' Laughton keeps her voice low and her eyes on Maya. 'Someone even threatened to cut her, did you know about that?'

Maya's eyes flick up for a moment then away to the side.

If Laughton saw this kind of behaviour in court or on a police interview tape she would view it as evasive and suspicious. But Maya is just a teenage girl unexpectedly being quizzed by an adult, so maybe it was nothing.

'If you know something, it won't come back on you if you tell me, I promise.'

Maya glances around the playground, still noisy with kids hurrying between classes but beginning to thin out. She obviously needs to go.

'Please, Maya,' Laughton says, 'if someone in this school is carrying a knife and threatening people with it then something needs to be done about it.'

Maya looks up, her expression now changed to the universal teenage look of *you-adults-just-don't-understand*.

'This is St Mark's,' she says, and starts to move away. 'Lots of kids carry knives.'

10

Celia Barnes sits in a featureless interview room somewhere on the first floor of Kentish Town police station. She stares unblinking at the cup of tea on the scarred table in front of her, a small, floating island of bubbles turning slowly in the centre of liquid the same colour as the cardboard cup. She doesn't see the bubbles, or the tea, or the cup. She sees Kate Miller, lying in a dark circle of red, and in a small, detached part of her brain she still worries about how she'll ever manage to get the stains out of the rug, and the sofa, and the white-painted walls. If they let it dry, she'll have no chance.

Was it dry when she found it?

She can't remember and she starts to feel anxious in case this is one of the questions the police are about to ask. She tries to calm herself by concentrating only on the things she does know.

The walls can be repainted, of course, no point in trying to scrub the stains out, and the sofa was leather and fairly new, so maybe that can be saved too.

But not the rug.

No amount of salt, or white wine, or baking powder, or any of her other housekeeper's tricks is going to shift those stains from that rug. It'll have to be replaced. That's the only way they can make the room neat and tidy and perfect again, the way Kate Miller likes it.

Kate . . .

Celia pictures her again, her blood soaked into the ruined white rug, that horrible mask across her eyes, and all those strange objects arranged around her.

The sound of the opening door makes her jump. She looks up as the nice girl who brought the tea enters the room carrying a briefcase and a laptop. She says 'girl' but she's in a uniform so she must be a WPC, though Celia imagines they probably don't call them that any more. PC then, though it feels wrong somehow to call her that.

The girl smiles in a kind but professional way and sits down opposite.

'How you feeling, Mrs Barnes?' she asks, placing the briefcase on the floor and the laptop on the table by a small, flat microphone, taped in place and connected to a bulky recording device bolted to the wall.

Celia opens her mouth to answer but can't find any words. The truth is she doesn't feel anything. Despite the horror of her morning she feels numb and wrung out, like she's been crying, though she hasn't been. She can't seem to manage any tears.

The girl continues to smile kindly at her. Alice – that was her name, a nice old-fashioned, comforting name. She reminds Celia of her niece, same colouring, same reddish hair, same freckled milky skin and pale green eyes. Probably about the same age too. What was it they say about knowing you're old when the policemen start looking younger? Imagine being as young as this girl and having to deal with things like what she saw in the Millers' living room that morning. It makes Celia feel even older. Old and unworldly, like she is the child and this young girl is the grown-up.

'I need to take your fingerprints, just so we know which ones in the house are yours so we can eliminate them and help us identify any that shouldn't be there. After that I'm going to ask you some questions, OK? About the house, about your employers, things like that, all right?'

Celia doesn't want to remember, but she does want to help the police catch whoever did that to Kate Miller, so she nods, because the thought that someone, some*thing* like that could still be out there makes her feel afraid.

A fingerprint scanner is produced from the briefcase and Celia rolls her fingers and thumbs across it as instructed, then the girl in the uniform presses a button on the recording device and a red light comes on. She looks at her watch.

'The time is 10.05 a.m. on Tuesday the fifteenth of September. PC Alice Eades taking an initial witness statement from Mrs Celia Barnes in relation to case number 45201/D.' She looks up, the kind smile in place again. 'Now I know this may be difficult, Mrs Barnes, but I need you to talk me through exactly what happened this morning in as much detail as you can, OK? Start with what you did before entering the house. Try and remember any cars you may have noticed, anybody out on the street. Don't worry if it seems trivial, every detail at this stage might be important, so just tell us anything and everything you can remember.'

Celia nods and pulls the tea towards her, feeling the warmth of it through the cardboard. She doesn't drink it. Instead she starts to talk, describing her morning leading up to the discovery of Kate Miller's body. And even as she frowns and tries hard to recall the particulars of her horrible morning, she feels increasingly anxious and useless. She wishes she could remember more, useful things instead of the boring details of empty streets, and what cupboard she took the bleach from, the listing of her dull morning routine only serving to underline exactly how mundane and pointless her life is and has always been. And it is the realization that nothing she can do or say will help them catch Kate's killer or stop Kate from being dead that finally brings tears.

The PC produces a small packet of tissues from somewhere and slides them across the table.

'Sorry,' Celia says, dabbing at her tears and blowing her nose.

'It's OK. Take as much time as you need, Mrs Barnes.'

'I just wish I could be more helpful, that's all.'

'You are being helpful. Knowing where you walked and what you touched in the house is a massive help to the forensics teams. You're doing great. Just let me know when you're happy to continue.'

Celia nods. 'I'm fine.'

'OK. Do you have a key to the Millers' house?'

'Yes.' She fumbles in her handbag and pulls out the key ring holding all the keys to the houses she cleans, the one her Derek says makes her look like a jailer. She separates a silver and green security key from the rest. 'This is the Millers'. Apparently you need a special ID card to get a copy made.'

PC Eades takes the key and studies the complex pattern of pits and grooves cut into the long, rectangular blade. 'For the record, Mrs Barnes is showing me a security key with a green fob and the brand name Mul-T-Lock printed on it.' She looks up at Celia. 'We'll need to take this into evidence, if that's OK.'

Celia hesitates. When she took the job with the Millers, Mike was very specific about the need to be extremely careful with this key.

Promise me you'll keep it very safe, he had told her, the twinkle in his eye taking the edge off the serious tone of his voice. And she *had* promised, blushing slightly as she did so, as if they were sharing a secret.

But this is different, this is the police, and the promise she made to him back then was on the other side of the huge chasm that now runs through her life, the one that separates before Kate's death and after. And she realizes with a swift and sudden sadness that she doesn't need the key any more because that life, the one where she cleans for the Millers every Friday and every other Tuesday, is now part of the 'before' and she won't ever be going there again. So she works the key off the ring with fumbling fingers and watches the nice PC take a small plastic evidence bag from the briefcase on the floor and seal the key inside it.

'How would you describe Kate and Mike Miller's relationship?' the PC asks as she starts filling in the exhibits paperwork.

Celia blinks, wrong-footed by the abrupt change of subject. Ordinarily she would never talk about her clients to anyone, but again, this is no ordinary situation.

'They're lovely together,' she says, 'absolutely devoted.' A torrent of memories rushes through her head. 'I would probably say they're about the nicest couple I know. I don't know how long they've been together, but they still act like newly-weds.' She blushes as she realizes what this implies. 'I mean, they're so sweet with each other, really attentive, always holding hands and sitting next to each other. I mean, not in an icky way, just – natural.' She smiles at a memory.

'One of the things I always had to be careful with was the pollen from all the flowers Mike bought for Kate. She loves lilies, you see, white lilies – beautiful flowers but the pollen is a bugger for staining.' She glances at the red light on the audio recorder. 'I mean, it can stain really badly if you're not careful, especially on white surfaces, so in that house, well you can imagine. The best thing to prevent it is to cut off the stamens but Kate liked the look of the whole flower so I couldn't do that, so I asked if they wouldn't mind getting me one of those rechargeable dust busters, you know the handheld job, so I could suck up all the fallen pollen and stamens. You can't wipe them up, you see, because that stains too, I mean it's as bad as turmeric, and you know what that's like if you get an Indian take-away and it spills on anything. Anyway Mike got me one – a Bosch, top of the range – and that was how we got round that. I think after that he bought more flowers than ever. He was always buying her flowers, flowers, and cards, and little gifts. It was like every day was special, like a birthday or an anniversary.'

'So no problems that you were aware of? No arguments or signs that things might not be quite right, sleeping in separate bedrooms, that kind of thing?'

Celia shifts in her chair. She knows they have to ask these questions but she still feels uncomfortable talking about Kate and Mike in this way, like she's gossiping about them to a stranger. Then a sudden realization strikes her and her eyes go wide. 'You don't think Mike did this?' She starts shaking her head. 'No. He would never, he couldn't . . .'

'At this stage we're not discounting anything, Mrs Barnes, but it's important for us to build a picture of what their relationship was like in case there were any tensions that might possibly have flared into something more serious. So if you did notice anything, especially in the last few weeks or so, it would be very useful for us to know about it.'

Celia continues shaking her head, shocked that they're even thinking Mike could have done such a thing. But then her mind slips back to the other side of the divide, back in the 'before' where something *did* happen.

It was about a month ago, a nothing-y kind of thing really, but still. It was the only time she ever witnessed Kate lose her temper, and even as she remembers it now, in light of the enormous and awful thing that has happened since, it seems like even less of something. And if she mentions it to the nice PC she'll read all sorts of things into it, things that just weren't there, and it will muddy the waters and get in the way of them finding whoever it was who really did this. And didn't her dad always tell her to speak well of the dead or not to speak of them at all?

'They were the loveliest, happiest couple you could ever hope to meet,' she says, 'and Mike would never, ever do

62

anything to harm Kate. Whoever did this, it wasn't him. Once you talk to him, you'll realize . . .' A new thought strikes her. 'Oh God, he doesn't know. Someone needs to tell Mike. You need to find him and tell him what happened. He's away somewhere.' She stares back down at the swirling island of bubbles in her tea, dredging her memory for something Kate said in passing the week before. 'I think he's on a yoga retreat, abroad somewhere. India, I think. Oh God, poor Mike, he's going to be absolutely devastated. Someone needs to call him and let him know what . . . someone needs to tell him about . . .' The tears come again and drown the end of her sentence.

PC Eades pulls another tissue from the pack and hands it to Celia. 'We have tried contacting Mr Miller,' she says, 'several times in fact, but he's not answering his phone.'

Celia dabs at her eyes and scrunches the tissue into a tight ball with the first one. 'Well . . . maybe he's asleep. It's probably still night-time where he is. Can't you find out what resort he's staying at and get someone to wake him?'

'We will,' PC Eades says. 'We're doing everything we can to locate him.'

'He didn't do it,' Celia says, shaking her head again. 'Mike didn't kill Kate. He couldn't have done that to . . .'

PC Eades smiles her kind, professional smile. 'I'm sure you're right, Mrs Barnes. But, until we can speak to him and rule him out of our investigation, Mike Miller is our number one person of interest.'

11

Tannahill shrugs off his paper suit, balls it up and stuffs it into one of the crime scene refuse sacks in the field office. Across the hallway in the living room the Crime Scene Manager and his assistant slip large bags over Kate Miller's outstretched arms, cable-tying them in place to seal in the evidence. He pulls his phone from his pocket and checks the time. He has just over an hour to get across London. He also has four missed phone calls – two from the office and two from his mother – the closest he gets to any kind of work/life balance these days. He heads to the front door and looks up to see DS Baker heading down the stairs.

'You off?'

'Yep. You found the husband yet?'

'Yeah, turns out he was upstairs all along.'

Baker pulls an e-cig from his pocket and follows Tannahill to the front door, his blue plastic shoe-covers whispering across the expensive, polished wood.

'He's proving to be a bit of an enigma, our Mr Miller, as is his missus. Nothing on the electoral register, no online presence, no National Insurance numbers listed for either of them, no employment histories, no paper trail of any kind. According to the records, they don't exist. They're ghosts.'

They step through the front door and out on to Swain's Lane.

'What about bank statements, bills, anything like that?'

Baker fires up his e-cig. 'So far we've found no paperwork anywhere in the house. No filing cabinet, no laptops, no computers, nothing. It's almost like they only just moved in, only we know from the neighbours that they've been here about a year, though that's about all. They didn't join the golf club, or the gym, or any of the usual social groups, so no one seems to know them at all, not where they came from or how they made their money.'

'Well keep digging' – Tannahill looks up at the front of the house – 'no one makes the kind of cash you need to buy a place like this without leaving some kind of trace, or making enemies along the way.'

Baker blows a long stream of white vapour up into the misty air then shakes his head. 'I still think it was him. Who else could have got in without tripping the alarm? Who else could have got out again and reset it – the cleaner who found the body said the alarm was on when she arrived.'

Tannahill nods slowly. 'Whoever killed Kate Miller certainly did it with a degree of anger, rage even, which suggests it might have been personal, a crime of passion. But then the clean-up was so calm and dispassionate, almost clinical.'

'That's because he read the book, didn't he?' Baker takes another draw on his e-cig and shakes his head as he blows out a long white stream of strawberry-scented smoke. 'Laughton Rees. Helluva name for a girl, no wonder she hates her father so much – I'd be mad at him too for lumbering me with a handle like that.'

Tannahill pictures the woman he saw only once from a distance. 'It suits her, actually.'

'You know her?'

'I went to one of her lectures when I was studying for my sergeants' exam, right after I'd read her book. I was intrigued.'

'Any good?'

'The book or her?'

'Either. Both.'

'The book's great. Clear. Insightful. She's pretty good too. Surprisingly young. Really sharp. Scary focused. She'd probably have made a great detective.'

Baker grunts. 'Not if her old man had anything to do with it.'

Tannahill nods. Like every cop in the Metropolitan Police he's aware of the bad blood between the big boss and his estranged daughter but has always deliberately chosen not to dig into it, figuring it was none of his business and he'd rather not know. But now a textbook she wrote on crime scene procedure has been found at an apparently cleansed crime scene – his crime scene – it has become his business. 'So what's the deal with the chief and his daughter?'

Baker turns to him, a look of puzzled amusement on his face. 'You don't know?'

'Only the headlines. I know the chief's wife was killed by someone he put away and his daughter blames him for it.'

Baker snorts. 'She doesn't just blame him, she hates him, like *really* hates him. I was around when it all went down and it was ugly. I mean, we all have family stuff to deal with, but not like this, and not played out for months on the front page of every newspaper. It was a huge story; look up the McVey case, you'll see. Apparently she went totally off the rails in the wake of it all, complete breakdown, refused to live with her dad, even lived on the streets for a while and fell pregnant before she pulled herself together. Now she's a lecturer in police procedure and writes books telling us all how we should be doing our jobs, and you don't need a psychologist to figure out what that's all about. It's like she's made it her life's work to lecture her father about what he did wrong and how he really should have done it. I'm glad you're going to be the one telling the chief about all this and not me.'

A bus rumbles by. A young woman in an upper window spots the two of them standing by the police van, jerks her phone from her ear and points it at them just as the bus moves on. It was probably too quick for her to snap a photo. Probably.

'You think maybe we should close the road,' Baker says, tucking his e-cig back in his pocket, 'stop the Snapchat vultures from getting too close?'

Tannahill thinks for a moment then shakes his head. 'A few blurry pics on social media are probably better than the increased attention we'd get from blocking off a main road on a bus route. Let's leave things as they are for now, keep a cordon around the house and the cemetery closed and don't say anything to anyone. If any press do show up, tell them an official statement will be issued in due course. But let's be careful about the removal of the body. You can stop the traffic for that if you need to.'

'Got it.'

Tannahill checks the time again: 11.58. Half-hour Tube journey to Westminster, ten-minute walk to Highgate station, ten-minute walk from Westminster to New Scotland Yard, press conference starting at one. He has time. Just about. He pulls several sheets of printed paper from his jacket pocket and glances through all the data he'd hoped to memorize that morning.

'How bad are the crime stats?' Baker asks, trying to get a peek at the pages.

'Bad,' Tannahill says, 'particularly knife crime. That's why we can't let the press get anywhere near this until we know what it is. If the tabloids find out a book on forensics, written by the chief's daughter, has been found at a forensically cleansed "multi-million-pound-mansion-murder-scene" it'll be all over the front page. And I definitely don't fancy explaining *that* to the chief.'

12

The email arrives at exactly midday.

Brian Slade – cane thin, perma-dressed for running, standing at his adjustable desk in the corner of the newsroom – does not see it at first. He is in the zone, up against deadline, writing the main body of an article about Darren Platt, the Premier League striker who may or may not have had sex with an underage girl in a hotel room with two of his friends. The verdict is due today, tomorrow at the latest, and will be front page of *The Daily* the moment it drops.

Slade takes a sip of water from his bottle and shifts from foot to foot, shaking each leg out in turn, flicking away his nervous energy. It doesn't matter to him which way the verdict goes. If Platt is found guilty Slade has a string of ex-girlfriends and assorted conquests lined up who'll pose in not very many clothes for a few grand a piece and give chapter and verse on the footballer's many kinks and shortcomings in the bedroom and as a person. If Platt is found *not* guilty – which past history and the fact he gets paid two hundred grand a week so can afford the best defence money can buy suggests he will – then Slade will use the threat of all these exes telling their sordid little tales to leverage an exclusive interview with Platt himself. Either way he gets an exclusive and *The Daily* gets its front page. Sex, sport, money, and glamour, that's what shifts newspapers and drives click-traffic, always has and always will. He just needs the verdict so he can slap an ending on his story.

He stretches some stiffness out of his lower back, takes another sip of water and is about to dive back into his story when a calendar alert pings up on his screen.

Police Press conference – 1 pm.

If sex and scandal are Slade's bread and butter then 'the-police-are-shit' stories are more like his hobby, and the release of the annual crime stats is usually good value. Slade has already seen how bad they are, courtesy of a copper on his payroll, and doesn't want to pass up the opportunity of watching Commissioner Rees squirm as he tries to put a positive spin on the pile of dog turds he has to deliver. If Slade can finish this article and park it in the next five minutes, he'll have plenty of time to run over to New Scotland Yard and get in position for all the fun and games. He clicks on the calendar alert to close it, then spots the email, the subject line snagging his attention:

DS GEORGE SLADE – RIP

Slade experiences the usual rush of emotions whenever he encounters his father's name: hatred, disgust, fear – still fear after all these years. He looks around the office to see if he can spot anyone smirking or pretending not to look his way, but everyone is staring at their screens. Whoever sent the email is either not in the room or doing a good job of keeping their head down.

He checks the sender – justice72@yahoo.com – could be anyone, a standard newsroom wind-up, find a person's weak spot then poke it relentlessly, and everyone knows everyone's secrets in this place, it's a matter of survival as much as anything: come for me and I'll come for you, mutually assured destruction, survival of the shittest.

Slade clicks open the message, expecting to see a picture of someone's arse, or a still from a gay porn video with his face Photoshopped on to some bloke getting shafted by another dude or something equally witty. Instead a series of large image files start downloading.

The first photo shows a white room with blood, lots of blood, and what appears to be a dead woman lying in the centre of it. The next shows the woman in life, beautiful and blonde but with a knife driven through her smile, the blood on the blade staining her perfect teeth. She is cuddling up to a blandly handsome man who looks like he might be a celebrity, though Slade doesn't recognize him so he can't be. Together they look like a couple in an advert selling something aspirational like investments or high-end cruises. A caption beneath the photo reads *Kate and Mike Miller*.

Slade googles them, clicks on the image tab and scrolls through the results looking for a match but finds none.

Interesting.

Who doesn't come up in a Google search these days?

Slade switches back to the email and stares at the picture of the smiling couple with the knife driven through it. 'Hello, Kate and Mike Miller,' he murmurs, 'who are you, I wonder?'

The next image downloads, an exterior of a house, a big, modern-looking thing with a wall of glass rising behind mature trees and what look like gravestones in the foreground. It's a strong image and the slowness of the downloads shows that these are large files, print quality, though the crime scene photos all have a time and date stamp on the bottom right corner which will need cropping out. Slade can see this house image sitting nicely beneath a headline, but what's the story? The subject line mentioned his father, but he can't see what connects him to these images other than it's a crime scene and his dad was once a detective in the Met, before they kicked him out. He checks the date stamps on the crime scene photos. Today's date. Not one of his old cases then. So what is it?

Another photo opens, a closer shot of the dead woman's body, her blood vivid against the white rug she's lying on; and there's something else, something Slade had missed in the wider shot. He leans forward and squints at the image, trying to make out the objects arranged so carefully around the dead woman. As if in response another image opens showing a close-up of one of them, a book, and Slade instantly knows what the story is and exactly how to spin it.

Laughton Rees.

He hasn't thought about her in years, not since he was reporting on the McVey case almost twenty years ago.

He snatches up his phone, finds a number in his recently called menu and dials it.

Laughton Rees, one of the lead characters in his first proper scoop, the gift that kept on giving as her life spiralled into tragedy. But then she'd pulled herself together and ceased to be of interest. And now she was back, her name swimming out of a room full of blood in a millionaire's mansion.

Money. Murder. People in high places. He could write it in less than five minutes, he just needed to check it was true, or true enough to hang a story on.

The phone starts ringing and he scrolls back through the photos looking for the picture of the house. There can't be many houses like this, built right next to an old cemetery, not in London at least. It might be in another city of course, but he doesn't think so.

'What do you want?' a low voice murmurs. 'I've already given you the crime stats.'

'I'm not calling about that, I'm calling about a murder. Victim is a woman. Blonde. Nicely put together. Somewhere

71

in her thirties, maybe forties but well preserved, or she was until someone stuck a knife in her multiple times. The house she was killed in is one of those wanky, architect-designed steel-and-glass boxes, looks like a dentist's or the offices of a tech company. It's right next to an old cemetery, big trees, headstones with moss on them. Maybe Highgate, maybe Stoke Newington.' He hears a sigh then the muffled sound of a keyboard being tapped. 'How recent?'

Slade glances back at the timestamp on the corner of the photographs. 'This morning.'

More typing. 'OK, I got it. Victim is Katherine Miller with a "K". Age thirty-nine. Found dead in her Highgate house by her cleaner.'

Slade opens his notebook and starts scribbling. 'Does the cleaner have a name?'

'Er . . . Celia Barnes.'

'Any suspects? Anyone in custody?'

'None yet, though we're looking for the husband, one Michael James Miller, forty-eight, current whereabouts unknown. What's your interest?'

'Not sure yet. Is there anything else?'

'Not much. The scene's still being processed so the case file won't get fully updated until they get back and upload it. The cleaner's been interviewed and there's an audio file of that.'

'I'll have that. Anything else?'

'Not really. There's a brief initial report from a DS on the murder squad that describes the scene as being very clean.'

Slade looks back at the photo of the woman lying in the centre of a room decorated with her blood. 'What do you mean "clean"?'

'I mean forensically clean – no fingerprints, no DNA, like it's been wiped down by someone who knew what they were doing.'

'Really?' Slade scrolls back to the book and smiles when he re-reads the title, the story taking solid shape in his mind now. 'Is there anything in the file about some objects that were left by the body?'

'Nothing. Sounds like your information is more up to date than mine. Who you getting all this from?'

Who indeed?

'What time was it called in?'

'Er . . . seven fifty-seven a.m.'

Slade scrolls back through the email, checking the timestamps on all the crime scene photographs and smiles.

'You're not my only friend in high places,' he says. 'Keep me posted about any new developments and I'll call back later for an update.'

He cuts him off and opens a new document, all thoughts of Darren Platt and his court case now forgotten. There's only one story that's going to be on the front page of the evening paper and it's not going to be about shagging footballers.

13

Laughton Rees explodes into the tiny office on the third floor of London Metropolitan University, dumps her bag on a chair with orange foam showing through worn fabric and slams the door behind her.

'SHIT!' she says, venting some of the rage she's built up on her furious march from her daughter's school.

She checks the time. First lecture in fifteen minutes – two minutes to get down to the lecture hall, call it four if the lifts are on the wrong floors, ten minutes spare. Just about enough to make a start.

She collapses into the worn swivel chair she shares with a colleague, logs on to the ancient, beige-coloured desktop PC she also shares and taps in her password, the only thing that is uniquely hers.

'Shit,' she says again, quieter this time, then one more time to round it up to three as Maya's casually chilling words echo in her mind:

This is St Mark's. Lots of kids carry knives.

Well sod that for a game of soldiers. There's no way she's going to leave Gracie in that place a day longer than she has to, not with *Call-me-Jonathan* and his fridge-magnet philosophy manifesto in full-blown denial.

The desktop blinks into life, the London Metropolitan crest filling the screen, a black knight's helmet and a hand holding a fish that always makes her think she's lecturing at the University of Monty Python. She opens a browser, googles 'Best Private Schools in North London' and clicks the first result.

A homepage loads showing a gorgeous red-brick building that looks more like a hotel spa than a school. Laughton dials the contact number and scrolls through pages of professionally taken photographs showing happy children cheerfully engaged in music, and chemistry experiments as she waits for it to connect. It looks amazing, inspiring – safe. It also looks expensive.

She scans the keyword menu running up the side of the page, spots the word FEES and clicks on it just as someone picks up.

'Highgate and Holloway School for Girls,' a posh but friendly woman says. She sounds nice, a complete contrast to the grumpy harridan who mans the St Mark's reception desk.

'Hello,' Laughton says, 'I was just wondering if I could talk to someone about a possible place for my daughter.'

'Of course,' the friendly woman trills, 'I'll just pop you through to Mrs Wilson in admissions.'

The line clicks and soothing classical music fills the gap, making Laughton think of lazy summer afternoons on shady lawns. She scans the 'fees' page, a frown forming as she adds it all up in her head: seven grand a term, twenty-one thousand a year, five-grand deposit on accepting a place, plus a hundred and fifty quid application fee (non-refundable). Happiness comes at a price, it seems, and that price was roughly twenty-six grand for the first year alone.

'Shit!' she whispers, just as the summery music cuts out and another friendly voice takes its place.

'Hello, my name's Holly Wilson, I'm director of admissions

75

at Highgate and Holloway. I understand you're interested in a place for your daughter?'

'Yes, that's . . . yes.' Laughton is instantly flustered and worried that this nice friendly lady just heard her say '*shit*'.

'Lovely. Well let's start with a few details, shall we,' the woman continues, sounding thankfully like she did not. 'What's your daughter's name?'

'Gracie, er Grace Rees.'

'Grace, what a lovely name. I don't think we have a Grace here, so she'll be our first.'

Laughton hears the sound of keys being slowly tapped. She glances at the time on the top of her screen, aware that she has tricky questions to ask and not much time to ask them in.

'And what year is Grace currently in?' Mrs Wilson continues.

'Year nine.'

'Right, so she's making her GCSE choices.'

'Yes.'

Just ask the question. It's a perfectly legitimate question. Stop being intimidated by the nice posh lady.

She takes a breath, moves the mouse to an empty part of the screen, clicks the button three times then says:

'Sorry, Mrs Wilson, I've got to cut this fairly short because I'm at work and need to . . . The truth is, the fees are going to be a bit of a reach so I was wondering what the situation was regarding scholarships.'

'Oh, right, of course. Well, we do offer scholarships in each year group based on exam results and performance during term time.'

'And how much of a discount do they give?'

'Well it's on a sliding scale, depending on results, but it can be as much as twenty-five per cent.'

Twenty-five per cent.

Laughton does the sums in her head. She'll still need to find another fifteen grand a year from somewhere – after tax

– not to mention five grand for the deposit, plus the cost of the uniform, and that's only if Gracie gets the full 25 per cent discount in the first place.

'Is there any other kind of financial assistance available?'

'Well . . . we are a registered charity so a number of our pupils are financed either partly or wholly by grandparents, which can be very tax efficient.'

'That's not. I mean, Gracie doesn't have any grandparents.' The lie comes easily. As far as this conversation goes it's true anyway because there's no way she's going to ask *him* for help. 'What about grants for local children? We live in Holloway, so . . .'

'Well then yes, we do offer means-tested financial support to a small number of local pupils each year whose families can't afford the full fees. I can send you some details if you like?'

'Yes, that would be great, thank you.'

'Or maybe I could give them to you in person – have you visited the school yet?'

'No, I . . .'

'Well, I'd be more than happy to arrange a visit for you and Grace, she could even sit the entrance exams at the same time.'

'Entrance exams, yes.' Laughton starts tapping the thumb of her spare hand along her fingers in patterns of three and is instantly annoyed at herself.

This is what she wants, isn't it? To get Gracie out of that shitty school and into one where she can go about her day without being threatened by someone with a knife. So why was she hesitating? It wasn't the money – well, partly it was the money, but she could figure that out somehow. She could do more consultancy work, work more hours, write a crime novel – *something*. She looks at the clock on the screen and realizes she's out of time.

'Listen, Mrs Wilson, I've got to dash. Let me talk to Gracie tonight and I'll get back to you tomorrow to hopefully arrange a time to visit, OK?'

'Of course. May I just ask one quick question?'

Not really – she thinks. 'Of course,' she says.

'Why are you looking to move schools?'

Because the headmaster's a dick.

Because apparently everyone at the school carries a knife.

'Because I don't think her current school's quite right for her,' she says. 'I think she'd benefit from a bit more . . . structure.'

'Of course,' Mrs Wilson replies, the smile evident in her voice. 'I'm sure Grace will fit right in here at Highgate and Holloway. I look forward to hearing from you.'

Laughton hangs up, grabs the memory stick with all her lecture slides loaded on to it and roots out a couple of books from the pile on her desk – *The Numbers Game: Why everything you know about football is wrong*, and a slim volume one of her students ordered on Amazon and brought in for her to sign. She glances at the cover as she hustles out of her office, the outline of a body beneath the title – *How to Process a Murder.*

Maybe she should get all of her students to buy signed copies. The royalties could help pay Gracie's new school fees.

14

Tannahill makes it to Highgate underground station just as a southbound train pulls away from the platform. He blows out a long breath and checks the board. Four minutes until the next one. He strolls up the platform, enjoying the breeze rinsing down the platform, conjured by the departing train.

There was a time, so the old boys tell him, that the fastest way around London bar none was in a squad car with the blues and twos blaring. Nowadays, with all the budget cuts and the hellish London traffic, the quickest way from one side of the city to the other is the same for the police as it is for everyone else.

Tube. Bus. Bike. Walking.

He pulls the cheat sheets from his jacket pocket, a *Reader's Digest* version of all the historical crime and knife stats he's compiled ahead of today's press conference, but his mind is too distracted to concentrate on it. All he can think about is the Miller house, and the strange objects surrounding the victim, and the book written by the Commissioner's daughter – the daughter no one's allowed to mention.

Look at the McVey case, Baker had said.

Tannahill stuffs the notes back in his pocket, pulls out his phone and googles *Laughton Rees McVey*.

The signal in the station is weak and Tannahill can already hear the screech and rattle of the next train approaching so he walks along the platform holding his phone out in front of him like a water diviner, looking for a stronger signal.

The train squeals to a stop beside him just as the results page loads. He taps the top hit as the doors rumble open and steps on to the train, staying by the doors to catch as much signal as he can before it moves off.

The banner loads first, showing he's on *The Daily* website, then the headline follows:

'Masked Monster' suspect brutally murders wife of police officer who arrested him

- Adrian McVey, the man accused of killing 8 children over a 10-year period and attacking dozens more, walks free after bungled investigation causes the case to dramatically collapse
- Hours later McVey savagely murders wife of DCI John Rees, the detective who led the investigation against him
- DCI Rees's daughter, Laughton Rees, 15, witnesses her mother's murder

By BRIAN SLADE for *The Daily* and Laroux Publications

The doors slide shut and the train lurches forward, knocking Tannahill off balance. He grabs a rail with his spare hand and scrolls down the article with his thumb, making sure it's all there so he can still read it once he loses signal when they leave the station. The article is complete but the photographs are still downloading, fuzzy at first then sharper as data trickles in, people and faces emerging from digital fog. One shows a man in his early fifties, thinning red hair brushed forward, rectangular, metal-rimmed glasses reflecting the flash so his eyes seem to glow.

Adrian McVey, the caption reads, *suspected 'Masked Monster'*.

Another shows a young girl, petite, blonde, huge eyes staring through the camera as she is led away from a house and towards an ambulance by a paramedic.

Laughton Rees, 15, the caption reads, *who witnessed the brutal murder of her mother at the hands of Adrian McVey*.

The train lurches again and the windows of the carriage go black as they rattle into the tunnel. Tannahill's signal drops to one bar, then none, and the photos stop downloading.

He walks down the carriage, jostled by the movement of the train, finds a seat then scrolls back to the top of the article and begins to read.

Adrian McVey, 52, chief suspect in the long-running 'Masked Monster' paedophile serial-murderer case, was arrested last night after brutally murdering Grace Rees, 48, wife of Detective Chief Inspector John Rees, lead detective in the case against him.

Earlier in the day McVey had been dramatically released from custody after his case had been thrown out by Justice Robin Plenderleith. As McVey was being led from the court he pointed at DCI Rees and shouted:

'You ruined my life. How would you like it if someone ruined yours?'

It now seems he planned to do exactly that.

Shortly after 11 p.m. a neighbour heard screams coming from the Rees family home in Acton and raised the alarm.

Police officers arrived on scene within minutes and discovered Grace Rees, 48, bloody and unresponsive. She had been stabbed multiple times as she apparently attempted to defend her teenage daughter, Laughton, who police believe was McVey's intended victim.

Mrs Rees and her daughter were rushed to nearby Hammersmith hospital where Mrs Rees later died of her injuries. DCI John Rees was not at home at the time of the attack.

McVey was found at the property brandishing a bloodied kitchen knife and wearing an animal mask – the trademark of the 'Masked Monster'. He was subdued and arrested then taken to a secure psychiatric unit where he is currently being held.

This shocking attack raises again the question of whether or not McVey was in fact the Masked Monster. The police have so far issued no comment, but McVey's lawyer Ruth Cottington-Bray QC gave the following statement.

'Since Mr McVey's name and identity were made known in connection with this case my client has been through hell. Anyone would have been pushed to the edge of reason as a result of the intolerable scrutiny and hate he has had to endure and though I, of course, sympathize with the victims of this violent act, it is important to remember that my client is a victim too.'

It remains to be seen whether the tragic events of last night were the act of an innocent man driven to insanity, as McVey's lawyer suggests, or if it will finally mark the end of the so-called Masked Monster's reign of terror.

Brakes squeal as the Tube train slows.
Doors open. People get off. People get on.
Tannahill notices none of it as he continues to read.

Ten-year reign of terror

It began on 16 July 1995 when a six-year-old girl, playing in her garden in Brockley, south-east London, was snatched in broad daylight while her mother stood just a few feet away making sandwiches in her kitchen.

Minutes later she heard crying and found her little girl on the railway embankment backing on to her garden. At first her mother thought she had hurt herself climbing over the fence, but then her daughter, known as X to protect her identity, said these chilling words that revealed something far more sinister had happened:

'The rabbit man hurt me,' she said, 'the rabbit man grabbed me and hurt me.'

A medical examination later showed that the girl had been sexually assaulted. When police later interviewed Girl X to try and gather details about her attacker, she drew a picture of a grinning cartoon rabbit with big black eyes, later identified to be a child's rabbit mask with one terrifying difference. The attacker had made the eyes on his mask bigger. So began the reign of terror of the serial paedophile attacker known as 'the Masked Monster'.

Over the next eight years he struck at least twelve more times, all in the Greater London area, each attack more violent, and each time wearing a child's animal mask with enlarged eyeholes.

As his infamy grew so did speculation as to the significance of the mask. Clearly it was to hide the attacker's identity, but why did he make the eyeholes larger? Was it simply to make his appearance more horrific to the terrified children he targeted? Whatever the reason, the similarities of each attack proved that a serial attacker was at large. And as the number of attacks grew, so did public outrage, particularly at the police who seemed nowhere nearer to catching him.

Then, eight years and one month after the first known attack, the Masked Monster's reign of terror took an even darker turn.

On a warm August evening in 2003, ten-year-old Esme Lord was taken from the bedroom of her basement flat.

Her body was found the following morning on a nearby building site. She had been sexually assaulted and strangled. Lying next to her body was a child's mask of a cat, the eyeholes made larger, leaving no doubt as to who had committed this awful crime.

The Masked Monster had killed his first victim – but not his last.

Four more children would lose their lives to this monster over the next two years, Eloise Fraser, Matilda Jones, Isabella Morrison, and Ruby-Mae Brown, each new victim striking fresh fear into parents not just in London but across the entire country as they asked themselves as they locked their doors and tucked their children into bed at night – who was the Masked Monster, and when would he strike again?

On 4 September 2005 we had an answer. Police, who had been criticized for their lack of progress and inability to stop the killings, finally arrested a man. His identity, initially held back for legal reasons, was later leaked in the lead-up to his trial and spread widely online, robbing the suspect of his anonymity.

The man was Adrian McVey, a 52-year-old part-time caretaker in a local primary school in Honor Oak Park, South London, close to where most of the attacks had taken place.

Described by shocked neighbours as quiet, friendly, and always polite, McVey was a familiar figure in an area he'd lived all his life. Known for cycling everywhere in a shirt and tie, and woollen sweaters knitted by his late mother, he lived alone in the house he'd been born in.

The house, a Victorian terrace on Grierson Road, also

happened to back on to the same railway embankment where the Masked Monster's first victim had been attacked, just half a mile away in Brockley.

After his identity was revealed his house was repeatedly vandalized, the rose garden McVey had planted in memory of his mother, Rose McVey, destroyed by fire. McVey himself received numerous death threats and after one violent attack that left him almost blind in one eye, he had to be kept in solitary confinement in Rampton Secure Hospital where he was being detained while awaiting trial.

Throughout all this, right up to the much-publicized trial at the Old Bailey, McVey repeatedly protested his innocence. His defence team, led by Ruth Cottington-Bray QC, claimed they would prove his innocence and insisted that he had been the victim of a police force so desperate to find a suspect and obtain a conviction for these crimes that they were prepared to frame an innocent man. They singled out Detective Chief Inspector John Rees, lead investigator on the case, as someone who'd 'had it in' for McVey and had steered the investigation in a way that both targeted and victimized him.

The trial began as planned on 14 June and was expected to last for at least eight weeks, but before the jury was even sworn in, Justice Robin Plenderleith dramatically dismissed the case following a pre-trial meeting called by the defence.

In a statement, Justice Plenderleith said:

'Justice is at the heart of everything we do here, and there is no greater role for the criminal justice system than to conduct itself in a fair and just way. In this case the police failed to properly disclose, and in one instance attempted to conceal, key pieces of evidence germane to the fair conduct of this trial. Having seen proof, provided by the defence, convincing me of these grave truths, I regretfully have no other choice but to rule that, in light of this, there is no case to answer here and the accused is therefore free to go.'

It was in the uproar that followed this statement that Adrian McVey accused DCI John Rees of ruining his life and threatened to get revenge. Little did anyone know how serious he was . . .

(Click here to view more . . .)

Tannahill automatically taps on the link to expand the article but gets a new window with a *Page can't be loaded* message instead.

He looks up at the black windows of the carriage, the train so deep underground as to kill any signal. He has lost track of time and has no idea where he is or what station they are approaching.

He looks back down at his phone, returns to the previous page and scrolls past adverts for holidays and investments to the comments section.

Golferman, United Kingdom, 3 days ago
Should of been given the death sentence.

Dave, United Kingdom, 1 week
Bring back hanging for scum like this.

BritishBulldog, United Kingdom, 2 weeks ago
The police and the courts is no better than the crims. Defund the police now!

(Click here to view more . . .)

Beneath that are links to related stories:

Police cleared of all wrongdoing in 'Masked Monster' investigation

The inquiry into police mishandling of the investigation into alleged 'Masked Monster' Adrian McVey ended yesterday with all officers involved being cleared and returned to full duty with no further action required. DCI John Rees, who headed up the investigation and came in for the heaviest criticism, said he was looking forward to returning to work. 'Nothing can change what has happened,' he said in a brief statement, 'I hope everyone involved can now heal and move forward with their lives.' . . . *(read more)*

Daughter of masked monster detective leaves home, blames father for mother's death

Laughton Rees, the tragic girl at the centre of alleged 'Masked Monster' Adrian McVey's brutal revenge slaying of her mother, has quit her family home and voluntarily entered social care saying she no longer wishes to live with her father, whom she holds responsible for her mother's death. Miss Rees (15) has no other family and intends to stay in care until she reaches her 16th birthday . . . *(read more)*

Tragic daughter of masked monster cop now a single mum on benefits

The Daily can exclusively reveal that Laughton Rees (18), daughter of DCI John Rees who headed up the investigation into the notorious Masked Monster is now living in a rehabilitation shelter with her baby daughter after a period of being homeless. She has had no contact with her father since her mother's tragic death three years ago . . . *(read more)*

Tannahill reaches the bottom of the page and looks up as the train slows and pulls into a station.

Tottenham Court Road. Four stops left, one change, still no signal.

He scrolls back to the top of the page and looks at the photo of the young girl being led away from her home.

Fifteen-year-old Laughton Rees, eyes wide with shock, and any chance of a normal life already gone before it's really begun.

She reads his name out loud, a ritual she started on her first day on the job and has continued for almost three decades to respectfully acknowledge each person who passes through her care. He has a police tag too, but not an urgent one, and she scans their report, reading how the boy had jumped, or fallen, or been pushed from the Hornsey Lane Bridge at around six thirty that morning, tumbled thirty feet on to the A1 below, then been struck by two cars and a bus before the traffic finally stopped. The attending paramedics also found stab wounds on the boy's back, though they couldn't determine whether these, or the fall, or the vehicle impacts were the main cause of death. This will be for her and the pathologist to establish. But not yet.

In a mortuary, where rigid systems and protocols lie beneath the surface like bones under flesh, the boy will have to wait. Because he was just a street kid, a runaway from the broken care system, someone who lived and died on the fringes of society. No one stayed awake through the night wondering where he was, no frantic call was made to the police to report him missing; and so, in the practical world of an overstretched and underfunded mortuary, he is not a priority. He is just another statistic, another young victim of knife crime.

Arlene McManus places his notes gently back down on the steel table next to the bag containing the broken remains of his body and glances up at the orderly re-entering the cold room ready to transport the first body next door, the tinny whisper of lively music leaking from his earbuds and sounding out of place in this sombre room. Arlene moves across to the woman who arrived with the red police tag. She studies the dead woman through the translucent white body-bag, her face framed by expensively cut, salon-blonde hair darkened now by blood. Death is supposed to be the great leveller but Arlene knows this is not true: the evidence is lying before her, embodied in this woman who has just arrived and yet will be seen first, and the boy who must wait until last, even in death. The blonde woman looks like someone who never waited in line in life either, though this is one queue she undoubtedly never expected to join so soon.

Arlene stares down at her in a private moment of remembrance then scans her notes, looking for hints of who she was in life – daughter, sister, wife, mother – all just words now sketching the vague outline of a person passed. She sees with surprise that she too is a victim of knife crime, and, in her final act of remembrance, reads her name out loud.

Kate Miller.

'Sorry?' the orderly pulls a bud free from his ear and the tinny music sounds even louder.

'She was called Kate Miller,' Arlene replies, gesturing at the woman in the white plastic shroud.

The orderly nods and looks nervously at her, like she's asked him a question he doesn't know the answer to. He is young, and lanky, and eager – a gap-year medical student who'll be gone as quickly as he arrived. No one stays here very long. Only her.

'Could you take Mrs Miller into the lab please,' Arlene instructs him, too tired and too busy to explain her ritual to this boy. 'And tell Dr Collins we're ready for him now.'

Jake Stevens nods, fits the earbud back in place and releases the wheel brake on the steel table the woman's body is lying upon.

Kate Miller – the name seemed familiar somehow.

He wheels the table over to the door leading to the main mortuary and glances down at the body-bag, unnerved at the thought that someone he knows might be inside it.

He can see the vague outline of the woman's face through the white plastic shrouds they used rather than the thick, black body-bags you saw in films. It was one of the many weird little things he'd learned since taking this job because his mother had insisted he get some 'life experience' after messing up his A levels, though how wheeling corpses around was 'life' experience he wasn't quite sure. It sucked, that was for sure, especially when some of his equally slack mates were currently sitting on a beach in Thailand waiting for *their* re-sits.

Then it dawned on him.

His mother had texted him earlier asking if a Kate Miller been admitted to the hospital and to find out what she was in for. She must be a friend of his mum and she obviously thought she'd just had an accident or something.

Jesus! She didn't know. He would have to tell her.

He pushes the steel table through the doors into the main lab, feeling a little shocked but also vaguely pleased that for once he would be able to demonstrate to his hard-to-please mother that he could actually be useful sometimes.

He was due a break soon. He would text her then.

He lines up the body next to the stainless-steel autopsy table, applies the wheel brake and slides the body over, starting with the head then moving the feet across to join them. He takes his phone, turns off his music and glances up at the door, waiting for Nurse Arlene and the two police officers to walk through it. He hears the clang of a storage locker door next door and it occurs to him that he could snap a quick picture of the body.

No one would know.

Then he dismisses the idea as stupid and gross.

Besides, he would get fired if anyone caught him, it was practically the first thing they told the porters on their induction – no photos, no messing around, this was a place of respect and professionalism. And imagine having to explain to his mother that he'd lost his job trying to take a picture of her dead friend.

No. He'll just text her with the bad news in a minute. Maybe even call her in case she gets upset.

He releases the wheel brake and pushes the now empty steel table back out to the cold room to be disinfected and rotated back into circulation, ready for the next arrival, and the never-ending parade of the London dead.

16

Tannahill emerges from Westminster Tube station into a damp mist that turns the buildings lining the Thames into looming grey shapes. He dials a number as he heads along the Embankment and presses his phone to his ear to block out the traffic noise. He can still smell the chlorine from the nitrile gloves on his hands. Baker answers on the second ring.

'Any news?' Tannahill ducks round a couple of tourists who have stopped to consult a map on their phone. 'Preferably of the good sort.'

'Not really. The cleaner said Mike Miller was away on some foreign retreat somewhere, so we did a search and found a Michael Miller booked on to a British Airways flight to Goa last Tuesday, but he apparently never turned up so at least he's still in the country. Except he can't be, because he doesn't exist and neither did his missus.'

'Did you run her prints?'

'Yep. Nothing pinged on the database on a preliminary search, but we'll keep looking. Ditto the set we managed to lift from one of the bathrooms, which we're assuming belong to the husband. We managed to lift thumbprints from the scanners front and back. The one by the front door is the cleaner's. The one at the back matches one of the prints we lifted from the bathroom.'

'Mike Miller.'

'Most likely. That's it though; there's nothing else useful in the house. As suspected, it's totally clean, thanks no doubt to the information in the book written by our dear Commissioner's daughter.'

'What about the house? There must be some kind of paper trail for the sale or, if it's rented, solicitor's details, estate agency files, that kind of thing.'

'Well that's another thing. I checked with the land registry and the Millers don't actually own the house, it was bought by a company based in the Cayman Islands just over a year ago. The same company, Twilight Holdings, is also listed on all the utility bills. We'll keep digging but . . .' Tannahill hears a hiss as Baker takes a drag on his e-cigarette, 'bloody Cayman Islands. Good luck following the money on that one. There's a good reason people set up companies in the Cayman Islands.'

'Because they're crooks.'

'That's one of them, yes.'

'Well then maybe they were on the run from something. Maybe they made their money doing something dangerous – drugs, money-laundering, something under the radar that paid handsomely but went sour so they had to change their identities and move somewhere no one knew them. We should check with NCA to see if they were Protected Persons, though I doubt it, this seems way too rich for their blood.'

The white block of New Scotland Yard emerges from the mist ahead, reminding Tannahill it's time to get his head out of the Miller case and back into the crime stats.

'And stick an extra-urgent flag on the forensics. Maybe Kate Miller's DNA can tell us who she really is, either directly or through a familial screen.'

'Will do, though even with a red flag we won't get any

results before tomorrow afternoon at the earliest, and we'll only get a direct match if her DNA is already on the database.'

'Well if they're buying houses through blind trusts and using false names they're clearly dodgy, so you never know, she might be on it.'

'Bet you a tenner she isn't.'

Tannahill walks up the steps to the glass reception area and pauses by the door. 'No bet,' he says. 'We should look at those items we found by the body too. Maybe the medals are traceable, the keys must fit a lock somewhere, and that blue one might be something we can get a lead on. And what about the toy unicorn, what's that doing in the house of a childless couple?'

He pulls open the door and sees the press already filing into the briefing room. He's been dreading this moment for weeks but now it's here it seems like little more than an annoyance, an obstacle to get over as quickly as possible so he can get back to work. 'Got to go,' he says.

'Enjoy the grilling,' Baker replies. 'And good luck telling the gaffer his daughter helped a killer clean up a crime scene.'

17

Commissioner John Rees – tall, slender, old-school authoritarian in his dress uniform – regards himself in the mirror of a too warm toilet on the top floor of New Scotland Yard.

Despite the polished service medals and the looping red braid denoting his high rank there is a vaguely worn air about him. It's there in the slight hollowness of his cheeks, accentuated by harsh overhead lighting. It's in his hair, almost white now, cropped tight on the sides and upright on top, rising from a forehead corrugated by too many years of too much responsibility. At least he still *has* some hair. He runs his hand upward to make it stand fully to attention, adding an extra inch to his six feet of actual height.

When he joined the police you had to be five foot eight minimum to even apply, a restriction long since lifted after the police stopped being a respectable profession to aspire to and they started struggling to attract any applicants at all. He's seen new male officers walking down corridors recently who might be better employed as munchkins. Still, new men in uniform at a time when the job was getting ever harder made them worth their weight, no matter how slight that weight happened to be: beggars in an impoverished world could not afford to be choosers.

Rees breathes deeply and catches the whiff of warm piss beneath the pine scent of the deodorizing mats lying crooked in the urinals. He glances down at the sheets of paper in his hand, bullet-point reminders of the crime statistics. He hates press conferences at the best of times, and this is always the worst, like an annual ambush he knows is there but has to walk into anyway.

He's had the figures for a few weeks now and has had to endure several meetings with various public relations experts as a result, professional liars sent down from the Home Office, well versed in the black art of taking one thing and talking about it in such a way as to make it seem like something else. They had all agreed that knife crime was the stand-out turd in this year's sea of shit and had advised him to refer to it as 'street crime' instead, which was technically correct as almost all of the reported incidents took place there. Rebranding it as 'street crime', the PR people argued, softened the scare factor because the vast majority of home owners with cars (otherwise known as voters) didn't spend that much time on 'the streets' so would feel it didn't really affect or pose any threat to them.

Rees had nodded and dutifully changed all mention of 'knife crime' in his statement to 'street crime', knowing it was a thin layer of varnish on what was still a turd because whatever words he used the figures remained the same and were the worst since records began back in 1946.

That was the headline right there. He could picture it, a big, bold, scary banner designed to terrify people into buying a paper or click on some link in order to find out exactly how bad things were and how scared they needed to be about the way things were heading in their already shaky world.

Rees studies his reflection, runs his finger round the slight gap between his neck and shirt collar. He tightens his tie a little. Attempts a smile but it only makes the creases in his hollow cheeks deepen so he lets it fade.

Street crime.

He reaches into his pocket, thumbs the lid off a small jar of painkillers and tips one into his palm. 'Come on then, you broken-down old bastard,' he murmurs, and the figure in the mirror murmurs it back. 'Let's get this over with.'

He pops the pill in his mouth, swallows it dry, then turns and walks away from his reflection.

18

Tannahill excuses his way through knots of journalists, heading to the raised stage at the back of the press room. Everyone else is already there – Ed Murray, chief press officer, Ian Duncan, commander in charge of Specialist Crime, some woman in a corporate suit he doesn't recognize who's probably been drafted in for the same reason he has, namely to improve the diversity and equality optics: one woman – tick; one brown person – tick. Fortunately the Commissioner isn't there yet, so technically he's not late, though the CPO glares at him anyway. Tannahill nods a silent greeting to him and the others, takes his place alongside them and pulls his notes from his pocket, wishing for the hundredth time that the facts they contained were in his head and not in his hand as he turns to face the room.

There are a lot more people here than he had imagined. A *lot* more. At the back two TV cameras squat on top of tripods, their lenses pointing over the heads of the seated journalists at the lectern standing empty at the front of the stage. The room feels too hot after his brisk walk from the Tube and he can feel sweat prickling beneath his jacket and shirt. He blots his forehead with his sleeve, dimly remembering something a police media coach once said about how Richard Nixon sweated his way through the first ever televised presidential debate and lost the election as a result. Good job he's not running for president.

He glances down at his notes one last time, his eyes sliding uselessly over the dense blocks of stats, then the burble of conversation stops abruptly and he looks up to see the Commissioner of Police of the Metropolis John Rees step on to the platform and take his position behind the lectern.

'Good afternoon, ladies and gentlemen,' the Commissioner says, his voice a low rumble, 'I believe you have all been given a copy of the latest crime statistics but, for the purpose of clarity, and the benefit of the television cameras, I will run through them now then throw to the floor for questions.'

He lays a single piece of paper on the lectern then looks back up at the room and proceeds to run through the stats, looking at everyone and no one, never once glancing down at his notes, which makes Tannahill feel even worse about the amateur-hour performance he's about to give.

He listens to the numbers, his heart sinking lower as the figures get higher: homicide up 6 per cent; robbery up 9; domestic violence up 1; knife crime – sorry, '*street* crime' – with forty-three thousand separate incidents up 12 per cent; total violent crime up 19 per cent over the course of the whole year.

Rees opens up the room to questions and Tannahill almost rocks back on his heels with the force of everyone speaking at once. Rees points at a ruddy-faced man in tweeds sitting in the front row.

'Thank you, Commissioner. Bill Nicholson, *Daily Telegraph*. These figures seem unusually high, any comment on why?'

'Well, post-Covid we are in a particularly challenging economic climate, which traditionally goes hand-in-hand with higher crime rates. The jump in domestic violence can also be directly tied to lockdown periods caused by the virus, and we expect those numbers to drop back down now. Also, recent technological improvements in crime reporting means many more crimes are being recorded and categorized more accurately than ever before, particularly in areas such as street crime.' He turns and gestures towards Tannahill. 'To give a little more detail and background on these street crime figures in particular I'm going to hand over now to DCI Tannahill Kha—'

'Why do you keep calling it "street crime"?' The shouted question cuts Rees off and makes him turn back to the room.

Tannahill scans the crowd for the speaker. 'Why do you keep calling it "street crime"?' a bald, skinny, suntanned man in running clothes repeats as he stands up and turns slightly towards the TV cameras. 'What you're clearly talking about is "knife crime".'

'Well the figures include more than just knife crimes,' Rees replies, 'and as knife crime does tend to be restricted to the streets it's a perfectly accura—'

'What about the woman knifed to death in her house last night?'

The sound man by the TV camera angles a microphone in the bald man's direction and Rees hesitates, aware that both sides of the conversation are now being recorded.

'Well, as you know I can't comment on active ca—'

'Lady in Highgate,' the bald man cuts in, addressing the room now, 'stabbed to death in her multimillion-pound North London mansion.' He turns back to Rees. 'Looks like "street crime" is no longer confined to the streets.'

Rees pauses for a moment. 'Well, as I said, I can't comment on current cases, so—'

'What if a book explaining how to cover your tracks at a murder scene was found next to this dead woman's body, a book written by your daughter, Commissioner Rees – would you comment then?'

A murmur sweeps through the room, punctured by the click of cameras and the frantic scribbling of notes.

'No,' Rees replies, 'I would not – though I would be very interested to know where you're getting this information from.'

The bald man smiles. 'I bet you would.' He turns back to the room: 'Check *The Daily* website in about half an hour and you'll see what *street crime* really looks like.' He does air quotes with his fingers when he says 'street crime'. 'That's *The Daily* dot com, always first with the news.' He looks back at Rees, winks, then heads away to the exit.

Hands fly up and the room fills with noise as everyone shouts for the Commissioner's attention.

Rees glances back at Tannahill, as if he's about to hand the press conference over to him, then he turns to the room and the clamour intensifies.

Commissioner!
Commissioner!!!
Is knife crime out of control?
Has it left the city streets and spread to the suburbs?
Did your daughter write a book showing how to get away with a crime?
Commissioner!
Commissioner!!!!
Commissioner!!!!!!

Rees scans the room and the noise subsides as he opens his mouth to speak. 'Thank you, ladies and gentlemen,' he says, his voice a low rumble beneath the noise of the room, 'any further questions can be directed to the press office.'

Then he steps off the stage and leaves the room.

Tannahill watches, his brain trying to catch up with what just happened. He looks down at the notes, weeks of work rendered irrelevant. The officers next to him start filing off the stage and he follows automatically, glancing across at the room full of journalists, their attention already elsewhere, talking to each other, or into phones hidden behind cupped, conspiratorial hands as they tell their desk editors what just happened here. He was supposed to try and help defuse the bomb of the crime stats, try and 'take control of the narrative' by attempting to put a broader, more positive spin on the stories these journalists might write. But there was only one story that was going to run now, and he was lead detective on the case at the centre of it.

He steps off the stage, walks through the side exit and almost collides with Ed Murray, the chief press officer, red-faced at the best of times but now practically scarlet.

'Could be Slade grandstanding to sabotage the press conference,' Murray says, addressing the group from the stage who have now formed a tight huddle around Commissioner Rees, 'certainly wouldn't be the first time. I'll call North London, see what case he might be talking about, and issue a denial if he's got any of his facts wrong.'

'He hasn't,' Tannahill says, and all faces turn to him. 'I came here straight from the crime scene he was talking about. Everything he said is true.'

Murray glares at him as if all of this is his fault. 'Including the bit about the book?' he barks.

Tannahill nods.

'Ah Jesus! Why the hell didn't you tell me about this before the press conference? Did you not think the press might get hold of it and use it in an ambush?'

Rees holds up his hand to silence him. 'If he'd tried to talk to you, you'd have told him to stop wasting your time. Isn't the whole point of an ambush that you don't see it coming?' He shifts his attention to Tannahill. 'Go after the journalist,' he says. 'Try and find out what else he knows and how he knows it. His name's Brian Slade. His dad's ex-police, which is a whole other story, but basically he knows all the rules so don't bother trying to lean on him, just offer him an inside line on the investigation, an official one in exchange for cooperation. See what you can find out, then report back to me.'

Tannahill nods but doesn't move, unsure what the protocol is.

'Go!' Rees says.

Tannahill goes.

19

Laughton Rees throws her Post-It frilled copy of *The Numbers Game* on to her desk and collapses into the ancient swivel chair in a puff of orangey foam dust.

On the walk back to her poky shared office she decided to attack the problem of Gracie's schooling the same way she tackles any other problem she encounters in life, with intense and exhaustive research and forensic scrutiny.

She pulls a cereal bar, a bottle of water and her notebook from her bag, turns to a fresh page and writes SCHOOL, FEES, SCHOLARSHIPS, BURSARIES along the top, draws vertical lines down between each word to form columns, then starts working her way through the Google results for 'Best Private Schools in North London'. By the time Laughton has nibbled her way through the cereal bar the page is filled with data. She had hoped Highgate and Holloway School for Girls would prove to be one of the more expensive options but if anything it sits somewhere in the middle of the price range. There are cheaper options, but these schools are all further out of town and are *way* down in the academic tables. Clearly you get what you pay for. And Laughton can't afford any of it.

She leans forward, places her head on the desk and closes

her eyes, the weight of everything settling suddenly and heavily upon her. She can just about do this most days – work, parent, make the right choices, or at least spot the bad ones and try and steer away from them. But occasionally something flies out of nowhere to smack her in the face and reveal how terrifyingly close to the edge she is. It's at times like these that she feels like tuning it all out and disappearing into the welcome escape of work.

But she can't do that. Not ever.

Because that's what her father had done.

He had been a mysterious, glamorous and mostly absent figure, up early, back late, sometimes not back at all, passing through their orbit like a comet, the legend of him burnished by her mother's bedtime stories where she often had to talk about him and all the things he did to make up for the fact that he was almost never there.

Your father catches bad men, she had said. *He hunts them down and locks them up so they can't hurt anyone. And bad men never rest, which is why he can't be here to read you stories, or take you to school, or help with your homework, because who's going to protect us from the bad men if your dad's always home?*

He had become a hero to her in this way, his legend mingling with those of the princes and knights that populated her other bedtime stories. Even when she hit her teenage years his hero status remained intact because everyone watched the cop shows, and she knew that's what her dad did for real. So she forgave him his absence, and gladly accepted his sacrifice as her sacrifice too. She would lend the world her heroic dad, even though she missed him, because they needed him more than she did. And besides, she always had her mum.

But then one day he caught a really bad man, the worst one of all, and he didn't lock him up, and he wasn't there to stop her or her mother getting hurt by him either. And just like that, his legend was shattered. He was no hero, he was just a shitty, absent, dad, like all the other shitty dads, worse even: because if the estate agent, or shopkeeper, or factory worker dads messed up at work no one died. Her father had sacrificed family life, his own daughter's childhood, and ultimately his wife's life – and for what? For nothing. She was never going to let her daughter down the way he had. Nothing was more important than her daughter, not work, not even her own personal happiness. Gracie was everything.

Laughton lifts up her head, picks up her desk phone and dials the first number, tapping the table with her spare hand, three times with each finger, hoping to manage all five before someone answers. She makes it to her middle finger when her mobile starts buzzing in her bag. She glances at the caller ID – *Withheld*.

'City of London School for Girls,' a woman's voice says suddenly in her ear.

'Oh, yes, er hi,' Laughton stammers, stabbing the off-button on her mobile to silence the buzzing.

'How may I help?' the woman prompts. She sounds even posher than the last one and Laughton feels instantly intimidated.

'It's, yes, er . . . it's about my daughter.'

Jesus this was going to be harder than talking to convicted psychopaths, but she'll do it if it's for Gracie.

'I was wondering what level of scholarships and bursaries you offer . . .'

20

Tannahill weaves through the knots of journalists clogging New Scotland Yard reception, searching for the bald man in the running clothes.

Slade, the guv'nor had called him, *Brian Slade*. Said his dad had been in the force. Maybe that was how he'd got his information, by tapping into some murky old boy network.

He pushes on, out the main doors and over to the low wall at the top of the steps to get a clearer view of the street. The mist has cleared a little and he can see the river now. He looks right towards Westminster Bridge, as far as the mist will allow, then left along the Embankment Gardens and the Ministry of Defence building: plenty of people, none of them the guy he's looking for.

He can't have vanished that quickly.

Think.

Slade had said he worked for *The Daily*. Their offices were in Kensington, so he would probably head back there and the fastest way was by underground. But Slade had also been wearing running gear. And why wear running gear to a press conference then take the Tube back to the office? A runner would take the most direct route, the greenest route.

He heads down the steps towards the Ministry of Defence

and ducks into Victoria Embankment Gardens, peering ahead through the mist. A few tourists drift along the pathways, staring at their phones or up at the sombre statues dotted throughout the park. Still no sign of the man he's looking for.

Tannahill breaks into a jog and can feel the gravel through the thin soles of his shoes. He veers over on to the grass, half-expecting some angry military type to shout at him from an upper window. He still hasn't eaten this morning and his body is not happy with this latest turn of events. He can already taste copper in his mouth. He passes a stone plinth with an oriental-looking cat on top that looks like it's laughing at him when a voice behind him calls out, 'Looking for me?'

Tannahill slides to a halt on the damp grass and looks back.

Slade is leaning against the plinth, arms folded, phone in hand, a lopsided, vaguely slap-able grin on his face. 'I thought your boss might send someone after me.'

He has the look of a gym junkie – sunken eyes, zero body fat, black T-shirt and running shorts that appear painted on. He looks more like a long-distance runner than a journalist and his lack of hair makes it hard to pin an age on him. Could be thirty, could be fifty or anywhere in between. He steps forward, closing the leather cover on his phone. 'Brian Slade,' he says, nodding a greeting. 'And you are?'

'DCI Tannahill Khan. I'm lead detective on that case you seem to know so much about.'

'Really? You barely look old enough to be handing out parking tickets. Is the Met struggling to recruit grown-ups these days?'

Tannahill forces himself not to rise to the provocation. 'You seem very well informed about my case,' he says. 'I don't suppose you'd consider telling me where you're getting your information?'

Slade smiles, showing small white teeth that remind

Tannahill of the porcelain in toilets. 'No, I don't suppose I would. Unless of course you're prepared to give me something in return.'

'Like what?'

'Like tell me about the scene,' Slade folds his arms so his phone rests against the knot of his left bicep. 'Was it clean? I mean, forensically speaking.' The smile broadens. 'I already know it was messy.'

Tannahill feels a surge of dislike for Slade. How can he know the scene was 'messy', or have seen what he saw in that room and smile about it? He glances down at Slade's phone, realizes he's probably being recorded and his dislike turns to borderline hatred. 'Sounds like you don't need me to tell you anything,' he says.

Slade shrugs. 'OK, you don't want to play, fair enough.' He opens his phone case, pulls out a business card and hands it over. 'You want to know what I've got? Log on to *The Daily* website in about five minutes. You'll see.'

Tannahill takes the card. 'Five minutes!? You said half an hour.'

'Yeah, but that was before we had this little chat. I was hoping we might be able to work together on this, but if you're going to be all coy, I'll just run with what I've got. Besides,' he glances at the time on his phone, 'cat's out the bag now. I need to get this story out before any of my esteemed colleagues puts out a spoiler.'

He turns on his heels and starts moving away. 'That card has all my direct contact details on it, by the way. You might want to call me after you see the article.' He smiles one last time then starts jogging away, raising his phone to his ear as soon as he's out of earshot.

Tannahill watches him bobbing away past the tourists and civil servants, shoulders back, chest puffed out like a bantam chicken. Even the way he runs is irritating. He pulls his own phone from his pocket and calls DC Baker.

'Yo!' Baker answers before it even rings.

'You need to widen the security cordon around the house,' Tannahill says. 'Call in some extra uniforms and close the street off now.'

'OK. Why the urgency?'

'Because somehow *The Daily* got hold of details of the investigation and they're about to run a story, so expect a lot more press interest and a whole bunch of rubberneckers heading your way in the next ten minutes, if not sooner.'

'Oh crap! OK.'

'How we doing on forensics? Anything new?'

'Nothing. Looks like our suspect definitely read the book. Have you managed to tell the guv'nor about it yet?'

'No, but he already knows.'

'Oh bollocks!'

'Yeah.' Tannahill leans back heavily on the stone plinth with the laughing black cat on top. 'Just close the road and dig in,' he says. 'Let's see how bad this article is, then take a view. I'll be back as soon as I can.'

21

Laughton ends her call to another achingly polite admissions person and checks the time. Her next lecture starts in just over ten minutes so she could probably squeeze in another call, but her heart's not really in it – there's only so much of the kindness of posh strangers she can take in one day.

She closes the browser showing the list of schools and opens her research folder instead, defaulting to her usual mode of sinking into work and the ghosts of crimes past whenever the present day gets too much for her. She turns her mobile phone back on then clicks on a file named 'IAN COULTHARD', ready to seek comfort in a double murder in Edinburgh in the mid-eighties, when her mobile phone buzzes. Again, the number is withheld, and, again, she is about to ignore it when a sudden thought assaults her.

Gracie!

Something might have happened to Gracie and this is her panicked school calling her. She snatches the phone from her desk and answers it.

'Hello?'

'Hi, am I speaking to Laughton Rees?' The voice is male, unfamiliar, a bit breathy like he's running, which is vaguely creepy. It's not 'Call-me-Jonathan'.

'Yes, this is Laughton. Who am I—'

'I wondered if you were aware that one of your books was found at a murder scene this morning?'

Laughton feels relief that the call is not about her daughter but guarded suspicion about where it might be heading. 'Who is this?'

'The title of the book is *How to Process a Murder* and it seems the murder scene was wiped clean using information gleaned from your book.'

'That book is a procedural guide for investigators,' Laughton says. 'It's not a manual on how to wipe away fingerprints or get away with murder.'

'Yeah, but given who your father is, the presence of your book in particular at a crime scene is still pretty embarrassing, no? I mean there's plenty of books on forensics and investigation procedure, but it was *your* book specifically that was left at the scene. I would be very interested to talk to you about it.'

'I don't have anything to say. I don't work on active cases.'

'So I understand, however you're already part of this one so I thought you might make an exception. I can pay you, of course.'

Laughton's standard response would be to say 'thanks but no thanks', probably not that politely, end the phone call and carry on with her day.

'With your distinguished credentials,' the voice continues, 'as well as your personal ties with the Commissioner, we'd easily be talking five figures, maybe even more if the story has legs.'

Five figures.

Her eyes drift down to her notebook and the list of private schools with their yearly fees, also five figures. 'Let me think about it,' she hears herself saying.

'OK, but don't take too long. I'll ping you over an email with my contact details so you can get in touch directly. Look forward to hearing from you.'

He hangs up abruptly, leaving Laughton frowning and listening to the dialling tone. He never did say who he was or what paper he worked for. Not that it would make much difference. Laughton has had an instinctive mistrust of journalists ever since they camped out on her doorstep following her mother's death. She starts tapping her fingers in patterns of three at the ghost of this memory. All those shark-eyed cameras and shouted questions whenever she left the house. The feeling of being exposed and vulnerable at a time when all she wanted to do was disappear, like her mother had disappeared.

Her PC pings softly as an email arrives.

BSlade@TheDaily.com – subject line: *Interview request.*

The Daily. Of course he's from *The Daily*, biggest beast in the gutter with the biggest circulation too. No wonder he could afford to wave his big fat cheque book at her.

The first story is about to drop, the email says. *You're already in this one for free so if you want to be paid to be part of the next one, give us a bell. Might as well be on the bus rather than under it. :) x*

Underneath is a link.

Again Laughton feels the stirring of something unpleasant and half-forgotten. There is a very good reason she doesn't work active cases. All her cases are old, and obscure, and low-profile. They don't get picked up by the newspapers and turned into circuses. Active cases are messy, uncontrollable, dangerous. They can bring unwanted attention. They can even be deadly.

She checks the time.

Her next lecture starts in less than four minutes but the lift is working so she can get there in two. She clicks the link and a new window opens, displaying the shouty colour of *The Daily* website.

The lead story is about some footballer she's never heard of, on trial for something grubby. There's a large picture of him leaving court wearing a suit that manages to look both expensive and cheap at the same time. More stories are stacked along the right-hand side like a colourful tower of kids' building blocks, more people she doesn't recognize looking glamorous on red carpets and beaches, or looking terrible as they emerge from cars and drab front doors.

She scrolls down the page, scanning the headlines, her stomach feeling like a stone is forming inside it. She pauses at the ones with red EXCLUSIVE banners pinned to them, figuring these must be the scoops, but they're all about celebrities – singers, reality stars, movie stars, more footballers.

None of them seem to be about a recent murder.

She refreshes the page, clicking the button three times out of habit but the page comes back unchanged. She checks the time. Three minutes to her next lecture.

Three.

She sees this as a sign, clicks the refresh button three more times, grabs her notebook and leaves her office.

She doesn't see the page refresh behind her, the picture of the footballer replaced by the cover of a book with her name on it, lying on a blood-soaked carpet.

22

Tannahill heads up to the Commissioner's office on floor eight of New Scotland Yard, feeling like he was sent to do a job and is returning empty-handed. It was always going to be a long shot asking Slade to cooperate with them, but that doesn't make him feel any better.

The lift doors open and he makes his way down the corridor past glass-walled meeting rooms and open-plan offices filled with senior management staff. He is aware of all the glances sliding in his direction but returns none of them. Everyone will know what happened at the press conference by now.

His phone buzzes in his pocket and he pulls it out, hoping it might be Baker with some timely news about the case, but it's his mother. He's about to ignore it when he remembers the two missed calls earlier and guilt and the chance of any distraction from the sly scrutiny of the entire eighth floor makes him answer.

'Hey, Mam.'

'What happened?'

'What happened when?'

'At the news conference. I was watching the live feed on the website and it cut out before you came on.'

'Oh, I didn't go on.'

117

'What? Why not?'

His 't's come out soft, almost sibilant, his mother's Dublin accent still hanging in there after forty plus years in the UK.

He takes a breath, ready to launch into an explanation, but realizes it's way too complicated and he hasn't got time. 'They changed their minds,' he says.

'But you were there, I could see you in the background. You looked tired.'

'Thanks.'

'They work you too hard. When was the last time you had a day off?'

'Sunday!'

'Sunday doesn't count, everyone's supposed to have Sunday off. And if you had the day off why didn't you pop in and see me? I haven't laid eyes on you in weeks.'

Tannahill smiled. He'd been trained in the most sophisticated interrogation techniques but he could still get outmanoeuvred by his mother.

'OK, Mam, you got me, I was working Sunday too. I had to prepare for that press conference that didn't happen.'

'Well, a right waste of time that was then. Tell your boss you need a few days off. Tell him your mam said so.'

Tannahill smiles again and rounds the corner into the executive offices. Ahead of him the door to the Commissioner's office stands open and ready.

'I've got to go, Mam,' he says, the brief comfort of talking to her already evaporating. 'I'll call you later, OK?' He hangs up before she can say anything else.

The Commissioner's PA looks up at his approach. 'They're waiting for you in there,' he says, nodding at the open door. No smile. No clues. All business.

Tannahill walks up to the door, clears his throat, then steps through it.

The Commissioner's office is grey and surprisingly empty, just a desk, a couple of chairs and a floor-to-ceiling window filling the room with a soft light. Commissioner Rees stands in front of it, looking out at the misty world. Ed Murray, the chief press officer, is bent over a laptop lying open on the Commissioner's desk and looks up as Tannahill enters.

'What did he say?'

'Not much. He asked if the scene was clean, forensically speaking, which suggests he either doesn't know or was sounding me out.'

'And is it?'

'Pretty much. The main scene is messy, but the rest of the house is spotless.'

'Yes, we can see that,' Murray says bitterly. 'Take a look.' He spins the laptop round so Tannahill can see the screen.

KNIFE ATTACK AT MULTI-MILLION-POUND MANSION

WOMAN (39) STABBED TO DEATH IN HER LUXURY HOME AS KNIFE CRIME HITS ALL-TIME HIGH

Tannahill leans over and scrolls through the article. The first image is the photograph of Kate and Mike Miller with the zombie knife driven through her smile, the colours boosted to make the green of the knife handle and the red smear of blood extra vivid. Next is a wide shot of the Millers' living room with Kate Miller's body visible but pixelated at the centre, as if that was the most upsetting part of the image and not the numerous stripes of blood left untouched by the Photoshopper's brush.

There are pictures of all the objects too, their red-spattered backgrounds blurred but the pumped-up colours leaving no doubt as to what it is. The one of the book is slightly larger than the others so the title and name of the author can be read.

A book written by Laughton Rees – Commissioner Jack

119

Rees's daughter, the caption reads, *found by the victim's body*.

Below it is a picture of Rees at the press conference captioned: *Commissioner Jack Rees reveals worst crime figures on record. Knife crime at an all-time high.*

'It's a total shitshow,' Murray says, glaring at Tannahill. 'How the hell did Slade manage to get hold of the crime scene photos? I mean, what kind of security have you got in place, if any?'

'The scene is secure,' Tannahill says, scrolling through the rest of the article.

'Well clearly it isn't. You need to give me a list of everyone who set foot inside that house – witnesses, uniforms, HAT personnel, everyone. We need to find the leak and plug it.'

Tannahill glances up at Commissioner Rees silhouetted in the floor-to-ceiling window.

'I think maybe you need to warn your daughter about this, sir. Slade mentioned he might contact her.'

Rees continues to stare out at the mist, his silence and stillness unnerving. Tannahill isn't sure he even heard him until his voice rumbles a reply: 'She won't listen to anything I have to say. Maybe you should talk to her, bring her up to speed on what's happened. Tell her I'm happy to talk to her too . . . if she wants.'

'Never mind about any of that,' Murray says, pacing the room and staring at his phone. 'We need to find the mole in your investigation and tear them a new one. I don't want Slade getting hold of any more information or photographs, understood?'

Tannahill nods and scrolls back up to the top of the article, stopping at the photograph of the book, something about it gnawing at the back of his mind. Then it hits him. He looks at the photograph again to make absolutely sure he's right before speaking.

'It's not one of ours,' he murmurs.

'What?'

'This photograph, it's not one I took. Look,' he turns the laptop so Murray can see, 'the book in this photo is lying on the floor face up. But when I entered the scene it was face down. I know this because it was only after I'd picked it up that I realized what it was and who'd written it. The only pictures I took of the book's cover were size reference photographs, but there's no scale rule in this picture.'

A new thought seizes him. He scrolls back up to the top of the article to the main photograph of the front room with Kate Miller's body lying in the centre. He points at the wall of windows at the back of the shot. 'It's dark outside,' he murmurs.

'So?'

'So, by the time we got there it was light. These photos must have been taken before we got there.'

He stands up and looks across at Rees, who has finally turned away from the window and is now looking right at him.

'That's why Slade asked me whether the crime scene was clean. He genuinely didn't know. The person giving Slade his information is not us, it's whoever killed Kate Miller.'

III

THE MASK

Extract from *How to Process a Murder*
by Laughton Rees

A murder is like a slow explosion.

It starts off small, a single act of violence.

But very soon the consequences of this singular act start to spread, like ripples on a pond, ever widening until they can stretch as far as the horizon all around. This is why the time immediately following a murder is crucial, the so-called 'golden hour', when these ripples are still small, and clear, and centred around the original act where the connection between them is still easy to see.

But the longer an investigation continues, the harder it is to see these connections, and the further these ripples travel until their outlines become blurred by the weight of evidence, and public conjecture, and by conspiracy theories that weave fiction with half-truths then take on the appearance of fact.

Therefore the longer you can keep your slow explosion contained, the more you can stretch out your 'golden hour' into hours, or even days where the facts are still close and in your control, the better chance you have of catching your killer and seeing justice served.

23

– *It's on the news!*

The message on the Highgate Book Club WhatsApp group pops up less than a minute after Slade's article goes live. There is the briefest of pauses where people see the message, google the story, read it, then the phones of Highgate start buzzing and skittering across the granite and marble worktops once again.

– *She was killed with a knife!*

– *We just had the police at our door. They asked us about Mike.*

– *We've had them too. LOTS of questions about Mike. They definitely think it's him.*

– *Would Mike really kill Kate? And with a knife!!? I can't believe it.*

– *The article says knife crime is moving off the streets. Maybe it was some mad druggie.*

– *Makes you feel unsafe in your own home.*

– *IKR. George has already been on the phone to ADT.*

– *OMG, so has Richard. He wants to get cameras installed.*

– *The Millers had cameras, and a swanky alarm. Didn't help poor Kate tho.*

– *That's what makes me think Mike must have done it. Who else could have got past that security?*

– *OMG it's on LBC right now.*

A battalion of retro-looking radios and Alexas are activated and tuned to the local London radio station, where an earnest newsreader is halfway through a report on the knife murder of a woman in her Highgate home.

Brian Slade listens too, smiling as he runs along Kensington High Street, his phone streaming the radio station to the Bluetooth buds jammed in his ears. He used to get mad when other news outlets jumped on his stories, now he sees it as an endorsement. 'Let them follow, as long as you're the lead,' an old editor had told him once, an old-school Fleet Street wreck, sixty-a-day, long pub lunches, dead at fifty-six, but someone who had certainly known his way around a story. 'If it bleeds, it leads' was another of his pearls, and boy, was that one ever still true.

Slade slows to a jog and enters the central soaring atrium of *The Daily* building. He swipes his identity card to get through security and glances over at the large display screens behind reception. The central screen is permanently set to *The Daily* website and he smiles again when he sees his story sitting pretty at the top of the scroll. Let the others follow if they want, he knows he can stay in front of them all because he's the only one with the inside line.

He takes the stairs to the second floor, using it as a warm-down after his run, and checks his phone to see if he's had any more emails from justice72@yahoo.com.

Nothing.

No matter, the story has got its own momentum now, like a big dirty snowball rolling downhill, getting bigger and picking up all kinds of shit as it rumbles along. Right now it's still just about small enough to steer and he's the one who'll decide which way it goes. The police are clearly not going to give him anything, not officially at least, but as long as the killer is at large their ongoing failure to catch him will be a story in itself and give him plenty of opportunity to re-run his exclusive crime scene photographs. Then there's the fascination with the victim too, all that blonde-ness and good looks, the handsome husband who ends up killing her, and all that money! The more he can build them up to be the perfect couple living everybody's dream, the more tragic their story will feel. Build them up, then knock 'em down.

And what about that house? There's a whole feature right there; find the estate agent who last sold it and get exclusives on all the photographs and any other media they have, hopefully even a virtual tour they can tie up with an exclusive and stick on the website – *Take a tour round murder mansion* – who's not going to click on that then share it with all their bored friends?

So many angles. So much to do.

He enters the newsroom and strides towards his desk, aware of the glances from the other hacks as he passes by but ignoring them all. Suck it up, you bunch of losers. He never has been much of a team player. Never seen the point. Running's not a team sport either and when he runs he gets further and faster on his own, without other people slowing him down and stealing his oxygen.

He grabs his water bottle from his desk and takes a long drink while staring at his new assistant, Shakila, who looks up at him, eager and expectant, waiting for him to tell her what he needs. He continues to drink and winks at her; she smiles back because what else can she do, roll her eyes and call him a dick? That's not how the power balance shakes out in the newsroom and the smart ones realize it. Jury's still out on how smart Shakila will turn out to be. Slade stops drinking and wipes his mouth with the back of his hand.

'I need you to do some digging and get hold of a few people for me.'

Shakila picks up her notebook and a pen. Old-school. He likes that about her. No mimsy voice memos or tippy-tappy notes on her phone. Maybe she'll be old-school Asian too, walk a few steps behind him and treat him like a king. He might take her out to dinner later and find out. He flips open his own notebook and scans the notes he scribbled earlier when speaking to his police contact.

'OK, first find out anything you can about Michael James Miller, age forty-eight, and his wife Katherine Miller, thirty-nine, of number three Swain's Lane, Highgate. Don't bother googling them because nothing comes up. You're going to have to be creative, check through the black files and run their photos through Clearview, see if that throws up any IDs or aliases.'

The phone on Shakila's desk starts ringing.

'I also want biographies, photos, names and contact details of any relatives or significant business associates. We're looking for anyone who knew the Millers and can give us either the human angle, or some useful background info, preferably both. Also, try and find anyone who currently works for them; they're minted, so we're talking driver, nanny, gardener, that kind of thing. There's definitely a cleaner because she found the body.' Slade checks his notes and Shakila takes the opportunity to pick up the ringing phone to silence it.

'Cleaner's name is Celia Barnes,' Slade says, 'start with her.'

He looks back up and clocks the serious expression on Shakila's face. 'What?' he says.

'Police,' she says. 'They're downstairs and they want to see you right now.'

24

Things moved pretty fast once they realized the killer had sent the photos to Slade. Commissioner Rees fast-tracked a warrant and sent a unit from the DFT – the Digital Forensics Team – to *The Daily* offices to seize Slade's phone and computers and take them into evidence. Digital image files also contain a host of other information that could reveal what camera or phone the pictures were taken on, when and where they were taken, even the phone's number and the name of the contract owner. Whatever method had been used to deliver the photos – email, file link – could also possibly yield valuable information. Tannahill half-wishes he could have gone along just to see the look on Slade's face when he saw the warrant, but his need to get back to North London and brief his team outweighed it. At least the escalation of everything meant he got a ride back and didn't have to face the Tube again.

He sits in the passenger seat of the squad car heading rapidly north, returning a call he missed while he was in with Rees. The call was from a number he doesn't recognize, so he's guessing it's probably the morgue. Ordinarily he would have attended the post-mortem but the press conference and everything that followed threw a spanner in the face of that particular plan, so he asked the Crime Scene Manager, who did attend, to get the coroner to call him and give him the details of his findings the moment he had them. He listens to the ringing tone as the grey London streets flash past outside.

'Collins.' a tired-sounding voice answers.

'Hi, this is DCI Khan.'

'Ah yes, the stabbing, or one of the stabbings, I should say.' Tannahill hears papers being rustled. 'Well, she was definitely stabbed, but I imagine you probably figured that out for yourself. Total of thirty-eight different puncture wounds – some defensive, most not – varying in depth between 1.5 and 20 centimetres, all apparently from the same knife. The presentation of the stab wounds suggests a blade of around 25 to 30 centimetres with one straight edge and one serrated, a hunting knife most likely.

'Official cause of death is exsanguination due to multiple stab wounds. If I was a betting man, which I am, I would put my money on the mortal blow being a 6-centimetre stab wound on the neck between the cricoid cartilage and the mandible, which caused severe arterial damage to the external carotid.'

'Any idea of time of death?'

'Well, due to the acute blood-loss, lividity is minimal, but body temperature and rigor indicators suggest it would have been sometime between midnight and two o'clock.'

'OK. Anything else?'

'Blood alcohol was point two, so she probably had a large glass of wine at some point in the evening. Drug screen results are negative. No stomach contents. Examination of the pelvic area indicates the victim had not experienced any sexual violence. She was also not pregnant at the time of death and had not given birth. I have taken samples of vaginal fluid for further analysis, but I can see nothing here suggesting any obvious sexual motive.'

'What about other injuries?'

132

'Nothing of note.'

'Anything historical? Anything that might suggest she'd experienced recent violence?'

'She doesn't bear the marks of domestic abuse, if that's what you mean: no healed metacarpal fractures, no maxillo-facial trauma, no corneal haemorrhaging. The only notable historical scarring was from fairly standard cosmetic procedures: breast augmentation, rhinoplasty, a minor face-tuck, evidence of liposuction on the thighs and stomach – all top-end and very subtly done.

'There is one thing I would add, however, though this is merely a personal observation rather than a robust clinical opinion. In the admission notes it puts the victim's age at thirty-nine. I would say, anatomically speaking certainly, she seems more like a woman in her mid-forties, well preserved undoubtedly, but definitely more in that kind of ballpark. I don't want to put it in the notes because, as I say, it's just an opinion, but I thought it might be useful for you to know, in case . . . well, in case it's useful.'

'Thank you,' Tannahill says, 'it is. And thank you for turning this around so quickly.'

'Not up to me, I just do what they tell me.'

Tannahill smiles. 'Me too. Thanks anyway.'

He hangs up and looks out of the window, trying to see where they are, but the driver is obviously taking some obscure back route to avoid traffic. A sign flashes past with NW1 written in red after the street name. Camden. North London already.

He watches the streets slide past and tries to still his mind and use this moment of calm to look at the case objectively. The killer contacting the press has shunted everything sideways and shone a spotlight on the case. Why would a man on the run, a man who had gone out of his way to remain anonymous in his daily life, contact the press and send them photos of his crime? But then why would he kill his wife in such a frenzied fashion then carefully arrange her body and surround it with weird objects either? He thought about the objects, each one now labelled, and bagged, and in the process of being subjected to the highest level of forensic scrutiny.

The book, the mask, the keys, and the unicorn were all mass-produced, so are unlikely to be of much value in the way of leads through retail or manufacture channels. The lab will conduct a bank of tests on them, including VMD which can lift prints off fabric, and fibre analysis through microscope and chemical analysis to try and match it to a specific manufacturer, but he won't get the results of any of that until tomorrow at the earliest, even with the full weight of Commissioner Rees pushing it along.

The keys might yield something, the blue finish on the Yale made it more distinct and therefore more likely to be able to trace. As well as checking both keys for material transfer, the lab techs will also be able to identify the alloys they're made from, which, along with cuts, duplication marks and analysis of the keyway, will help identify where the keys are from and therefore what doors they might open.

Then there were the medals, far more specific and therefore much more likely to lead to something. Both were six-pointed stars, one inscribed with the words THE ATLANTIC STAR and the other THE 1939–1945 STAR. He has seen this medal before, twenty-odd years and several thousand miles away.

He had been eleven, maybe twelve, and it had been his first time on a plane, which he was way more excited about than where it was taking him. Pakistan, and everything it represented, was something he didn't want to acknowledge, let alone visit. The trip had been sudden, just him and his father and hastily packed bags heading across the world to see his sick grandmother.

They had flown direct to Lahore and stepped off the plane into heat like he'd never known before. His uncle Ali, one of his six uncles, had picked them up in a car that looked like it had been hammered together from bits of scrap, and driven them at terrifying speed through the packed streets to his grandparents' house, a crumbling, pre-partition building in the Old Town with splintery shutters barely clinging to their rusted hinges. They entered through a doorway into a surprisingly neat and cool interior with tile floors and ceiling fans, where his grandmother lay propped up on a bank of pillows like a queen, surrounded by a large group of people who turned out to be a small fraction of his extended family.

They had taken it in turns to pat Tannahill on the back, pinch his cheeks, and jabber at him in machine-gun Punjabi, a language that he had refused to learn. Pakistan and his connection to it had always been something he'd been ashamed of, a secret he'd tried his best not to acknowledge, as if by ignoring it long enough it might eventually go away. But there was no ignoring this place. It demanded to be acknowledged – the colours, the noise, the unbelievable heat, the regular wail of the muezzin drifting through the air, calling people to prayer five times a day, and the battalions of relatives all smiling and hugging and shoving mouth-tingling food at him, saying – *try this, try this* – literally cramming his culture into him. The trip had transformed Pakistan from a word he had only ever associated with a kind of nameless shame to something real, and solid, and mighty, something he not only felt proud of, but a part of, like some hidden, exotic superpower he'd never known he had.

On his last day, his *paṛadādā*, his grandfather, had taken him into a room he called his study, crammed with mementos of his time spent in the British Army and the Punjab police. He had shuffled about opening drawers looking for what he called *khazānā*, treasures from the family's past. One of these was a six-pointed star.

'See this, boy?' he had said, pulling the medal from a rusted tobacco tin and holding it up for him to see. 'This is all the bastard British gave me for fighting their war.' He bit into the yellow metal. 'Not even bloody gold plate. Bastards! But we got the last laugh,' he wheezed, tossing the medal to him. 'The British taught us how to fight so we could fight their war for them. Then we turned around and kicked them out two years later!'

It was the only time Tannahill had ever seen any of his father's family. They had returned home, his grandmother died a few weeks later and the whole trip quickly faded into something that felt like it might never have really happened. His dad had been almost less interested in his Pakistani heritage than Tannahill was and so he'd grown up feeling far more Irish because of his yearly trips to Ireland with his mam to visit her even larger, even noisier family.

The squad car turns a corner and passes an Irish pub, a few people smoking by the door and cosy, orange lights inside, and another sign flashes past – N7 now.

A thought strikes him and he takes his phone and googles 'London Metropolitan University'. Laughton Rees had been at London Metro when he'd crashed her lecture that time when he was studying for his sergeants' exam. He opens the homepage then scrolls down the Staff menu. She's still there. He hovers the pointer over her name and a diary box pops open. She even has a lecture this afternoon. It's already started but won't finish for another hour.

He looks out of the window again.

The forensics are all in hand, and he won't get any results back for an hour at least. Baker is running the door-to-door enquiries. The DFT have only just seized the photos sent to Slade, so there won't be anything back from them for a while, and there's a whole team of people back at the office doing a deep background dive into Kate and Mike Miller to find out who the hell they are. The only lead from any of the objects not currently being thoroughly investigated is the author of the book.

He glances at the driver.

'How far are we from London Metro University?'

'About five minutes, sir.'

Tannahill thinks for a moment then nods as if agreeing to some unspoken question. 'OK,' he says. 'Slight change of plan . . .'

25

Celia Barnes stands in her kitchen, half-listening to the news.

Her kitchen may not be as grand as the ones she cleans but her radio is just as posh. It's a Roberts, suppliers of radio receivers to the Queen and the Prince of Wales, it says so on the badge. Her Derek bought it for her fiftieth. She wishes he was here now; he did offer to miss his physio session and come home early, but it's such a nightmare trying to rebook a missed appointment that she told him she was fine and not to worry.

She leans against the sink, staring out at the grey slate and red brick of Archway, feeling the stillness and emptiness of the flat pressing in behind her.

. . . *Found dead of apparent stab wounds at her North London home this morning* . . . the newsreader says in a serious voice. *Police are appealing for witnesses and anyone who may know the current whereabouts of her husband Mike Miller* . . .

Hearing their names read out like this makes Celia feel like she has let them down somehow.

There's an unspoken contract between any cleaner and client that being allowed inside someone's home means they expect you to keep whatever you may see there private. As someone who's never been particularly comfortable with gossip, this has always suited Celia just fine. So to hear Kate and Mike Miller's names read out on the news along with details of what happened within the privacy of their home feels like a betrayal. She was the one who rang the police and set all this in motion, after all. And even though she knows it was the right thing to do, she never for one second imagined it would end up on the news.

The sudden chirp of her mobile phone makes her jump. Normally the sound would make her heart lift a little because very few people have the number and she's always happy to speak to any of them. Today it feels like just one more thing she can barely deal with.

She tugs her phone free from the pocket of her coat, still draped over a kitchen chair, and frowns when she sees the *No Caller ID* message on the screen. She definitely can't face talking to some well-meaning salesperson about broadband or whatever, so she puts the phone down on the worktop and stares down at it, waiting for the ringing to stop and voicemail to kick in. The phone chirps two more times then falls silent. Celia immediately feels anxious again. Maybe she should have answered it. It might have been the police wanting to ask her some more questions about the house, or Kate, or Mike, or something else. She picks up the phone, ready to answer the moment it rings again with the voice message, but the home phone rings instead.

The ring is turned up to maximum so she and Derek can hear it over the TV, and sounds much too loud in the silent flat. Celia snatches it off its cradle to silence it, her heart hammering at who might be calling so urgently and what it might mean.

'Hello?' she says, her voice small and wary.

'Hi, am I speaking to Celia Barnes?'

'Yes.' She doesn't recognize the man on the end of the line.

'And am I right in thinking that you work as a cleaner for Mike and Kate Miller?'

'Yes, I . . . yes.'

'Good, I was just wondering if I might ask you a few questions about them.'

Celia frowns. She's already been through this with the nice PC at the station. 'What kind of questions?'

'Just a bit of background,' the man continues, 'what they were like, what kind of couple they were, what sort of life they led.'

'Who is this, please?'

'My name is Brian Slade. I work for *The Daily*.'

'The newspaper?'

'Britain's most popular. We're running a story on the tragic death of Kate Miller, and I know people would be interested to know more about the real person, who she was, what she was like, that kind of thing.'

'Well she . . . I'm not sure I should be talking to . . .'

'I totally understand. You must be shocked about what happened. Were you very close to Kate Miller?'

'No. I mean she was . . . we weren't friends. I just worked for her, but she was always nice to me.'

'I'm sure she was. She looks lovely. I'm sure she would want people to know that about her, that she was a nice person. Did she do any charity work? She looks the sort of lady who might. The kindly sort.'

'Yes, she was very kind.'

'How so, was it the way she acted, something she did?'

'She, er . . . I don't know . . .'

'What was it she did for a living, by the way, or was it just her husband who worked?'

'They were both . . . I mean . . . neither of them . . .' Celia feels like she's being swept along, like she's no longer in control. 'I really don't think I want to . . .'

'If it would make it easier, I'd be more than happy to pay

140

you for your time. Or make a contribution to a charity of your choice, or perhaps one that was close to Mrs Miller's heart.'

The mention of money is like a slap across the face. It was probably meant to loosen her up and get her talking, but instead it brings her to her senses and shuts her down completely. She opens her mouth to say something but then does something else entirely, something she has never done before in her life, even to the most persistent of cold callers. She hangs up.

She stares at the phone for a moment, shaken by both the unwanted intrusion and what it prompted her to do. The phone rings again and she picks up the receiver and puts it right back down again. She removes it from the phone and places it down on the worktop, the soft purr of the dial tone humming low in the silent flat.

Her mobile phone starts chirping again.

No Caller ID.

She flicks the switch on the side to silence the cricket sounds but the phone continues to buzz, like the insects are trapped inside, wanting to get out. She presses the button on the side to turn it off altogether then stuffs the phone into her coat pocket and becomes aware of another noise in the kitchen, like a siren getting louder and louder. She looks around in panic for the source and realizes it's coming from the phone receiver, some kind of warning alarm to let her know it's been left off the hook. The noise grows steadily louder like something bad drawing closer. Celia snatches up the receiver and jams it back on its cradle with a bang of hard plastic. There's a brief moment of silence then the phone starts ringing again.

Celia stares at it for a moment, wondering what she can do to stop it, then she grabs her coat and handbag and heads for the front door. She can ignore it, that's what she can do, sit in the cafe on the corner and nurse a pot of tea until Derek gets back from the physio. Maybe the phone will have stopped ringing by then. If it hasn't, she can get him to answer it, he's always much better with the nuisance calls than she is. He'll just tell them to sod off then put the phone down.

She fumbles the safety chain off, installed by Derek after the break-in last year, and squeezes through the door on to the open walkway outside.

She slams the door closed behind her, double locks it with the Chubb key, then walks swiftly away, buttoning her coat against the damp chill as she goes, the steady sound of her footsteps gradually drowning out the sound of the phone still ringing in her kitchen.

26

'Anyone here play any sport? Please raise your hand.'

Laughton looks up to see almost every hand in the lecture theatre go up.

There are around forty people in the room, arranged on a steep bank of curved seating that could have been specifically designed to be intimidating. The first time Laughton had lectured here she'd almost had a panic attack, now she feels more comfortable here than pretty much anywhere.

'OK, now keep your hand up if you play something other than football.'

A low murmur rumbles through the room and two-thirds of the hands drop down. Laughton surveys the remaining dozen or so, an even spread of men and women, mostly in their early twenties but with a few older students in the mix.

'Akim,' Laughton points at a young man in the second row who's so tall he looks like he's standing up, 'basketball, right?'

Akim smiles and his face lights up. 'By the time I was twelve I was already six three,' he says, 'my games teacher didn't give me no choice.'

Laughter murmurs through the auditorium and a number

of the female students, and some of the men, lean forward to get a better look at him.

'But you could have played football too, I'm guessing?' Laughton asks. 'Your height would be just as useful in goal or in defence? So why basketball?'

Akim shrugs. 'You get to score more points. It's indoors, so you don't get muddy and cold.'

Another ripple of laughter.

'Smaller team too, right?' Laughton says. 'More chance to shine. So who's the superstar in your team, who scores the most points?'

Akim smiles and looks away, like the question has embarrassed him. 'Me, probably.'

'All right, Akim!' Laughton starts clapping. 'Let's hear it for the superstar.'

Others join in and Akim continues to smile bashfully, staring down at the floor, half enjoying the attention and half hating it.

Laughton looks up as the door at the back of the lecture hall opens and a man wearing a suit steps in and takes a seat. The applause dies away and she returns her attention to the class.

'All right, let's not blow Akim's head up too much. The truth is, it's easy to spot the stars in basketball because it's obvious who's scoring the most points and the rest of the team leans towards that player. Now could all you football players stick your hands back up.'

Laughton looks around the lecture theatre, her attention lingering for a moment on the newcomer at the back. 'Stella,' she points to a young woman sitting a few rows in front of him. 'Who's the superstar in your team?'

Stella thinks for a moment. 'Depends on the game and who we're playing. Last week we played a really good side and our goalie played a blinder and kept us in it. Week before that we played a bunch of donkeys and she barely had to do anything. Our midfielder is pretty steady, but there are no real superstars. The team is the star.'

Laughton smiles. 'The team is the star, interesting. Thank you, Stella.'

She turns to the display board, pushes a button on the remote in her hand, and a caption flashes up:

WHAT TEAM SPORTS CAN TEACH US
ABOUT CRIMINAL INVESTIGATIONS

The lecture theatre fills with the rustle and tap of the words being copied into paper and digital notebooks.

'So, unlike basketball where a superstar player can control the ball and win games more or less on their own, football is all about the team, which means you're actually only as good as your weakest link. Stella, who's the best football player in the world right now?'

'Lionel Messi, probably, or Cristiano Ronaldo.'

'Ok good, and who does Ronaldo play international football for . . .?'

'Portugal.'

'And where did Portugal finish in the last World Cup, 1st, 2nd, 3rd?'

'Nowhere. They barely made it out of the group stages.'

'Exactly, so we have one of the best players in the world but his team didn't even make it to the quarter finals of the World Cup. Why is that?'

Stella shrugs. 'His team sucked.'

Laughton nods. 'The *team* was weak, so it didn't matter how good their best player was, they still crashed out early and went home. That's because football, unlike basketball, is a weak-link sport. One superstar does not make a difference at the higher levels.'

She presses the button and two new titles pop up on the display screen:

145

STRONG-LINK TEAM
WEAK-LINK TEAM

'David Sally, a former baseball pitcher turned behavioural economist, and Chris Anderson, a former goalkeeper turned football statistics guru and professor at Cornel, wrote a book called *The Numbers Game: Why everything you know about football is wrong*. In this book they did a statistical analysis of the best teams in Europe and discovered that they would win more games and score more goals if they upgraded their poorest players instead of blowing the budget on a superstar. Their findings revealed that every goal generally came after a series of eight or nine passes ending with the superstar doing something sublime. The problem was that if any one of those passes reached the worst player in the team, who then messed up and gave the ball away, the superstar might as well not even be on the pitch.

'Now, if we transpose this idea to a criminal investigation where the goal is to get a successful conviction, then we can view those various passes as the different steps in the chain of evidence. Like football, a criminal investigation is a weak-link game and when you think of it in those terms you can start to see how each individual part is crucial to the successful outcome of the whole.'

Tannahill sits at the back of the lecture theatre.

Unlike the students he doesn't need to take notes so he just sits back and enjoys the show. The lecture he'd attended on the same subject when studying for his sergeants' exam had been nothing like this. No one here is stifling yawns or fidgeting on the hard seats. Every single student hangs on every word, their collective attention fixed on the small, energetic woman at the front of the lecture hall who has somehow managed to turn this driest of subjects into something compelling and clear. He remembers how she had pulled a similar trick at the other lecture of hers he'd attended when she'd held another roomful of people spellbound for almost an hour on the singularly unsexy subject of 'Long-range familial DNA and its impact on the solve rate of cold cases'.

It's even more remarkable in light of the life he knows she has led. He can still see traces of the wide-eyed, traumatized, fifteen-year-old girl in the impressive woman now holding court.

He settles deeper into his seat, enjoying this unexpected moment of peace in the middle of his turbulent day. He could happily sit here for hours, listening to her speak, watching her command the subject and this room full of people, but the lecture is over way too quickly, and he sits up in his seat as the room starts to empty, feeling slightly nervous that he now has to go and talk to the star of the show.

He stands and weaves his way through the crowd of departing students, making his way down to the front of the lecture hall where Professor Laughton Rees is chatting to one of her more eager students. He stands to the side and slightly back, keeping to the shadow of the auditorium, not wishing to overhear what might be a private conversation. He is surprised by how Laughton looks even younger up close. He can still see no family resemblance with her father.

Laughton forces herself to focus on the student in front of her, though she is keenly aware of the man in the grey jacket standing close by. The student asks for the name of any other books she should read on the subject and Laughton reels off a list, which the student slowly scribbles into a notebook. Laughton shoots an apologetic look at the waiting man. He has the unmistakable air of police about him, though she doesn't remember teaching him. Finally the student stuffs her notebook and laptop into her 'Books Are My Bag' tote then hurries away.

'Great lecture,' the stranger says, stepping forward into the light, 'almost makes me want to go back to school again.'

Laughton smiles, momentarily distracted by his eyes. Standing in the shadows she had thought he looked Asian or possibly Mediterranean, but his eyes are so blue they seem almost Aryan. 'Thank you,' she says, 'DS? DI . . .?'

He smiles. 'That obvious, huh? It's DCI actually. Tannahill Khan.'

'Wow, you must be on the super fast-track, you barely look old enough to be out of uniform.'

'Well, you don't look old enough to be a professor either.'

He fixes her with those ice-blue eyes that seem oddly warm and there's a moment of silence that should be awkward but isn't.

Tannahill Khan, she thinks, *Pakistani or maybe Bangladeshi Irish? Interesting heritage.*

'I'm working with your dad,' he adds, utterly ruining the moment.

'Good for you,' she says, turning away and ducking down behind the lectern to retrieve her memory stick.

'That's not the reason I'm here, though. I caught a case this morning, a homicide, and I thought you might—'

'I never work live cases.'

'I know that. I thought you might want to look at this one, though, because—'

'Because a book I wrote was left at the scene?' Laughton enjoys the look of surprise that appears on Tannahill's face. 'A journalist called me about it before my lecture.'

'Slade!' he says, like he's tasting something bitter.

'He wanted a comment and I told him the same thing I'm telling you: I don't work live cases.'

She pushes past him and heads for the exit.

Tannahill follows her out into the corridor. 'His article is already online,' he says, keeping pace. 'I was hoping to talk to you before he published, but I was at the crime scene up until about an hour ago, then I had this press briefing and . . . anyway I came here as soon as the article went live.' Laughton reaches the lift, jabs the button to summon it. 'It mentions you and your book, so you should probably brace yourself for more press attention.'

Laughton leans against the wall, feeling like the floor is falling away from under her. She has spent her entire adult-hood building walls between her work and her private life to keep herself and her daughter safe. Now it feels like those walls have crumbled and the world outside is about to crowd in along with all the dangers that brings.

'This is why I never get involved in live cases,' she murmurs. 'Journalists don't ring up and hassle you when you start looking into a twenty-year-old murder. This is just . . . it's . . .'

She jabs the button again but the light refuses to stay on so she twists away and heads for the stairs, craving the quiet security of her office.

'Listen,' Tannahill says, 'I know you don't normally get involved with live cases, and I totally understand why, but I thought as you're already part of this one you might recon-sider. Because of who you are and who your dad is, they're not going to leave this one alone until it's solved. So why not try and help us solve it?'

Laughton bursts into the stairwell and starts heading up to the third floor. She feels sick, like the darkest chapter of her life is re-emerging from the place she buried it, that death and danger are being brought to her door and, yet again, her father is the cause of it. She'd hoped by cutting him out of her life she might insulate herself and her daughter from all of this. She had been wrong.

'The sooner the case is solved the sooner it'll all go away,' Tannahill says, his voice echoing in the concrete stairwell. 'I need to talk to you anyway and investigate any possible reason why your book in particular was left at the crime scene.'

Laughton spins round to face him. 'It's obvious, isn't it? To embarrass him. It's not about me, it's about him. It's always about him. I'm just . . . collateral damage.'

'Maybe, but you wrote in your book that you must never be distracted by the obvious.'

'Oh please,' Laughton says, turning away and heading up the stairs again. 'Don't start quoting me at me.'

'Your book was not the only thing left behind at the scene. There were four other objects, I can show you them,' he adds, pulling his phone from his pocket. 'The pictures are online. Just take a look and tell me what you think. Five minutes, then I'll leave you alone.'

She stops at the top of the stairs and turns to look down at him frowning at his phone as it struggles with the notoriously weak Wi-Fi signal. Somewhere outside a siren starts wailing. It reminds Laughton of the one from that morning and her mental note to find out what it was all about in case it might be useful. Well here was her chance.

Tannahill looks up at her with those oddly blue eyes. They seem like scraps of summer sky in the gloom of the stairwell. Below them a door bangs open and voices echo up the stairwell as a knot of students start heading up.

'Five minutes,' Laughton says. 'We can use the computer in my office.'

Then she turns and barges through the door to the third-floor corridor, before she has a chance to change her mind.

27

He listens. Eyes closed. Concentrating.

The news murmurs in his ear, fed through a Bluetooth earpiece linked to his phone.

The Miller murder is now the top story nationally, not just in London. All the major news outlets are leading with it. #KnifeCrime and #MurderMansion are trending on Twitter.

It feels unstoppable now, like a train rumbling along, gathering speed towards a destination only he knows.

He opens a drawer, pulls out an old, worn laptop and starts it up.

For a long time it was just a fantasy, a slowly evolving story of revenge he pieced together over months and years and told to himself over and over, running it in his head like a soothing mantra. And unlike real life, where justice was slippery and fickle, in his head he controlled what happened, so justice was his to decide and dispense. In his mind the guilty were exposed and punished and the innocent walked free. But the more he told himself this story in his head, the more real it felt, like it was something that had actually happened and he was simply remembering it.

Then, miraculously, the story began to take form as the players and different elements presented themselves one by one, like he was somehow willing it all into being, or the universe was lining things up for him, setting the stage until all he needed to do was whisper 'Action!' to set it in motion.

The laptop creaks and chunters as it slowly boots up, a cheap model bought even cheaper at a liquidation auction.

Lots of owners. Complicated sales history. Hard to trace – but not impossible. He had to leave some breadcrumbs along the trail for others to follow. This was part of the story too.

The start-up screen finally blinks to life showing a logo of a sunflower with the earth at the centre and a progress bar that creeps slowly forward as he half-listens to the news, catching the odd phrase:

. . . multiple stab wounds . . . objects left around the body . . . links to the Commissioner . . . husband still missing . . .

The story in his head now being told by others out in the real world. It had a feeling of inevitability about it, like it was always going to happen, no matter which path he had taken, no matter what decisions he had made. He had never really gone in for any of that predestination crap before. You write your own stories, that's what he believed, you write your stories, own your actions, and create your own endings. But that wasn't true. Death came to everything, that was everybody's end, and there was nothing anybody could do about it.

The start-up sequence ends and the desktop loads revealing the same sunflower logo, a shortcut to an app, and a series of folders arranged in a line, each with a number and a title:

1. THE HOUSE
2. THE BOOK
3. THE MEDALS
4. THE KEYS
5. THE LION AND THE UNICORN

He opens the third one to reveal a series of photographs, video clips and documents, about twenty in total, laid out in a line and labelled.

The train was rolling now but it would need more fuel to keep it moving.

He clicks on the shortcut to open the VPN app, giving him an extra level of security to the already anonymous Yahoo account. There is a chapter on digital forensics and the use of Virtual Private Networks in Laughton's book, something the press will undoubtedly pick up on once his emails come to light and the police are unable to trace them.

He launches his Yahoo account through the VPN and opens a new email which he addresses to Slade, his willing accomplice, too blinded by the white heat of a hot story to realize that he is a part of it. He has a folder on him too, but that is for later.

He copies some photos into the email, along with one of the video clips and a PDF of a company prospectus, also with the sunflower logo on it. The police, or Slade, would have found this document eventually, but as it took him several weeks to chase down this copy he can't afford to leave it to chance. He needs the information it contains to come out sooner, while the story is still at the forefront of everybody's minds. He needs Slade to see it, then show it to everyone else.

He finishes the email and schedules it to be sent at eight the following morning, after a couple more news cycles have passed and the first story has had a little longer in the spotlight to grow, and spread, and snag everyone's attention. For now, he's given them quite enough: the glamorous victim, the missing husband, the strange objects.

Let them try to figure out what that all means for a few hours longer before he delivers the twist in the next chapter.

28

Laughton barges into her cramped office, startling a skinny man in a tank top, a bow tie and Tintin hair. He spins round in the office chair, eyes wide with surprise behind round, tortoiseshell glasses.

'Oh!' Laughton says. 'Sorry, Dave, forgot you were in today.' She turns to Tannahill. 'This is Dave, er – Dr Easton. We share this office.'

Dr Easton regards Tannahill with an approving look. 'By "share" she means she messes it up and I try and keep it tidy. And you are . . .?'

'Name's Tannahill.'

'Great name.' Dr Easton shoots Laughton a mischievous and quizzical look, which she knows means – *Boyfriend?*

'*DCI* Tannahill Khan is working on a murder case he wants me to look at,' Laughton says, deliberately using his formal rank to signal that this is a professional relationship. She sees the disappointment register on Dr Easton's face. 'I need to use the computer to look at the files.' Laughton nods at the shared PC. Dr Easton continues to smile up at Tannahill. 'Sensitive files,' Laughton adds.

'Oh.' Dr Easton's smile falters. 'So basically you're telling me to bugger off?'

'Yeah, basically. I mean, if you're in the middle of something, we could . . .'

'No, no, it's fine,' Dr Easton scoops his leather satchel from the desk and smiles at Tannahill as he squeezes out of the office. 'Three's a crowd. I'll leave you two to look at your – sensitive files.'

He says 'sensitive files' in a way that makes it sound like 'dirty pictures'.

Laughton closes the door after him and flumps down in the battered chair. 'Sorry about that.' She logs Dr Easton out and herself back in.

'Google *The Daily* website.' Tannahill steps up behind her, his eyes on the screen. 'The Highgate murder is the top story, or it was forty-five minutes ago.'

Laughton opens the website.

Knife Attack at Multi-Million-Pound Mansion is still the lead story.

She studies the lead image of the knife stabbed through the victim's face for a moment then scrolls down to the next image showing the Millers' living room with Kate Miller lying at the centre. She leans in and studies the body, the way it is displayed with the arms outstretched, the objects arranged around it.

'How did the paper get hold of the crime scene photographs?'

'They didn't. These aren't ours. The killer took them and sent them directly to the paper.'

Laughton nods. 'Interesting.'

'Have you come across anything like that before?'

'Not exactly. There are a few cases where killers have sent letters or objects to the press – Jack the Ripper, the Zodiac Killer, Son of Sam – but they tend to arrive days, weeks, sometimes even months after the initial crime. It's usually an attempt to extend the thrill of the original kill by boasting about what they did, or describing what they're going to do,

155

often with taunts to the police about how they'll never catch them. Also they tend to be in response to existing news stories, but this is different. These were sent before a story had even been written. In fact, by sending these photos directly to the press the killer created the story. Was there any message with the photographs?'

'Yes. We seized Slade's computer and phone from *The Daily* offices and the DFT recovered the email used to send the photos. The subject line was DS GEORGE SLADE – RIP. George Slade is the father of the reporter who wrote this story. He'd been a detective sergeant on the Flying Squad at the tail end of the good old, bad old Sweeney days. Good officer, by all accounts, but a shitty human being. He had a long list of black marks in his personnel files, things that should have been investigated but were all swept under the carpet: several call-outs to domestic disturbances at the family home, numerous public drunk and disorderlies, eight separate ABH charges spanning almost two decades and one GBH toward the end of his career. In the end it all caught up with him and he was kicked off the force a few years short of his pension. Dishonourable discharge.'

'Wow, what did he do, kill someone? Normally they get to keep their pensions no matter how bad they are.'

'George Slade's dismissal was part of a root-and-branch overhaul of what was seen as outdated and unacceptable policing instigated by the then incoming commissioner.'

Laughton looks up from the screen as she realizes where this is going.

Tannahill nods. 'Yeah, basically your dad fired him. As you can imagine, the son of someone who lost his job, his pension, and then drank himself to death is not going to be much of a fan of the person who caused it. The killer must have known all this and counted on the fact that Brian Slade would jump on any opportunity to embarrass your father. We're also thinking the timing of the murder with the release of the crime figures is not accidental. It all adds up to the perfect media storm with your father at the centre of it.'

'Did the DFT find anything else?'

'Not yet. The photographs are all encrypted and the email address the photos were sent from was a Yahoo account.'

'Untraceable.'

'Unfortunately, yes.'

'Sounds like the killer read my book.'

'Again, unfortunately, yes.'

'Any suspects?'

'There's a missing husband we want to talk to.'

'You think it was him?'

'We haven't discounted it. Could be a domestic that got out of hand.'

Laughton looks at the crime scene then up at him. 'You believe that?'

Tannahill opens his mouth to say something then thinks better of it. 'Not really, no.'

She nods and turns her attention back to the photograph of the Millers' living room, the red stripes of blood vivid against the white floor and walls, the objects carefully arranged around the pixelated body in the centre. 'I'm assuming the knife in the first picture is the murder weapon.'

'It matches the wounds.'

'Where was it in relation to the body?'

'Stuck in the wall on her right-hand side.'

Laughton draws back and looks at the whole picture again. There's something there but she's not sure what yet. 'Where was it in relation to her right hand?'

'Er, well she was pretty much pointing at it.'

Laughton nods. 'Apart from a copy of my book, what else was left at the scene?'

'If you keep going down you'll see.'

She scrolls down the article, past the photo of the outside of the house until she reaches the close-ups of the objects.

She studies the photo of the two medals balanced on the victim's finger. 'This was on her left hand?'

'Yes.'

'And there was something on her face in the wide shot.'

'An eye mask.'

She continues scrolling through the article, looking at the rest of the photographs: a set of keys; the copy of her book; a toy unicorn.

Laughton physically jerks away from the screen when she sees it.

'You OK?' Tannahill says.

Laughton stares at the toy unicorn, its big button eyes staring blankly back at her, the caption beneath like a cold whisper from her past. A toy found by the victim's body.

'What is it?' Tannahill moves round the chair, looking at her and not the screen now. 'You want some water? You look like you've seen a ghost.'

Laughton stares at the unicorn, her mouth dry.

No, not a ghost. A monster.

Laughton scrolls down until the photo of the unicorn disappears and the shadow that fell across her lifts a little.

'It's Justitia,' she says.

'What?'

'The victim has been arranged like Justitia, Ancient Roman figure of blind justice: arms outstretched, eyes covered, something like a sword by the right hand, the approximation of scales in the left. The symbolism is all very deliberate. The keys probably represent something too, maybe a secret to be unlocked, maybe something imprisoned. And the unicorn can represent all kinds of things: rarity; magic; innocence; a symbol of Christ, take your pick. I think the only outlier here, the only thing that doesn't really follow the pattern is my book. There's no obvious symbolic meaning, knowledge perhaps, but I think it just is what it is and may have been left behind to guarantee the murder got attention because of

158

the connection to my father. If I were you, I'd be looking hard at the victim and her husband to find out who they were, what they did and what kind of dangerous enemies they might have made. Whoever did this is settling a score. This is all about justice.'

Tannahill smiles. 'The email address the killer used to send the message was justice72@yahoo.com.'

'There you go.' She scrolls to the bottom of the article and flinches again when she sees the photo of her father. He looks older and thinner than the last time she saw him. There's a picture of her book next to him, blood clearly visible behind it. She clicks the browser to close the window, stands from her chair and opens the door.

Tannahill looks at her, confused. 'Is that it?'

'Five minutes you said, five minutes you had. I've got to be somewhere and, like I already said, I don't get involved in live cases.'

Tannahill stares at her for a beat then shakes his head and moves to walk out of the office. He reaches the door and pauses.

'I don't understand,' he says. 'You said yourself police work is a weak-link game like football. So why do you choose to play it like basketball? I want to find whoever did this and I would love you to be a part of the team that does it. You've already helped.' He reaches into his pocket, pulls out a business card and hands it to her. 'So if you decide you want to join the team and help some more, give me a call.'

Extract from *How to Process a Murder*
by Laughton Rees

There is a certain and peculiar intimacy to a murder investigation. It's a relationship of sorts – dysfunctional, very one-sided, somewhat obsessive.

The lead investigator will get to know everything about the victim and see them at their most unguarded and unflattering. They will have to cross the lines of usual human interaction, force open doors the victim chose to keep shut, rifle through drawers and documents never meant for public scrutiny, ask questions of the victim's family and friends that in any other circumstance would be both egregiously intrusive and grossly impertinent. A murder investigator's job is to shine the brightest of lights into the darkest corners of a person's life. Ultimately, in order to discover who ended a life and why, an investigator must take that same life, and also destroy it, by pulling it apart piece by piece.

In this respect the killer and the detective are closer to each other than either would care to acknowledge.

29

By the time the evening news rolls around, the Miller story is a juggernaut.

Every channel on TV and radio is running it. Most are leading with it, including several of the more serious news programmes, who frame it in the context of the latest crime statistics and peer at it through the lens of the loftier issue of whether this case proves that knife crime is becoming a broader problem everyone should now worry about. By 'everyone' they really mean white, middle-class people, not just the poor and brown people living on estates and benefits who are traditionally the ones who experience knife crime. Thirty-eight young men and boys – all poor, black, or Asian – have died already this year at the edge of a blade and yet this is the first knife murder that has led the news. An ex-Home Secretary and a retired chief constable are wheeled out to frown and give their thoughts, which are: yes, knife crime is a real and growing problem; yes, something urgent needs to be done about it; and yes, the current Commissioner has some serious questions to answer about how much crime in general and knife crime in particular has increased on his watch. The ex-Home Secretary goes slightly further by saying that maybe Rees is no longer up to the job and, after several years at the top, perhaps it's time for him to consider his position and make way for fresh blood.

For the more tabloidy online news channels and newspapers there is no such pretence to higher ideals or attempts at state-of-the-nation debate. For them it's just the usual, straight-up battle for eyeballs and circulation figures, with the trifecta of Murder, Mystery and Money providing the perfect click-bait.

Slade has already written three follow-up stories to feed the beast: one on the mystery of the victim and her missing husband with a tip-line for information and rewards offered; the second featuring the macabre objects left by the victim's body, with a sidebar of famous historical serial killers who also left or collected 'trophies'; the third, written for the evening print editions, is exclusively about the book and the fact that Commissioner John Rees's daughter wrote it, and how it appears from anonymous police sources that it may have helped the killer leave no evidence behind. This story also has a sidebar retelling Laughton's tragic past, detailing the whole Masked Monster/Adrian McVey saga, the murder of her mother and the troubled relationship with her father that followed.

Commissioner John Rees – the article ends – *the most senior policeman in the country who couldn't, in the end, even protect his own wife and daughter from a psychopathic killer.*

In Victoria train station a man wearing a long coat and a black baseball cap stands in WHSmith's. He picks up a copy of the evening edition of *The Daily* and skim-reads the article, his breath quickening when he sees the Masked Monster is mentioned. He picks up one copy of all the evening newspapers, then heads over to the self-service station to buy them before disappearing in the crowd.

But it's online that the story really explodes and goes inter-national. #MurderMansion starts to trend as hundreds, then thousands, then millions of people share the story. By far the biggest draw is the *Virtual tour of murder mansion*, Slade's idea made manifest after his assistant Shakila managed to track down the architectural firm who originally built the Miller house and produced a high-end video tour as part of a submission for a modern architecture prize. *The Daily* paid them five figures for an exclusive licence and the back-room, techy boys and girls – not one of them older than twelve, as far as Slade could tell – had re-packaged and re-edited it, adding a creepy music track which turned the slow, steady glide of the camera through the rooms into something altogether more sinister. They'd added other captions and images too, info bites that fade up and down revealing things like how much the house was worth, how it was built on the edge of Highgate Cemetery, then the names and smiling photographs of Mike and Kate Miller, her name with the subtitle *Victim*, his with *Wanted for questioning*. Finally, as the camera drifts into the living room and the creepy music reaches maximum tension, the crime scene photos flash up along with *Psycho*-style violin stabs. It has been live barely two hours and has already racked up over four million views, the number ticking up exponentially as it spreads like a virus across the super-connected globe.

The ladies of the Highgate Book Club all see it, are mostly appalled by it, then share it on the WhatsApp group and their Facebook pages so everyone they know can be as appalled as they are. Celia Barnes sees it too after a friend shares the link on her Facebook page. She watches numbly as it autoplays, reliving her own journey through the house that morning and raising her eyebrows when a caption fades up answering a question she had almost forgotten asking. Six point eight million, that's how much the house is worth, about three million more than she'd estimated – so much for her career as an estate agent. The camera drifts on, down the hall, through the door, into the living room and she quickly closes the app, too raw to see that room again or relive that part of her morning.

Somewhere over India, the finance director of an Australian sportswear company watches it on his phone using the free Wi-Fi in business class then shares it with his teenage son in Sydney who binge-watches true crime series.

In a Seoul semi-basement apartment that smells of mould and garbage, a family of night cleaners crowd round a phone before heading off to work, marvelling at the expensive-looking house then shrieking in horror and delight at the jump-scare ending.

And in a thatched rattan hut, tucked in a beachside coconut grove in Goa, a sinewy, tanned woman slides beneath thin cotton sheets, rearranges the mosquito net to cover any gaps then scrolls through her emails and messages, frowning at the continued lack of contact from the one person she wants to hear from most.

Shonagh O'Brien stretches as she scrolls through her Twitter feed, feeling the pleasant ache of days of doing nothing but yoga as she looks at what's trending and listens to the *shush* of the nearby ocean and the chirp of frogs in the palms overhead, outside in the tropical night.

She clicks on the top result and glances at the text accompanying the video clip but is too tired and distracted to take it in. The clip autoplays and she lies back on the white cotton, watching a camera glide through a beautiful house, still not really sure what she's watching. Then Mike's photograph fades up and Shonagh sits bolt upright, eyes wide, instantly awake.

Wanted for questioning, the caption beneath his photograph reads.

Her eyes flit across to the other photograph and the caption: *Victim.*

Shonagh stares at the screen, the sound of frogs and cicadas mingling with the creepy music leaking from her phone's tiny speakers. The video clip plays on and Shonagh unconsciously draws the phone closer to her face, her stunned mind scrambling to make sense of what she's seeing. Then the camera enters the living room and the sudden stab of violins makes her drop her phone. She stares down at it, frozen and shocked, like it has turned into a snake and any movement might make it strike.

'Mike!' she mouths, but no sound comes out. 'Oh my God!'

The clip ends and her phone is just a phone again. She snatches it off the bed, fumbles her way to her contacts and calls the number listed under 'Mmmmmm', trying to remember what time it is in the UK. It must be around six thirty in the evening, a time she's *not* supposed to call. But this is different. There's something wrong. Very wrong. Mike's number rings and rings then voicemail kicks in.

'Mike?' she says. 'I saw the news. What happened, are you OK? Call me, please. I need to know you're all right.'

She hangs up and stares at her phone, wondering if she should try again. She feels guilty now for being pissed at him ever since she got the message on her way to Heathrow:

Something's come up. You go on ahead I'll join you when I can. Don't try calling me I need to fix something here. I'll explain when I see you. M x

The bloody images flash into her brain again, the woman lying in the middle of that room. All that blood.

Is this what he needed to fix?

She remembers the photos too. Kate Miller – *Victim*. And Mike – *Wanted for questioning*.

It didn't say *suspect*.

She calls him again but again it goes straight to voicemail. Maybe he is in trouble. Maybe he needs her, like *really* needs her.

She hangs up, opens the Cathay Pacific website and looks to see how soon she can catch a flight back to London.

30

Laughton has not seen the murder mansion video. After the first article dropped and her phone started ringing constantly with journalists all wanting to talk to her, she turned it off. She'd been photographed leaving work too, which had disturbed her more than anything, a man appearing suddenly, saying her name then blinding her with flashes the moment she looked up. What if he'd had something other than a camera in his hand? What if they started going after Gracie? The thought makes her feel sick. She has carefully structured her entire life to cocoon her daughter from the dangers she experienced herself and sees at arm's length in her work. But danger has still found them.

She stands in her kitchen, focusing on her breathing and waiting for the kettle to boil, a mirror of her morning, the quality of the grey evening light almost identical to the dawn. She drops a peppermint teabag in a mug, a post-noon ritual designed to allow her caffeine levels to drop and give her a fighting chance of getting some sleep. She never has been a good sleeper, not as long as she can remember. Not since her mother died at least.

She had to turn her phone on again to access the timer and it rang three times in the sixty seconds it took to fill the kettle.

Three times.

She can't work out if this is a good sign or not.

It feels like she's under siege, like the journalists are not just on the other end of the phone but gathering outside the walls, closing in, pressing in on her carefully tucked away, anonymous life. She feels exposed, vulnerable.

She hears the front door open and experiences a mixture of relief and more anxiety.

Gracie is home.

She takes another mug and drops a teabag into it, listening for clues as to what kind of mood Grace is in. The door slams hard and she hears her stomp down the hallway and into her bedroom. Another slam.

Laughton closes her eyes and suddenly feels weary.

They used to be best friends, as close as it was possible for two people to get. Then the teenage hormone gods arrived and Grace had become increasingly colder towards her, secretive and withdrawn. She'd tried to talk to her about it, but it always ended in arguments and accusations.

You're my problem, Gracie would scream at her. *You watch me all the time, control every detail of everything. But I don't need protecting. I'm not a kid any more.*

She was the same age now Laughton had been when she left home. And look how that had turned out; it was a miracle she'd survived at all, and it was a miracle that had saved her. Gracie. She was the miracle. And now it was her chance to save her from the dangers that lay ahead of her. God knows there'd been no one to do it for her.

Behind her the kettle clicks off. She counts to three slowly, letting the water cool to just below boiling, then pours it on to the peppermint tea bags. She takes a deep breath, picks up both mugs in one hand and heads out towards Gracie's bedroom.

She pauses outside the black door and listens. The door is black because she promised Gracie she could paint her new

171

bedroom any colour she liked when they moved here. That 'colour' turned out to be Lamp Black, and 'painting your room' apparently also included the outside of the door. 'Gracie' is written across it in dripping red paint that reminds her of Kate Miller, lying in the middle of a room decorated with her own blood. She shakes the thought away and taps on the door – three times.

'Hey, hon? I've brought you some tea.'

No answer.

'Hon?' She twists the handle and opens the door.

Gracie spins round, eyes ablaze. 'Jesus, Mum!' She is half undressed, her clothes crumbled in piles at her feet and blending in with the general mess. She stabs a finger at her phone to silence the music being beamed to her earphones, grabs her bathrobe – also black – from the unmade bed and covers herself.

'Sorry,' Laughton blurts, 'just bringing you some tea.'

'How about knocking.'

'I did knock.'

'And did I say "come in"?'

Laughton places a mug down on a small pile of books, practically the only horizontal space in the room.

'I had a meeting with your headmaster earlier.'

'I know,' Gracie says. 'Everybody in the school knows that my crazy mother came in and swore at one of the special needs kids.' She barges past on her way to the bathroom. 'Thanks for the help, really appreciate it.'

Laughton watches her storm away down the corridor, bathrobe flying behind her like Batman's cape, then she disappears into the bathroom with another loud slam.

'So that went well,' Laughton murmurs.

She turns and studies her daughter's cluttered room, the black paint and framed band posters crowding the walls making it feel smaller than it actually is. Piles of clothes spill out of half-open drawers and collect on the floor in drifts, what Laughton sometimes refers to as the 'freshly burgled look'. She has looked through this door many times before but this time it's different. This time she realizes she is surveying the room with the scrutiny she normally reserves for crime scene photos. Consciously or unconsciously she is looking for things that are out of place. And there is something.

Down the hallway she hears the hiss of the shower, telling her where Gracie is, and, more importantly, where she is going to be for the next ten minutes.

She stares at the thing she has spotted, glowing now like it has a spotlight on it.

Should she ignore it, respect her daughter's privacy and her secrets?

The self-help books she's read all say a healthy parent–child relationship is built on trust. Lose that and you risk losing everything. But Laughton knows that mistrust could also be a force for good, the lesser of a much greater evil – her entire career has been built on it.

It was all part of the shitty deal you got as a mother, a duty to be suspicious and watchful over the person you loved most in the world. Or maybe it wasn't like this for everyone. Maybe it was simply another added bonus of being a lone parent where she didn't have the luxury of being able to talk things out with someone who shared the immense burden of bringing up a child. She was on her own in this, which meant all the decisions were hers. And all the mistakes too.

Down the hall the cascade of water continues.

She remembers her conversation with Maya, and the way she had shrugged as if sharing a simple fact of life when she'd said, *This is St Mark's. Lots of kids carry knives.*

She has to know. Without further thought, Laughton picks her way through clothes, make-up, empty food wrappers and the packets of painkillers Gracie hoards for when her period is particularly bad, over to where her school bag has been neatly tucked under the small desk that also serves as a bedside table.

Neatly tucked.

Despite her slammy mood when she came home the bag had not been angrily dumped on the floor the moment Gracie stepped into her room. Instead she had carried it as far from the door as it was possible to get, then deliberately placed it under something else. In a room full of mess and chaos, it was the only thing that had been properly put away.

Laughton sets her tea on the desk then crouches down. She glances over her shoulder nervously, the sound of the shower much quieter in the room, the whisper of it almost smothered by the noise of her hammering heart. She turns back, unclips the flap on the front of the bag, opens it and peers inside.

Gracie's school bag is like her room in miniature, books and folders crammed together haphazardly with a random collection of torn bits of paper and sweet wrappers packed into the remaining gaps. Laughton slips her hand inside, working her way with her fingertips between the folders and books. It would be much easier to tip the contents on to the bed, but she doesn't have long and is still hoping her suspicions might yield nothing and she can leave no evidence behind of this gross betrayal of trust. She pushes her hand deeper into the bag until it reaches the bottom and touches something cold and hard. She jerks her hand away and stares at the bag for a moment like it just bit her. Then she grabs it and upends it on the bed, all caution now abandoned. She needs to see it, needs to confirm with her own eyes what she already knows is there.

The knife looks evil against the soft, black backdrop of her daughter's bed, its black rubber handle and silver blade obscene among the school books, sweet wrappers, and the worn-out Star Wars pencil case Gracie got when she was eight after she decided Leia was a way cooler princess than any of the Disney ones.

Down the hallway Laughton hears the hiss of the shower.

In a minute or less it will stop and Gracie will walk down the corridor and into this room and they will have to talk.

She has no idea what she is going to say.

Her mind has been disconnected from any calm, rational function by the fight-or-flight response sparked by the cold metal blade of the knife.

Lots of kids carry knives, Maya had said.

And her fifteen-year-old daughter was apparently one of them.

Laughton sits numbly on the edge of the bed and waits. She listens to the distant hiss of her daughter showering, thinking about what she will say when Gracie walks back into the bedroom and finds her there. How do you even start a conversation like that?

In the end she decides to fall back on a standard police interview technique where a piece of evidence is simply presented to a suspect along with silence to draw out a response. She will make Gracie begin the conversation, because Lord knows she has no idea how to start it.

Down the corridor the shower stops then she hears the door to the bathroom open and her mouth goes dry at the sound of approaching footsteps and soft fluffing of wet hair. Gracie steps into view, anger darkening her face at the sight of her mother. Then her eyes drop down to the knife lying on the bed. She stops drying her hair and there is a moment of silence, which hangs between them like an open door that neither of them wishes to step through. Then Grace looks up and her expression hardens.

'You went through my bag,' she murmurs.

Laughton says nothing.

'Why did you go through my bag?'

'Because I was worried you might be hiding something from me.'

Gracie shakes her head. 'You don't understand,' she turns around and walks away.

'No, I don't.' Laughton follows her into the hallway and on to the living room. 'Have you any idea how many people die every year from stab wounds.'

'Actually, yes – it's all over today's news.'

'And do you know how many of those victims are stabbed with their own knives?'

'No. Do you know how many people *don't* get stabbed every year because they *were* carrying a knife, have you got that little statistic to hand?'

'That's a ridiculous argument. That's like gun nuts in America calling for more guns every time there's another mass shooting.'

'No, it's not. A three-year-old with a gun can kill themselves or someone else, a toddler with a knife can't, so it's not the same thing at all. You want to talk about the knife crime figures? OK let's talk about them. Let's talk about the fact that if you live in certain parts of London, eight out of ten young people will be carrying a knife, not because they're violent idiots but because it makes them feel safer. And guess what? We live in one of those areas. So what would you rather have me do on my way to and from school: cross my fingers and hope for the best?'

'Yeah but Jesus, Gracie – a *knife*.'

'Mum, just because I carry one doesn't mean I'm going to stab anyone with it.'

'Then what's the point of having it?'

Gracie slumps down on the sofa, takes a breath and blows it out slowly. 'OK, so in nature, a lion meets a zebra, zebra has a pretty high chance of being killed. But when a lion meets a lion, they roar at each other for a bit, then both walk away. At my school, if you don't have a knife, you're a zebra.'

176

Laughton sits back in her chair, feeling like the worst parent in the world for sending her to that school. 'Why didn't you tell me things were so bad?'

'Mum, you worry about whether you've flicked the light switch the right number of times. You can't do anything without putting a timer on it or counting to three every few seconds. How can I possibly talk to you about anything as major as this?'

Laughton dies inside a little. And her sadness and worry, already fathoms deep after the discovery of the knife, plummet deeper still.

'I'm sorry,' she says. 'I'm sorry I'm such a weirdo, but I want you to know I'm actually quite tough. I can handle the big things. And all the light-flicking and the counting . . . all the quirkiness – that's nothing. It's me, it's about me, it's my issue, it shouldn't affect you.'

'Of course it's going to affect me,' Gracie says quietly. 'We live together and you're my mum. I get that it's all to help you deal with stress and things, but I can't deal with things the same way you do. I can't just run away and hide.'

'That's not fair. You make me sound like some kind of hermit. I don't hide, I work, I take you to school, I don't lock myself away.'

'Yes, but when was the last time you had any friends over? When was the last time your phone rang for any reason other than work? When was the last time you went on a date?'

Laughton opens her mouth to speak then closes it again because she has no answer.

'You say I should talk to you,' Gracie continues, sounding like the grown-up now, 'but you never talk to me, not about anything important. You don't talk about your past, you don't talk about your work, and God forbid I should ever try and bring up the subject of family.'

'There's nothing to talk about,' Laughton says, covering her eyes with her hands and shaking her head. 'Nothing you don't know already: my mum's dead – killed with a knife, by the way – and it was my dad's fault. I couldn't live with him after that so I left home and it was bad for a while, really bad, then your dad came along and . . . It was a dark, dark time and it really screwed me up and I'm still trying to work my way through it, which is why I'm such a basket case. But the best thing, the only good thing to come out of all that was you. And the most important thing to me is that you don't suffer the way I suffered. It damaged me, but I will not let it damage you.'

Gracie shakes her head then stands up slowly from the sofa. She looks down at her through a curtain of damp, messy hair like she's a fierce warrior princess. She seems so grown up in so many ways and yet she's still a child. 'You want me to start talking to you about my problems,' she says.

Laughton nods. 'Yes, I do.'

'OK,' Gracie says. 'But you go first.'

Laughton hesitates. A large part of the protective shield she has built around her daughter has involved keeping her own problems quiet and, given Gracie's fragile emotional state, talking about them now feels inappropriate and dangerous. 'I don't think now is the time for me to burden you with any of my crazy shit,' she says, smiling and trying to make light of it. 'Right now I just want to help you.'

Gracie nods sadly, then turns and walks out of the room.

Laughton hears her bedroom door closing, softly this time but in many ways louder than a slam. She feels numbed by the conversation, wrung out by the onslaught of emotions that came with it: anger, concern, frustration, and a kind of strange pride that her fifteen-year-old daughter somehow managed to flip her argument and dismantle it in a way many barristers earning hundreds of pounds an hour had failed to do in court.

She launches herself out of the chair and moves into the kitchen, head spinning, heart racing with the realization that things are worse than she'd imagined, *way* worse.

She grabs her phone from where she left it by the kettle and powers it up. She needs to get Gracie out of that school, any way she can and as fast as possible.

Her phone blinks to life and immediately buzzes with alerts for missed calls and new text messages. One is from Brian Slade.

I would be interested to get your take, he'd said to her earlier. *I can pay of course . . . With your distinguished credentials and personal ties with the Commissioner we'd easily be talking five figures.*

I don't work live cases, she had replied.

First time for everything.

31

Tannahill is hunched over a laptop updating the Murder Book and trying to order his thoughts before the briefing when his phone rings. He picks it up and glances over at the incident room where his team are already starting to assemble.

'Tannahill Khan.' He answers the phone without checking the number.

'Hi. It's Laughton. Laughton Rees.'

Her voice snaps his attention away from the gathering crowd. 'Oh hi. Are you OK?'

'Yes, I'm . . . yes. Listen, about your offer earlier – to consult on the case.'

'Yes?'

'Does it still stand?'

'Of course.'

'OK. Then I will. I mean, I want to.'

'Really!? Great.'

'But I'll need to do it properly.'

Tannahill frowns. 'What do you mean?'

'I mean you're going to have to . . . you'll have to contract me properly, as an outside consultant.'

'Oh right.'

'I'll have to invoice for the hours I work and charge my normal consultant's rate.'

'Of course, yes, I'm sure that's fine.'

'It's bound to be quite a lot of hours. The way I work means I'll have to go over everything multiple times, so . . .'

'Yeah, don't worry . . . Your da— I've already been given authorization for any extra resources I need, so I'm sure it won't be a problem. I'll need to run the appointment past the NCA, but I can't see them having any objections.'

'OK, that would be . . . thanks.'

'No problem. So when can you start?'

'Well if you send me whatever files you can share, I can start now. Though I was thinking . . .'

'What?'

'I was wondering if I could see the crime scene.'

'Yes of course. If you send me your email address I can send links to all the media files, which include a 360-degree walk-through so you can effectively—'

'No, I mean can I go to the actual house?'

'Oh right. Well, there's a lot of press buzzing around it at the moment, and with you being part of the story . . . it's probably not a good idea.'

'Oh, OK.'

He can hear the disappointment in her voice. He checks the time and glances out of the window at the grey street outside, the evening light already fading fast.

'Can you get to Highgate in about an hour?' he asks.

'I can get there in twenty minutes,' Laughton replies, 'I live just off the Holloway Road.'

'OK, let me see if I can sort something out and I'll call you back. Is this the number to reach you on?'

'Yeah. This is the only number I have.'

'Great. I'll call you back in half an hour or so.'

He hangs up and smiles. He hadn't really expected to see

Laughton a second time, now he was going to see her again today.

An email pings into his inbox from LaughtonRees@londonmet.org with *This is me* in the subject line.

He smiles, hits reply and quickly sends her copies of the media files, the witness statements, and latest forensic reports from the Murder Book, then picks up his laptop and heads to the briefing room.

The chatter quietens a little as Tannahill enters the room.

'I know we've all got things to do,' he says, capitalizing on the momentary quiet, 'so let's keep this brief.'

He places his laptop on the podium by the large smart screen that fills the back wall and hits a command to connect it. A picture appears on the screen showing Kate Miller in an evening dress, smiling down at the team assembled to catch the person who killed her.

'Sometime between midnight and two a.m. this morning a person, or persons, disabled a highly sophisticated alarm and security system at number three Swain's Lane, Highgate. They then proceeded to murder the lady of the house, Kate Miller, in a frenzied knife attack.'

He clicks on another photo and the image on the screen changes to one showing Kate Miller's body, arms outstretched with the objects around her.

'The killer or killers then laid her body out on the floor and placed four objects around it: a set of keys; a child's unicorn toy; two military medals; and a book on murder scene protocol and process, written by Laughton Rees who, for those who don't know, also happens to be Commissioner Rees's daughter. The killer also appears to have read the book and used the information it contains to clean up the scene afterwards, but we'll get on to the forensics in a minute.

'The killer or killers then took photos of the crime scene – the timestamps on the photos put this at around four thirty, which the DFT have confirmed is accurate. The killer or killers then sent a selection of the photographs directly to the press via a Yahoo account, which is untraceable. We have, however, found digital traces on the images that suggest they'd been saved on an old Compaq laptop, between ten and twelve years old, prior to being emailed. It's not much but it will hopefully help tie the killer to the evidence once we find him. Anyway, as a result of these images being sent to the press, as well as the family link with the Commissioner, this case is now big news and the spotlight is very much on us, so the faster we can wrap it up, the better.'

He taps a key on the laptop and the image on the screen widens to show Mike Miller standing next to his wife in a white dinner jacket.

'Meet our main suspect, Mike Miller, husband of the victim, current whereabouts unknown.'

'We should look for him in a casino if that's how he dresses!' someone calls out, and a ripple of laughter loosens the room.

'Or the penguin house at the zoo,' someone adds.

Tannahill smiles and lets the laughter settle before continuing. 'At the moment we're considering four possible hypotheses . . .' He turns back to the screen. 'One, that Mike Miller killed his wife and has either fled and/or come to harm; two, that a third party did it and Miller has either fled and/or come to harm; three, a third party did it and Miller is currently unaware; and four, a third party did it at Miller's direction. Either way, without a clear motive the easiest way to find out which one of these is correct is to find Mike Miller. Bob, what's the latest?'

'The latest is that Mike Miller is still a ghost.' Bob Chamberlain – grey hair, grey suit, grey sky demeanour – looks down at a notebook as old-school as he is. 'The only official records we've managed to find are for a passport and a driver's licence, both issued at round the same time just under a year ago. Same story for his wife, which suggests a total identity switch. I contacted the PPS to see if they might be in witness protection but they're not. From the autopsy we have a couple of breast implants that we're in the process of tracing and we're waiting on the DNA to see if we can get a match from that and I'm presuming there might be budget to screen for familial matches too if the first screen draws a blank?'

'You presume correctly. Whatever it takes, that's the word from the top, so don't worry about anyone dicking you around about your overtime. I've already requested an outside consultant to assist with this investigation.'

Tannahill reads the silence in the room. No one likes outsiders coming in, a question of professional pride.

'It's Laughton Rees,' he says. 'She's a highly regarded criminologist in her own right and the presence of her book at the scene means she's already part of the investigation anyway. Now, forensics. Any joy?'

A hand shoots up and Tannahill points at the person attached, a young DC whose name he can't remember. 'Yes, sir. Forensics found partial prints on one of the pages inside the book. They're still processing it, but the tech I spoke to doesn't think they're a match for any of the other prints taken from the house.'

Tannahill nods. 'Maybe it's a good thing our perp read the book after all. Let me know as soon as you know any more. What about the other objects: anything distinctive about any of them, anything we can trace that might give us a lead?'

Another hand shoots up. 'I've been looking into the medals, sir.' The speaker is DS Watson, rugby-player solid, ex-Navy not from choice and still a tiny bit chippy about it.

Tannahill clicks on a new photo and the image of Mike Miller is replaced by the two medals.

'The medals themselves are nothing special,' Watson continues. 'There are millions of 1939–1945 stars out there because they were given to everyone who served in the war, even the RAF.' He smiles knowingly and looks around but no one gets the joke.

'Isn't the 1939–1945 medal supposed to have a name inscribed on the back?' Tannahill says, remembering his grandfather's medal.

'Only the ones issued to South African, Australian and Indian forces.'

Tannahill nods, the mystery of his grandfather's named medal now solved. Pakistan had still been part of India back in 1944.

'The Atlantic Star is a bit more specific as these were only issued to sailors and pilots, but the thing I noticed about this one, sir, is that the ribbon's wrong. It should show pale bands of blue, white and sea-green to represent the waters of the Atlantic, but the one on this medal is crimson. Crimson is the ribbon for the Victoria Cross, which – as I'm sure you know – is awarded for valour and is the highest and most prestigious award of the British honours system. And though hundreds of thousands of Atlantic Crosses were issued in the Second World War, only one hundred and eighty-two VCs were awarded during the entire campaign.

'So I cross-checked the list of VC recipients with the list of those who also got the Atlantic Star and came up with thirteen names. All of them are now deceased; in fact many died while earning their VCs. The last survivor up until a year ago was Cyril Lawson, the only merchant seaman to receive the award. He died in a nursing home in Cleethorpes. There was a bit of an outcry about it at the time because of the quality of the care he received prior to his death, a few "Abandoned Hero" headlines in the press, that kind of thing.'

Tannahill nods. 'Good work. Keep on it and see if he has any surviving relatives. Anyone else?'

'Sir!' Another hand lifts up, this one belonging to DC Anderson, a man so blond he's almost transparent. 'I found something in a CCTV trawl,' he says. 'It's in the file with the other security camera info from the house.'

Tannahill finds the tab on the laptop, clicks the image to open it on the big screen and the whole room seems to lean forward to peer at it.

The image is fairly low-res and blurry, but in colour: a screen grab from a CCTV camera taken at night. It shows the street, and a brick wall, and a street lamp, and a tall man wearing a big coat and a baseball cap with what looks like a pale blue surgical mask covering his face. A date and time-stamp on the image shows that it was taken at 1.30 a.m.

'This is from the onboard camera of a night bus which follows the route down Swain's Lane past the Miller house,' Anderson explains.

Tannahill studies the man, his height and build difficult to accurately gauge because of the big coat, but certainly close enough. 'Could be our suspect,' he says. 'Canvas the neighbours again and ask if any of them went out for a stroll at one thirty last night, or if they saw or heard anything at that specific time. And see if we can't sharpen this image up a bit; mask or no mask, there might be something about the coat or the cap or his shoes even that we can use further down the line.'

He turns back to the room. 'Anything else?'

Heads shake and notebooks are closed.

'OK then, back at it. Let's see if we can't find Mike Miller before tomorrow morning's papers give us another kicking.'

32

The news that Laughton Rees is joining the investigation raises all kinds of eyebrows. Baker is impressed Tannahill managed to talk her into it; Bob Chamberlain, knowing the backstory and bad blood better than most, is surprised he managed to clear it with the big boss. The rest of the team, who don't know much more than what was printed earlier in *The Daily*, google her name and quickly realize that their own various slightly dysfunctional family lives are like a sun-drenched sitcom compared to the Rees family saga.

Commissioner John Rees finds out from the head of the National Crime Agency after he forwards Tannahill's email notifying them of his intention to hire Professor Laughton Rees as an expert consultant on the Miller case with a one-line question.

Any objections?

A simple question with a complicated answer.

Rees looks up at a framed photograph he keeps on his wall showing a slim man with a sharp, intelligent face wearing the full dress police uniform of a Metro Police Commander. The man is Peter Fairweather, Rees's first boss, the person who had taken him under his wing and taught him more about police work than possibly anyone else in his life. He had become a good friend too and in the absence of a wife or anyone else close enough to trust had often been the one Rees called whenever he faced tricky personal decisions like this one.

On a professional level Rees has no objection to Laughton consulting on the case, he knows her credentials and has followed her work enough to know she would be an asset on any complex investigation like this. But as a father, even one as remote as he has become, he still feels protective towards her and therefore hesitant. Once she becomes part of the investigation she will become a target, fair game for the professional haters, whose job it is to conjure outrage, and the slimy legions of trolls who then feed on it and crap it out as online anger. If he objected to her appointment he would protect her from all that, though she would know it was he who had blocked her appointment and it would add another reason to hate him to her already stacked pile.

He stands and moves over to the window. Outside, the grey autumnal light is fading to nothing and the lights of London glow through the dirty mist.

In the beginning he had reached out constantly, offering her anything he thought might help rebuild the bridge that had gone up in flames when Grace had died: financial help, a place to stay, a place of her own, anything. And after every direct approach had been angrily rejected, his relationship with her had changed, become more indirect, more secretive.

He had helplessly watched from a distance as she spiralled down, keeping painful tabs on her through intel gleaned from street informers, arrest sheets, and social services reports. It was through one of these he'd found out she was pregnant and addicted to prescription meds. He'd pulled strings to funnel her into the best rehab and social care streams without ever letting her know he was behind it. He'd found out who his unborn grandchild's father was and dealt with him too.

Shelby Facer, a charming snake twenty years Laughton's

senior and a known associate of some pretty bad street-level people, was like a modern, sleazier version of Fagin. On the surface he seemed like a glamorous, old-school piece of Eurotrash, cash to burn but with no discernible means of employment, on first-name terms with every nightclub doorman in London, a one-man rolling good time. In reality, his public school accent, not-quite film-star looks and charm masked a calculating, borderline sociopath who groomed a succession of 'girlfriends' through dates and good times until they got addicted and he got bored then he'd introduce them to his associates who would put them to work in the sex industry – porn shoots, escorting, whatever paid best. He was a scumbag, but also a cunning and dangerous one, and Rees sought to surgically remove him from his daughter's life.

It had taken him two months and pretty much every favour he could call in to first introduce Facer, then push him as close as he could to the centre of a huge, international drug-trafficking sting operation that was already underway. It ended with Facer flying first-class to Miami to meet what he thought was the US contact to finalize details of the shipment only to be arrested by a group of undercover DEA agents instead. By this time Scotland Yard had given the US authorities everything they had on Facer, certainly enough to make sure he was going to spend most of the rest of his life in a US supermax penitentiary. That was the kind of parenting he practised.

How much his unorthodox parental intervention contributed to Laughton coming out of her tailspin and pulling her life together he was never quite sure. What he did know was that her attitude towards him remained unchanged, even when she became a mother. He had hoped motherhood might mellow her a little, change her perspective on life enough to cool the fires of her hatred towards him, but nothing had changed. He had watched his granddaughter grow up from a careful distance and learned to harden his heart against his situation, for his own emotional protection as much as anything.

As time wore on, it got easier. He could almost pretend his relationship with his daughter was normal because plenty of fathers hardly ever saw their grown-up children. They watched them from afar, proud but distanced, just like he did. Just like he always had. Laughton is grown up now with a family of her own. She doesn't need him to look out for her any more. She should stand on her own two feet. He turns back to his laptop, hits reply on the email, types 'no objections' then sends it.

He glances at the photograph of his old boss then looks back out of the window, and down at the people walking home along the embankment eight floors below him, back to their homes, and their families, and their relatively uncomplicated lives. He stays like that for a long time.

33

Brian Slade is also walking, but not towards home. He is on the corner treadmill in a dimly lit room lined with smoked glass and concealed lighting, earbuds in, laptop open when the email alert flashes up. He normally keeps alerts off when he's working out here but not when a killer is sending him emails that generate headline stories.

He opens the email.

Laughton Rees is consulting on the Miller case, it says. *Just received a group email to the investigation team asking us all to be nice to her.*

Slade compresses his mouth into a tight line. 'Well fuck you very much,' he murmurs, then checks around to make sure no one else heard. He nearly got thrown out once for 'language' and though he normally doesn't care who he offends, he likes this gym enough to keep a lid on it.

The Crypt is a private gym built in a deconsecrated church about half a mile from his office. It is not the nearest gym to him but it's easily the most expensive and it's also stripped down enough to keep most of the amateurs away. People who come here are serious about fitness. They come to actually work out, not sit around in Lycra, sipping smoothies, pretending their bodies are the product of hard work and discipline rather than a skilled surgeon and their husband's money. Another significant section of the clientele at the Crypt are celebrities. As a result there are no cameras anywhere in the building, which means he can work while working out without fear that some security guy, bribed by a rival paper or someone he's doing a story on, might zoom in on his screen and snatch screenshots.

Slade comes here a lot, especially in winter, so he can do his daily miles without getting filthy black London water splashed all over him by the passing buses and cabs. He always thinks better when he's running. It also means the idiots at work can't interrupt him with their office bollocks and inane small talk.

Slade closes the email. He had thought Laughton might take him up on his offer, so had pulled all the old stories on her and any other documents on file to reacquaint himself with her backstory before speaking to her again. So much for that. Now she's chosen the wrong side he will use it as ammunition against her instead. Win-win for him – as usual.

Slade is already casually familiar with Laughton's story because he wrote about most of it, starting with her mother's murder. Since then she has always been more of a supporting player, a stick to beat her more high-profile father with. You can see it in the headlines that have chronicled her existence, always second fiddle to her more famous father.

Tragic daughter of top cop in rehab as she fights for custody of baby daughter

Police chief's estranged daughter to follow in Dad's footsteps as she lands scholarship to top university

Tragic story has happy ending as Met Police commissioner's daughter graduates top of her class – but dad stays away

Maybe now she might finally make it to top billing, especially given her rejection of his offer: so much for my enemy's enemy being my friend.

He ups his pace until his heart rate settles to 120 bpm then goes back to reading, looking for the hook he can hang his story on. The documents currently open on his screen are all from the black files, private documents sold or leaked to the paper and filed away in case they may one day prove useful. The first document is a transcript of a psychiatric evaluation Laughton had undergone after being picked up in a police raid on a squat where drugs were reportedly being sold and used:

Subject (L) calls herself Laura but fingerprint records have identified her as Laughton Rees (17), whose personal trauma is acute and has been extensively documented. L refuses to talk about her mother's death or the breakdown of her relationship with her father – a high-ranking police officer and therefore an especially strong patriarchal authority figure.

Anecdotally L has been living rough for several months and her condition is fair with some signs of malnourishment and vitamin deficiency (B1, B6 and C). A pregnancy test also confirmed that L is pregnant, her physical appearance suggesting she is in the late stages of the second trimester, though – again – L refuses to discuss this or reveal who the father is. A drug test and search also shows L to be clinically dependent on Temazepam.

Her mental state is anxious and borderline manic, and she exhibits signs of acute compulsive behaviours, often centring on the number 3, which appear to be connected in some way to the trauma of her mother's death, though L has been consistently evasive when questioned about this.

Interview conducted by Dr Elizabeth Courtney-King (CK).

CK Tell me about the number 3.

L   Three. That's the tragic number.

CK Why tragic?

L   How high's the water, Mama? Three feet high and rising. Am I under arrest?

CK No.

L   So I can leave?

CK That's what we're here to decide.

L   Who's we?

CK Well you're technically a minor, so the state has a duty of care towards you and your unborn child to make the best decisions on your behalf to ensure you are both healthy and safe.

L   Safe? The state wants to make sure I'm safe?

CK Yes.

L   Ha!

CK We can find you a place in a hostel, help you to stop taking the meds you're on, which are not particularly . . .

L   Oh no, they calm me down. They help me sleep.

CK Well yes, but they're also very addictive and certainly not recommended to be taken during pregnancy.

L   Baby needs to sleep too. Sleep is good. Dreamless sleep is the best.

CK You're tapping your fingers in patterns of three again. Could you tell me about that?

L   One then two, and then comes three. Always after two, you see. Why do you think there were three wise men? Shadrach, Meshach, and Abednego. Or were they the ones who got thrown into the fire? They survived though, didn't they? Power of three, you see.

CK Why does the number three have power?

L   It just does. You know it does. Everyone knows it.

Look at the evidence. Three strikes and you're out. Three's a crowd. Holy Trinity – Father, Son, Holy Ghost. Two billion Christians can't be wrong, can they? Or can they? Can I leave now?

Slade smiles. Total mental case. That's a juicy angle. Is this woman really fit to head up a high-level investigation?

He skips to the next document, a first-year tutor report compiled for the trustees of the education scholarship she qualified for when she was in recovery, presumably the report was to make sure she was doing some actual work.

Laughton Rees is exceptional, the report begins, mincing zero words:

She has a near superhuman instinct for criminal study and a work ethic I have rarely encountered, qualities that are all the more remarkable given the extreme difficulties and trauma of her early life.

Example:

In the first semester I run a little experiment to introduce the new year group to the unreliable nature of 'testimony'. I do this by recreating something William Marston, one of the inventors of the lie detector, did in his American university lectures back in the early twenties.

The experiment is called 'the Messenger'.

I begin my lecture talking generally about testimony then am interrupted a few minutes in by a young man wearing distinctive clothes and carrying three books of different colours and an envelope. The messenger hands me the envelope and while I read the contents he does a number of pre-scripted things, such as slipping a second envelope into my pocket, producing a small knife and scraping the finger of his gloved left hand with it, and other notable things of that nature.

When he leaves I tell the students to take a sheet of paper and write down as many facts about the messenger as they can remember. There are 147 distinct facts the students can observe and record, and each year they generally get around 30 to 40 of them. Many don't even notice he had a knife, all of which clearly demonstrates how little eyewitnesses generally notice and can accurately remember.

When I ran this experiment for the class Laughton Rees was in, however, it didn't work because she got 128 of them – that's 46 more than the previous high score set over twenty years ago by the man who is now chief constable of Greater Manchester.

I initially thought she must have been tipped off about the lecture by a previous student, but subsequent examples of her almost preternatural abilities to observe, process and recall information have proved to me that she genuinely is that good.

In short, I cannot begin to express how impressed I have been with Ms Rees on such brief acquaintance, or how highly I consider her natural investigative talents to be, other than to say that if ever I am found murdered – and bearing in mind I have taught thousands of students, many of whom now hold senior positions within law enforcement – that Laughton Rees would be top of my list to investigate my demise.

Slade closes the document and takes a long drink from his water bottle.

If she really was as good as this professor said she was, then that could work for him too. Imagine if she goes on to solve the Miller murder; that would be pretty embarrassing for her dad – civilian amateur wanders in and makes his professional cops look like idiots.

Or – she might muck it up, and he could roast Rees senior for that too.

Top cop hires bungling daughter.

All very promising.

He steps down from the treadmill and carries his laptop into the changing room so he can shower and change and start work on the next story.

Maybe he should build her up first, reveal her involvement in the case then retell the story of her tragic life and show how far she's come since, set her up nicely to be either the father-shaming heroine or the embarrassing liability, depending on which way the cards fell.

It was a lose-lose for family Rees either way, and a win-win for him.

Just the way he liked it.

34

Night has settled damp and dark by the time Laughton arrives at the entrance to Highgate Cemetery. Tannahill texted her directions and a time to meet but she hates being late so has arrived early. The DCI is already there, standing by a gate, chatting to a stout woman in a green tweed skirt suit with severe, grey hair bobbed like a helmet. He looks up, sees Laughton and smiles. She experiences a moment of panic, like she was trying not to be seen but has been spotted. She could still back out, tell him 'Sorry, I've changed my mind' then run back home and hunker down, cancel everything for a few weeks and wait for the storm to pass. But deep in the darkness where her grief resides she knows this is not really an option. And considering the toxic atmosphere at home right now, visiting a fresh and bloody crime scene actually seems like the better option. So she forces a smile and keeps on walking.

'Evening,' Tannahill says, turning to the lady in tweed. 'This is Mrs Buchanan, she's a trustee of Highgate Cemetery and is kindly letting us in round the back so we don't have to run the gauntlet of reporters.'

The lady inspects Laughton with a look on her face that

seems to say *Who is this child standing in front of me?* – a look Laughton is used to.

'This is *Doctor* Laughton Rees,' Tannahill says, picking up on the vibes, 'one of the country's leading criminologists.'

'Oh! Dr Rees.' The woman frowns in thought for a moment. 'Wasn't it your book they found by the . . . at the house?' Her accent is as tweedy as her suit and still carries a hint of heather despite three decades of living in London.

'It was,' Laughton says. 'Thank you for letting us in.'

'Oh no, always happy to help.' She takes a key from a jingling jailor's bunch and slides it into the gate lock. 'We've had all sorts trying to get into the cemetery to catch a glimpse of the murder mansion. We had to close the graveyard.' She pushes the gate wide. 'Welcome to Highgate Cemetery.'

Laughton smiles and they step through the open gate on to the gravel path.

'I'll need to lock you in again, if that's all right,' Mrs Buchanan says. 'Just give me a buzz when you want to be let out. I only live round the corner.'

'We will,' Tannahill says. 'Shouldn't be too long.'

'Oh take as long as you like, it's absolutely no trouble. Just do what you need to do so we can all get back to normal again.'

Amen to that, Laughton thinks. The gate clangs shut and Mrs Buchanan strides off into the night like she has something very important to do and is already running late.

'Shall we?' Tannahill leads the way into the dark cemetery along a path that curves through a line of ancient trees. Laughton has never been in Highgate Cemetery before, but it doesn't feel creepy at all. Maybe it's because there's enough ambient light from the city to make it appear more like twilight than full dark. Or maybe it's because Tannahill is striding along so confidently it feels unimaginable that anything bad could happen to them, even though crooked headstones are now emerging from the dark on all sides. Laughton breathes in the loamy smells and the super-oxygenated air, listening to the soft crunch of their footsteps across the gravel path. It feels nice, like taking a stroll in the park in the middle of the day, like a date almost. The thought makes her feel instantly awkward, so she does what she always does when faced with emotions or situations that make her uncomfortable, she focuses on work.

'What's the latest on the case?' she asks.

'Husband's still missing and still our main focus of interest.'

'He's still not your killer.'

'Maybe, but we need to find him, question him, and eliminate him from our enquiries, one way or another.'

'Before someone else finds him and eliminates him from theirs.'

'You think he was the intended victim?'

'It's possible. Someone comes looking for him, finds the wife and kills her instead to send him a message. It would also explain why the killer sent photographs to the press, to make sure he saw that message. What do we know about the victim and her husband?'

'Not much. We've been unable to track down any extended family, even with the press coverage, and none of the neighbours seem to know much about them. Both have driving licences and passports issued a year ago, but that's about it.'

'No social media?'

'Nothing.'

'Phone records?'

'We've requested them but all their bills are run through an offshore company so there are extra data protection hoops to jump through. All of which does suggest they were hiding and wanted to stay hidden for some reason. The question is, who from and why?'

They emerge from a tunnel into one of the oldest sections of the graveyard where stone angels, crooked crosses, and leaning obelisks poke through laurels and other evergreens. Tannahill presses on to the far side of the clearing towards what looks like a huge black mirror.

'Is that the house?' Laughton asks.

'Yes. Impressive, isn't it?'

'It's creepy,' she says. 'Who'd want to build a modern house like that in an old Victorian graveyard?'

Tannahill shrugs. 'A really rich goth?'

Laughton smiles. 'A rich goth would buy an old church and paint it black.' She studies the huge panels of glass reflecting the night sky, creating the illusion that there's nothing there at all. 'Can you see inside the house when the lights are on?'

'To a degree, though if someone's standing towards the back of the room they're hidden because of the angle. I guess it was designed to give the owners some privacy.'

'Yes, that and the fact that the neighbours are all dead. How secure is it?'

'Extremely. You'll see in a minute.'

They reach the edge of the clearing and Tannahill wades into the longer grass towards a ten-foot-high box hedge, then looks back over his shoulder at Laughton. 'Do you like magic?' he says, then takes another step forward and disappears.

Laughton blinks, waits a second for him to reappear, then follows when he doesn't, freaked out slightly that she's suddenly alone in a graveyard at night. She wades through the grass until she reaches the spot in the hedge where he vanished and sees the gap, trimmed and angled in such a way that it's invisible from the path. She steps through it and follows a narrow curve of clipped hedge until she catches up with Tannahill.

'Cover your eyes,' he says, then he steps through to the other side of the hedge and the night explodes into headache brightness.

Laughton squints through the white light, up at the back of the Miller house and down into the deep concrete trench that lies between her and it. The trench is maybe fifteen feet wide and deep with a twenty-foot-high fence rising up from the bottom to finish just above eye-level. It's clever. A twenty-foot-high security fence hidden behind a hedge that appears regular height until you got up close to it. The fence also looks to be about the same strength and specification as the type used in maximum-security prisons. A narrow concrete bridge spans the trench and passes through the fence via a security gate. Tannahill leads the way across to it now, pointing up at one of several compact boxes perched along the top of the fence like weird metal birds.

'All the cameras have heat and motion detectors as well as infra-red capabilities in case the lights fail. There are similar ones at all points of entry with face-recognition software that triggers a silent alarm if anyone it doesn't recognize enters or even approaches the house. And even if you do manage to get close to the building, you still need a specially issued security key to unlock the door, *and* there's additional code and thumbprint security required to deactivate the alarm. The Millers had it installed before they moved in. We tracked down the company that did it and got them to deactivate the face-recognition software for us during the investigation so it doesn't go off every time one of our people walks through the door.'

'Did they have to come to the house to do this?'

'No.'

Laughton nods. 'And was the alarm tripped on the night of the murder?'

'No. The cameras were turned off, but the alarm wasn't triggered, and you need the right key, the right code and the right thumbprint to gain access.'

He takes a short, stubby-looking key with a yellow plastic fob from his pocket, unlocks the gate and pulls it open. A soft beeping sounds and Tannahill steps up to a keypad.

'Interestingly even the security company couldn't deactivate the alarm, it's designed to be permanently armed. They've simplified the codes for us so we can gain access, and authorized any thumbprint to authenticate for the duration of the investigation, but it's always on.'

He types 999 into the keypad and places his thumb on the scanner, instantly silencing it. 'So that means on the night of the murder the alarm was fully armed, which means the person who gained access had to have the right code and thumbprint. We dusted this scanner for prints and pulled one that matches several we found in Mike Miller's bathroom. It seems the last person to access the house, aside from the cleaner, was Mike Miller.'

Laughton studies the back of the house as she steps through it, counting the cameras – eight as far as she can tell – pointing inwards as well as out. Behind her the gate shuts with a solid clang. 'What time were the cameras turned off?'

'Midnight on the dot, which makes us think it was probably on a timer.'

'And what was the time of death?'

'Somewhere between midnight and two a.m. The first timestamp on the photos the killer sent to the press is four thirty-six a.m., so we think probably more like two.'

'Who has admin privileges to turn off the cameras?'

'Only Kate and Mike Miller, which is another reason to think it was him.'

Laughton shakes her head. 'Kate and Mike Miller were not the only ones with admin privileges. You said the security company deactivated the alarm remotely, so there must be a back door built into the system. Someone at the company could have switched the system off, or it could have been hacked.'

'Unlikely. This is a top-end security company we're talking about, commercial, not residential, and they mostly specialize in bank security, so pretty hard to hack.'

'Hard but not impossible. And banks get hacked all the

time, they just go out of their way to keep it quiet because no one's going to stick their money in a hack-able bank.' Tannahill leads the way across the narrow bridge to a solid concrete wall with a metal door set into it. 'And why did this company agree to install a house alarm if they specialize in banks?'

'Because the Millers had tons of money?'

'Yeah, but lots of people have tons of money. Maybe Mike Miller was already known to them because he'd done business with them before. Worth checking that out.'

'I'll get someone to call the security company in the morning, find out how they knew the Millers and ask them if they've ever been hacked.' Tannahill pulls a pair of blue nitrile gloves from his pocket and hands them to her. 'The CSIs have finished inside, but still – good practice, is good practice.'

Laughton takes the gloves and wriggles her fingers into them. Tannahill snaps his on, then unlocks the steel door and pulls it open.

Most domestic doors open inwards but not this one. Doors that open in are easier to force. This door is also made from solid steel and hung on heavy-duty hinges anchored some-where deep within the concrete. It feels more like the entrance to a nuclear bunker than a house. Whoever designed this place had prepared it for a siege. But someone had still got in. They had got in and then they had got out again without leaving a trace of how they'd done it.

Tannahill steps aside, holding the door open, and Laughton peers into the gloomy building, the shadows inside made deeper by the bright, exterior security lights. 'You first,' she says.

'Oh yes, sorry. Just trying to be chivalrous.'

'What, by letting me go first into a house where a violent murder recently took place?'

Tannahill laughs. 'Yes, sorry. You didn't cover crime scene etiquette in your book.'

Laughton smiles. 'I'll stick in a new chapter next time I update it.'

Tannahill steps inside and lights flicker on automatically, revealing a long, white hallway with three dark wood doors leading off it and a modern-looking wooden staircase rising up to the other floors. Laughton catches the smell of bleach and something ferrous coming from inside the house and feels suddenly cold with much more than night. Up until this moment everything has felt familiar and detached, an intellectual puzzle of the type she is well used to solving. But once she steps through this door, *if* she steps through this door, it will become something else.

Way back at the start, when she'd first started studying crimes purely as a form of therapy, she had made a deal with herself. She had promised herself that there was a line she would and should never cross. Theory only, that was the deal; old solved cases for study, cold cases at a push, but never, ever live ones. She had already suffered too much, been too badly burned by exposure to the white-hot heat of an active case. So far she had stuck to that deal, even when something that started as therapy turned into a career. Yet now here she was, standing by the open door of a house that smelled of blood and industrial cleaning products.

She doesn't have to step through this door. She can still turn away, walk back across the concrete bridge and away from this house. But then tomorrow another news story will come out, dragging up her past, reuniting her in print with the father she has spent her life distancing herself from. And the next day will be the same, and none of this will stop or return to normal until the murder is solved and people's curiosity drifts elsewhere. This story, her story, needs an end. And she can help give it one. And she is really good at this. It's the one thing she's confident about. And she hasn't really chosen to break her rule anyway. It was the killer who left her book at the crime scene and sent a picture of it to the

205

papers. It was the killer who brought her into this, and she hates them for doing it, whoever they are. She hates them so much she's even prepared to break her rule and personally make them regret it.

So she takes a step, one small step but as big in her life as the one that put a man on the moon, and she enters the Miller house.

35

Laughton can sense the cavernous emptiness of the house above her the moment she steps across the threshold. She pauses inside the door, still ready to bolt if the panic overwhelms her, taking in the polished concrete walls, the concealed lighting that seems to emanate softly from the edges of the floor and ceiling. The only indication that someone actually lives here is a large photograph of a smiling couple in evening wear. The woman is blandly pretty, blonde hair falling over her face as she leans against her equally blandly handsome husband. He is in full dinner jacket – white jacket, bow tie, cummerbund, the whole bit – and stands facing the photographer with a cat-got-the-cream smile, his hand resting territorially on the small of the woman's back, fully exposed by the backless cocktail dress she's wearing.

'Tell me about her,' Laughton says. 'Tell me about the victim.'

'Katherine Miller, thirty-nine, no middle name, no record of any employment, no family, or none that we've managed to find so far. Her phone is missing, but we're assuming she had one.'

'Did she drive?'

'She did.' Tannahill steps over and opens the door on the left and the dark room beyond blinks into brightness, revealing a silver Porsche 911 convertible with a maroon roof and a chunky-looking grey car with darkened windows. 'The Porsche is hers, your basic chic, expensive little city runabout. The other's a Tesla SUV, eco-friendly, very expensive. Both are leased through the same offshore company that owns the house, so there are no ownership documents as such.'

'Have you run the plates through ANPR?'

Tannahill frowns. 'The cars are right there.'

'I don't mean to find them, it just might be useful to know where both cars have been, particularly in the last week. If we can find out where Mike Miller was, it might help us find out where he is.'

'He was supposed to be out of the country on a yoga retreat in Goa but never made the flight.'

'Was he travelling alone?'

'According to the cleaner, yes.'

Laughton looks back at the photograph, the pose, the dinner jacket. It was all so staged and self-aware. 'Do we know what the Millers' relationship was like?'

'Blissful, by all accounts. As you can see, love's young dream. Young-ish dream.'

Laughton nods. 'And yet he was going off on holiday alone. Might be worth checking the flight manifest to see who was booked in the seats next to him.'

'You think he might have been going away with someone?'

'I think a man with a large picture of himself looking like some kind of James Bond figure is telling us something. And if he's jetting off to some exotic foreign location, maybe he had a Moneypenny with him. *Cherchez la femme*.'

'OK. I'll run an ANPR search on both cars and check the flight manifest. We've been told we can have whatever resources we need, so I might as well start using them. I need to start behaving like I'm in a TV cop show and start barking orders at my many underlings.'

Laughton smiles. 'I was asked to consult on one of those

once. I had one meeting where they clearly realized I was going to unravel all their stories with my annoying details about proper process and I never heard from them again.' She points at the stairs. 'Up there?'

Tannahill nods. 'Next floor up.' He heads up the stairs first and more hidden lights fade up automatically, making the stairwell glow. Laughton notices that he keeps to the edge of the steps, avoiding the area of main traffic, even though the scene has been processed. She follows him and does the same. Good practice is good practice.

The smell of bleach and iron is stronger on the next floor and a memory resurfaces, something a fellow student who delighted in grossing out his peers had whispered to her in a particularly ripe morgue:

All smells are particular, he had said, meaning she was now breathing in microscopic particles of a murder victim's blood, drawing them into her own body until they inevitably became a part of her. Laughton stops walking as it strikes her with sudden force that this is a real crime scene. Ahead of her is a door with crime scene tape stretched across it and beyond it are things she only normally experiences through the detached medium of photographs.

Tannahill turns to her. 'You OK?'

'Yes, I'm . . .' She stares at the door.

'Listen, you don't have to go in if you don't want to.' His voice is soft. 'I can show you the photographs, if you'd prefer, and we can just talk it through.'

She looks at him, and the careful concern in his face instantly makes her feel safer.

'I'm fine,' she says, 'thanks.' And to prove it she takes three steps forward, ducks under the tape, and enters the room.

Soft, concealed lights fade up. Laughton already knows what to expect from the photographs, but even so the violence on display here is astonishing. Her eyes trace the arcs of blood on the ceiling and walls, reading the pattern of them like words on a page telling her the story of what happened here and how. The body has been removed but she still feels its presence. She feels it in the heavy iron tang hanging in the air, and in the blank, white rectangular space where the rug had been. She looks across at the spot where the photograph had hung above the white marble fireplace, and recalls the photograph of the knife stabbed into Kate Miller's face, blood from its blade staining the canvas.

'Odd,' she murmurs.

'What?'

She turns to Tannahill, unused to having a witness to her crime scene reveries. Normally she conducts her investigations alone, locked away in her office at work or at home in her bedroom with the door closed, music on low to smother her mutterings so her daughter doesn't overhear them. Talking to herself is part of her process, she has realized, becoming both detective and sergeant so she can bounce thoughts and theories around, obsessively making notes as she sinks deeper into the varied strata of evidence and information that makes up the geology of each case. It's a kind of fugue state, a deep and focused concentration where time stretches and cups of tea go cold.

In the early days, when they threw handfuls of different therapies at her to try and make her sane – her words, not theirs – she learned about mindfulness. In theory, it had sounded good, exactly the sort of thing her febrile and anxious brain needed to help tune out the bad stuff. In practice, however, all the concentrating on your body and breathing through your feet never really worked for her. She could never fully focus, her restless, atomized mind always slipping out from beneath the yoke of her good intentions and latching on to something else – a passing worry, a sudden fear that she hadn't carried out the correct number of repetitions in one of her many counting rituals.

It was only when another therapist suggested she look at

the details of her own case as an attempt to face her real anxieties through exposure therapy that she finally found the focus required for mindfulness to work. She had disappeared into the details of the case file, fascinated by the dispassionate account of something so intimately connected to her and yet also apart and detached. It had felt safe, like watching a documentary about sharks but not actually swimming with them.

Studying criminal cases, it turned out, was her own, dark form of mindfulness. But it had only ever worked before when she did it alone.

'You said something was odd,' Tannahill prompts.

'Yes.' Laughton turns back to the room, slightly uncentred by his presence. She walks over to the wall where the photograph had hung, studies the crater where the plaster has been removed at the spot where the knife was embedded.

'Why drive the knife through Kate Miller's face? Defacing someone's image is usually a form of acting out a repressed desire. But by the time the killer stuck the knife in her photograph she was already dead, so that desire had already been expressed.' She taps on the wall with her knuckle, listening to the hard knocking sound it makes. 'Do you know how tall Mike Miller is?'

'About five nine, according to the neighbours. Why?'

She stands back and studies the crater. 'Because your killer is a six-foot male, give or take.'

Tannahill smiles. 'How do you know that?'

'These walls are solid concrete with a plaster skim. Whoever killed Kate Miller stuck the murder weapon into it with one blow and at a height I'd need to stand on a box to reach. Sounds like Mike Miller would too. Not many women are that tall. Not many women could stick a knife into a hard wall like this either, especially not considering how exhausted they must have been after killing Kate Miller.' She looks up at the arcs of blood on the ceiling and walls.

'Lot of energy expended here before that knife ended up in this wall.'

She does a slow pan of the room again, enjoying the novelty of being able to look wherever she likes without having to flip through crime scene photographs for the angle or detail she wants. It's exhilarating and a little terrifying. She catches her own reflection in the wall of glass, an insubstantial version of herself in a ghost version of the room she's standing in.

'This is such a weird house,' she says, walking over to the window. 'It's full of contradictions: ultra-modern but built in the grounds of a Victorian graveyard; hidden away and yet exposed; set up like a fortress, yet anyone could be out there in the shadows, watching us right now.'

She stares out at the graveyard but can see only darkness and the distant lights of London, peeking through trees.

'We did a sweep of the cemetery,' Tannahill says. 'We thought someone might have used it to case the house, but we didn't find any evidence. We also canvassed the neighbours to see if anyone saw anything suspicious either last night or in the past few weeks but all we got was the usual sightings of joggers, dog walkers and cemetery tourists.'

'Cemetery tourists, is that a thing?'

'It is here. All kinds of famous folks buried out there, Karl Marx, George Eliot, George Michael.'

She turns to him. 'George Michael is buried here!?'

'Apparently.'

'All that money and fame, yet everyone ends up the same.' She looks back out at the night.

He looks up at her, looking out.

He is tucked away among the trees and the gravestones, in the same place he stood when he watched Celia Barnes discover Kate Miller.

It was a risk to come back here so soon but he is glad he took it because there she is.

He watches her at the window, staring out at the darkness, staring out at him. She cannot see him, he knows this. He has removed the surgical mask that might show up in the dark and he has stood in the room where she's standing. Even with the lights off, the cemetery at night is a formless place of darkness and shadows. She won't be able to see him. She won't be able to see anything but the distant lights of the city and her own reflection. He almost can't believe she is here, can't believe he has managed to draw her out into the open, that she has taken the bait.

Once, in one of the few times he remembered ever doing anything vaguely father–son normal, his father had taken him fishing. He must have been seven or eight at the time. They had driven for an hour or so up the Thames, the radio on in the car the whole time so his dad didn't have to speak to him, and hired some gear from a shop filled with fishing stuff that smelled like maggots. He remembered his dad asking for things he had never heard of before, like pulley rigs, and big-mouth hooks, and wondered what they were, and how he knew these things, and if maybe he was going to teach him about them though he never did.

They had bought a bucket of live peeler crabs that made a clicking sound in the plastic pail as they moved around inside. He had thought maybe these were for him to play with while his dad fished and he had pulled the lid back to see them and got shouted at for doing it.

They're not toys, his dad had barked. *That's bait for catching the thornbacks.*

He had no idea what a thornback was but it sounded fierce and he remembered being afraid. He didn't want to see a thornback, he just wanted to play with the crabs.

They had stood on a sea wall for the rest of the day, his father swearing as the crabs nipped him and the hooks got caught in the skin of his fingers. They never caught a damn thing, but he did find out what a thornback was.

213

Looking back now over the distance of time it's clear that his father didn't know what he was doing.

This is fun, isn't it? he'd kept saying like he was willing it to be so. *I did this with my dad too.*

That was what it had all been about. The fishing trip had come not from a place of love or genuine desire to spend time with his son but from a lack of imagination. His dad had taken him fishing, so now he was taking his son fishing, because that was what you did. You didn't question it, you just did it.

The fishing trip had ended abruptly when another fisherman appeared and caught a thornback almost immediately, pulling the weird, flat-looking fish out of the water and showing it to him, the frill of its skate wing rolling like a wave, its long tail like a spike. They had driven home in silence after that and never gone fishing again.

But his dad had taught him something on that trip. He had shown him that it wasn't enough just to be in the right place with the right equipment and the right bait. If you wanted to catch something you also needed to know exactly what you were doing.

Up in the house, Laughton turns from the window and disappears from sight.

After a minute the lights in the room fade to black then the security lights at the back of the house explode back into daylight.

He sinks back into the shadows, far enough from the path so that they don't see him watching them as they walk slowly by a few minutes later, talking about who might have killed Kate Miller, totally oblivious to the fact that the answer is close enough to touch them.

36

Tannahill pushes open the door to his tiny studio flat and drops his keys on the countertop that juts into the room defining which bit is kitchen and which is living space. The sofa bed is still pulled out and unmade from the last time he slept in it, which feels like about a week ago but is in fact only a day.

He fills the kettle, sets it boiling, then opens his laptop and logs on, glancing up at the room as he waits for the latest case updates to download. You could fit his entire flat in the Millers' living room twice. He'd found the flat in a hurry, between court appearances and long days, a temporary solution picked for location and, in London terms, relative cheapness. It was supposed to have been a stepping stone to something better, something he'd more suitable for a man of his age and professional stature that he planned to find when work eased off a bit. He's been living here for over two years now. Work never eased off, and so the stepping stone has turned into a tiny, bare island where, apparently, he now lives.

He picks a dirty mug out of the sink, sniffs it, rinses it out then looks in a cupboard for something to put in it. He finds a strip of instant miso soup portions, tears one off and squeezes brown paste into the mug.

The updates to the case file finish downloading and he scrolls through them.

Still no conclusive forensics from the lab on any of the objects.

Still no new information on either Mike or Kate Miller.

Still no new leads, not even with all the press attention, though they've had plenty of calls, most of them time-wasters: people claiming to have seen Mike Miller; people claiming to *be* Mike Miller; people claiming to be the killer; people claiming it's all part of some broader conspiracy involving Russia, or Israel, or Satanists. High-profile cases like this always bring out the crazies. Kick over a large enough rock and there they always are.

The kettle boils and he pours water into the mug, takes a teaspoon from a drawer and stirs as he checks his phone.

Missed calls from the office and his mother. He should call the office back but feels filled to the brim with work already and wants to process everything from his trip to the Miller house with Laughton Rees first.

Laughton.

He'd meant to ask about her name but the right moment had never really presented itself. When is the right moment to ask personal questions while poking around a murder scene? Didn't write about that in her book, now, did she?

He half collapses, half sits on the edge of the unmade bed, drags his laptop off the counter and clicks on a shortcut to the Automatic Number Plate Recognition portal.

When he was a baby uniform on the force, you had to pick up the phone and talk to an actual human who would run a plate for you while chatting about the weather or football while you waited. Now everything that can be automated has been or is being automated, which means he spends half his life hunched in front of a screen, filling in forms and sifting through the responses.

A new window opens on the laptop and he copies the case

file number from the Murder Book along with the registration plates of Kate and Mike Miller's cars into the relevant search fields. He then clicks on a calendar, selects a time period dating back a month to keep the results manageable and submits it.

A wheel starts spinning on the screen telling him something is happening. Someone in IT once told him these things are called 'throbbers' but he suspects they might have been winding him up. If he had the energy he would google it, but he takes a sip of his miso soup instead, the hot, salty liquid tasting way better than it should.

His phone buzzes. His mother again. He hasn't really got the energy to talk to her either but then he also hasn't got the energy to keep ignoring her, so he lets out a long sigh then answers it, putting it on speaker.

'Hi, Mam.'

'You still at work?' His mother is never one to waste time with 'hellos'.

'No.'

'Good. Did you eat yet?'

'Yes.'

'What?'

Tannahill glances at the miso soup. 'Japanese.'

He hears a deep sigh on the other end of the line. 'There's no goodness in those instant soup things, Tanny – you might as well eat the bloody packet. What time did you get home?'

'Just now, I was at a crime scene with a consultant.'

'And this fella's more important than calling your own mam, is he?'

'She.'

'Oh!?' He hears the immediate interest in his mam's voice and wishes he'd never said anything. 'Is she single?'

'Mam, we were at a crime scene, we weren't on a date!'

'What, people don't meet at work any more? Is she attractive?'

'Mam!'

'You didn't answer, so I'll take that as a "yes".'

Two new windows pop up on the laptop screen showing the ANPR results for both number plates. 'I have to go,' he says. 'I'll call you tomorrow. Promise. Love you, Mam.'

He hangs up before she can ask any more questions and sips his soup as he scrolls through the results for Mike Miller's car.

The ANPR results take the form of a list of dates, times and locations running down the left-hand side and a map filling the rest of the window with red markers corresponding to each camera that recorded a hit. They are densely clustered around the Miller house, and he goes through these first, clicking each camera in turn and unchecking them from the list to leave just the results from slightly further afield.

There's one that jumps out immediately, a red marker just south of the river, about six miles from the Miller house. This camera captured Mike Miller's licence plate four times in the last month, the last time a day before his missed flight to Goa.

Tannahill hovers the cursor arrow over the last entry and a new window pops up showing the image captured by the camera. Mike Miller's car fills the centre of the frame. A silhouetted figure is just visible behind the wheel at the top of the frame – someone who looks an awful lot like Mike Miller. Someone else is sitting next to him. Someone smaller, dark-haired, female – someone who is not Kate Miller.

He clicks through the other three hits: same car, same driver, and in the last image, same passenger.

Tannahill zooms into it but the image quality is too low and pixelates into nothing without revealing more detail.

'Who are you then?' Tannahill murmurs.

He returns the image to normal size and studies it. Mike Miller's car is turned off the main road slightly and he is looking at the woman, like they're mid-conversation and he doesn't need to pay attention to the way ahead, like he's waiting for a gate to open or something.

Behind the car on the opposite side of the street he can see a pub with tables spread out along the front of the building. Next to that is a cafe and what looks like a fancy card or gift shop. It all looks expensive.

He checks the location information of the ANPR camera – 72–76 Borough High Street. Sounds about right. Nice area, lots of bars, good food, perfect for the modern man about town cheating on his wife. Southwark was also south of the river, which in London terms meant it might as well have been in a different country from Highgate. No one would have spotted Mike canoodling down there. Different crowd. Lots of tourists.

Tannahill opens Google Street View and types in the camera's address. The picture zooms down to street level, revealing more shops and a large set of double iron gates with MAIDSTONE BUILDING MEWS written across them in metal letters and a leafy courtyard beyond. It looks like an old factory or a warehouse that's been turned into an apartment building. Cool city lofts. Good security, which is obviously very important to our Mr Miller for reasons still unknown. It also looks like a great place to lie low if you'd just killed your wife and the whole world was looking for you.

He pecks out an email to Chamberlain asking him to run a background check on the building, pull the current list of residents and see if Mike Miller is listed as living, owning or renting there, then looks back at the photo of the car. The two people inside are looking at each other, easy and casual with each other as they head into the luxury loft development.

Cherchez la femme, Laughton had said. And here she was.

He finishes his soup, almost chewing the sediment that has settled at the bottom and searches back through the case file until he finds the passenger manifest of the flight Mike Miller missed. He'd had a business class ticket for 63B on the upper deck of a 747. Tannahill has only ever flown economy, so imagines business is the same only with more leg room, but after a few minutes searching online he finds a seat layout map for a 747 and sees that the business class seats are staggered and face each other with a divider between them. He checks the names of the passengers either side of the empty seat. Both are women – Andrea d'Almond and Shonagh O'Brien.

He looks back at the outline of the dark-haired woman sitting in the car next to Mike Miller. His money is on Andrea. She looks like an Andrea. Andrea d'Almond also sounds way more like femme fatale material than a Shonagh. He makes a note in the file to do background checks on both of them in the morning then leans back on the bed, kicks off his shoes and closes his eyes.

He can feel sleep tugging at him, pulling him down like gravity, but he fights it. Instead he opens a new case file – Kai Mustafa, fifteen years old, stabbed for apparently no reason other than he was alone and weak, killed by oncoming traffic after he jumped, fell or was pushed off a bridge. He was the twenty-second knife homicide in the capital that year but his murder had not made it on to the front pages of any newspapers. And because Kate Miller's death had, it meant the already scant resources allocated to delivering justice for Kai and the other twenty-one cases had now been diverted to her. And though it would be the easiest thing in the world to sign off Kai Mustafa's case as unsolved and file it away, he can't, because everyone deserves justice, not just the people with money and status. So he stares at the photo of the unsmiling boy, fixing it in his mind along with the knowledge that this boy died alone and afraid, living on the streets, abandoned by society, and starts working through the evidence, looking for the patterns beneath the surface, looking for the connections that might unlock the case, looking for justice for Kai.

37

Laughton Rees does not go home.

The weight of the day plus her trip to the Miller house has left her feeling spiky and on edge. She had expected her first visit to an active crime scene to be difficult, unsettling even. What she had not expected was that she would find it exhilarating. Going home also means facing Gracie, and she definitely can't risk that, not with a day's worth of anger and jagged energy fizzing inside her, so she does what she always did at times like these – she heads to Harry's.

Harry's Gym and Boxing Club occupies an old Victorian bathhouse halfway down the Holloway Road and has trained boxers ever since anyone can remember. Laughton pushes through the door and heads past old contest bills and black-and-white photographs showing fighters captured in their prime, breathing in the familiar mix of sweat and leather. She changes quickly into loose gym clothes she keeps in a locker, grabs her water bottle and heads into the main space where a full-sized boxing ring stands beneath a high, vaulted roof. A couple of fighters spar inside the ring, their long-sleeved Lonsdale shirts rendered two-tone with sweat.

She stops at the drinking fountain and starts the minute countdown on her phone, stretching her arms, legs and shoulders while the seconds tick down, then standing ready with her water bottle by the stream of water so she can start filling it the moment the timer hits zero.

Three. Two. One.

She fills the bottle to the top and drinks from it as she makes her way over to the corner of the room where the punchbags hang.

It was her last therapist who had introduced her to 'punchbag therapy', back when she still listened to what therapists said.

'Just go to a gym, find a punchbag and hit it,' she'd said. 'It can't hurt.'

So she'd booked a taster session at a local boxing club, gone straight to the heaviest bag and hit it – oh man, had she hit it – she'd hit it, and kicked it, and screamed at it until the coach had to pull her away because she was freaking out all the other people in the gym. 'Guess you needed that,' he'd said.

Boy, had she ever.

The next day Laughton had thanked her therapist, told her she'd really helped – though didn't tell her exactly how – then cancelled her remaining sessions and used the money to join the gym instead.

She kicks off her shoes and starts to stretch, concentrating on the feeling of the floor, like Yut had taught her, the second revelation on her path of punchbag therapy.

Yut had appeared in the gym one morning, a slight figure from Chang Rai in Northern Thailand. Laughton had been boxing for a few months by this time, loving the bag work and the blissful release it gave her but hating the maleness of the gym, and the fact that membership required everyone to spar at least once a week. Her size meant she ended up being paired with kids who were either cringingly embarrassed to be fighting a woman or, on some rare and unpleasant occasions, violently relished it.

Yut had kicked off his shoes, stretched for a short while, then walked up to the speed bag, leapt effortlessly into the air and kicked it so hard the noise had brought the place to a standstill. He had then worked the bag like no one else she'd ever seen, kicking and punching it in balletic, blistering combinations, her first introduction to Muay Thai, 'the art of eight limbs', national sport of Thailand.

Yut was not much bigger than Laughton, but when it came to the end sparring session that day they put him with one of the biggest boxers in the place, a tower of muscle called Otis whom no one ever wanted to be paired with. It had been a novelty bout, a David and Goliath contest between the gym's local hero and the impressive stranger, and the whole gym had gathered to witness it: one round, traditional boxer versus Thai boxer, a straight-up contest with a point for each blow landed.

When they touched gloves at the start she had noticed how Yut's hands were roughly half the size of Otis's. Then the bell sounded and Yut sprang forward, lashing out with his shoe-less foot in a blur of movement that caught Otis hard on the bulging grapefruit of his left bicep, drew a gasp from the crowd and pissed Otis off royally. As a straight-up boxer, Otis was not used to being kicked. He was also the local boy with a reputation to uphold and the honour of the gym resting on his massive shoulders, so he had to put this guy down.

He had steamrollered forward, aiming fast jabs at the smaller man's body, hoping to catch him with one and knock him off balance so he could follow through and finish him off. But Yut was too fast and Laughton was transfixed, not only by his technique as he used his size and speed to avoid trouble and spin his punches and kicks into devastating counter-attacks, but also by his calmness and his courage. He seemed utterly unafraid of the pile of muscle in the shape of a man charging at him with arms thick as legs. She doubted she had ever felt as in command of herself in the face of

223

potential danger as this man in the ring. And when the bell rang again and Otis had not managed to land a single punch, Laughton waited until the crowd of congratulation dispersed, then walked up to him and said simply,

'Teach me.'

She completes her stretches, feeling the tension and anger built up by the day crackling inside her like a poison she needs to get out. Usually she would start with the speed bag, working up a rhythm to elevate her heart rate, get some heat going and give her something to focus on other than whatever particular toxic crap her mind had decided to fixate on that day. But today she needs raw release so she heads for the heavy bag, a near solid column of sand and scarred leather suspended from the roof by thick chains.

She straps on a pair of training gloves, sets her feet apart slightly then starts to punch, jabbing from the shoulder, fast and precise, savouring the satisfying jolt of each blow as it shudders through her body and starts to shake loose the solid lumps of tension that have formed there. And as her muscles loosen and the strength flows she begins her own brand of therapy, dredging up all the bullshit from her day and focusing all her aggression on to it.

First she pictures Call-me-Jonathan, picking a spot on the leather bag at the approximate height his face would be, remembering the look of something like pity on his face that appeared upon learning she was a single mother. She springs up, spinning round to plant a firm kick right in his imagined face and the heavy bag jerks away with the impact. Laughton lands in a crouch then springs again, following the kick with a flurry of punches, elbow jabs and shin kicks that would have put the headteacher in hospital if she'd done it to him for real. Laughton finishes the melee attack and bounces lightly from foot to foot, shaking her hands down by her sides to keep them loose, watching the bag sway and settle in front of her.

Next she pictures the journalist, recalling the photo from his byline and switching her focus to a spot six inches down from the fresh dent in the leather because he seems shorter somehow, a tiny cowardly man who casually toys with people's lives. A growl rises from somewhere deep within her and she springs forward, landing a flurry of punches on his imagined face, letting the growl out in ragged fragments, and ending with a yell and a vicious roundhouse kick that jolts the heavy bag so hard it makes the chains rattle.

Laughton bounces on the balls of her feet, shaking out her hands and feet again until the sting from the blows fades. She scoops her water bottle off the floor and takes a long drink, moving around the bag and picking a new spot on the mottled leather before diving deeper into her personal store of pain.

This time she pictures her father, remembering the photo in the online article, his neat dress uniform and service medal ribbons evidence of the distinguished career he built despite his failures as a husband and a father. She twists her body, her planted feet turning her into a tightening spring, then throws herself into a spin, releasing her anger and energy in a full-force kick that lands with a loud smack in the middle of the bag.

She cushions her landing, sinks low then springs back up, twisting in the air and lashing out with her other foot to catch the heavy bag at the top of its swing and send it rocking right back in the other direction. Her breathing is heavier now, her heart rate elevated, pumping hot blood to hungry muscles. She is angry, strong, focused, and finally ready to face *him*.

He was shorter than her father and she moves around the bag, looking for the worn patch of leather she has focused her anger on so many times before. She steps back with her right foot, planting it on the ground and shifting her weight as the bag turns and the worn patch of leather slowly slides into view. She takes a breath then summons the memory she keeps buried deepest of all.

First she pictures the mask he wore, a child's mask, too small for his adult face but with the eyeholes made larger – a unicorn mask.

She sinks lower as the image takes form, almost as if she's cowering from the thing she has conjured. In life she had screamed then ran while her mother stayed to fight. Now she roars and attacks.

Her legs straighten and launch her up and forward, lashing out at the leather bag with her left leg, driving her foot through the spot where the mask would be to shatter it and reveal the face of the monster behind.

Adrian McVey: round, soft face; pale grey eyes; thinning red hair, the picture that had stared from the front page of every newspaper during his trial. Such a bland face, so ordinary – such a clever disguise for a devil.

Laughton explodes forwards, all technique abandoned now, her hands flailing wildly, beating at the leather bag, raining blows on the spot where she imagines his soft round face to be. She howls and rages, pouring every drop of her jagged energy out of herself and into him.

All energy comes from somewhere and for a long time Laughton believed the source of her energy was anger. Some therapists told her she was angry at her father because he represented a betrayal of security and safety. Others said she was angry at her mother for effectively abandoning her through death. But anger was only part of it. Anger did not explain the crippling need to control everything in her life down to the tiniest detail. It did not explain the crushing and terrifying loneliness that was only ever soothed, but never fully cured, by the unexpected miracle of having a child of her own to care for. So the source of her dark energy had to come from something else.

With one final leap, Laughton throws the last dregs of her rage at the leather bag, no longer a column of sand and leather but the pale stranger who had reached into the sunlight of her life and dragged her down into his darkness. Both her feet drive into the spot where his face would be with enough force to shatter bone and push the jagged fragments back into his brain. The bag jerks away, rattling loudly on its chains, and Laughton falls to the floor, exhausted.

Grief is the thing that fuels her energy.

Grief for her mother. Grief for herself. Grief for the life that was taken from her.

Anger may burn brightly but it fades eventually, whereas grief burns black and is never extinguished.

38

Night shifts and moves over London, deepening the shadows and creeping down rain-drizzled streets.

Laughton goes home to a closed bedroom door and no response to her tentative knock. She leans in, listens, and can feel her daughter's anger radiating through the black door like a fire is raging on the other side of it.

She heads to bed, hoping her early start and trip to the gym will have bought her some sleep, which it does – for a while.

She wakes at three from a dream, not of knives in school bags, or her daughter's fury, but of Kate Miller, lying on her back. She lies awake staring up at her ceiling in the dark, her own arms outstretched like hers had been, wondering where the anger that violently ended Kate Miller's life had come from. Such anger. And she realizes in the quiet dark that it's an anger she understands and wonders if whoever killed Kate Miller was grieving too, like she still grieves.

A few miles south, Tannahill sleeps fully clothed on his sofa bed, the screen of his open laptop flicking on and off inter- mittently like a faulty neon sign as updates to the Miller case file continue to come in. He dreams he's at the press confer- ence, standing at the lectern while journalists ask questions he can't hear but suspects are all about the woman who was killed in her own home. He has no answers to these unheard questions but the questions keep coming anyway, just as the automated updates continue to flash up on his screen, all through the night and on to morning.

West of them both, on the far outskirts of London, a woman emerges from a glass-and-steel building and hurries through drizzle to a waiting Uber, dragging a large suitcase behind her. She sinks into the back seat of the car and feels her travel fatigue settle on her like a dirty duvet. Apart from a few snatched hours on the plane, Shonagh O'Brien has now been awake for almost twenty-nine hours. The driver stows her case in the back then drives off, heading into Central London. She watches Heathrow slide away outside. A plane takes off, its lights twinkling against the pre-dawn sky. She wonders where it's going and has a sudden urge to be on it.

Funny.

Since discovering Mike was missing, her entire focus has been getting back to London, but now she's here all she wants to do is run away again. Some of this stems from her brief but terrifying glance at the huge amount of news coverage now swirling around Kate Miller's murder and the continued search for Mike.

Manhunt – that's what most of the papers are calling it, like he's an escaped lunatic or a monster on the loose.

She checks her phone for messages. She has called him whenever she could at every step of her journey, telling him she was coming and how long it would take her to get to London. She has still heard nothing back.

On the flight – in the cramped standby economy seat that was all she could get – she had played out a million scenarios in her head about what this silence might mean and what she should do when she got back to England. Her instinct was to go to the flat and see if he'd been there, or was maybe there still, hiding out, frightened and confused. But then the image of the bloody room on that video clip would flash back into her head and she would think maybe she should call the police instead, tell them what she knew and where she thought Mike might be. Not to turn him in, of course, but because if he hadn't killed Kate – and he can't have done, he just can't – then he needed to stop hiding. He needed to turn himself in and start helping the police find who really did do it, and the sooner he did that the better.

But there was also something else she kept turning over in her mind.

As the 'other woman' – horrible term – she had naturally entertained thoughts about Mike possibly leaving his wife for her one day. And though, in these quiet fantasies, she had never imagined anything as horrible as this, there was still some detached, pragmatic part of her brain that kept whispering the inescapable truth that Kate *was* now out of the picture. And wouldn't Mike cling to the woman who stood by him and helped him through all this? Wouldn't he owe an unpayable debt to whoever came to help him, and still believed in him when the whole world seemed to be against him? Would not that man end up loving that woman far more than, say, one who called the police on him, no matter how well intentioned it might have been? Right now, Mike needed her more than he ever had before and possibly ever would again, and the thought made her feel powerful.

She eventually decided – somewhere over the Middle East, when London was still several hours away – that she would go to the flat first. She would go to the flat, see if he was there, *then* decide what to do next. But now the consequences of her decision are only twenty minutes in front of her, her stand-by-your-man resolve is starting to waver.

She looks up at the sky, the lights from London bouncing off low cloud and the faintest hint of the new day behind them. It will be brighter still by the time she gets to the flat and this comforts her a little. Entering somewhere at dawn is a lot better than doing it at night. Everything is easier in daylight.

So she sinks into her seat and decides to stick with her original plan. She will go to the flat, see if Mike's there, and if he isn't, then she can call the police – maybe.

39

Tannahill wakes with a jolt to the sound of his ringing phone.

'Yeah, hello,' he says, not even checking who it is before answering.

'Morning.' Bob Chamberlain's voice on the other end sounds way too perky for this time of night. Then Tannahill registers the fact that he said *Morning* and glances over at the window to see dawn beginning to lighten the grey sky. 'Did I wake you?' Chamberlain has always been an early bird. He often sends emails of little urgency first thing in the morning just so people can see the timestamp on them and register what time he started work.

'No,' Tannahill lies. 'What's up?'

'I managed to get hold of that list of residents for Maidstone Building Mews you emailed me about last night.'

Tannahill looks across at his laptop, his brain trying to catch up with what Chamberlain is saying. Kai Mustafa's photograph stares back at him with what feels like reproach as he closes his file and switches his attention back to Kate Miller's. 'Yes, the, er, the ANPR hit on Mike Miller's car.'

'Yeah, he's not listed as a resident in the building.'

'Oh.' Tannahill feels annoyance creeping into his crispy morning mood. Did Chamberlain really have to call him so early to tell him this non-news? He clicks back to the ANPR portal where the photo of Mike Miller in his car with the unknown person is still up. 'What about . . .' he clicks through to another of the windows still open from last night, looking for the passenger manifest from the flight to Goa Mike Miller missed. 'Andrea d'Almond?'

'Erm . . . no she's not a resident either.'

So much for his hunch about the femme fatale. 'What about Shonagh O'Brien?'

'Shonagh O . . . yes. There she is.' Tannahill sits up, instantly awake. 'Shonagh O'Brien lives at number 27, the penthouse flat.'

Tannahill's mind races, processing what this means and what his next move should be. She caught the flight but Mike Miller didn't, which means the flat would have been empty for almost a week, a flat he presumably had the key to.

'We need to fast-track a search warrant and organize an immediate enter-and-arrest op,' he says, springing up from the bed and unbuttoning his shirt.

'Really!?'

'Yes. Possible arrest of our main suspect, we don't know if he has a firearm but he's resourceful and has not surrendered himself yet, so we should expect resistance if he's there.' Tannahill pulls a fresh shirt from a hanger and drops his old one on the floor. 'Let's not take any chances. If we mess this up the press will crucify us. Run it directly through the Commissioner's office.'

'OK. Anything else?'

Tannahill grabs a can of deodorant, ready to deploy it the moment he's off the phone. Borough was a couple of miles south of his flat and there was a Specialist Firearms Command centre half a mile north. 'Get one of the inbound Trojan units to pick me up en route,' he says. 'If Mike Miller is there, I want to be there too.'

40

The sky is lightening to a flat, dirty grey by the time the Uber drives through the metal gates of Maidstone Building Mews into a courtyard surrounded by old warehouses. Shonagh looks up at the fourth-floor windows of her flat as the car slows to a stop. The blinds are down, just as she'd left them when she departed for Goa a week ago.

She steps out on to the damp cobbles, watching the windows for any twitch of life as the driver hauls her suitcase out of the car and dumps it next to her before driving off. She stands for a moment, looking up, feeling the damp cold through clothes she had put on in jungle heat. It looks empty and still.

She drags her case noisily across the uneven ground to the front door then pauses again. She presses number 27 and a light comes on over the entryphone camera. She attempts to arrange her face into . . . something, though her exhaustion, jet-lag, and peaking stress levels never really let her settle on what. She holds the look of concern, or compassion, or whatever it is in place until the light over the camera goes out, then lets it fall, further exhausted by the effort of it.

She checks the time on her phone. It's after seven now.

He still hasn't called or messaged. She rings him one last

time but it goes straight to voicemail: *This is Mike, leave a message and I'll call you back.*

Hearing his voice gives her comfort somehow and she takes a deep breath, taps in the security code and enters the building.

Tannahill hears the Armed Response Vehicle before he sees it, a speeding car in an otherwise quiet morning. He finishes tying his tie just as the black BMW X5 appears round the corner and drives straight at him, the three figures inside dressed in the black tactical uniform of the Special Firearms Command unit.

The car lurches to a stop in front of him and the back door flies open.

'Chop-chop,' a voice orders, and Tannahill jumps in, fumbling for the seatbelt as the car takes off again at speed.

'Sergeant Rook,' the officer in the back says as she hands Tannahill a headset and a Kevlar vest with POLICE written on the front and back in white letters.

'DCI Khan,' he replies.

'So what's this we're going to?'

'Block of luxury flats possibly containing a murder suspect,' Tannahill says, struggling into his vest as they hurtle down London back streets. 'Suspect's name is Mike Miller, age forty-eight, been missing for a week, his wife was murdered two nights ago.'

'This is the case that's all over the news.'

'Yes. Address we're going to belongs to a woman we believe to be Mr Miller's girlfriend, mistress, whatever you want to call it. We don't know if he's there but there's a strong chance he might be, and if he is he's likely to be in a desperate state and will need taking down fast to stop him from hurting himself or anybody else.'

'Do we know what floor this flat is on?'

'It's the penthouse.'

The officer nods. 'Course it is.'

'A minute out,' the officer in the passenger seat says, consulting a scrolling map on what looks like an armoured iPad.

Tannahill tries to swallow but his mouth has gone dry, he's not sure if it's from the adrenaline, the tiredness or just because he skipped breakfast again. Whatever the reason, what seemed like a good idea five minutes ago now seems less so, sitting in this car with these pseudo-military types. He is not fully tactical firearms certified, though he has done a large chunk of the course so is eligible for ride-alongs on missions related to his cases. He'll be at the back, though, which is fine by him. The officers with the guns and all the training will be on point.

The ARV turns a corner into a dead end where another ARV and a police van are already parked with at least ten officers in tactical gear kitting up next to it. 'We're here,' the driver says.

They lurch to a stop and everyone jumps out of the car, Tannahill scrambling to keep up. Even though he set all this in motion, he now feels like a passenger.

The firearms officers nod silent greetings at each other and Sergeant Rook turns to Tannahill.

'Are we waiting on surveillance?'

Tannahill shakes his head. 'If he's here, he'll be holed up in the flat. No point in waiting around to see if he shows. We need to get in and get him out.'

Sergeant Rook nods and holds up the armoured tablet so the other team leaders can see the screen.

'OK, so this is the schematic of the building.' She points at a door at the end of the cul-de-sac. 'That's a service entrance leading to a staircase. We have an admin entry-code from the caretaker.' She looks up at Tannahill again. 'Do we have keys to the flat?'

'No.'

'Any idea of security level?'

236

Tannahill thinks of the fortress that was the Miller house. 'Assume it's going to be heavy.'

She nods and looks back down at the screen. 'OK, so bring the frame spreader, a hoolie bar, and an enforcer. We'll take lead. Team two will cover the front door and stop anyone coming in or out. The rest of us, that's teams three through five, go in the back. We disable the lift then work our way up floor by floor, two men on each floor for containment, until we get to the flat on the fourth floor.'

Sergeant Rook taps a new tab and the schematic is replaced by what looks like a floor plan from a sales brochure. She locates flat 27 and zooms in.

'OK, so it's at the end of a corridor, only one main entrance, but there's also what looks like a balcony inside the flat with possible access to the roof.' She looks up at one of the other officers. 'Your team covers the roof. We'll wait until you're in position then hit the door hard. Shield man through first, three in support with X2s and sidearms ready in case of resistance. Any questions?' She looks around the group and gets only head shakes. 'OK, team two, get into position at the front of the building. The rest of you get kitted up and ready to move on my command.'

The group breaks up, each team leader heading back to their own MPV where the driver of each vehicle is now acting as quartermaster, handing out individual SIG MCX carbines and X2 tasers from the weapons locker in the back. One of the MPVs pulls away and heads off up the road.

Sergeant Rook checks her rifle and turns to Tannahill. 'You come with us but keep way back and when I say stay, you stay, understood?'

Tannahill nods.

Behind her, one of her team slings a solid red metal pipe with two handles across his back. This is 'the enforcer', otherwise known as 'the big red key', sixteen kilograms of tempered steel that can unlock any door if you hit it enough times.

Another officer shoulders a hydraulic spreader bar and a third takes a ballistic shield, a dark grey rectangle of lightweight Kevlar with a viewing panel set into it. Everyone checks their weapons then holds them in the ready position, listening to radio updates from the team covering the front of the building. It seems to take an age but is probably less than a minute.

'In position and ready,' the message finally comes through.

Sergeant Rook gives Tannahill one last look, holds up her hand in a fist then points to the building.

'Go,' she says, and everyone moves forward in a low crouch run, weapons cradled tight to their chests, twenty officers in total moving as one and flowing smoothly towards the building.

Shonagh O'Brien roots around in her handbag as the lift carries her silently up to the fourth floor. She pulls her keys free from a tangle of earphones, receipts, and other travel detritus, separates the bright blue door key and holds it up, turning it so it catches the overhead light.

Mike had given it to her almost a year ago as a surprise when she was having trouble with her old flatmate who'd recently split from her own philandering husband and strongly disapproved of Shonagh seeing a married man. He had casually handed her a box at lunch one day as if he was giving her a bracelet and the shiny blue key was inside it. The colour of the key was electric blue, a cute reference to a Bowie song they both loved.

Blue, blue, electric blue, that's the colour of my room.

She'd moved in the next day, blasting out a Bowie playlist in the cavernous flat, her meagre possessions utterly dwarfed by the high ceilings and large rooms, as if they'd been shipped in from a smaller-scale life. Mike had also bought a ton of new furniture for the flat and they'd unpacked it and arranged it all together, sofas, tables, beds, like they were a regular couple moving in to their first home. He had seemed really happy that day. He'd also revealed, when 'Sound and Vision' played for about the twentieth time, that his wife didn't really like Bowie, which as far as Shonagh was concerned was clear grounds for divorce. She had thought then that one day he might leave her and they would be together, though she had never imagined it would happen like this.

The lift doors open and she stands there, frozen. It is quiet in the building and she feels the silence pressing in around her.

She stares down the corridor, her front door standing at the far end of it, dark and silent. The lift doors start to close and she automatically shoots out her hand to stop them.

Come on, Shonagh. Mike might be in there, and he needs your help.

She steps out of the lift and pulls her case out on to the corridor.

The doors close behind her and the silence floods back.

She takes a deep breath then starts making her way towards her front door, the wheels of her case whispering across the carpet.

She feels uncertain again, like a dumb character in a horror movie, walking like a lamb towards the dark room with the monster in it. She could still call the police, that would be the sensible thing to do, that's what she would be shouting at her character if she was watching this scene play out in a movie. But if she calls the police she'll have to explain who she is, and about her relationship with Mike, and it will make the police think badly about him. It might even make them think she was his motive for killing his wife, though it wasn't, she's sure it wasn't, she's pretty sure he didn't kill his wife at all.

She thinks back to his last message to her.

I need to fix something here. I'll explain when I see you. M x

The police will find that message, won't they? They'll find it and read something sinister into it and use it as evidence against Mike. The papers will find it too, and they'll crucify him for it, for having an affair, for everything, and it will all be her fault for being too scared to walk down a corridor, and unlock a door that's now just a few feet in front of her.

She reaches the door.

Pauses.

Places her ear against the surface.

All she can hear is the whisper of blood in her ear and the hammering of her heart in her chest.

Come on, Shonagh.

She checks her phone one last time in the vain hope that Mike might finally have got back to her.

He hasn't.

In the movie this would be the point where she decided to call the police only to discover she had no signal. But she does have signal. She has full signal and full Wi-Fi.

Phone or key.

Key or phone.

She takes one last breath – and slides the electric blue key into the lock.

The lead officer taps in the door code then stands aside. The teams flow into the building in reverse order, first-floor containment unit going first and Sergeant Rook's flat-entry team bringing up the rear carrying the door opening equipment and ballistic shield. Apart from two officers staying back to cover the door, Tannahill is the last to enter the building.

Up ahead he can see Sergeant Rook leading the way, up one flight, check round the bend then hold position so the next officer can overlap then repeat – check and move, check and move – all the way up to the fourth floor.

Tannahill does his best to keep up but tactical officers are notoriously fit and the Kevlar vest is heavier than it looks.

By the time they make it to the fourth floor he is breathing hard, sweating, and smelling strongly of the deodorant he doused himself in before leaving his flat.

Sergeant Rook points at a ladder leading to a skylight and two officers head up it and gain access to the roof. She turns to Tannahill, holds up a hand telling him to 'stay', then peers through a small window in the door. The corridor beyond is all exposed brick and steel girders, loft living chic. She points left then pulls the door open a little.

The officer carrying the ballistic shield ducks down, peers through the gap to check the corridor is clear, then surges forward, shield first. Sergeant Rook and another armed officer follow close behind, weapons readied, while the officer with the door opening equipment follows.

Tannahill sticks his foot in the gap to stop the door from closing and listens for sounds of their progress. The floor plan had shown the stairwell to be on the opposite side of the building to the penthouse so they'll need to turn two corners before they get to it. He leans his head into the corridor a little more, listening hard, but he still can't hear anything. There are now twenty armed police officers inside the building and not one of them is making a sound.

The first thing that hits Shonagh as she opens the door is the heat, closely followed by the smell. It billows out of the room like something foul that's been trapped inside and is desperate to get out. She rocks back on her heels, trying to steady herself, fighting a fresh urge to run.

She tells herself the smell and the heat are nothing to panic about. It's probably just something manky she left in the bin a week ago in her haste to make it to the airport because she'd been in such a rush. She could easily have left the heating on too, or maybe it's just broken, which wouldn't be the first time something went wrong with the flat. The conversion had clearly been done slightly on the cheap and there were all kinds of little things that kept going wrong, windows that jammed, the timer on the under-floor heating having a mind of its own, it was probably just something like that.

Even so, she leaves the door open slightly and her suitcase in the hall and covers her face with her arm before stepping into the flat.

The front door leads into a short, open-ended corridor with a cloakroom and a guest bedroom leading off. She checks the cloakroom first to see if the smell is coming from there but it's clean and unused, as is the guest room.

She looks ahead to the main living area, the leather sofa and big Union Jack flag on the wall behind it framed by the doorway. She drops her arm down to check the smell and nearly gags at the solid strength of it in the confines of the flat. On her second day in Goa, pissed off at Mike's absence, she had gone on a jungle walk with a flirty guy on the retreat and they had come across a dead monkey on the path. This smells exactly the same.

She wonders if she should call out to see if Mike is here but decides against it. Instinctively she doesn't want to make any sound or draw attention to herself, and besides he can't be here, not with this smell peeling the paint off the walls. He would have done something about it. She clamps her arm back over her nose and mouth and moves tentatively forward into the main living area.

The smell is much worse here, even with her arm covering her nose. There are flies too, big black ones circling in the air and bashing sluggishly against the large skylights set into the sloping wooden ceiling.

She looks over to her right where the open-plan kitchen stretches along the length of the wall and the room thermostat is fixed to a section of exposed brick. It's on constant and set to 'Max'.

How the hell did that happen?

Maybe she did it by mistake, pressed the wrong button as

she was heading out, distracted and in a rush. She turns it off and moves over to the bin, a big, old-fashioned, galvanized zinc number she bought because she thought its industrial look matched the flat. She grabs the handle, screws up her face behind the barrier of her arm, then yanks it off like a chef revealing something delicious but expecting quite the opposite.

The bin is empty, not even a black bin-liner inside, and she remembers now dropping it down the chute as she struggled along the corridor with her suitcase on the way to the airport. So where the hell is that smell coming from?

She turns back and surveys the room, all neat and tidy, exactly as she'd left it.

She looks up to the mezzanine that serves as the main bedroom. It might be her imagination but the flies seem thicker up there.

Maybe she forgot to close the doors to the roof terrace and a pigeon got in and died. That's all she needs. A dead pigeon on her bed and maggots and flies everywhere when all she wants to do is take a shower and have a long lie-down.

She opens the cupboard under the sink, pulls a bin-liner from a roll then marches over to the stairs leading up to the mezzanine, determined to deal with the pigeon or whatever the hell it is before she has a chance to change her mind.

She walks steadily up the stairs, rising into trapped heat, and clouds of buzzing flies, and the smell that now feels like something solid and contains strong notes of shit and piss.

The master bedroom comes into view step by step and she squints slightly in some vague attempt to lessen the impact of whatever disgusting thing she's about to encounter.

Tannahill hears the scream echo down the corridor and is sprinting towards it before he even realizes he's moved.

He hears shouts up ahead, Sergeant Rook, telling someone to raise their hands and get down on the floor.

Another scream rings out as he rounds the corner and sees a door open ahead of him, a large suitcase standing next to it, movement in the flat beyond framed by the doorway.

A woman is being restrained by one of the officers. She is clutching something black and shiny in her hand and half-shrieking, half-sobbing.

Tannahill catches the smell halfway down the corridor and knows instantly what it is. He reaches the door to the flat and heat billows out, carrying the stench with it. The woman is on the floor now, just a few feet away from him, arms pinned to her sides to stop her scratching as she struggles and babbles hysterically.

Mike oh God Mike oh my God Mike Oh my God.

'Shonagh,' Tannahill says, using her name to try and get her to focus. 'Shonagh, it's OK, we're not here to hurt you or Mike, we're here to help.'

The mention of Mike makes her head snap round and she stares at him for a moment, like she's woken from a nightmare, then she looks back into the flat and starts howling again.

Mike Jesus Mike Oh my God Mike Jesus oh my God . . .

Eyes wide and staring up the stairs to the mezzanine where one of the armed officers looks over the top of his rifle then turns away, a look of disgust clearly visible on his face.

'He's up here,' he says, moving back down the stairs, rifle aimed at the floor, clearly no longer needed.

'Flat's clear!' Sergeant Rook shouts, emerging from another door on the far side of the flat.

Tannahill steps into the flat and walks past the officers attempting to calm Shonagh O'Brien. He waits for the officer to reach the bottom of the stairs leading down from the mezzanine, then heads up himself, making sure to tread in the same places and on the same steps he trod, his mind ticking through a checklist put there by Laughton Rees's book.

244

One in, one out. Preserve evidence. Keep to the edges of rooms and stairs.

The bedroom above comes into view step by step.

And so does the horror on the bed.

Mike Miller, lying on his back, arms outstretched, clearly dead for some time, and surrounded by strange objects.

V

THE MEDALS

Extract from *How to Process a Murder*
by Laughton Rees

The human mind is designed to look for patterns in everything and find meaning when it spots them. This is how tea leaves in the bottom of cups, and the creases of a human hand, end up being possible indicators of the future. We like patterns because we like order. We like them so much that we can seemingly conjure them out of chaos. And remarkable though this talent undoubtedly is, it can be both an asset and a liability in a murder investigation.

Because a murder scene *is* chaos.

The natural order has been upset, often violently, and the investigator is tasked with the job of making sense of this senselessness and finding answers where initially there are only questions. Naturally they will instinctively look for the patterns in this chaos and try to formulate a narrative about what happened and why.

The key in any murder investigation is to train the mind to see only the patterns that are actually there and not the ones you might simply be willing into existence through a strong and instinctive desire to impose order.

Sometimes chaos is just chaos.

41

The ladies of the Highgate WhatsApp group wake to a new twist and fresh information.

Tragic daughter of top cop now leads Miller murder investigation

The Daily headline blares loudly and incorrectly. Even so, the link is rapidly shared and the news is gobbled up along with coffee, yoghurt, granola, and power smoothies.

Laughton Rees, whose book on how to clean up at a murder scene and avoid detection was found by the body of Kate Miller yesterday, has been controversially included in the investigation. Her father, Met Police Commissioner John Rees, refused to respond yesterday to accusations of nepotism and his continued questionable leadership amid increasing calls for him to stand down in the wake of the latest disastrous crime figures. His daughter Laughton Rees was also unreachable for comment.

Ms Rees, 33, a single mother, is no stranger to personal tragedy after witnessing the murder of her mother Grace at the hands of alleged Masked Monster Adrian McVey.

Adrian McVey, who never admitted to the multiple child murders and attacks of the Masked Monster, was jailed for life for the killing of Grace Rees and died in Broadmoor almost a year ago of lung cancer.

Laughton Rees has been estranged from her father since the age of 15, which makes her high-profile appointment on a case where her father's future hangs in the balance seem all the more bizarre and intriguing . . .

All the other news sites and papers carry variations of the same story, rehashing the details of the murder, speculating about Laughton Rees's surprise involvement, and using it as an excuse to retell her own tragic backstory.

Celia Barnes sees it on the front page of her Derek's copy of the *Mirror* while he's reading the sports pages, still feeling anxious for Mike, and sad about Kate, and numb to just about everything else.

In a small, dingy room containing little more than a single bed, a man drops a pile of morning newspapers on to the butchered remains of yesterday's evening editions. He takes a pencil and gets to work, reading through every new story about the Miller murder, underlining key names and new pieces of information. When he's read all the papers he takes a scalpel and carefully slices through the paper, surgically removing the best photographs to add to all the others decorating the wall facing his bed. When he's finished he stares at the wall for a long time, almost in meditation, then takes a child's exercise book from a box and starts writing in it in neat, cramped and intense handwriting, capturing his thoughts and feelings and trapping them all between the neat blue lines of the book.

Brian Slade lies in the rumpled bed of the Z-list reality TV star he booty-called last night, scrolling through the news feeds on his Twitter account and feeling increasingly pissed off that all the other papers have jumped on the Laughton Rees/tragic daughter angle he has. In twenty-four hours he has gone from clear front-runner to just another member of the pack.

This is what happens when you ease up for one second: everyone else catches up. And he hates not winning. HATES it. It feeds into everything his dad always said to him growing up – that he was small, that he was weak, that a little boy like him was never going to add up to anything in this man's world.

'Shit!' he says, scrolling past another *Tragic Police Commissioner's daughter* headline.

'Whassup, babe!?' A tangled blonde head with dark roots showing rises from the pillow next to him, one eye closed, the other squinting up through a false eyelash that hangs off her lid like a squashed spider.

'Nothing,' he says, vaguely disgusted by her now. 'Shut up and go back to sleep.'

She grunts and turns away.

Maddie, not her real name, is a balloon-breasted tabloid regular after being the first contestant to be booted off the last season of *Love Island*. She's also part of a roster of D- to Z-list 'celebs' Slade has groomed by writing the odd story about them, or killing others to help protect their so-called image as they try to cling to the scrap of fame they've managed to snag. Like everything in Slade's life, the relationship is transactional, and he saw collecting on these investments from time to time as being no different from a landlord collecting the rent. They all knew it, and if they didn't then they were even dumber than they seemed, which was impressive. Cum dumps he calls them, though not to their faces obviously. He called Maddie last night after Shakila was 'too busy' to grab a drink with him to celebrate their scoop. Now there was a girl who needed to wise up about the transactional nature of things.

He opens his email account to see if justice72@yahoo.com has sent him anything new, but he hasn't.

He wishes he'd gone harder now on Laughton Rees in his story, made much more of her mental state and her unsuitability to be part of such a major police investigation. He'd held back so he could use it later, but now he thinks he should have just led with it, given her the full broadside as punishment for turning him down.

He opens a new email and addresses it to justice72@yahoo.com:

Today's news is moving away from you and on to the police – he writes, hoping to appeal directly to the ego – If you've got anything new for me, now would be a good time to let me have it. Can't help you if you don't help me.

He hits send and feels a hand close around his dick.

'Don't be grumpy,' Maddie says, super-pouting with her cosmetically enhanced lips, her hand moving gently up and down.

He's about to tell her to piss off but his dick's response is way quicker.

He puts his laptop on the floor and flips Maddie over so she's facing away. An angry fuck will probably do him good right now, clear the tubes and burn off some of his jaggy energy. He spits on his fingers, rubs it over the end of his dick, slides it between Maddie's butt cheeks and starts to push. Maddie moans and Slade wishes she wouldn't. She's a crappy actress and the porn sound effects are really distracting.

They make it harder for him to imagine it's Shakila.

42

Laughton is mid-argument when Tannahill calls.

She is standing in her kitchen, laptop open with the website of the Highgate and Holloway School for Girls filling the screen in all its happy, expensive glory. Gracie glares at it like it's a picture of someone torturing a puppy.

'I'm not going there,' she says as Laughton quickly declines the call to stop her phone from buzzing. 'I'm not going to some poncy school where everyone plays lacrosse and thinks I'm a massive povo.'

'It's not like that.'

'How do you know it's not like that? Have you been there?'

'No, I thought we could go and see it together today.'

'No! No way.'

'Why don't you just think about it?'

'Because I don't need to. Look at it. It's all bullshit, all those swotty uniforms and fake smiles.'

'Gracie, that's what happy kids at a decent school look like. Why don't we just go and see it?'

'Because I don't need to go and see it to know it'll be rubbish, and the kids'll be shitty, and the teachers will be patronizing because they're all posh and stuck-up. You can't afford to send me to a school like that anyway.'

'I can if you get a scholarship.'

'No way. I'm not going to a school where I'm some kind of charity case.'

'Scholarships are not charity.' Laughton's phone starts buzzing again. She silences it without even looking to see who's calling. 'Scholarships are there specifically to help smart kids gain places.'

'Well that's me out then.'

'Oh shut up, you're really smart. Even your crappy head-teacher admitted you were bright.'

'Maybe compared to the morons at my school I am, but that's not difficult.'

'You're really smart. You're like . . . top one per cent smart.'

Gracie closes her eyes and seems to deflate a little, like the comment has caused her actual pain. 'I'm not, Mum. I'm not smart, and I'm not beautiful, and I'm not special.'

'Yes you are. You need to stop being so hard on yourself.'

'That's a joke, coming from you.'

'OK, yes, you're right. I'm not the best example of someone who goes easy on themselves, but that's exactly why I don't want you to fall into the same trap. And I don't want to argue about this either. Why don't we just go to this school and have a look round at least before we make our minds up about it?'

Gracie shakes her head. 'You've already made your mind up about it and so have I. Look at it. I don't belong there.'

'Well you don't belong at St Mark's either.'

'No, I don't. I don't belong anywhere.'

'Oh stop being so dramatic.'

'It's true. I don't fit in at school, I don't have any friends. I'm just a prisoner in this flat.'

'No you're not, that's—'

'Yes I am. I'm a prisoner and you're the warden, constantly watching over me. I daren't even cough in case you think I've got Covid or something. I can't tell you I'm tired or I've got a headache because you'll immediately have me down to the hospital getting tests. Whenever I actually do get ill, I have to pretend I'm not, to stop you from having a meltdown. I can't keep worrying about you worrying about me all the time. It's exhausting. I can't deal with it any more.'

Laughton stares at her, embarrassed and ashamed because she knows it's true. She would never say this out loud to anyone, not even herself, but her greatest desire in everything she does is to protect her daughter like her mother had protected her and steer her away from all the rocks her own life has been wrecked upon. Basically she wants to stop Gracie from becoming her. She opens her mouth to say something, not this, but *something*, when her phone rings for a third time and Gracie glares at it with a look of deep and weary sadness.

'Answer it,' she says, turning away and walking out of the kitchen. 'It's probably something more important. It always is.'

Laughton watches her leave, feeling wretched and powerless, and once again wordless when faced with the full eloquent fury of this stranger who she now shares her life with.

She glances at the screen, sees it's Tannahill and answers, grateful for the distraction, and shamefully recognizing that this reaction has just proved her daughter's point.

'We found Mike Miller,' he says. 'He's dead, looks like he's been dead a while, certainly long enough to give him the perfect alibi for his wife's murder. Listen, the body was . . . it was arranged in a similar way to Kate Miller's . . .'

'Was my book left behind again?'

'No, which I suppose is a good thing, given this morning's news.'

'What!? What news?'

There's a pause. 'You haven't seen the news yet?'

'No.' She hears Gracie's bedroom door open and turns, ready for a possible round two.

'Look, it's not a disaster,' Tannahill says, 'and it's nothing

257

we didn't expect, but the press have picked up on your connection to the chief and run with it. You're on the front page of pretty much every newspaper this morning.'

Laughton closes her eyes and feels like going back to bed and staying there.

'Don't worry, we're gearing up to release the news that Mike Miller has been found dead, so by lunchtime that will be the only thing anyone's talking about. The forensics team are moving in now to process the scene, but we need to announce this before it leaks so we're moving quickly. I don't know what you're up to today, but it would be great if you could come down and give us your input.'

'To the crime scene?'

'Yes, I'm here now. It's off Borough High Street.'

A loud slam echoes through the flat, leaving the chain rattling on the front door. Laughton looks down at the laptop and the images of happy pupils at the knife-free school she had hoped to visit today.

'Give me the address,' Laughton says wearily, closing the laptop. 'I'll be with you as soon as I can.'

43

Movement catches his eye as the heavy front door of the mansion block swings open and Gracie Rees steps through it.

She looks up the street, her eyes seeming to linger on the spot where his car is parked, almost like she knows he's there. He keeps perfectly still, weathering the scrutiny, knowing that if he doesn't move she can't see him.

The building Laughton and Gracie Rees live in is called Fairview Mansions, a rather grand name for a somewhat shabby block of purpose-built flats. There are six floors in Fairview Mansions, four flats per floor, twenty-four in all, with a live-in caretaker occupying number 1 and Laughton all the way at the top in 24.

Gracie looks in the other direction as the front door continues to swing slowly shut behind her. She is careful. Watchful. So like her mother that sometimes it takes him a moment to tell the one from the other, especially now the weather is colder and woolly hats and heavy coats blur their identities further.

In terms of security, Fairview Mansions is not in the same league as the Miller house, nevertheless it still presents certain challenges. The road is on a bus route, so is effectively patrolled regularly by mobile CCTV cameras. There is a row of shops and a bank close by, with the additional cameras and heightened police awareness they bring. Then there's the added complication of witnesses.

The Miller house – remote as it was, and secure as it was – was also far removed from other people and only had two people inside it for most of the time. Fairview Mansions, by comparison, has sixty-seven permanent residents and a constant ebb and flow of visitors.

Noise had also not been an issue at the triple-glazed, concrete constructed Miller house, but here in the densely populated, thin-bricked building, it could prove problematic for a person with dark intentions. Yes, in many ways the problems posed by Fairview Mansions are equal and opposite. If getting into the Miller house undetected had been the hardest part, getting out of Fairview Mansions without being seen would prove to be just as hard, just as it had been in Maidstone Building Mews.

The front door finally closes behind Gracie and she leans on it to check it has shut before stomping up the street towards him, heavy boots on skinny legs, shoulders hunched against the gathering cold.

He lowers his window a little and adjusts his position very slightly so he can watch her approach in his wing mirror. She looks just like her mother, acts like her too: fearful but fierce; watchful and wary. Her eyes scan the street ahead as she slips headphones over her ears.

Headphones, the mugger's friend, both alerting them to the presence of a phone and hiding the sound of their approach. Gracie's mother should tell her to be careful about wearing them on the street. You never know who might be watching.

He watches her grow larger in the mirror and pulls his phone from his pocket so he can look down at it and hide his face when she passes by. She is almost upon him now, barely two cars back, and he reluctantly looks down at his phone, pulling his eyes away from her face and forcing them to focus on the glowing screen instead.

She walks past the car, so near he could reach through the open window and touch her. He feels the faint puff of displaced cold air and he breathes it in, catching the faint traces of her – strawberry soap, and scrubbed skin, and fresh, minty breath.

He looks up and watches her moving away, her teenage awkwardness evident in her clenched body and the slight heaviness of her steps. He could so easily slip out of the car, fall in step behind her and walk in her wake, so close he would be breathing in the minty, strawberry scent of her. She wouldn't even know he was there.

He watches her reach the row of shops and hesitate outside the pharmacy, like she's forgotten something. She looks back down the street to Fairview Mansions, her face seeming almost haunted, then disappears inside the pharmacy.

In his hand his phone buzzes but he ignores it, glancing in his rear-view mirror instead to see what it was she was looking at.

Someone else has just passed through the front door of Fairview Mansions on their way out, another resident, no one of any importance. They hurry away from the building letting the door swing slowly shut on its automatic closer. It takes almost seven seconds for the door to shut, plenty of time for someone to slide in, easy as a knife between ribs.

The phone buzzes again and he looks down and reads the message.

He checks the time.

Almost eight.

He drives away slowly, glancing through the window of the pharmacy as he slides by for one final glimpse of Gracie, standing by the till, pointing at something behind the pharmacist's head.

He picks up speed and heads back to town, his eyes scanning the way ahead above the surgical mask that hides his face.

44

Slade finishes with a grunt then slides out of Maddie and straight out of bed.

Maddie turns over and squints up at him again with her dead-spider eye. 'You off then?'

He doesn't reply, just grabs his clothes and feels a sudden and urgent need to get the hell out. He'll run over to the Crypt and shower there because he's sure as shit not going to stay here and run the risk of having to endure another 'career' chat with Maddie.

His phone buzzes and he glances at the number before answering. 'What?'

'Mike Miller.'

'Seriously?'

'An armed response squad just bashed in the door of a shag-pad he was keeping in Borough and found him dead in bed. The CSIs are in there now but advance word is it's similar to the other one.'

'Similar how?'

'Well I don't know much because there isn't even a case file yet, but apparently it wasn't suicide, the body was lai' out in the same way and there were objects left behind.'

'Do you know what kind of objects?'

'Not yet, this is all fresh off the wire. There's going to be an official announcement in about an hour.'

'Right, listen to me. Whatever they're going to say in that press release, I want to know it from you half an hour beforehand, understood? And there's BIG bonuses for any photographs you can send my way.'

'Got it.'

Slade hangs up and steps into his trousers. 'Shit!'

'What?'

'Nothing.' Slade drags his skinny jeans on and snatches up his shirt, desperate to get out of there as fast as he can. He doesn't normally stay the night anywhere but last night he was so tired he fell asleep before he could bail and now he's paying the price.

'You weren't in such a hurry five minutes ago,' Maddie pouts.

Yeah well I am now. Slade grabs his shoes. Somewhere outside, church bells start chiming eight o'clock, reminding him that time is against him.

He grabs his bulky borrowed laptop and is about to close it when he spots a new email in his inbox from justice72@yahoo.com – subject line, DS GEORGE SLADE – RIP.

Slade sits on the edge of the bed and opens the email.

'Thought you was off?' Maddie sneers.

'Shut up!'

'Arsehole!' She slumps down on the bed, her back to Slade, which is fine by him.

As before the email is filled with photographs.

The first shows an ancient-looking man lying in a single bed with leather straps around his wrists and a gag over his mouth. The old man's eyes are open and wet and stare helplessly through the camera as if he's drugged or dead.

The next is of an unmade bed, the sheets twisted and stained with something dark and brownish that could be shit, or blood, or both. An empty water jug and dusty glass are visible on a nightstand at the edge of the frame, as well as a couple of cards saying 'Happy Birthday Nanny'.

The next attachment is a video clip, also low quality, showing a small, plain room with a single bed pushed against a beige wall. A woman lies in the bed, a mess of curly white hair sticking out from under dirty sheets. A timestamp on the bottom shows 04:27. Slade clicks the 'play' arrow and the seconds tick forward.

Two stout female orderlies wearing pale blue smocks enter the frame.

Come on you, old bitch, says one, roughly shaking the elderly woman awake. The low sound quality makes her voice extra harsh and the fixed frame suggests it was recorded on a hidden camera. *Have you gone toilet in your bed again?*

I'm sleeping, the old lady pleads, sounding confused and frightened. *Leave me alone, I'm all right.*

The orderlies grab her wrists and jerk her violently upright. One leans forward and peers at the bed.

Oh, you filthy animal! She backhands the old lady full across the face then throws her back down on the bed. *You can lie in that for a bit, you dirty cow, teach you a lesson.*

The orderlies leave.

The old lady draws the sheets up to her face then lies there making a low noise that is both pathetic and awful. The clip ends.

'What is that? That's 'orrible.'

Slade turns away from Maddie so she can't see the screen. 'Nothing, it's nothing. Fuck off out of the room, will you, I'm working.'

'You fuck off, this is my bedroom.'

He feels like turning round and smacking her across the face but knows it'll probably turn him on and he hasn't got time for round three, so he grabs his stuff and leaves the room instead. He rests his laptop on the pink marble countertop in the kitchen so he can go through the rest of the attachments, hoping there's something juicier in what's left than what he's seen so far.

It's all very sad and everything, old people getting abused, but it wasn't exactly his department and it sure as shit wasn't front-page material. Apart from anything else, it was old news. There had been a public outcry a year or so back when one of the big care home companies had been mired in scandal then gone belly-up owing millions in unpaid compensation claims. It was a good enough story for the bleeding-heart libtard broadsheets, but not for him. The only interesting thing he could remember about it was that the company's owner had disappeared along with about fifty million quid, which made him a bit of a legend as far as Slade was concerned.

He clicks open the next document, hoping it will finally make sense of what this is all about, and is disappointed to discover what looks like the brochure for a care home company. There's a sunflower logo on the front with the earth at its centre, which is vaguely familiar, as is the name and slogan beneath it:

SunnySet
All the care in the world

That was it, the name of the company that went to the wall. This really was old news.

Slade clicks through the pages of the brochure, skimming the text and becoming increasingly annoyed at all the pictures of smiling old people staring out of windows at lovely views with cups of tea in their gnarly old hands. Jesus, you could almost smell the piss and lavender coming off the screen. What the hell was this?

He'd been hoping for something about Mike Miller, some pictures of the latest murder scene, maybe a rambling confession from the killer explaining why he'd killed Kate Miller, or Mike Miller, or both, that God told him to do it – *something*. He had no use for crumblies, and sob stories, and cups of tea.

At the back of the brochure *A word from our founder* dribbles on beneath a photograph of a smug-looking man leaning back on a large desk. The statement is signed *Mark Murphy*, which stirs another vague memory. That was the name of the dude who did a runner with all the cash. He'd been public enemy number one for a bit, until some other scumbag had come along and everyone had forgotten about him. Mark Murphy, the scumbag millionaire who'd made a fortune by exploiting the elderly and their families, then pissed off into the sunset.

Slade clicks to the last page of the brochure, where a video clip has been added to the PDF file. He clicks play and the picture of the cheesy dude from the previous page fades up with *Mark Murphy* written across it. It holds for a few seconds then slowly mixes through to another photo.

Slade leans in. The image holds for a beat then mixes back to the original photo, back and forth, back and forth on a loop. The hair is different and there's been a few alterations around the eyes and nose, but seeing them presented like this makes it clear and undeniable.

Mike Miller, the man police wanted for questioning in relation to his wife's murder and who has just turned up dead in a bed, is actually Mark Murphy, scumbag millionaire and former public enemy number one.

Now *that* was a story.

45

The corridor on the fourth floor of Maidstone Building Mews is now a makeshift field office. CSIs in white paper suits organize evidence bags, paperwork, and plastic bins beneath the large warehouse windows leading to the open door of number 27.

Laughton Rees steps out of the lift and is met by a uniformed police officer who hands her a pen and turns the crime scene log round on the portable table. The logbook records all the ins and outs at every murder scene. She has looked at hundreds of these, thousands even in her career, but this is the first time she's ever written her own name in one, and she has a momentary out-of-body experience. She imagines a future version of herself, reading the name she is about to write, making connections between her and things that have already happened, and things that are still to come. Adding her name to this official record, the ball of the pen indenting the page, will leave behind an indelible record of her presence here. The thought makes her feel exposed and panicked.

She starts tapping her thumb along her fingers in series of threes and looks up into the confused face of the police constable, her mind riffling through excuses – a forgotten work commitment, her daughter taken unexpectedly ill, anything so long as she doesn't have to sign her name in this book, walk down this corridor and step through that open door at the end of it.

Then a voice calls out down the corridor.

'Laughton!'

She looks up and sees Tannahill framed in the open door, standing next to a table covered with audio-visual equipment. He smiles at her, and even from this distance he looks tired from too much to do and not enough time to do it in. This is the difference, she realizes. On the cases she works, the clock has stopped. No one will die if she takes her time, but here they might. They already have.

She takes the pen, signs her name, and walks down the busy corridor to the open door of number 27 where Tannahill stands adjusting something on a monitor until a wobbly image appears showing a spacious and airy loft apartment. 'This is a direct feed from DS Lyons's camera,' he explains. 'She's about to do the primary walk-through and this will allow us to look over her shoulder without stepping on anything or contaminating the scene.' He slips a headset on with a microphone and taps it with his finger. 'Can you hear me, Rhona?'

'Yep.'

'OK. Whenever you're ready.'

The image on the screen swings round to a piece of paper lying on the kitchen worktop with the case number and DS Rhona Lyons written on it. A 'record' message flashes on the screen and a date and timestamp appears, with the seconds ticking steadily forward. The image holds for a few seconds then swings back round and starts moving towards a flight of stairs leading up to a mezzanine level.

'It's pretty messy,' Tannahill warns her.

'I've seen messy before,' Laughton replies. And she has, though never before when the body is lying only thirty feet away.

The camera starts climbing the stairs, the operator keeping to the right where a walkway has been marked out with tape.

Laughton starts counting again, tapping her thumbs against the fingers of both hands out to in, then in to out, pausing each time before she gets to three.

1, 2 – 3
1, 2 – 3
1, 2 – 3

Then the bed comes into view and the camera holds on a wide shot that records the whole macabre scene.

Mike Miller is lying on his back on sheets so filthy they look like they may have been soiled multiple times. The blandly handsome man from the photo is now almost unrecognizable, his tan turning mottled with lividity and the beginnings of putrefaction. Flies move across his greying skin, laying eggs on the open sores visible on his lower body and where thick, blue nylon straps stretch across his body at the chest, waist and feet, binding him tightly to the bed. There is a drip attached to a needle in his arm and a large saline-type bag on a stand, and he has been arranged in the same way as his wife – mask over his eyes, arms stretched out on either side, and four objects placed around the body.

But unlike his wife the violence here seems more focused though no less vicious. His right hand has been pinned to the bedside table by the same kind of knife that killed his wife, and balanced on his left finger is something that looks like a short rope, like woven leather maybe. At his feet is a pile of newspapers, stacked on a chair, and the final object, placed at the head of the victim, is a stuffed toy, a lion this time.

'How long do you think he's been here like this?' Laughton murmurs.

'The timeline suggests he went missing on or around last Tuesday when he failed to get on the flight to Goa, so if he was picked up then he could have been here for a week. Long enough to die from dehydration, especially with the heat turned up in the flat the way it was. I don't know what's in that drip bag, but I imagine it's not there to keep him alive; keep him quiet, maybe. The pathologist will be able to give us an approximate time of death and we've also got a forensic entomologist on their way in who'll be able to tell us what the fly evidence says, but I can't see any sign of maggot infestation yet, so he can't have been dead that long. I would say our man may well have still been alive this time yesterday.'

Laughton nods. 'So he was still alive when Kate Miller was murdered.'

'Yes, but I don't think he would have been in any kind of state to have killed her, do you?'

'I wasn't thinking he did it. I was thinking he might have helped. Can we have a closer look at the right hand?'

'Yep,' DS Lyons's voice replies, picking up the request through Tannahill's microphone.

The camera moves closer. A large black fly buzzes through the frame and settles on the handle of the knife that has been driven through the palm of Mike Miller's right hand. It's a zombie knife, green and black, the same size and type as the one that killed his wife. The wound looks ragged, with congealed blood around the blade, and a raw redness stains the tips of two fingers.

'Look at the fingernails,' Laughton murmurs. 'Two are missing. His thumb's missing too. Looks like our killer may have tortured the victim.'

Tannahill nods. 'It's because he needed the security codes for the house. He also needed someone with admin privileges to switch the cameras off. Once he had those, the only thing he needed to access the house was a key and an authorized thumbprint. Looks like he took them.'

The camera captures all the violent details of Mike Miller's ruined right hand before pulling wider and panning across his chest, following the line of the blue nylon strap where flies have laid clusters of long white eggs, like miniature grains of rice, in the sores that have formed where skin and nylon meet. The camera reaches the other hand, which has been bound tightly to the edge of the bed by another, thinner strap and moves in to start recording the details. Laughton leans in too, squinting at the strange length of leather rope, tapered at one end and fatter at the other, beige with dark spots and draped over the end of his curled finger, like the medals had been balanced on his wife's dead hand. The focus on the camera shifts then settles and Laughton involuntarily flinches away when she realizes what it is.

'Is that a snake?' Tannahill says.

'Yes,' DS Lyons's voice replies on the monitor. She moves the camera down a little to show the underneath. 'It looks like it's been stuck to the finger, I can see drips of something clear running down the skin. We'll take samples and test it, but it definitely looks like glue of some kind.'

'Guess you don't want your snake falling off your finger,' Tannahill mutters.

'It has to be like that,' Laughton says, thinking out loud. 'It has to be balanced. The arrangement of everything is the same as before, even if some of the objects are different.'

'A snake can mean all kinds of things,' Tannahill says, 'poison, deception, cunning. We'll find out what species it is too, maybe that's a clue.'

'Or maybe it's something more obvious.' Laughton points at the screen, outlining the diamond shapes on the snake's back. 'What's a snake covered in?'

Tannahill shakes his head, not sure where she's going with this. 'Snake skin?'

'Scales,' Laughton says. 'A snake is covered in scales. In the first murder scene the medals stayed in place because Kate Miller was already dead when they were placed on her finger, but here he was still alive when all this happened to him, so the glue was necessary to make sure the snake stayed where the killer put it.'

The camera pulls wide again, confirming that the arrangement of the body is the same as it was for Kate Miller.

'He needed everything to stay in place so the tableau was right,' Laughton says, pointing at the screen, 'the mask, the outstretched arms, the scales in the left hand, the knife representing the sword in his right. It's Justitia again, blind justice, same theme, slightly different tune.'

The camera continues its tour of the body, up to the head next, pausing to hold on the mask covering Mike Miller's eyes. 'Same type of mask as before,' Tannahill says. 'Only he's wearing it this time. Last time it was only draped across the eyes.'

'Again, that must be for the same reason as the glue on his left hand: to make sure it all stayed in place.'

The camera moves up to the stuffed lion toy above his head. 'It's interesting the points of difference here,' Tannahill says. 'I can see why some had to be different, like the mask being around the head instead of placed over the eyes, but what's the significance of the lion this time instead of the unicorn?'

Laughton studies the lion and remembers the unicorn from the first scene, its big glass eyes reminding her of a child's mask from her past. Even recalling it like this makes her anxious and she takes a breath and starts counting to three again under her breath as she taps her thumb along her fingers, hesitating before she gets to three each time, something she only ever does at times of extreme stress.

1 – 2 —— 3
1 – 2 —— 3

Get a grip. Focus.

'They're facing different ways,' she says, forcing herself to concentrate on the screen and the problem at hand. 'Last time the unicorn was facing right. Here the lion is facing left. I think maybe we're meant to look at these two crimes scenes as a whole.'

'What makes you think that?'

'Well, bearing in mind the whole *justice* fixation our killer seems to have, where else have you seen a lion and unicorn facing each other before?'

Tannahill thinks for a moment. 'In court.'

'Exactly. It's the seal of the United Kingdom which hangs behind the judge's chair in every courtroom in the country. I think these two crime scenes together represent a kind of courtroom for our killer, only one where he is judge, jury and executioner.'

The camera moves again, down to the pile of newspapers at Mike Miller's feet. They are stacked on a chair and lying face down so the front pages are hidden. The pages seem yellowed with age. The camera records them first as they were found, moving round to show where they are in relation to the body, before a blue gloved hand reaches in and turns the top copy over.

For a moment the shift of light makes the paper blow out a little, the over-exposure delaying the reveal of the cover. Then the camera adjusts and settles, the headline comes into focus, and Laughton feels the ground fall away beneath her:

DAUGHTER OF MASKED MONSTER DETECTIVE LEAVES HOME, BLAMES FATHER FOR MOTHER'S DEATH

The headline is more than a decade and a half old, half her lifetime ago, but seeing it like this, in this setting, makes it feel like it only just happened.

The blue gloved hand lays the first newspaper aside then turns over the next:

TRAGIC DAUGHTER OF TOP COP IN REHAB AS SHE FIGHTS FOR CUSTODY OF BABY DAUGHTER

. . . THEY'RE ABOUT ME . . .

The realization screams in Laughton's head.

. . . THEY'RE ALL ABOUT ME . . .

'You OK?'

She realizes Tannahill is looking at her and tries to say something but she can't form any words so she just shakes her head then turns and stumbles away down the corridor, away from the screen and the dead man in the flat. Away from the newspapers that have reduced her life to screaming headlines. Away from the darkness of her past that always catches up with her and swallows her whole, no matter how fast or how far she runs from it.

46

Commissioner Rees sees the armed police guards stiffen as they spot him. He nods a hello then enters the steel-and-glass block of a building.

A meeting with the minister as soon as is convenient, the message had said.

Well, here he was.

No.2, Marsham Street, also known as the Home Office, was the government department in charge of the internal affairs of England and Wales, which included policing. The current Home Secretary, Charles Nixon – one of the Prime Minister's closest advisers and possibly next in line for the top job – was the minister Rees had been summoned to see. The message hadn't said why he wanted to see him so urgently, but Rees had a pretty good idea.

He steps into the elevator and presses the button to take him to the sixth floor. The lift is glass, as is most of the interior of this fishbowl of a building, and Rees watches the floors flash past, the business of government passing through the open-plan offices like food through the gut of some giant, transparent creature, often with similar end results. Rees was not a big fan of politicians or the machinations of government.

He reaches into his pocket and thumbs the lid off his bottle of pills. He's not a fan of open-plan offices either, modern panopticons that make everyone feel like they are being watched all the time. Jeremy Bentham had developed the idea in the eighteenth century as a type of architecture suited to prisons, insane asylums, and any other institution where surveillance was necessary. The basic idea was that people who felt they were constantly being watched would self-police and be more productive as a result. Now the whole world was a panopticon, which said all you needed to know about modern society.

He palms the pill and pops it in his mouth under the disguise of a cough, knowing he is probably being watched right now – by the worker bees in their open-plan offices, by the surveillance cameras within the lift and the outer atrium, by the whole damn country after the shitshow of yesterday's press conference.

The lift slows and the doors open on to the executive floor, revealing a large seal of Her Majesty's Government on the opposite wall, lion and unicorn rampant either side of the crown. Rees heads past it and along the main corridor where a host of assistants look up from their desks. He knows he's supposed to tell them he's here and wait for a summons, but he's in no mood for petty power plays today so marches straight up to the door of the minister's office, raps once on the wooden surface, then opens it.

Charles Nixon is behind his desk, a large slab of something dark and expensive covered with stacks of documents and the morning papers. Laughton's photograph stares out from most of them.

'Ah John,' Nixon says, 'thanks for coming over at short notice.' He gestures at a thin, grey man sitting opposite, 'I think you two have already met.'

The grey man unfolds himself from his seat and extends a pale hand. He is pencil-thin, long nose, rimless glasses and beady eyes, boring but expensive grey suit. He looks like a rat made human. He's vaguely familiar, but Rees struggles to place him. Civil servant probably, one of the grey men of government, quite literally in this case.

'Spencer Bates,' the man says, giving Rees a bony handshake. 'We met very briefly last autumn at our AGM.'

'Oh yes, Shield Group,' Rees says, remembering the corporate waste of time he'd been forced to attend. 'How are you?'

'Good, thanks. Great, actually, business is booming. Whoever said crime doesn't pay clearly never worked in the private security sector.' He laughs at his own joke. Rees does not. He looks back at the minister, who is staring down at the acreage of newsprint on his desk. 'Bloody bad timing, all this. I mean, we knew the crime figures would cause a few ripples, but this Highgate knife murder has turned it into a bloody tsunami. Any closer to catching this missing husband?'

'Actually, sir, we've found him.'

'Really!?'

'We traced him to an unlisted address and sent in an armed task force to make the arrest.'

'So he's in custody?'

'No, he's on his way to the morgue. He was murdered, seemingly by the same person who killed his wife.'

Nixon shakes his head and looks back down at the newspapers. 'They're going to have a field day with this. Now they're going to say we have a serial killer on our hands.'

'Well, sir, technically a serial killer is someone who kills three or more people over a period of more than a month.'

'Oh come on, John, don't be naïve, the tabs don't give a shit about dictionary definitions. I must say I'm concerned about the way you've handled all this – it demonstrates a worrying lack of judgement. At a time when the Home Office and policing policy in general are under intense scrutiny, you seem to be going out of your way to give the press a stick to beat us with. We knew the latest crime stats were going to generate some negative press, that's why we sent the spin doctors down to help you manage the message.' He picks up *The Daily* and waves it in front of him. 'Hiring your own daughter to help investigate a high-profile knife murder is not managing anything, especially when it seems her book helped this "not technically a serial killer" cover his tracks.'

'With respect, sir, I didn't hire her, and Laughton Rees is a highly respected academic in the field of criminology who is eminently quali—'

'She's your daughter, John. Doesn't matter how well qualified she is, hiring her or allowing someone else to hire her was a huge mistake. Smacks of nepotism.'

Rees glances across at the thin grey man whose name he has already forgotten again. He would normally be circumspect in the presence of a civilian, but Nixon invited the man here and seems to be speaking frankly enough in front of him, so Rees decides to do the same. He turns back to Nixon.

'I agree it was unfortunate timing that a wealthy white woman in a posh neighbourhood went and got herself knifed to death on the same day the crime stats were published. Maybe if it had just been another black teenager in Tottenham the press wouldn't have cared so much and we wouldn't be having this conversation.'

'That is absolutely not true!' Nixon glances uneasily at the grey man. 'The government is just as concerned as you are about every single crime.'

'Then tell me who Kai Mustafa is.'

Nixon shoots his guest another uncertain look. 'Kai . . .?'

'Mustafa. Fifteen years old. Died after jumping or being pushed off a bridge to get away from a knife attack. He was killed just a few hours before Kate Miller, but I notice you didn't pull me into a meeting to ask me how *that* investigation is progressing, or any of the other twenty-one knife-related deaths this year. If you really cared about crime, sir, then you and your party would not have cut the police budget by nineteen per cent over the past decade and you wouldn't need to employ teams of spin doctors to try to disguise the annual crime figures.'

Nixon sits back in his chair and regards Rees for what seems like an uncomfortably long time. 'How long have you been commissioner now, John – six years, seven?'

'Seven. Eight in January.'

Nixon nods slowly. 'That's a long time on the front line. All that censure, all that pressure – you must be worn out. To be honest, you do look a bit tired, John.'

Rees studies the Home Secretary, soft stomach straining against expensive, high-thread-count cotton, and plump, pink, manicured hands laced together and resting on top. Rees is probably fifteen years older than Nixon, but he'd like to take him out on a 5k run and see which of them looked tired after that. 'It's been a tough week,' he says instead.

'Of course,' Nixon replies, 'and I do have sympathy. In fact I organized an emergency meeting last night with the PM and the Chancellor, where we discussed policing, among other things, and agreed to allocate an additional four hundred and fifty million to the police budget, spread over two years.'

Rees is floored. A large chunk of his time in office has been spent campaigning for greater investment in the force and now here he is, effectively being promised a huge bag of cash on the back end of a bollocking. It didn't make sense. There had to be a catch, and somehow it involved the man in the grey suit sitting next to him.

'Thank you, sir,' he says.

'Don't thank me yet. This increase in funding comes with two conditions. The first is that we want to formally announce it in the spring statement, so not a word is to be whispered about it before then.'

Rees nods. He could do with the money sooner and wonders why they're waiting when an announcement now would instantly change the narrative about policing. Then he realizes what the second condition must be.

'You want me to step down,' he says, a statement, not a question.

Nixon shakes his head. 'I don't want you to go, John. I know we've butted heads a few times, but it's never felt personal; you're doing your job, I'm doing mine. But the simple truth is that every elected official has a sell-by date. Doesn't matter how good you are at your job or how many successes you have, the longer you stand up there in the full glare of the public's gaze, the more shit they throw at you and the more it sticks until no amount of PR polishing or water under the bridge can wash it away. And this current situation, this high-profile case, a double murder now with your name tied to it through your daughter, it's just too much. You've become the story, John. So if we announce the budget hike with you still in charge it would be like giving someone a pot of gold in a dirty bucket. That's why we need to clear the decks first, appoint someone new so we can announce the extra funding as part of their succession. The police get their funding. Your successor gets a flying start. Everybody wins.'

Rees fixes him with an even gaze. 'Almost everybody.'

Nixon smiles. 'No, everybody wins.' He turns to the man in the grey suit. 'Spencer has a proposition – go ahead, Spence, tell him what we discussed.'

'A position has become available on our board,' he says, as if he's selling insurance, 'a non-executive director role that you would be eminently suited for.'

Rees nods. 'Convenient.'

'We're always looking to bolster our boardroom expertise at the senior end of security work, and you, with your years of experience, would be an absolutely perfect fit. It's not a full-time position, so you would be free to pursue any other interests you had, such as charity work, or golf, or whatever

281

else you haven't had much time for over your many distinguished years of service.

'Your salary package would, of course, be commensurate with your experience and high standing in the security field and would start at three hundred and twenty thousand a year, plus share-linked bonuses and a full healthcare package. We can hammer out all the details later but, well, there it is. We would be more than delighted to have you on board at Shield Group, if you choose to join us.'

Nixon creaks forward in his chair. 'Three hundred grand, John. That's more than you're getting now, only without all this crap' – he grabs another newspaper and holds it up – 'plus there'll be another little bonus in next year's New Year's honours list. *Sir* John Rees. How's that sound? You'll never have trouble getting a table reservation again, not with that on your company credit card.'

Rees looks at the thin, grey man. Private security firms like his made their fortunes by plugging all the gaps in national and domestic security left by government policy, either deliberately or through incompetence. 'It's a very generous offer,' he says. 'Can I think about it?'

'Of course.' Nixon rises abruptly from his seat and heads over to the door with the clear intention that both men should follow. 'Though we've scheduled a press conference for this afternoon to announce you're stepping down, so it would be great if you could make your mind up by then.'

He stops by the door, leans in and lowers his voice so only Rees can hear.

'Don't make me fire you, John. The press might enjoy it, but I certainly wouldn't.' He pats Rees on the shoulder and opens the door wide. 'Sorry to rush you, gentlemen, but I've got a policy meeting in five minutes.' He smiles and points a finger at Rees. 'Go catch your killer, John, then you can go out a hero. Like I said, everybody wins.'

He smiles one last time then closes the door.

Rees stares at the closed door for a moment then turns to the grey man.

'Nice to meet you again, John,' he says, holding out his hand.

'Likewise,' Rees says, shaking it.

He still can't remember his damn name.

47

By the time Tannahill catches up with Laughton, she's almost made it down to the third floor.

'I can't do this,' she says, half leaning, half sliding down the wall of the stairwell. 'It's . . . I just can't do it.' She trips on a step and stumbles.

'Whoa there.' Tannahill grabs her arm to steady her and she catches his scent, like fabric softener and leather. 'Sit down for a sec. Take a breath.' Laughton slump-slides down on to a step and puts her head in her hands. 'I should never have asked you to be part of the investigation,' Tannahill says, sitting next to her on the step.

'It's not your fault. I didn't have to say yes, and it wouldn't have made any difference anyway, you saw those headlines – the killer pulled me into this, not you. I never had any choice.' She takes a deep breath and blows it out slowly, feeling a little calmer now. 'Sorry I freaked out back there.'

'Hey, don't worry, I think anyone would freak out if they found a stack of newspapers filled with stories about them next to a corpse. I also don't necessarily think it's personal.'

'Feels pretty personal to me.'

'I'm sure it does, but look, we already know from the Kate Miller murder that our killer wants to draw maximum attention to his acts and also to embarrass the police in the process. Leaving your book behind in a forensically cleansed scene was a middle finger to us more than you, given who your father is. And sending photos directly to the press to coincide with your dad's press conference made sure it became a big story where both he and we look like idiots, but again, not you.'

'Don't call him that.'

'What?'

'Dad, don't call him "dad", it makes him sound like he's some benign figure in a jumper pottering around the garden with a cup of tea. That's not who he is.'

Tannahill takes a deep breath and lets it out slowly. 'Look,' he says softly. 'I know what happened to you, about your mam and everything, and I'm not going to even attempt to try and imagine what that was like or how it affected you. But I do know John Rees, and he's without question one of the smartest, hardest-working people I've ever met. There are plenty of other people in the force, people in high positions I don't have much respect for, but he is not one of them. No one has more integrity than he does or uncompromising commitment to the job, and he's made plenty of enemies because of it, on both sides of the criminal divide, many of whom are quite capable of killing people to get what they want. So without wanting to bash your ego or anything, I think this is far less likely to be about you, and way more likely to be about him. He is also much higher profile than you are, and though those newspapers back there are about you, they're about him too. And you said it yourself, this is all about justice. Maybe whoever did this feels the police generally, possibly even your father specifically, failed to deliver justice and let them down in some way, so they're settling scores for themselves and making us look stupid in the process.'

Laughton feels her usual, nameless anger expanding within

her at any mention of her father. But Tannahill's right, it is much more likely to be about him than it is about her.

'You should draw up a list of people who hate my father,' she says. 'But whoever did this hated Kate and Mike Miller just as much. Both of these murders are far too violent and rage-filled to not be personal, and clearly the intention here was not just to kill Mike Miller but to make sure he suffered too. So if you find someone who had reason to hate both Kate and Mike Miller enough to do this to them, and also someone who was let down by the police generally or my father specifically, then you'll have your killer.'

'Agreed.' Tannahill arches his back to stretch some of the tension out. 'The only problem is, at the moment, we still have no idea who Kate and Mike Miller really are.'

The sound of a door banging open and hurrying feet makes them both look up to see the anxious face of the uniformed officer who'd met Laughton when she stepped out of the lift appear on the stairs above them.

'Sir,' he says, holding up his phone. 'A story just appeared on *The Daily* website.'

Tannahill nods wearily. 'I guess we should have expected this. The killer must have let the press know already that Mike Miller's been found.'

'Yes, sir, but that's not all,' the PC says, hurrying down the stairs and handing his phone to Tannahill. 'The story also reveals Mike Miller's real identity.'

48

– *OMG Mike Miller has been found dead.*

The news detonates like a bomb in the Highgate Ladies WhatsApp group.

– *Really, when?*

– *Look on The Daily website, I just got an alert.*

There's a pause as phones are grabbed and full attention can be focused on the only thing any of them will be talking about for the next few days.

– *OMG Mike Miller was actually Mark Murphy, I don't believe it!!!*

– *I KNEW there was something not right about the Millers.*

– *What about poor Kate?*

– *What about her? She must have known who he was. She enjoyed the money as much as him. I don't feel sorry for her at all, living in luxury because of other people's misery.*

– *George had an uncle who died in one of his homes. He was helping them out with the court case, or he was until Murphy disappeared with all the money.*

– *My auntie was in a SunnySet too. Fortunately my sister got her out, but not before they'd made her sign up to some hideous finance deal.*

– *It's on the radio now. I just heard it.*

– Which station?

– Radio 2.

Across the wide, leafy expanse of Highgate anyone listening hard enough at that moment would have heard a collective chorus of '*Alexa – play Radio 2*' through the chill autumn breeze, then silence as everyone leans in and listens to the breaking news story, their faces softening into smiles as they realize that the Millers were in fact not like them after all, and the violence that reached into their comfy, cosseted world might not touch them now, because the Millers deserved what happened to them, whereas they did not, because they were all good people, and bad things never happened to good people, so everything was fine again in their world. Order had been restored.

In her kitchen, Celia Barnes stands immobile by the sink, the cloth in her hand paused mid-wipe.

In the background the radio burbles.

She stares out of her window at a world so familiar but utterly changed because of what she just heard on the news. A single tear brims then runs down her left cheek.

The news report ends, breaking the spell, and she drops the cloth, wipes the tear away with the back of her hand and upends her handbag on to the countertop, looking for the card the nice PC gave her.

Celia Barnes almost never gets angry but she is angry now, angry at herself for being taken in by the money and the easy charm, angry that she had covered for the Millers, brushing dirt under the carpet for them, thinking they were nice people and respecting their privacy when all along it was Mark Murphy she was protecting.

She finds the card and dials the number, clearing her throat nervously as she waits for it to connect.

Well, she's not clearing up for them any longer.

*   *   *

In his office Commissioner Rees is informed of the breaking news and, like everyone else, he takes his phone, logs on to *The Daily* website and scans the article exclusively revealing that Mike Miller has been found dead at an address in Borough, and – second exclusive – that the paper has also learned that Mike Miller is actually Mark Murphy, the infamous care home magnate who went missing a year earlier.

Rees sits at his desk watching the video clip embedded at the end of the article, Mike Miller's face dissolving into Mark Murphy's then back again in an endless loop.

If there was any residual hope in his mind that he could fight to hang on to his position, this has blown it away in an instant. He knows how this will look, the police yet again being outmanoeuvred by a newspaper, and with the added freight of his daughter being both subject and part of the investigation. At least these new revelations have knocked her off the top of the news agenda.

Small mercies.

He slips his phone into his pocket, opens the drawer of his desk and pulls out a laptop, ready to get back to work. In his eight years sat at this desk he has always endeavoured to clear it by the end of each day. Today, it seems, he may well be clearing it for the last time.

He sits in a steamy cafe, blandly anonymous amid the morning crowd, his coffee going cold as he tries to capture his fresh, glistening thoughts in the child's exercise book. He's overheard that Mike Miller's been found dead, the news already online but not in the papers yet. He almost wishes he had a phone that could connect to the internet so he could find out what's happened, but he knows that's too dangerous. McVey had told him about phones and computers and how they could be used to trap you. McVey had only ever written things down on paper, and that's why he does the same.

One copy. One owner. No danger.

Two girls arrive at the table next to his, excitedly talking about the latest news. He looks up, watches a video over the nearest one's shoulder showing Mike Miller's face changing from one person to another, and listens in on their conversation:

. . . I thought he definitely killed her . . .

. . . same . . .

. . . and he was that bloke who ripped off all the oldies . . .

. . . I know . . .

. . . so who do you think killed him, then? . . .

. . . I don't know . . .

. . . They found those old newspapers by his body, din't they? All about that kiddy-fiddler.

. . . Yeah. He's dead though, in'e. Whassis name, McVey . . .

His skin tingles at the mention of the name.

Because of the Miller murders, people are talking about McVey again, and something surges inside him whenever he hears the name whispered on a stranger's lips, or sees it spelled out in bold, black newsprint.

McVey – dead, but not forgotten, not any more, and never by him.

McVey had been the only one who had ever made sense about who he was. Everyone else had treated him like a creature of shame, because of those things he had done when he was a boy, because of all the thoughts he had. But McVey, only McVey, had understood him. It was he who had given him permission to be true to his nature and taken away his shame. He had shown him how to be, and also what to become.

He closes the child's exercise book, slides it into his pocket then heads out into the damp, grey morning, taking his cold coffee with him, thinking what it would be like to sit behind these girls in a few days' time, and listen to them talking about what's coming next.

49

Slade enters *The Daily* newsroom to a round of applause.

Most of the large TV screens dotted around the place are displaying the video of Mike Miller, his face morphing into Mark Murphy's then back again, each one smiling smugly down at the newsroom like some game-show-host version of Big Brother.

Slade's back is slapped and he is high-fived all the way to his corner desk, and he smiles his way through it, half-loving, half-hating it. He raises his adjustable desk to standing height, logs in and clicks on the shortcut to the Black File database.

'You must be feeling pretty chipper this morning,' Shakila says.

Chipper!? – who the hell uses a word like 'chipper'?

'Not really,' Slade grumbles.

Shakila's smile falters and he almost feels sorry, because it's such a very nice smile.

'Everyone else is going to be on this like flies on shit,' he says, 'so we need to stay in front. Go through all the files on SunnySet, we're looking for anyone who knew Murphy – old friends, business associates, people who worked for him. Find them and throw money at them to stop them speaking to anyone else, and give me anything you find the moment you get it.'

Shakila frantically writes it all down in her notebook and he watches her long, elegant fingers as they grip and guide the pencil and imagines them wrapped around his dick. He looks away, forcing his mind back to the task in hand. It's a curse, it really is, what he calls 'Achilles' Cock', the rule that no matter how successful a man is, and no matter how disciplined, his dick will always prove to be his weak spot and trip him up in the end. Speaking of which . . .

He opens his own notebook and flicks through it until he finds the page containing notes he scribbled down from his insider source on his way in to the office. He types 'Shonagh O'Brien' into the search engine and gets a few hundred pages of hits.

Yes, thank God for 'Achilles' Cock'; without it he'd be out of a job.

He opens the search tools to fine-tune the search. His police source said she was late twenties to early thirties, so that should narrow it down a bit. Add in 'London' and hopefully he'd have a small enough sample to be able to find her mobile number and get hold of her before someone else does.

He hits 'return'. Sixteen pages. That's more like it.

He starts working through them, using the image search so he can discount the mingers. Old Goldenballs Mike Miller, or Murphy, or whatever he was called didn't seem the type to set up a shag-pad with any old dog. The Shonagh he was looking for would be a sort, a head-turner, which was also good news for the photos they'd want to use of her to accompany the exclusive interview he has his sights fixed on.

Yep, it was just like running; getting ahead was one thing, staying there was another story – literally in his case.

Slade starts working through the Shonaghs, rejecting the frumpy, the fat and the objectively unfuckable, like he's on some clunky version of Tinder. He's about halfway through the results with six strong candidates for further investigation when his phone makes a sound like a cash register.

He snatches it up. After the first email from justice72@
yahoo.com had come in he'd set up an alert on his PC and
phone for anything new from that address and the cash-
register sound seemed appropriate given the bonuses it was
earning him for every front page he secured.

He sees the familiar subject line, opens the new mail and
frowns at the contents.

No pictures this time, no click-baity videos, just a name,
an address and what looks like half a phone number.

2, Lucan Place, SW3
Adam
070753

He scrolls to the bottom of the email to check there's nothing
else, then puts the address into Google Maps. Lucan Place is
in Chelsea, about a mile or so south-east of him, a decent
run in normal circumstances, but he has no idea what kind
of circumstances these might be. Just because the killer has
been his friend so far doesn't alter the fact he's a killer. Slade
wasn't about to pop round for a breakfast meeting.

He switches from 'Maps' to 'All' on Google and clicks on
the top hit, a local history website. An old black-and-white
photo of a large corner building loads, and as it does something cold slides down Slade's back and the skin on his scalp
tightens. The street in front of the building is filled with cars
from the 1950s and a man in a police uniform is walking
out of a large front door with POLICE STATION written
above it. Slade has a flash memory of being dragged through
those same doors by his mother when he was about seven,
and standing by the sergeant's desk while she had a blazing
row with his father. Then she'd walked out and left him there.
He shudders as he remembers what came next and his eyes
flit back to the subject line: DS GEORGE SLADE – RIP.

He had assumed it had been added purely to grab his

attention, but maybe it was more than that. But what did his old man have to do with any of this? He was off the force and in the ground long before the SunnySet scandal hit.

He scrolls down the local history site, skim-reading the article beneath the photograph, and sees that the station was closed the previous year and sold to a property developer.

He drums his fingers on the desk, considering his next move. The TV screens all around the room continue to display his story on *The Daily* website, the video of Mike Miller/Mark Murphy playing on a loop. He can feel it becoming old news by the second. He always has this same feeling whenever an exclusive drops, an initial burst of fist-pumping euphoria then a rapid crash as he feels the pack closing in behind him. It's the same in running, it's great to be out in front but it means everyone else can see you and is chasing to catch up.

He looks at the email again. He should go and have a look at the place at the very least. He doesn't have to go in if he gets a bad feeling about it. He'll do a lot of things for a story but he won't walk into an ambush. He's not stupid. He looks up at Shakila, her glossy black hair scraped back from an oval face now creased in concentration.

'Call us an Uber, would you, love?'

He likes calling her 'love' and 'darling' specifically because in the modern PC world he's not supposed to, and also because there's nothing she can do about it.

'Where to?' she asks.

'Chelsea police station.' He smiles when he sees the look of surprise on her face.

'I'm going to turn myself in for all my wicked, wicked ways,' he says, giving her a wink like he's sharing a secret.

'If I'm not back for the morning editorial meeting, send someone over with bail money, would ya.'

50

Laughton stares out of the squad car window at the grey smear of London outside. The siren is on and the slow London traffic parts before them as they duck into bus lanes and push through red lights on their hurried way back to Kentish Town. Tannahill sits beside her in the back seat, phone clamped to his ear, getting the latest updates on the case.

Tannahill ends his call. 'We have a couple of new leads, one really good one by the sounds of it, and the Millers' cleaner just called to say she remembered something that might be important; she's heading in to give another statement.'

Laughton had listened to the audio of the cleaner's first statement sometime in the small hours of the night and remembers how uncomfortable the woman had been, talking about her employer. Toward the end of the interview she had hesitated before answering a question about the Millers' relationship and Laughton had made a note that she was probably holding something back.

'She'll tell you the Millers weren't as happy as she previously implied,' Laughton says. 'She'll tell you they argued sometimes, maybe quite bad arguments. I think she almost told you in the first interview but she was still being loyal and professionally discreet. Now the news has broken that her boss was having an affair and was also an infamous scumbag, I imagine she no longer feels the same need to protect him.'

Tannahill smiles. 'Maybe I'll tell her not to bother coming in then, seeing as you already know what she's going to say.'

Laughton shrugs, already tired and wrung out from the day. 'I'm just thinking out loud.'

They stare out of their respective windows, the siren filling the silence between them as the driver continues to thread his way through the gridlock.

'I wish I could have one of these all the time,' Tannahill says. 'Usually it's either bus, Tube or bike.'

'What are the new leads?' Laughton says.

'OK, first, the DFT have managed to extract the serial number of the laptop the killer used to store the photographs and email them to Slade. It's an old Compaq model, bought as part of a large consignment for a U-based limited company that's no longer trading. The company's assets were sold at a liquidation auction, which unfortunately means the purchase trail goes cold at that point. Want to have a guess what the name of that company was?'

Laughton thinks for a moment, then shakes her head.

'It was SunnySet, the company Mike Miller ran when he was still Mark Murphy. It won't help us catch our man, but it will help convict him once we do catch up with him. But we've also found another SunnySet connection. After the first murder we ran a check on the medals we found balanced on Kate Miller's finger and found one of the ribbons was wrong. It was actually the ribbon from a VC – the Victoria Cross, highest award for bravery. They're so rare, only one hundred and eighty-two were issued in the entire Second World War. The last surviving recipient, a merchant seaman called Cyril Lawson, died just over a year ago in less than heroic circumstances.'

Laughton nods, already seeing where this is heading. 'He died in a SunnySet care home.'

'He did, and his grandson was not at all happy about it – guy called Neil Lawson, fifty-three. He was one of the plaintiffs in a big class action lawsuit suing both SunnySet and Murphy personally for huge damages and compensation on the grounds of gross negligence, industrial manslaughter, financial misconduct, a whole heap of grievances. Then Murphy vanished with all the cash – end of civil case, lot of seriously pissed-off people including one Neil Lawson, also ex-army, who saw two active tours of duty in Afghanistan before being demobbed as part of the austerity cuts. Also his wife divorced him two years ago citing irreconcilable differences and incidents of domestic violence. He's been picked up twice for brawling, several times for D and D, and once for vagrancy when he was found living in his car. Each time he got fines and suspended sentences, but there's definitely a pattern there. His combat experience also means he's been trained to kill.'

'Everyone in the military is trained to kill,' Laughton replies, 'few ever do.'

'True, but our man here did. On his last tour his unit was ambushed outside Kandahar and apparently Corporal Neil Lawson's rifle jammed but, get this, he managed to battle his way to safety using only his knife, killing one of his attackers in the process by stabbing him repeatedly.'

'Jesus! Any idea where he is now?'

'Currently of no fixed abode. "London" is the closest guess we have so far, based on the fact that the vagrancy pinch was in Acton. His name has also popped up a few times at a couple of British Legion shelters in South London, though nothing more recent than two months ago. We'll find him. He had the advantage when he was flying under the radar, but now Mike Miller's been crossed off the list he's our main person of interest so we're throwing everything we have at finding him. He certainly has the motive and the means. Judging by the two bodies, he also found the opportunity.'

Laughton continues to stare out of the window but is no longer seeing the blur of the outside streets. She's lining up the new information with what she already knows, looking for the patterns, the points of connection, and also the gaps. 'What about Kate Miller – what was his motive for killing her?'

'I don't know. Hopefully he can tell us when we find him.' He looks up ahead. 'Listen, we're nearly there – if you want, we can drop you off at Kentish Town Tube.'

Laughton thinks about the day stretching ahead of her. Her first lecture isn't until after lunch and she's too tired and too frazzled to re-engage with any of her ongoing research projects.

'Or you can hang around the station for a bit and sample the delights of police vending-machine coffee,' Tannahill offers, seemingly reading her mind. 'You can sit in on the interview with the cleaner if you like, see if your prediction is correct.'

Laughton sees Kentish Town Tube up ahead and growing nearer. In her mind the gaps and the questions continue to swirl. Stepping away from the investigation won't change anything. Not really. It will only ever give her the illusion of separation. Those newspapers with her name in them will still be stacked at the feet of a corpse. The stories inside them will still be true. She can deny her past all she likes. But she can never, ever change it.

'Exactly how bad is this coffee?' she asks, turning to Tannahill.

He smiles. 'You'll see,' he says.

51

Slade gets the Uber to drive slowly past the old police station, still not sure if he's going to go anywhere near it yet.

He studies the building as they cruise past, four storeys of ugly brick and concrete occupying a whole block of prime London real estate. The Dubai-based property development company that bought it had already submitted plans to knock it down and turn it into thirty-two super-deluxe flats. In the meantime it lay empty.

Except it clearly isn't.

Flags and other sheets of mismatched material hang across many of the windows like makeshift curtains, and as they swing round the block for a second pass a young, petite woman in what looks like a nurse's uniform slips out of the big, black front door and bundles herself into a parka as she hurries away down the street.

'Pull up ahead of that girl,' Slade tells the driver, and the car stops a few feet in front of her.

Slade slides out of the back seat, a friendly smile fixed on his face, and steps up to the young woman. ''Scuse me, miss, did I just see you come out of that building over there?' The woman looks up at him suspiciously. 'It's just I was given this address to drop off a package for a guy called Adam.' He holds up his bag as if it contains something. 'I thought I must have it wrong because that building looks empty, but then I saw you coming out.'

'Oh,' she relaxes a little. 'Yeah, no, it's not empty. There's about forty of us living in there. We're property guardians. We live there and pay cheap rent and stop squatters from moving in.'

'Oh right. Sounds like a good deal.'

'It's all right, apart from the shared toilets, they're pretty minging.'

'I bet. So do you know Adam?'

'Er yeah, I mean I've spoken to him a few times. I don't know if he's in or not, but you could go and ask. There's still people in there, if you want to knock. Sorry, I gotta go, I'm going to be late for my shift at the hospital.'

'Yeah, of course, no worries. Thanks.'

She hurries away and Slade turns around and heads back to the old police station.

Health workers at one of the capital's major hospitals having to effectively squat in a disused police station because they couldn't afford London rents. If he worked for a different newspaper and gave a shit there was probably a story in that.

He reaches the big double doors and the ghost of a memory surfaces of standing in front of them when he was about seven or eight. The building seems smaller now, shabby and pathetic. He reads the sign fixed to the door:

> VANGUARD
> WARNING!
> **GUARDIANS**
> IN OCCUPATION

He looks for a doorbell, finds none, then hammers on the door with his fist.

Guardians! Made it sound like the place was protected by

a squad of cape-wearing superheroes. He hears footsteps approaching then the door opens and a man with a pale, narrow face peers out.

'I'm looking for Adam,' Slade says.

The man continues to stare blankly back at him.

'Are you Adam?'

'No,' the man says. 'Adam's not in.'

'Right. Well, can I come in and leave him a message?'

The man stares at him for a long beat as if he hasn't heard the question then says, 'Only licensed people are supposed to come into the building. It's one of the rules.'

'Yes, of course.' Slade glances back at the sign on the door. 'I work for Vanguard. That's why I need to talk to Adam. It's about his licence. If you could just let me in and point me in the direction of his room, I can leave him a message.'

'Don't you have his phone number?'

'Yes, we . . . er . . . the number we have on record doesn't work. That's what I need to talk to him about. He's not in trouble, I just need to sort out his paperwork.'

'Right.' The man nods and seems to consider this carefully before finally pushing the door a little wider. 'OK then.'

'Thanks.' Slade musters a smile and steps quickly through the door before slowpoke can change his mind.

52

Celia Barnes sits in the same featureless interview room in Kentish Town police station with what could be the same cup of tea in front of her. She stares at the island of bubbles turning slowly in the centre of her tea, but in her mind she's back by her father's bed in the care home.

She remembers the nurse laying her hand gently on her shoulder, telling her he'd gone and giving her some documents to sign – release documents for the funeral directors, she'd said. Celia remembers letting go of her father's cold hand for what would be the last time to sign them, then sitting there while they removed his body, lifting him from the bed and on to a trolley. That was when she saw the sores on his legs and back, angry red blisters that had burst in some cases and stuck to the sheets.

They look worse than they are, the nurse had said, hastily covering them with a sheet, though she hadn't looked her in the eye when she'd said it. *Very common among the very old and bedridden.*

Celia had said nothing, too shocked and emotionally wrung out from the long days and nights sitting vigil by her father's bedside, hoping he might wake one last time so she could say a proper goodbye. And now he was dead, so what did it matter? What was the point of causing a fuss and making an already raw situation even more painful? So she had signed the papers and said nothing.

When she was growing up there had been a piece of embroidery framed above the fireplace. Her mum had made it when she was a girl. *The meek shall inherit the earth*, it said. Celia saw those words every day and thought it was like a secret message from God, telling her to keep quiet, not make a fuss and ultimately she'd be rewarded. Only that wasn't true, was it? The meek don't inherit the earth, they just get pushed about by everybody else. It was a lie, the meek inherit nothing, it's the devils who get everything. They always do.

Celia pictures the sores again, skin ulcers where her dad's body had been in contact for so long with the sheets of the bed he died in, and all the while her sitting right next to him and meekly doing nothing about it.

. . . They look worse than they are . . . Very common . . .
But that had been a lie too, hadn't it?

She stares at her tea, the cluster of bubbles like the centre of a sunflower and reminding her of the logo on the documents she signed.

SunnySet – the company that had a policy of getting grieving relatives to sign legal disclaimers while they were still in shock to protect them from any future legal action. The same company that had still been sued by hundreds of angry relatives in a coordinated civil suit which came to nothing after some clever restructuring deal Celia didn't really understand that meant they came away empty-handed, while the owner got off with millions in the bank and no personal liability.

SunnySet – Mike Miller's company. The company he had built up then sold for all the money that had paid for his golden life. She had ended up cleaning the house of the man who had squeezed the life savings out of her poor dad as he lay dying. She *should* have done more, made a fuss, or asked some questions, dared to be awkward for once in her life rather than meekly letting things drift by.

The door to the interview room opens and she looks up at a tall, dark man and a short, blonde woman. She recognizes the woman from the papers. She has an odd name, Leyton or something. The man looks like he might be Italian and her mind flashes back to Commissario Brunetti. He introduces himself and the woman – Laughton, that was it – and asks her if she needs anything. He has very blue eyes that Celia finds it hard to meet. They sit down opposite her and the man presses the button on the bulky recording device bolted to the wall and a red light comes on. He checks the time on his phone.

'The time is ten twenty-six a.m. on Wednesday the sixteenth of September,' Tannahill says. 'This is a follow-up witness statement from Mrs Celia Barnes in relation to case number 45201/D. Present are DCI Tannahill Khan and Doctor Laughton Rees.' He looks up and smiles.

'You told PC Eades on the phone earlier that you'd remembered something, something that happened between Mr and Mrs Miller a few weeks ago, something you thought might be important.' He speaks slowly and softly, like he's being careful not to startle her. 'If you could tell us what you remember, take your time and give as much detail as you can.'

Celia cradles her tea with both hands and stares down at the scarred tabletop.

'Well, like I said on the phone, it was something I didn't mention before because, well, I suppose I forgot about it, I mean it wasn't anything really. It happened about a month or so ago. It was a Friday, definitely a Friday morning, and it was still warm, like at the end of summer,' she looks up. 'Maybe you can look up when the last sunny Friday was so you can get a date, but I'm almost entirely sure it was in August.'

Tannahill smiles. 'We'll check. Carry on, you're doing brilliantly.'

'Anyway, I let myself in with my key and headed for the stairs, ready to start work. That's when I heard voices, down in the basement. Angry voices.'

'Did you recognize these voices?'

Celia nods. 'It was Kate and Mike. I stayed in the hallway. I didn't mean to eavesdrop or anything but . . . their voices were raised. I'd never heard them like that with each other before.'

'Did you hear what they were arguing about?'

Celia shakes her head. 'I didn't really want to listen, truth be told. I started tidying a bit – nervous habit, I suppose – and there was this envelope lying on the little table next to the stairs. It had been torn open, so I picked it up thinking it was rubbish, but there was something inside it, a scrap of an old newspaper. Then I heard someone coming up the stairs so I put it back down, hurried over to the front door and closed it loudly, you know, like I'd only just come in. I suppose I didn't want them to know I'd heard them. Silly really. I thought it might . . . embarrass them. They were always so private and . . . Well I mean, couples argue all the time, don't they, it's part of married life. It's nothing unusual. Except . . .' She shakes her head and frowns. 'I should have told you before, after what happened to Kate, I don't know why I didn't really. I think I was worried you might get the wrong idea about Mike, think that he was an angry or a violent person when it was just that one time. But then, all those things in the papers, about how he made his money, and those awful homes. It makes you realize . . . you don't really know someone at all, do you?'

She looks down at the floor, tears brimming in her eyes.

'It's OK, Mrs Barnes,' Tannahill says gently, 'we understand why you didn't tell us before and we're very grateful you've been brave enough to come forward now; it must have been very difficult for you. Just take your time, you're being very helpful.'

Celia nods and dabs her eyes with a tissue before continuing. 'Anyway, like I say, Mike came upstairs and he was all smiles when he saw me, like everything was fine and well. I started work and by the time I made it back up to the ground floor the envelope was gone and I forgot all about it. But now I think it was that envelope and what was inside it that had caused the argument.'

'Why do you think that?'

'Well, like I say, I couldn't hear them properly, but one thing I did hear was a name. It wasn't a name I recognized, and it didn't mean anything to me at the time, but with everything that's happened since I've realized what it was.' She pauses and stares at her untouched tea.

'Was the name O'Brien?' Tannahill prompts. 'Shonagh O'Brien?'

Celia shakes her head and looks up at Laughton, the tears back in her eyes. 'It was McVey. The name they kept saying was McVey, and the scrap of newspaper in that envelope was a piece of an article about what he did to your mum.'

53

Entering the disused police station gives Slade the strange and uncomfortable sensation of stepping back in time. It brings back memories, sudden and clear, of the last time he came to this place when his dad was still working here.

The entrance lobby is almost unchanged, the only difference being the collection of bikes and scooters propped up against one wall and a large SAVE THE NHS poster covering most of the screen where the desk sergeant sat. The walls still have the standard government-issue pale green paint on them and corkboards with old Crimestoppers and Neighbourhood Watch posters stapled to them.

Slowpoke leads the way through a door with a sign saying BOOKING into a large room where the daily arrests were once processed that has now been set up as a kind of communal living area with bean bags, and a large table made from pallets, and mismatched sofas that look like they've all been fished out of skips. An old pub pool table occupies one corner, its baize so threadbare it shines under harsh fluorescent lights that hum along the water-stained ceiling that someone has tried to disguise by draping strings of coloured bunting across it.

'Nice,' Slade says. 'What's your name, by the way?'

'Ben,' Slowpoke replies after his usual pause.

'Do you know Adam at all, Ben?'

'No. Not really.'

'No? You don't hang around in here of an evening, shooting pool, having a laugh with all the other . . . er, guardians?'

'No. Most people here work at the hospital, nights mainly, so . . .'

'Right.'

Blimey, right barrel of laughs this dude was.

They move through another door into a windowless corridor with more bunting trying valiantly to cheer up a place that was deliberately built to scare the crap out of people. One end of the string is tied to a key sticking out of an old-fashioned, wooden control panel with coloured lights and various labels like TAPE INTERVIEW ROOM ALERT, and PANIC BUTTON. The other end of the bunting is tied to a dart sticking out of a dartboard next to a large poster saying MAKE ART NOT WAR. Someone's tried, God bless 'em, but there is nothing cosy or welcoming about this place, particularly for Slade. It all just reminds him of his dad.

They pass through another door into a stairwell and start heading down to the basement past a sign saying HOLDING CELLS with an arrow pointing the way.

'Adam's room is down here, is it?' Slade says, still trying to warm up his host a little in the hope that he might reveal something useful.

'Yep.'

'Draw the short straw, did he?'

'What?'

'You know, most people try and avoid spending a night in the cells.' Slade smiles but Ben doesn't.

'They're the best rooms,' he says. 'The cells are private and quiet. Some of them even have toilets.'

'OK. Great! Toilets! Fancy.'

They reach the bottom of the stairs and pass a large holding cell now being used as a laundry room with lines of bedding hanging from clotheslines that criss-cross the room. They move past it and through a security door that has been jammed open with a fire extinguisher into a corridor lined with metal doors with letter-box-shaped slits at eye-level with sliding metal panels covering them. Each one has a locker-type keypad where the keyhole used to be. Makes sense. Much easier and cheaper to reset a door code every time someone new takes up residence, rather than hand out keys these idiots would probably lose.

They keep walking, through another security door, and into another row of cells. One of the doors is open, and Slade gets a glimpse inside – pale green walls, single high window letting in light from street level, concrete shelf along one wall that could either be a wide bench or a narrow bed.

Another memory surfaces, one that takes him by surprise because he'd buried it so deep he'd forgotten about it. He remembers his mum dragging him here and having some kind of row with his dad. His granny had taken ill and his mum couldn't get anyone to look after him so she told his dad he needed to watch him for once.

His dad's mates had all laughed, which had pissed him off even more, so he'd locked him in an empty cell to show what a hard case he was, then carried on doing whatever the hell it was he did for eighteen hours a day, seven days a week, that made him come home pissed and angry every night.

He'd cried and shouted to be let out and someone had gone to fetch his dad, who'd told him if he cried again he'd throw the next nonce they nicked in there with him.

After a few hours in there he'd needed to piss so badly he'd done it in the corner of the cell rather than call out again. There were no toilets in the cells in those days. When his mum finally came back to collect him, his dad gave him such a belt for pissing in the cell that his mum never left him with his father ever again. That had probably been his plan all along, be the shittest father and husband you could possibly be, then no one would expect or ask anything of you.

His dad was the reason he hated the police so deeply. And his hatred for Commissioner John Rees was not because he'd fired his dad a year short of his pension, it was because George Slade absent at work and occasionally drunk and violent at home was one thing. But George Slade at home, bitter and washed up, vodka in his tea every morning, chain-smoking himself to death and making everyone around him as miserable as he could, was another thing entirely. Firing George Slade for being a violent arsehole might have been in the interest of the force and the general public, but it did bugger all for him and his mum.

'This is Adam's room,' Ben says, pointing at a door at the far end of the corridor where the lights flicker queasily.

'Blimey. Popular chap is he, this Adam?'

Ben frowns. 'What do you mean?'

'I mean his room isn't exactly in the prime location, is it?'

Ben shrugs. 'Listen I've got to go to work, so . . .'

'Right, yeah, you go for it. Actually, just wait one sec.'

He bangs his fist on the cell door to double-check there's no one in before Captain Personality leaves him alone down here. The sound of it echoes away down the empty corridor. No one answers.

'Thanks again for your help,' Slade says, then watches Ben amble away down the corridor, his white trainers squeaking on the concrete leaving Slade alone with the flickering lights and his own sour memories. He waits until he passes through the security door and it closes behind him then twists the handle next to the keypad.

The door is locked.

Of course it's locked.

He tries sliding the plate across on the viewing grille but that won't budge either. He tries to wiggle it loose but it feels like it's welded in place. He examines it to see if there's something wedging it in place and sees drips of hardened liquid oozing out from under the plate. Slade picks at it with his fingernail but it's as solid as the steel door.

Superglue. A whole tube by the looks of things.

Somebody doesn't want anyone peeking inside and this makes Slade want to peek even more. He tries the handle again, shoving the door with his shoulder at the same time in case it was stuck.

Definitely locked.

He stands back and stares at the door, his mind working overtime now as he wonders what might lie beyond.

Who are you, Adam? What are you hiding in here?

Then it hits him with the same rush of realization he felt when he watched Mike Miller's face morph into Mark Murphy's. The number on the email wasn't half a phone number at all.

He pulls his phone from his pocket, finds the last email from justice72@yahoo.com and carefully copies the number into the lock, pushing each button home with a solid, mechanical click. He enters the final number then twists the lock and feels it open. He glances back up the corridor one last time, checking no one is there.

Adam's not in, Ben had said.

Well, OK then.

Slade pulls the cell door open and looks inside.

54

Tannahill raps on a door and opens it to find a startled woman behind a desk with wide, magnified eyes behind her reading glasses.

'Sorry,' Tannahill says, holding up his warrant card, 'Is there a terminal in here I could borrow for a few minutes?'

'Oh here' – she gets up from behind her desk clutching the copy of *OK!* magazine she was secretly reading when they burst in – 'use mine, I was just heading off for a break anyway.'

She taps her keyboard to log off then heads for the door. 'All yours,' she says brightly, stepping out into the corridor and away towards the entrance in search of nicer coffee.

'Right,' Tannahill collapses into her still-warm seat and taps in his log-in details. 'Let's see if we can find any connection between either Mike or Kate Miller and the McVey case.'

Laughton pulls another chair over and sits beside him. 'We should focus on Kate Miller,' she says, 'we already know quite a bit about Mike Miller, and there's no obvious connection.'

Tannahill logs into the central case file database. 'OK, so we know Kate was married to Mike Miller, so she must have known him back when he was Mark Murphy. Maybe we can find out who she was by looking at him.'

He taps *Mark Murphy SunnySet* into the search field, hits 'enter' and a small page of results appears on screen.

'I was expecting more,' Laughton says, looking at the short list of files. 'I thought it was a big case.'

'It was, but it only became a police matter after he disappeared. Everything before that would have gone through the civil courts and the various local health authorities. I can put in a request for all the files, but there'll be hundreds of them and, from experience, it will take a while to get hold of them; local health organizations have even fewer resources than we do.' He opens Mark Murphy's missing persons file and starts scrolling through the usual collection of documents that build up on every investigation – police reports, witness statements, photographs.

'Do we know who was defending Murphy in all these civil cases against him?' Laughton says. 'Our killer is fixated on justice, so that might be a good place to start.'

Tannahill clicks through to the end of the file where the interviews are filed and runs down the list. 'Here we go, phone interview with retained counsel for Mark Murphy and SunnySet Limited, Ruth Cottington-Bray QC.'

Laughton catches her breath and sits back in her chair.

Tannahill turns to her. 'What?'

'Ruth Cottington-Bray was the barrister who defended Adrian McVey. She's the one who got his case thrown out.'

'Charming client list she kept. Let's see what she had to say about Murphy.' Tannahill opens the document and they both skim-read the transcript, the barrister's impatience and reluctance to say anything radiating off the page like static as she responds to every question:

No, I had no idea Mark Murphy was going to abscond.
No, he has not been in contact with me.

313

No, we have no outstanding business with him and therefore no longer consider him a client.

No – I have no idea of the current whereabouts of either him or Kathryn Warren.

'Who's Kathryn Warren?' Tannahill scrolls back up to the summary report at the start of the transcript.

Interview with Ruth Cottington-Bray QC of CBC Law (the law firm retained by Mark Murphy) regarding his disappearance and also of Kathryn Warren – lead member of the legal team representing Mr Murphy – who disappeared on the same date.

'*Cherchez la femme*' Laughton murmurs. 'Is there a photo of her?'

Tannahill jumps to the Appendix and finds the media tab where all the photos are archived. Warren, K., is not there. He opens Google and does an image search for Kathryn Warren and thousands of results come back – social media profile pics, actor head-shots, several realtor sites, even a couple of gravestones.

'Add Adrian McVey to the search,' Laughton suggests.

Tannahill types it in and the results come back again. The images are now mostly of pages taken from high school yearbooks and group graduation photos where both names appear on separate photographs. But there is one photograph on the third row that stands out and Tannahill looks at Laughton when he sees it.

'Are you OK?' he says tentatively. 'I can finish this on my own if you like, there's no need for you to—'

'It's fine,' Laughton cuts him off. 'I'm fine. Open the image. Let's see it bigger.'

Tannahill clicks on the picture and it opens in another window, almost filling the screen.

It shows a crowd of people standing on the steps outside the Old Bailey Central Criminal Courts in London. Adrian McVey stands in the centre, head down, eyes watchful, thinning hair scraped neatly across his freckled scalp. On his right a bewigged, strident-looking woman appears to be mid-statement, her arm pointing at McVey but her attention directed at the unseen press. On McVey's other side stands another, younger woman, her long, dark, almost black hair framing her face and matching the dark, well-cut suit that accentuates her athletic frame. Laughton takes her phone, finds a photograph of Kate Miller on one of the news sites and holds it up for comparison. Despite the obvious difference in hair colour and some subtle changes around the mouth and nose, it's the same person.

Kate Miller is Kathryn Warren.

'That's the connection,' Laughton says, sitting back in her chair.

Tannahill deletes McVey from the search field, adds Mark Murphy and gets pages of results back, mostly showing Kate and Mike Miller back when they were still Kathryn and Mark, leaving various legal buildings, heads down, suits on, briefcases in hand. Tannahill clicks on the first image and a page opens – *The Daily* again – the article outlining the ongoing multi-million-pound compensation case against Mark Murphy and identifying the woman with him as Kathryn Warren, a rising star in the world of high-profile and contentious defence cases with a reputation built on the foundation of successfully defending 'Masked Monster' suspect Adrian McVey.

'Charming couple,' Tannahill murmurs. 'She keeps paedophiles out of jail and he kills old people for profit. They were made for each other.'

Laughton nods. 'What's your suspect's name again?'

'Lawson,' Tannahill replies, 'Corporal Neil Lawson. Looks like he killed Mike Miller because he was responsible for the death of his war hero grandfather, and he killed Kate Miller because she helped him get away with it then ran off to live the high life on all the cash he'd made.'

Laughton frowns as she thinks it through. It makes sense, mostly. 'Why send them the newspaper cutting in the post?'

Tannahill shrugs. 'Maybe he wanted to rattle them, let them know he knew who they were and where they lived. If that was his plan, it worked. You heard that witness: the Millers never argued, but they were arguing when they got that cutting.'

Laughton nods. 'Makes sense. It also ties in with the heightened, performance nature of the crime scenes: Mike Miller being forced to die in the same way his care home residents did, lying in his own filth and covered in bedsores. And Kate Miller arranged like the symbol of blind justice she was supposed to serve but clearly didn't.'

'You've got to admire it on some level,' says Tannahill. 'I mean, I know it's not the kind of justice we're supposed to applaud or uphold, but I bet you'd be hard pushed to find a single person out there who didn't think these two deserved what they got. I'm almost tempted to sit on all this and let him get away with it.'

Laughton smiles, then frowns as something new occurs to her. 'I don't think he expects to get away with it.'

Tannahill thinks for a moment, then says, 'The medals.'

'Yes. Why leave behind such a specific clue? He must have known it would eventually lead us to him. You think maybe he's setting himself up for suicide by cop?'

'I hope not, though he's obviously in an extreme mental state and I can imagine there's also a large degree of bitterness there. You serve your country, it turns you into a cold, efficient killing machine, then you come back home and find you don't belong. Not only that but that same country lets your war hero grandad die of neglect in a care home and the

316

authorities can't even bring the people responsible to justice. I looked up Lawson's grandad, by the way. He was the only merchant seaman to win a Victoria Cross in the Second World War. The ship he was skippering got hit by a torpedo a few hundred miles south of Greenland. It was carrying eight thousand tons of phosphate, so basically it was little more than a floating bomb. By rights, the ship should have been instantly vaporized, but for some reason the torpedo didn't go off; it pierced the hull and sat there ticking as the ship got pounded by the Atlantic.

'Captain Lawson evacuated his crew, but night was falling and the weather was awful and getting worse. He realized they were unlikely to survive the night in the lifeboats, so figured he had nothing to lose, jumped over the side with nothing but a rope and a crowbar, and basically set about whacking the torpedo until it either blew up or fell into the sea. Luckily for him, it was the latter. After that the crew came back on board, they patched the hole the torpedo had made, and sailed into port on schedule. Unbelievable bravery. And then he ended up dying of neglect in one of Mike Miller's grotty care homes after signing over everything he'd worked his entire life for to pay for his shitty treatment.' Tannahill shakes his head. 'I hope we find Neil Lawson alive, I really do. I'd love it if he got to tell his story.'

The door opens and they look up expecting to see the woman with the big glasses and a large Starbucks in her hand wanting her office back.

But it isn't her.

There's a moment of awkward silence, when nobody even seems to breathe. Then the man standing in the doorway looks over at Tannahill. 'Could you give us a moment, please,' he says.

Tannahill looks at Laughton, then back at Commissioner Rees.

55

Slade stands in the corridor, studying the cell through the frame of the open door. The room is barely larger than a garden shed with a neatly made narrow bed running along the left wall, and a stainless-steel toilet in the far-right corner, shining dully from the weak light streaming in from a single window set high in the back wall. The only thing that gives any indication that someone lives here is a battered book lying on the floor next to the bed.

Slade moves into the room, wondering why the mysterious Adam felt the need to superglue the door hatch shut when there's nothing to see. Maybe it wasn't him. Maybe it was a previous resident with a chronic porn addiction and no self-control.

He leans down and picks up the book. The black leather is worn from years of handling, and whatever title it once had has been completely rubbed off. He flips it open and snorts when he sees what it is.

It's a bible.

Of course it's a bible.

It never ceases to amaze him how the lowliest, poorest, most pathetic people are always the ones who spend their lives on their knees thanking God for the shitty cards he's dealt them. You didn't find too many millionaires or billionaires with old bibles by their beds.

He sees that some of the pages have been marked, the corners folded over in a way he felt pretty sure God would not approve of. He turns to one and sees a line of scripture that has been neatly underlined in pencil:

Lo, children are an heritage of the LORD; and the fruit of the womb is his reward.

He turns to the next marked page and finds another highlighted line:

And all your children shall be taught of the Lord; and great shall be the peace of thy children.

OK, so our mysterious Adam apparently has a child fixation and is looking for godly approval.

He turns to the next one, which is in the first book of the New Testament, so Jesus has now joined the cast.

At the same time came the disciples unto Jesus, saying, 'Who is the greatest in the kingdom of heaven?'

And Jesus called a little child unto him, he set him in the midst of them.

And said . . .

. . . whoso shall receive one such little child in my name receiveth me.

There's another one on the next page:

Jesus said, 'Suffer little children, and forbid them not, to come unto me: for of such is the kingdom of heaven.'

And he laid his hands on them, and departed thence.

Slade flips through the rest of the pages to see if there's anything else, then back to the front cover to see if there's an inscription or a name of the owner, but there's nothing. He places the bible back down on the floor, adjusts it so it's in the same position he found it, then turns around, wondering what all this has got to do with his story, and shock makes him step back and almost fall on to the bed.

Invisible from the outside corridor, the fourth wall is covered with hundreds of photographs, bits of paper, and news cuttings. Some are yellowed with age, others have been ripped from more recent editions. They are arranged in concentric circles with the older items at the furthest edges and the more recent ones in the centre. Slade sees familiar faces in the ragged collage – Mike and Kate Miller, Commissioner John Rees, Adrian McVey being led out of the courtroom, as well as photos of all of his alleged victims. But the person who appears the most, starting as a girl on the outer circles and growing into womanhood the closer she gets to the centre, is Laughton Rees.

Slade takes a step closer to the wall, his eyes fixed on the most recent image, ripped from the front page of that morning's *Daily*, fragments of his article still visible around the photograph he had chosen as the lead image. He had picked it because the pap who had taken it had surprised Laughton and that look of surprise on her face made her seem out of control, and young, and totally unequal to the job of being part of a major murder investigation. But now, here in this bleak and unsettling room, the photo takes on a new dimension. Here she looks scared, her eyes staring out not at the photographer but at the man who has clearly nurtured a long and intense obsession with her.

Slade reaches out and lifts up the ripped edge of the photograph to see what lies underneath, what previously occupied the literal centre of this man's attention. It's another photograph, but not one torn from a newspaper. This one has been taken using a decent camera with a long lens. It's of Laughton again but this time she's not alone. Standing next to her is a young girl, slightly shorter, longer hair but other than that identical. There's another photo next to it, just of the girl, her head turned slightly and looking back at the camera as if she knows she's being photographed. Written across the bottom of the photo in round, childish handwriting is a single word – GRACIE.

Slade pulls out his phone and starts taking pictures. He'll have to report all this, unfortunately, but he'll make sure he gets an exclusive in return: exclusive on the arrest, exclusive interview with Laughton, who won't be able to refuse this time because she's part of the investigation team. He'll be able to stay ahead of the pack with that lot for days as well as writing a few unaccredited hatchet pieces on the side just for fun – The Daily *solves murder mystery and brings the killer to justice while the police do nothing* – that kind of thing.

He steps back, takes a wide shot of the whole wall and notices an archive box tucked in the corner and partially covered by torn-up newspapers that make it blend in with the background. He takes a picture of it then crouches down, carefully removes the newspapers then takes off the lid.

'Jesus!' Slade murmurs, raising his phone so he can take a picture of the object staring back at him from inside – a child's mask of a unicorn, with the eyeholes enlarged.

He lifts it out and studies it. Writing about Adrian McVey and the Masked Monster murders had given him his first front page, so he owes that twisted fuck a lot, as does this guy, apparently. He places the mask down on top of the newspapers and peers back into the box.

Three old school exercise books lie on the bottom, each with *Suffer little children* written on the cover in the same round, childish handwriting as on the photo. He picks up the top one and opens it. Printed on the front page is – *Property of Honor Oak Park Primary School* – with a name and a date scrawled underneath.

Adrian McVey, 3 August 2005

Shit! This was written a month before McVey was arrested, back when he was still just an anonymous creepy janitor at a South London school. Slade flicks through the pages, his eyes scanning words crammed tight between the lines, as if the book can barely contain them. He spots a name he recognizes in amongst the dense text:

Matilda Jones – I didn't know her name at the time – but God gave her to me one sunny afternoon.

Jesus! Matilda Jones was the third victim of the Masked Monster.

She was plump and pale, like a peach, a fat, ripe peach fallen from heaven right into my open hand. Parents so rarely understand the true power of the gift they've been given in a child. You just have to see how they ignore them in the playgrounds and at the school gates. By taking their children I am actually giving them a gift. A wonderful gift. For only when their child is gone do they really appreciate the precious thing they once had. Suffer the children to come unto me. And how that soft, pink peach did bruise.

Slade blows out a long breath.

McVey had never admitted to being the Masked Monster, so if these were real, if these were genuine, then it could be the biggest scoop of his life. It was like finding proof of who Jack the Ripper really was.

He grabs the next exercise book and leafs through it. More dense text. More confessions. More creepy details.

Pure gold!

He grabs the third book and doesn't even bother looking inside. He just needs to get out of here fast, call the police so they can arrest Adam and start work on the bigger story of tying him to McVey before revealing that McVey had been the Masked Monster all along. It was a perfect domino story, one thing leading to another, each thing bigger than the last with the confessions contained in these exercise books as the jewel in the crown.

He could serialize them over weeks, months even, put facsimiles of the pages up on *The Daily* website, a new one every day to string it out. Or better still he could hold most of them back and write a book. Fuck the paper, he found these diaries, they were his property now. He could probably get a six-figure deal for a book proving McVey was the Masked Monster, seven even; people went nuts for true crime stories these days and there was no bigger modern-day story than this.

He stuffs the exercise books into his bag, takes a few more pictures, then attaches all the photos to an email and sends them to himself as backup. He checks he has signal and the email is sending then switches to video and starts doing a video pass of the cell.

He starts with the same view he'd had when he came in so he can replicate the shock reveal of the wall, which will play well on the website. He frames the whole room first then moves closer to the bed, lingering on the bible lying on the floor for a few seconds before moving right, past the toilet and round for the grand reveal.

Jesus! – Slade jumps again, not because of the shock of the wall, but because someone is standing in the doorway.

His body floods with adrenaline, then he realizes who it is and laughs with relief.

'Don't be creeping up on people like that, dude – you nearly gave me a heart attack.'

Ben stands silently in the doorway, his white trainers held loosely in his left hand.

'Turns out the door was unlocked,' Slade says, stopping the recording and getting ready to go again. 'Thought I'd just do a room check while I was here,' he turns around, holds his camera up and re-frames the room 'Actually, if you could just step out of the way a second so I can get a clean pass, that would be great.'

He starts recording again, holding on the view of the whole cell first before moving closer to the bible. He holds on it for a few seconds and something niggles at the back of his mind.

The trainers. Why is he holding his trainers in his hand?

The sudden bang on his lower back jolts the camera.

'What the fuck?' Slade spins round, angry that another take has been ruined. 'What are you . . .'

His words trail away.

Ben is no longer Ben. The unicorn mask over his face has transformed him into something else, something inhuman and terrifying.

The trainers squeaked, Slade realizes as he backs away, reaching for the spot on his side where he was hit and feeling something warm and wet. *He took them off so I wouldn't hear him coming back.*

He looks down at the trainers and sees the knife in the other hand just as his legs hit the bed and he falls backwards on to it.

'How did you find me?' Ben asks, his voice different too, lower and colder.

Slade shakes his head, confused. 'You,' he says, pointing up at him and seeing the blood on his own hand. 'You sent me emails.'

'No,' Ben says, dropping the trainers and clamping his hand over Slade's mouth.

'No, I didn't.'

56

John Rees stands silently by the door for a moment. His daughter looks up at him, her face unreadable. She looks so like his wife that it almost unmans him and he wheels a chair over from another desk and sits opposite her before he collapses to the floor.

'Sorry for the . . . ambush,' he says. 'I thought if I tried to arrange anything formally you would just refuse.' He pauses for her to say something but she remains silent.

'Listen . . . after your mother died we never really got to talk about – anything . . . You ran away from me and I left you alone because, well I thought that was what you wanted. And I . . . I just wanted to give you what you wanted.' He shakes his head. 'I only ever wanted what was best for you. I know you may not believe that, and that's OK. But it is true.'

He takes a breath and looks down at a spot somewhere in the space that separates them. He can't look at her, not directly, being this close is almost too much after so many years of distance.

'I was very pleased when you decided to consult on this case. I wasn't sure you would. I *hoped* you would. I've read everything you've written, followed your career and I'm . . .

I'm so, so proud of you and what you've become. Again, I know you probably don't care, but . . . There was always one thing that puzzled me. I always wondered why you chose not to go into frontline policing. I concluded that perhaps it was me, that you didn't want to have to work for me, even distantly. That's why I wanted to talk to you now.'

He looks up at her again and sees his wife staring back at him – same eyes, same heart-shaped face – and has to immediately look away. He clears his throat.

'This afternoon I'll be announcing that I'm stepping down as chief commissioner, effective immediately. I wanted to let you know in advance in case it has a bearing on any decisions you might make about continuing your work on this investigation or further. I heard this morning at the crime scene you were having doubts.' He holds his hand up against an objection that doesn't come. 'I wasn't spying on you; people just tell me things whether I ask them to or not . . . The thing is, if my position was in any way a factor in your career choices, then I wanted to let you know that, as of lunchtime, that will no longer be an obstacle.'

He looks up at her again, forcing himself to face the person he both loves and feels he has let down most in the world. He takes a ragged breath, ready to speak again. He wants to tell her so much, how he misses her every day, how he bears the cross of his failure through every waking moment, that he too has never forgiven himself for his part in her mother's death, but it's too much to say and this is not the time. 'I hope we have another chance to talk sometime,' he says. 'I hope we find the time, somehow.'

Laughton swallows and her eyes gloss with tears but he can see she's fighting them back. She opens her mouth to speak, and is on the point of saying something when the door opens behind him and a squeal of surprise shatters the moment.

'Oh, I'm so sorry, I didn't realize . . .'

Rees turns to the woman, who instantly drops her magazine when she sees who it is.

'It's OK,' Laughton says, finally breaking her silence. 'We're done here.'

Rees turns back to her, but she is already up from her seat and halfway to the door.

'Thanks for the use of your office,' she says to the flustered woman, 'you can have it back now.' Then she slips through the door and is gone.

57

Shakila checks the time on her phone.

The morning editorial meeting is about to start and Slade is nowhere to be seen. Normally when one of his stories is the lead he likes to be there to suck up all the plaudits, dick that he is. But he's not answering her calls or emails either, which is odd considering he'd given her a list of people to find and instructions to pass on any information the moment she got it. She also knows how time-sensitive an unfolding story is; every second counts, which makes his radio silence even more peculiar.

She tries him again. Straight to voicemail. She chews her lip and thinks.

If he doesn't show up soon she'll have to stand in for him and, as he never tells her anything, she's going to look like a total idiot, which might actually be his plan.

She scooches round his twatty, elevated desk and opens his emails to see if she can find any clue as to where the hell he's got to. She scrolls down to the last one Slade opened and catches her breath when she sees who it's from.

She opens it, frowns at the cryptic contents, then googles the address and gets the same results Slade got an hour earlier.

When he'd said he was going to a police station she'd thought it was just another one of his crappy jokes. Still, at least she can tell the rest of the editorial team where he is now. She spots an unopened email from Slade that came in ten minutes ago, clicks on it, and a series of photos start to download.

Her eyes flick up to the conference room where people are already beginning to congregate, then back at the screen where a photo of an empty jail cell is now being joined by one of an old bible lying on a scuffed, concrete floor. Then the third photo appears, the hi-res image gradually coming into focus as the data streams in, and Shakila's eyes go as wide as the ones on the unicorn mask in the picture. She knows what this means, she did all the background research for the article on Laughton Rees.

'Where's old golden bollocks then?' The voice makes her jump. She spins round and almost collides with Trevor Nolan, the crime editor, whose smile drops the moment he sees the look on her face. 'You OK?'

'Look,' Shakila points at the photo of the mask on the screen. Below it another photo is coming into focus, a wide shot showing the cell wall covered in photographs and news-paper clippings.

'What is this?' Nolan says.

'Brian sent them about ten minutes ago,' Shakila says. 'He went off somewhere after the killer emailed him.'

'Show me.'

She opens the email from justice72. Nolan reads it and chews his lip. 'Did he go to this address?'

'Yes, I think so. He ordered an Uber and said he was going to the police station and to send bail if he missed the editorial meeting. I thought he was joking, but . . . I haven't been able to contact him since.'

'Ah Jesus.' Nolan picks up the desk phone. 'Go and grab

330

Michael and get him to look at this stuff and start working it up into a story.'

He stabs a button to get an outside line and dials 999.

'Brian's going to bloody kill me for this if I'm wrong.'

58

Tannahill leans over the laptop showing a live feed from the lead Trojan unit entering the disused police station in Chelsea. He was too far away when the call came in to get there in time but at least his carte blanche on resources has given him this real-time, ringside seat.

Chamberlain and Baker watch too as the wobbly body-cam on the lead officer shows the front door opening and the shocked face of one of the residents shaking his head then pointing into the building in response to a question.

The unit moves on, through the reception and into what used to be the booking room, where more shocked faces shake their heads and point.

The unit pushes on along a corridor, into a stairwell, then down to the cells on the lower level, overlapping the whole way as they cover and move, their rifles pointing the way ahead.

On the eighth floor of New Scotland Yard Rees also watches as he pulls things out of his desk drawers and dumps them in a box. He hasn't told any of his staff he's going. He just wants to disappear without fuss the moment the press conference is over.

He opens another drawer, pulls out a laptop and drops it into the box, along with a photograph of him standing next to the Queen, and another of Grace holding Laughton when she was about two. Both of them are laughing.

On the screen the lead Trojan unit makes it to the basement and starts working its way down a dimly lit corridor past steel doors with metal hatches. Rees did a six-month stint in this police station back when he was still in uniform. It doesn't seem to have changed much at all.

The live feed from the body-cam settles as they reach the end of the corridor and a black-gloved fist bangs hard on the steel cell door.

'OPEN UP! POLICE!!'

There is a pause then the same hand punches a code into the numerical lock and, after a count of three, the door is pulled violently open.

Tannahill leans closer as the door swings wide, and the body-cam jerks around as the Trojan officer enters the room and rapidly sweeps all four corners to check it's clear.

In the blur of movement Tannahill sees something.

'There's someone in the bed,' he murmurs, as the camera swings back to settle on it.

'HANDS WHERE I CAN SEE THEM.'

The shape on the bed doesn't move. It is covered in a sheet, like a body in a morgue.

The black glove reaches in, grabs the sheet and pulls it back.

The man is lying on his back, blood soaking the bed, his face covered by a child's unicorn mask. The officer on scene shouts for someone to call an ambulance but Tannahill can see it's already too late. Behind the mask the man's eyes are open and lifeless.

The mask is left in place now this is a crime scene, but Tannahill doesn't need to see the face to know who's lying there. He recognizes the bald head and the running gear, and it was his editor at *The Daily* who had called this in.

Brian Slade. Now a lead character in his own story.

'LOOK AT THIS,' a voice calls out, and the camera swings round to show the wall opposite the bed.

Tannahill, Chamberlain and Baker lean in to the screen as the camera takes a moment to adjust to the gloom. Up on the eighth floor of New Scotland Yard, Commissioner John Rees does the same.

The aperture on the body-cam finally settles to reveal the whole of the back wall with the photographs, and the news-clippings of Adrian McVey's victims arranged in concentric circles. And there at the centre, like a bullseye in a target, the picture of Laughton Rees.

59

Laughton is in the lift, heading down to her first lecture of the day, when her phone rings.

She sees that it's Tannahill and answers it just as the lift doors open.

'Where are you?' he says. It sounds like he's running.

'About to go into a lecture, why?'

'I'm sending someone over right now.'

'What? Why?'

'There's been a development. Slade's dead.'

'Jesus!'

'Listen, where's Gracie?'

Laughton stops walking and her mouth goes dry. 'At school, why do you need to kn— what's happened? Tell me what's happened.'

'What school?'

'St Mark's in Holloway.'

'What's the security like there?'

'Jesus, there's gates and fences, I don't know. What's going on?'

'Slade got another email with the address of a disused police station and a name – Adam. He went there looking for him and was killed. In the cell where we found his body there was a kind of shrine to Adrian McVey and his victims. There was also a picture of you and Gracie.'

'Jesus Christ no, Jesus.' She starts running.

'Look, I'm sending a unit to you right now and another one over to Gracie's school. Just stay where you are and you'll be fine. Stay where you are, OK?'

Laughton hangs up, bursts out of the entrance and carries on running.

If someone's coming for her daughter then she needs to get to her first.

She finds the number for St Mark's in her phone and calls it, the cold autumnal air already feeling sharp against her heaving lungs. Ahead of her she can see a couple of Citi-Bikes in the stand, which means she can be at the school in ten minutes, maybe less. She looks around as she runs, everyone suddenly a potential threat.

The phone connects. 'St Mark's?'

'Hi, this is Gracie Rees's mum,' she says, speaking fast between breaths. 'I need someone to urgently fetch her out of lessons, please. Have her wait in the office until I get there. I'll be about ten minutes.'

'What is this regarding, please?'

Not today. Not today. She can't deal with the stone-faced jobsworths on reception today.

'Just pull her out of her lesson and get her to sit in the office. I'll explain why when I get there, which will be in about . . .'

'Wait a minute, please.' The call cuts out and is replaced with some jazzy hold muzak.

Jesus Christ, this BLOODY school.

She makes it to the Citi-Bike stand and punches in her code to release the lock but the solar-powered control panel, always slow to respond, seems glacial today. Laughton looks around again, checking everyone, not even sure what she's looking for.

'Mrs Rees?'

'Yes.'

'Gracie isn't in school today.'

'What!?' Laughton's stomach clenches like a fist. 'No, she's. She . . . she left for school at the normal time this morning.'

'Well I've just checked the register and she's marked down as absent.'

The world goes white for a moment and Laughton has to hold on to the bike to stop herself from collapsing. Then the control panel beeps and jolts her back to the present.

Gracie isn't at school.

Gracie is in danger.

She needs to find her.

Nothing else matters.

Nothing.

She yanks the bike out of the dock and hangs up without another word. She dials Gracie's mobile with one hand while turning the bike around to point up the road toward home.

If she's not at school, she must be home.

That's all this is.

She's bunking off school, and who can blame her.

No one at home is going to threaten her with a knife.

Oh God, please let that be true.

The phone connects without ringing and Gracie's voice tells her to leave a message.

Her phone is switched off.

Laughton catches her breath and tries to focus. She opens Find My iPhone and waits for her listed devices to load. Gracie's phone is located 0.8 of a mile away up the Holloway Road.

She *is* at home.

Thank God, she's only at home. Home is nearer than school. It's going to be OK.

Laughton throws her phone into the basket and kicks down

hard on the pedal, pushing herself forward and swerving off the path and into the bike lane.

Five minutes and she'll be there.

Tannahill holds on to the roof handle to stop the speeding squad car throwing him around too much in the back. His free hand is clamping his phone to his ear.

'St Mark's?'

'Hi, this is DCI Tannahill Khan. There's been a security alert raised for one of your pupils, a Gracie Rees.'

'Oh! I was just on the phone to her mum. She's not here.'

Tannahill's grip tightens as they chicane through a crossroads, weaving through the stopped traffic.

'OK, thanks.'

He hangs up and shouts to the driver. 'Change of destination. Head to London Metropolitan University instead.'

'No worries,' the driver shouts back. 'It's all in the same direction anyway.'

Tannahill braces himself against the seat, something niggling at the back of his mind.

I was just on the phone to her mum, the receptionist had said.

When he'd spoken to Laughton she'd said Gracie was at school, but she clearly wasn't. And now Laughton knows this too because she had just spoken to the receptionist. He opens his contacts and looks up the entry for Laughton where he'd copied her phone numbers and home address.

'Sorry, mate, can we go to Fairview Mansions, N7 instead?'

'We can go wherever you like, sir.'

'Fairview Mansions then, final offer.'

Tannahill settles back in his seat. He'd told Laughton to stay put but she wasn't the type to sit still and do nothing, not when her daughter's safety was at stake.

338

And the second she'd found out her daughter wasn't at school she would have done what he is now doing. She would head for home and hope she was there.

Laughton throws the bike on the ground next to the entrance to Fairview Mansion and grabs her phone from the basket. A sensible, civilized voice in her head tells her she should lock the bike or at least bring it into the building, but there's no time. She'll pay the fine if someone steals it, and happily, just so long as Gracie is OK.

Please let her be OK.

She lets herself in and stabs the button for the lift – three times – then runs for the stairs because she isn't physically capable of standing still while she waits for it. Her legs are tired and her lungs burn but she throws herself up the stairs three at a time because three is the safe number. Her flat is right at the top of the building on the sixth floor, a multiple of three. Safe again.

Please let it be safe.

She counts the steps in threes as she drives herself up them, collecting them like lucky charms.

3 – 6 – 9 – half landing.

3 – 6 – 9 – first floor.

By the time she makes it to the top of the building she's almost in a trance conjured from her fear and exhaustion. She pulls her key from her pocket and stumbles down the hallway to her front door, still counting her steps and adjusting her stride to make sure the last step to her door is another multiple of three.

She unlocks the door and pushes it open.

'Gracie!!'

No answer.

'GRACIE? You in?'

Her bedroom door is shut, but it's always shut.

She almost knocks from habit but opens it instead, happy to weather the storm of outrage if all she finds in the room is her angry daughter with headphones on.

The room is dark but Gracie is there. In bed. Tucked up. Safe.

Thank God.

'Gracie!' She moves into the room and sits on the edge of the bed. Then she notices the packets on the floor among the mess. Empty blister packs maybe twenty of them. She picks one up and reads the label.

LIQUID PARACETAMOL CAPLETS 500MG

'GRACIE!'

She is shaking her now, pulling the covers off, trying to wake her.

Gracie moans but does not rouse.

How many has she taken. Thirty? Sixty?

She looks at the blister pack again and sees that there had been sixteen pills in it, not a multiple of three, so not safe, Oh God, not safe at all.

She yanks Gracie over into the recovery position, opens her mouth and jams her fingers inside. Gracie gags but nothing comes out and Laughton howls in misery and helplessness.

She has failed to protect her daughter. She is now failing to save her.

She pushes her fingers deeper into her daughter's mouth, knowing it's a hideous invasion but having no choice. Then footsteps behind her make her head jerk round as a man rushes through the bedroom door and comes straight at her.

For a moment she panics.

The front door.

She left it open.

She has let this man in, just as her father let McVey in. She is not her mother, she never was her mother, she is her father after all.

Then the man drops down next to her and she sees who it is.

'What happened?' Tannahill says, his face dark with concern as he looks down at the girl in the bed.

'Pills' – Laughton holds up the blister pack helplessly – 'she's taken some pills and she won't wake up. I can't make her wake up. Help me wake her up, please. Please help me wake her.'

VI

THE UNICORN AND THE LION

Extract from *How to Process a Murder*
by Laughton Rees

I have written extensively here about the various intellectual and clinical techniques and processes of a murder investigation, but there is one other element that is essential to every investigation – courage.

The successful execution then prosecution of any murder enquiry requires enormous reserves of courage. It requires the investigator to gaze upon things, both physical and psychological, that we are hard-wired to turn away and run from.

To catch a killer you have to be brave. You have to confront all the nightmare, fairy-tale horrors you were warned against from childhood. You have to enter the abandoned house, the night-time forest, the dank basement, and not only search for the horrors that have been left there, but also follow the footprints that you know will lead to the monster. And then you will have to dig deeper still, to find your lion heart within, in order to face down these primal monsters of your childhood.

60

News of the third victim lands just before lunchtime.

As usual the ladies of the Highgate Book Club WhatsApp group eagerly share the links then discuss it. But they do not debate this one with quite the same shocked enthusiasm as the previous two murders. Maybe it's because they knew the Millers – kind of – and so felt more emotionally invested in what happened to them and why. It's much harder to feel anything much for a dead tabloid journalist, other than a vague sense that he probably deserved it.

And it's not just the ladies of Highgate who greet this latest plot twist with far more muted enthusiasm. In the league table of victims a tabloid journalist ranks much, much lower than an apparently tragic, attractive blonde woman in a mansion, and a central casting villain like Mark Murphy. This latest death seems off message somehow, not obviously connected to the main narrative of the SunnySet scandal, like an unconvincing plot twist in a previously excellent TV show.

The killer also has a name now, Neil Lawson, though the police are not calling him the killer yet, not exactly. What they're saying is they wish to speak to him to help with their enquiries, but everyone knows what that really means. But even this development has the effect of weakening the drama rather than enhancing it. Before, when he was a nameless, faceless, violent psycho, everyone was terrified. Now he is just a man with a pedestrian name and a sympathetic backstory, an avenging angel of a grandson seeking justice for his war hero grandad who'd died in one of SunnySet's appalling care homes. And that's not scary at all.

There is still the ongoing narrative of the bungling police to enjoy, of course, three deaths now and still apparently no closer to catching the killer. The papers are all piling in on that angle too, not surprising, given that one of their own has now been slain by this person the police can't catch.

Commissioner John Rees is due to make a statement at one with an update on the case, and, in an intriguing though seemingly unrelated development, his estranged granddaughter was also apparently rushed to hospital unexpectedly that morning, though, disappointingly for those hoping this might signal an exciting and unexpected twist, this is not being treated as suspicious.

61

Gracie Rees – pale, stable, sedated – is wheeled into a private room in the Kensington wing of the Chelsea and Westminster Hospital.

Laughton follows and watches the nurses adjust Gracie's bed, her meds, the temperature of the room. They are professional, efficient, calm. Laughton doesn't feel calm. She feels numb, like she's been scooped out and is watching all this from a distance while a small, accusing voice continually whispers in her head—

This is your fault.
  You did this.
    You allowed this to happen.

Outside in the corridor, Tannahill is talking to a uniformed officer, his face furrowed and serious. The officer nods a lot. Tannahill pats him on the shoulder then enters the room.

'Hey.' He smiles at Laughton then looks across at Gracie as one of the nurses adjusts the drip in her arm. 'We had her moved here because this wing is less public, more secure, and much easier to guard.' He points a thumb over his shoulder at the open door. 'Sergeant Harris will be on duty from now 'til nine, then a replacement will take the night shift through 'til six, when someone else will take over, so there's always someone outside the door. I'm assuming you'll want to stay here too?'

Laughton nods.

'Good. It's better for us. Easier to guard you both when you're in the same place. If you need anything from home we can arrange for someone to get it for you. You'll be guarded round the clock until we find this man, OK? You'll both be safe here.'

Laughton stares down at her daughter and tears stream uncontrollably down her face. She doesn't look safe. She doesn't look safe at all.

'Listen,' Tannahill steps closer and lowers his voice. 'We've found Neil Lawson.'

She looks up at him.

'Wait, it's not as good as it sounds. Turns out he was already in Wandsworth jail on a battery charge. He'd given a false name when they booked him because he knew he'd get a longer sentence if his actual record was taken into account, and his fingerprint check was still sitting in the booking sergeant's in tray so we had no idea we already had him until he heard on the news that we were looking for him and decided a murder charge was worse than 'fessing up to giving a false statement. He's been in jail for the last seven days, which means he couldn't possibly have murdered Kate and Mike Miller – or Brian Slade. He has the perfect alibi.'

Laughton nods. She is so wrung out that she can't even properly react to this news. She has no emotion left. She is empty. 'So who did kill them?'

'Well, according to the other guardians, the person who occupied the cell Slade was found in is one Adam Evans. No one knows much about him at all. He was your bog-standard, keep-himself-to-himself kind of character. He did choose to sleep in one of the old cells, which everyone thought was a bit weird. That's where we found Slade. Listen, why don't you take a seat?'

'Why?'

'Just take a seat.'

Laughton sits down, though what could be more shocking or devastating than what she's already been through today she can't possibly imagine.

'We also found three journals in the cell.' Tannahill sits down next to her and leans in so he can keep his voice low. 'Two of which appear to have been written by Adrian McVey.'

Laughton closes her eyes and shakes her head. Of course. This is the worst moment of her adult life, so of course he's there somewhere, lurking in the shadows.

'These journals, well they're pretty incendiary,' Tannahill continues. 'We're going to try everything we can to contain them, but there's a chance Slade may have sent some of the details through to *The Daily* before he was killed.'

'What's in the journals?'

Tannahill takes a deep breath before continuing. 'They outline, in detail, exactly how McVey stalked, captured and killed Eloise Fraser, Matilda Jones, Isabella Morrison, and Ruby-Mae Brown. So despite all his life-long protests and his slippery defence team, Adrian McVey *was* the Masked Monster all along.'

Laughton sits back in her chair. She doesn't feel anything about this news either. It's like the trauma of the morning has left her incapable of feeling anything. She always knew McVey was a monster, so the fact that he was also *the* monster doesn't mean that much to her.

'What about the third journal?' she says. 'You mentioned there were three.'

'Yes, the third journal was written by Adam Evans. Seems he was quite the fan of McVey, had been since he was a kid, can you believe. He writes about how he *admired* him because he dared to carry out the things he could only fantasize about.

351

'Anyway, when McVey was sent to Broadmoor, Adam volunteered there, purely to get close to him. They became quite the master and apprentice, it seems. In the journal Adam writes about how McVey taught him that, far from being wrong, his feelings and fantasies towards children were "sacred". Then, after McVey found out he had cancer and knew he was dying, he encouraged Adam to carry on his work and set him a task, a kind of rite of passage. He asked for a sacrifice. To prove he was worthy, Adam had to kill you – that was the price of entry. Then he could kill Gracie – that was his reward.'

Laughton looks over at her daughter, feeling helpless and wretched.

'I'm sorry about all this,' Tannahill says softly. 'I was wrong about the case. It *was* about you all along.'

'What about Mike and Kate Miller?' she whispers. 'How do they fit in?'

'Well, Kate Miller, or Kathryn Warren as was, was apparently hated by McVey. In one of his journals he goes into great, ranty detail about how his defence team set him free but ruined his life in the process by leaking his identity. He thought they should have done it another way so he could have kept both his freedom and his anonymity. He wanted to punish Kate for what she did and apparently got Adam Evans to send her death threats from him. This probably also contributed to Kathryn Warren becoming Kate Miller and riding off into the golden sunset with her scumbag Prince Charming.

'What's also clear from the journals is that McVey was obsessed with his legacy and hated the fact that the papers hardly ever mentioned him or the Masked Monster any more. We're thinking now that killing Mark Murphy, as well as extracting the security access he needed to get in the house was also a way of stoking the fires of tabloid intrigue and getting people talking about McVey again. That's why he sent

Slade the photos and why he left the old newspapers behind featuring Masked Monster stories. It was so that when you were eventually murdered the Masked Monster would be front-page news again. And I suppose he will be, for a while at least, so he got that wish. But he didn't get his main one; you're safe here now. No one can get at you in here.'

Laughton nods then looks at her daughter. 'She's not safe though, is she.'

'What do you mean?'

'She's lying in that bed because of me. She's lying there because I didn't listen to her, or hear her cries for help. She's lying there because I'm a terrible mother. Who's going to protect her from me?'

Laughton looks up as a woman in surgical scrubs steps into the room. She smiles at her and Tannahill and says, 'Are you Mum and Dad?'

'Oh, er, no.' Tannahill stands up and moves away from Laughton as if their proximity was what was confusing things. 'I'm just . . . I'm a work colleague. I was just going actually.' He turns to Laughton. 'We'll talk again later, but do not blame yourself for this. This is not your fault, OK. Call me if you need anything. I'll let you know of any further developments.'

Laughton watches him go, the door closing slowly behind him, then turns to the doctor who sits down opposite her.

'So you're Mum?'

'Yes, I'm Laughton. Gracie is my daughter.'

'OK, hi. I'm Doctor Hames, the on-call emergency surgical registrar. I was in the emergency room when we treated Gracie. Your daughter took an overdose of paracetamol and we performed an emergency gastric lavage to flush out as much of the drug as possible, and also orally administered activated charcoal, which helps bind any residual paracetamol in the stomach to stop it from entering the bloodstream. We then administered a sedative to calm her down and help her recover.

How much do you know about paracetamol poisoning, Mrs Rees?'

Laughton hasn't got the energy to correct her. This woman just saved her daughter's life, she could call her whatever she liked. 'A little,' she says. 'I know it affects the liver.'

'That's right. When too much paracetamol is present in the body the liver can't cope and starts metabolizing it via an alternative pathway. This produces a toxic metabolite called NAPQI, which the liver struggles but ultimately fails to detoxify. It can lead to liver damage, even failure. The reason I'm telling you this is because we took some bloods from your daughter to see if there were any of the molecules present we associate with the kind of liver damage we typically see in acute cases. I am sorry to tell you that we did find these molecules in your daughter's blood.'

'What!? But that can't be right. She only took the pills a few hours ago.'

'Well, her blood suggests she has been ingesting high levels of paracetamol for much longer. Clinically she's presenting as what we would term a staggered overdose.'

Laughton is floored. She can't process what the doctor is saying.

'What does that mean?'

'It means your daughter has been taking high levels of paracetamol for an extended period. Has she been showing any signs of anxiety? Depression? Moodiness?'

Laughton thinks.

Yes, of course she has, all of the above. She's an angry teenager. All teenagers are moody, aren't they, and she's been having a terrible time recently with school and everything, but not like this. Not this level bad. This is . . . she doesn't know where this has come from.

She flashes back to when she stole into her daughter's room the night before so she could search her bag for a knife. She remembers picking her way through the mess on the bedroom floor, the clothes, the tissues, the empty food . . . and painkiller packets. She had been so focused on one thing she hadn't even noticed the real danger lying right there on the floor beneath her feet.

Oh my God.

How could she have missed it?

How could she have been so blind and let her daughter down so badly?

'In terms of treatment, we have put your daughter on a course of intravenous acetylcysteine to help counteract the effects of the toxins,' the doctor tells her, then adds, 'A member of the mental health team will be along later to talk to you about why she may have attempted to take her own life.'

How is she even having this conversation?

Because she's a terrible mother, that's why.

She'd known her daughter was miserable, but rather than listen to her she had made her own mind up about what was wrong and how to fix it. She had ignored her daughter, and this was the result.

She looks up at the doctor, aware that the woman has just said something but, yet again, she hadn't been listening.

'Sorry?' she says.

'I was just saying that I have a daughter myself and know that, if I was in your shoes, I would want to know the truth about her situation. So I need to prepare you for the fact that your daughter is not out of the woods yet, not by a long way. She is still very poorly and there's a possibility her liver may already be too far gone to save. So we might be looking at a transplant – assuming we can find a suitable donor. All we can really do in the meantime is hope for the best but prepare for the worst.' She lays a hand on Laughton's arm. 'Please know that Gracie is getting the best medical help there is, of that I can absolutely assure you.'

62

Commissioner John Rees stands in his dress uniform, staring at his reflection in a toilet mirror for the second time in less than forty-eight hours. The lighting is slightly softer this time, emanating from some unseen source behind the mirrors. He still looks old, though. Old and tired.

He glances down at the single printed sheet in his hand, the resignation speech written for him by the Home Secretary's press office. It had been sent to him less than an hour after his meeting, suggesting it had already been written before the meeting even took place. It is short, to the point, and has been crafted in such a way as to make it sound like he's stepping down voluntarily because he's decided he's gone as far as he can in the job. He had attempted to rewrite it a little, mentioning the urgent need for more resources and not just a new commissioner so that he would be vindicated when those resources were eventually announced. He'd sent his amended draft back to the Home Office for the press secretary's approval. The response had been to return the original with a note: *We'd prefer to run with this version*.

Rees checks the time and a numb sadness settles on him as he realizes this will be his last official duty as Commissioner of the Metropolitan Police. His free hand automatically reaches

356

for the pills in his pocket, closes around the hard plastic bottle and he starts to unscrew the cap then stops. This pain he's feeling now is not the kind the pills are designed to ease. This is something else, something he wants to feel.

He takes his hand out of his pocket, fits his cap on his head like a soldier readying himself for the firing squad, and walks out to face the press.

The Home Office press room is too bright from the TV lights and warming up with the sheer number of people present. Every seat is taken, the late-comers forced to stand at the back, jostling for position and being tutted at by grumpy cameramen keen to protect their lines of sight. The stage is the only part of the room that remains clear.

The Home Office press room does not usually host crowds of this size, but word has spread that something big is being announced and, like sharks sensing a fish in distress, they've been drawn in, hoping this will turn out to be a meal big enough to satisfy them.

There is a murmur in the room, a ripple of energy from somewhere that makes camera shutters click and heads turn. An anonymous male Home Office staffer opens the door next to the stage and stands aside to let others file through. The news cameras reposition and another staffer steps through the door, a young woman this time but equally anonymous.

The assembled journalists shuffle restlessly, worried they might have misread the whispers. Usually the importance of a press conference can be gauged by the calibre and seniority of the first people who enter the briefing room – the more senior they are the bigger the announcement – but these people are nobodies. There is a moment of hesitation, a pause where everything seems to stutter and stall, then Commissioner John Rees walks into the room and everyone snaps to attention.

The dry whisper of camera shutters ripples through the

room and the TV cameras hold their wide shots until Rees settles behind the lectern centre stage before crash-zooming in to catch the beginning of his announcement.

The more senior correspondents already know what's coming. The only reason someone as senior and powerful as the Commissioner of the Metropolitan Police would hold a press conference here instead of New Scotland Yard and be preceded by such lowly staffers is because he's not that powerful any more and is just about to announce it.

Rees places the single sheet of paper on the lectern in front of him. Looks up at the eager, expectant faces and the bright TV lights.

'Full house,' he says, and a shallow wave of nervous laughter ripples through the room. Rees spots Bill Nicholson from the *Telegraph* sitting in the front row. He's not even smiling, and Rees can see in the serious set of his face that he already knows what's coming.

Six floors above, Nixon sits in his office, a laptop open on his desk showing a live feed from the press room. His chief adviser Tom Kenwright stands next to him, a printed copy of Rees's speech in his hand. On screen Rees glances down at his copy then back up at the room.

'You're all aware of the ongoing crisis regarding violent crime,' he says, 'especially knife crime in the country as a whole and particularly in the capital. I know you're all aware of it because you're the ones who keep reporting it in such outraged detail.'

Another ripple of laughter.

Kenwright looks up from his copy of the speech. 'He's going off script a little.'

Nixon nods and stares at the screen. 'He's just warming them up, give him a chance.'

In the press room Rees waits for the laughter to die down. He glances back down at the collection of spin-doctored sound

358

bites that make up his speech and his eyes drift up to the Home Office seal on top of the page and its French motto: HONI SOIT QUI MAL Y PENSE – *Evil be to he who evil thinks*. A needle of pain skewers through his gut and he grips the edge of the lectern, steadying himself until it recedes enough for him to look back up.

'Let's be honest,' he says, 'this is not the first time I've stood before you like this, dressed in my best uniform, to deliver some carefully worded speech about how the police are cracking down on this or that. We also know that, regardless of what I tell you and whatever assurances I give, you'll go away and write whatever you want to write anyway.' Outright laughter passes through the room this time. 'Generally, it'll be something along the lines of "the police are losing control of our streets", "Crime wave sweeps the nation", "the Commissioner needs to go" – that kind of thing. And the truth is, you're right. We *are* losing control of the streets. A crime wave *is* sweeping the nation. And so maybe I do need to go.'

A murmuring rises up in the room and Rees pauses a moment as a band of pain tightens across his chest. He grips the edge of the lectern and squeezes it hard.

Up on the executive floor Kenwright frowns at his copy of the speech. 'None of this is what we agreed.'

'Hmmm,' Nixon murmurs, as on the laptop screen Rees takes his own copy of the speech from the lectern and holds it up.

'This was written for me by the press office of the Home Secretary. I could read it to you, but the basic gist is I'm supposed to apologize for all the current failings in police policy, say something about how I've realized I've reached the end of the road and that a new broom is required, then tell you how it's been a privilege to serve before announcing I'm stepping down.'

Rees looks up.

'That last bit is true, by the way, it really has been a privilege to serve. Then, after I've spoken these carefully chosen words, I'm supposed to shuffle off to a nice, cushy job that's been set up for me at Shield Group, where I'll be paid a lot of money to do pretty much nothing, and you guys will no longer get to throw rocks at me on a regular basis. And all I have to do is read this speech and go quietly. Sounds tempting, doesn't it? Got to be a catch?' He waves the piece of paper. 'Unfortunately, this is the catch. Because I can't do it.'

He lets go of the sheet of paper and it flutters to the floor.

'For one thing I can't, in all conscience, go and work for an organization I consider to be part of the problem. If we really want to start tackling crime in this country, the first thing we have to do is strip Shield Group and all the private companies of their government contracts immediately. Public service should be about one thing: serving the public. It should not be about keeping shareholders happy. If the billions spent annually on these private contractors was put back into police budgets, then we'd have a fighting chance of doing our jobs more effectively, because, like everything else in life, you get what you pay for. I hate to think how much of my time in office has been spent in meetings arguing for more money, more resources, and constantly being told there isn't any, that we'll just have to try and do more with less. But then this morning the Home Secretary himself informed me that actually there *is* more money – four hundred and fifty million pounds, to be precise.'

Up on the executive floor Nixon throws himself backwards in his chair. 'You bastard!'

Kenwright folds his copy of the script into a tiny square. 'Can I assume, sir, that Commissioner Rees's name should be taken off the New Year Honours list?'

Rees moves out from behind the lectern now. 'He told me he'd met with the Prime Minister and the Chancellor of the Exchequer and they'd agreed to the budget hike I've been arguing for ever since I took up the post of commissioner almost eight years ago. Only I'm not supposed to tell you about it because they want to wait until the spring statement to announce it when it's politically advantageous. And the reason I'm breaking ranks and telling you about it now is not because I want to claim any glory for it, it's because we need that money now – kids are killing themselves on our streets today.

'You all know the latest crime figures, you've all been covering the Miller case and writing about how bad knife crime has become and how something urgent needs to be done – and you're right, something does need to be done. But if we really do want to solve the problem of knife crime in particular, we need to tackle the causes of it, not just focus on the end results and punish the perpetrators. We need to look at where crime comes from in the first place.

'We live in a society where poverty levels have been increasing for a decade and food banks have become normal, and when kids go hungry they will try to feed and look after themselves any way they can. For most, with limited opportunities and almost no resources, this means dealing drugs and joining gangs. Add to this the generational breakdown of families, the systematic closing of youth centres and other youth initiatives that traditionally provided a focus and instilled a sense of community, and you are creating the perfect breeding ground for an entire generation of kids with no options and an almost feral instinct for personal survival.'

Pain tightens across his chest and he throws his hand out to the side, grabbing at the lectern for support as he struggles for breath. He looks back up at the room, fills his lungs with as much air as he can and continues.

'Instead of giving billions to companies like Shield Group to lock people up, we should be putting that money into things that will stop these kids from needing to be locked up in the first place. We need to invest in people. We need to help rebuild communities and families. People are not born criminals. It's society that makes them so, and that's all of us, from government down. *We* are society. And if *we* genuinely want to make society better, then we all need to take responsibility and stop looking for someone else to blame. There is no "them" and "us". There is just "us". We are all in this together.'

The pain explodes in his chest, eclipsing everything – the room, the people in it, everything. Rees tries to move back behind the lectern to grip it with both hands and try to ride out the agony. He manages a step, knocks into the lectern and upsets the delicate balance he was only just managing to maintain. The lectern twists and wobbles, his grip slips and he collapses heavily to the floor.

Camera shutters click. The TV cameras zoom in.

Upstairs on the executive floor Nixon leans forward in his chair, watching it all unfold, his politician's brain already spotting the possible spin.

He turns to Kenwright, a hint of a smile on his shiny face.

'I think we can use this,' he says.

63

Night creeps back over London.

People on their way home, the late workers and the cheeky pint-ers, pick up their free copy of the *Evening Standard* from the piles left next to the ticket barriers, glance at the headlines then riffle through the rest of the paper, looking at pictures of houses they can't afford, filling the minutes before their trains arrive to take them home to the cheaper suburbs where they will eat something, then try and get some sleep before they have to do it all again.

In the Chelsea and Westminster Hospital white blinds are pulled down over night-blackened windows. An orderly does the rounds with a drinks trolley, handing out herbal teas to patients to help them sleep and coffee to the staff to keep them awake. The weary day shift hands over to the night, and medical information and gossip is exchanged. Because of its central position in the city, and the private facilities in the Kensington wing, there's often a celebrity or public figure to report. Today it's the Met Police Commissioner, rushed here after collapsing earlier and now in room 302. Laughton hears two nurses talking about it in the corridor outside Gracie's room.

Gracie has still not woken. The doctors tell her this is a

good thing and Laughton tries to believe them. The body heals itself best when that's all that it's doing, they say, so let her sleep. Yes. Let her sleep. But please God let her wake too.

Laughton looks up in response to a tap on the door and sees the eager face of the constable stationed outside the door. She forces a smile and waves him in.

'Just wondered if you fancied a brew,' he says. Behind him a skinny man in a green orderly's tunic stands expectantly by a drinks trolley.

'Oh. No thanks.'

He nods and she watches the door slowly close behind him, the number 322 above Gracie's name written on a printed sheet.

The nurse had said that her father was in room 302.

They were on the same floor.

She looks back at her sleeping daughter, the tube in her thin arm connected to a bag of clear liquid giving her saline, and glucose, and the drug to counteract the toxic effects of the paracetamol.

She looks so small.

Laughton stands and stretches to squeeze some of the tension from her back. Through the window in the door she can see the orderly with the drinks trolley opening another door down the corridor: 326. Her father's room must be in the other direction.

She looks back down at Gracie, watches the gentle rise and fall of her chest for a moment, this tiny and precious proof of life. She shakes her head, like she can't quite believe something she's just heard or thought, then she blows out a long breath, quietly opens the door and steps out into the corridor.

The sergeant looks up and moves to get out of his chair, but Laughton holds up her hand to stop him. 'Just stretching my legs,' she says. 'Will you keep a close eye on her for me?'

'Of course.' The constable holds up his cup. 'Black coffee, two sugars – should keep me nice and sharp until the morning shift takes over.'

She smiles. 'I'll only be up the corridor. Shout if you need me.'

'You got it.'

She heads along the corridor, following the decreasing room numbers past the nurses' station and around the corner where the floor becomes carpeted and the pictures on the walls a little bit nicer.

At the far end of the hallway another uniformed police officer sits on a two-seater guest sofa reading the *Evening Standard*. He looks up as Laughton approaches, eyes watching her over the headline:

Suspect in SunnySet murder case released without further charge

'I'm not supposed to let anyone in,' he says stiffly, lowering the paper to reveal a drooping grey moustache that makes him seem sad and disapproving.

'I'm not anyone,' Laughton says.

He'll know who she is. Her picture is on the front page of the paper he's just been reading. They stare at each other for a long few moments then he seems to relax and deflate a little.

'OK, five minutes' – he jerks his head at the door to room 302 – 'but don't touch anything.'

'Thank you,' Laughton says, then opens the door and steps into the room.

Her father lies in an elevated hospital bed, hooked to various machines that record and monitor the flicker and pulse of his life. Just like Gracie, he has a tube in his arm hooked to a bag of clear fluid but, unlike Gracie, he also has an oxygen mask covering his face.

She steps forward, pulls his medical chart out of the metal well at the foot of his bed and scans the single page of notes and drugs dosages recorded in a hurried and spidery hand. Her medical knowledge is limited and largely involves corpses, so the information on the page reveals little about what is wrong with him. It might as well be written in Mandarin.

'Heart disease.' The voice makes her jump.

She looks up into the half-open eyes of her father. 'Idiopathic Dilated Cardiomyopathy, if you want to get technical.' The oxygen mask makes his voice sound muffled. 'Terminal, unfortunately. Come into the light so I can see you.'

Laughton hesitates then places the chart back in the well and moves closer. He looks much older and greyer than he did earlier that day. He also looks small, like Gracie does. Maybe everyone lying in a hospital bed is diminished somehow.

'I got a doctor friend to check me over because I was feeling tired all the time, and my ankles started swelling up and then I fainted a couple of times. He discovered that I had an enlarged heart. I thought he'd give me some pills and tell me to stop eating red meat, but instead he told me I had only a fifty per cent chance of living another five years – and that was over a year ago.'

Laughton sits in the chair next to his bed. 'Is there anything they can do?'

'I could get a transplant. I'm on a list for one, but apparently healthy hearts are incredibly scarce. The doc gave me some meds to ease the symptoms and some diuretics to stop my lungs filling with fluid, and I made him promise not to tell anyone how ill I was. I'd helped him out when his eldest son had got into drugs and a few bits of trouble, so he owed me a favour. Thing that annoys me most was that I always ate everything you're supposed to eat, ran for miles every day, and yet here I am.' He looks down at the tubes coming out of his arms and the ECG monitor beeping softly next to him. 'Guess the cat's out of the bag now.' He looks across at her, the oxygen mask fogging with his every breath. 'I heard what happened with Gracie. She going to be OK?'

Laughton freezes in the headlights of his question, a question she hasn't dared ask herself because she's so frightened of the answer.

'Her liver is damaged,' she whispers, so quietly it's like she dare not say the words in case she makes them come true. 'They're trying to stop it getting worse, but she might need . . .'

She squeezes her eyes tight to try and stop the tears but they burst out anyway. Behind her she hears the door open and lowers her head to the bed, burying her face in her arms.

'It's OK, Roger,' her father says, and the door closes again.

'I'm sorry,' he says softly. 'Sorry about this, sorry about everything.' He strokes her hair, ending a decade and a half of distance. 'I had hoped, when I first found out how little time I had left, that it might be enough to make things right between us. Maybe it still will.'

Laughton opens her mouth to speak but the words won't come. Too much time has passed and her heart has become too hardened towards him.

'I don't know,' she finally manages.

Rees nods, the pain etched on his face from far more than the disease that's killing him. He strokes her hair and lets her cry.

64

Tannahill steps out of his shower pretty much straight into his kitchen. He towels himself dry and pours hot water into a mug with miso paste already squeezed into it.

The shower has made him feel slightly more human but no less tired. He stirs the soup, sending reconstituted seaweed strands swirling through the brown liquid and glances longingly at his still unmade bed. He has the strongest urge to lie on it, just for a few minutes, and close his eyes, but he knows if he does he'll blink and it will be morning, and he can't let himself sleep. Not yet. Not while a man who has killed three times is still out there. Not when that man's fourth and fifth intended victims are Laughton and Gracie Rees.

He takes a sip of the scalding, salty liquid, stands at the kitchen counter that divides the room and opens his laptop. He logs into the case file and reads through the latest updates as he pulls on fresh clothes.

Unlike the previous two scenes, forensics have pulled a ton of stuff from the police cell, including fingerprints that match the partial they found on the pages of Laughton's book at the Kate Miller murder scene and prints found on the newspapers left by Mike Miller's body. They tie Adam Evans to all three murder scenes. All they have to do now is find him.

Tannahill flicks to the next tab containing more witness statements from guardians at the property who'd been missed in the first round of interviews. One is from Nurse Erin Medford, who'd spoken to Slade as she'd left that morning to go to work. She seemed pretty traumatized by what had happened, even though she must be used to death in her job. You could see her distress in her answers:

. . . I can't believe Adam would do something like this. I mean I didn't really know him very well. He just blended in really . . . He was a bit quiet but he seemed just like everyone else . . . I mean I spoke to the man who died. I told him to knock on the door and ask for Adam . . . If I hadn't said that then maybe . . . I just can't believe what happened . . .

His phone rings. He checks the caller ID, sighs then answers.
'Hey, Mam.'
'You still at work?'
'No, I'm home.'
'I don't believe you.'
'I can FaceTime you if you like.'
'Oh God, no, I can't bear looking at myself.'
'You're not supposed to look at yourself, you're supposed to look at the person you're talking to.'
'Ah, everyone looks at themselves on those things. I've seen you fiddling with your hair when you're talking to me, checking your quiff.'
'I haven't got a quiff. Anyway no one uses words like "quiff" any more.'
'Well whatever you call it, I've seen you primping it. Have you eaten?'
Tannahill eyes his miso soup. 'Not yet. Been a bit of a manic day.'
'I know, I've been watching the news. Terrible thing. Mind

you, that Mark Murphy deserved to be killed if you ask me. Promise you'll never put me in one of those homes, Tanny!'

'I promise.'

'Good boy. Now tell me about the murders – you got any leads?'

'Mam, I can't talk about live cases, you know that. We're feeling confident with the direction it's going.'

'What about your lady friend?'

'Which lady friend?'

'The consultant I've been reading about in the paper.'

'Laughton?'

'Yes. What's going to happen with you two when this case is over?'

'Nothing! And I'm not quite sure where you got the idea there's something going on between us.'

'Because you like her, that's why, and I can tell you're too scared to do anything about it.' The phone starts beeping in Tannahill's ear. 'If your father had been too scared to ask me out, you wouldn't even be here now to be so annoying. No point fiddling with your hair and making yourself look pretty if you're never going to do anything about it. What's that bloody clicking sound?'

'I've got another call coming in.' He checks his phone and sees it's Baker. 'Sorry, Mam, it's work, got to go.' He cuts her off to answer the incoming call.

'You done for the day?' Baker asks, sounding about as weary as Tannahill feels.

'No, not even close.'

'OK. Well I'm done, literally and figuratively. I'm heading home now to remind my kids what Dad looks like and get glared at by the wife for a few hours, then I'll be back bright and breezy. I've uploaded the last few witness statements to the case file, if you want to have a look.'

'I was just reading them. Anything useful I should be looking out for?'

'Not really. Stuck record. Kept himself to himself, didn't really speak to anyone, seemed to keep odd hours. Mind you, a lot of them keep odd hours because most seem to be nurses and shift workers at various hospitals around London. I think they work even harder than we do.'

Tannahill glances back at his laptop at the name of the last witness whose statement he'd read – *Nurse Erin Medford* – and a cold thought forms in his mind.

'Get some rest,' he says, and hangs up. He opens his recently called log and dials a number, his eyes scanning back through the witness statement he'd just read.

. . . He just blended in really . . . Nurse Erin Medford had said, *. . . he seemed just like everyone else . . .*

65

Laughton wakes to the gentle buzzing of her phone in her pocket.

She looks up and sees her father lying asleep on his bank of pillows, his hand still resting on hers.

She gently pulls her hand free so as not to wake him and fumbles her phone from her pocket as she tiptoes to the door, smiling when she sees who's calling, then feeling a flash of annoyance when she sees how late it is. Why didn't the police guard come and find her? Then she realizes he probably did and her father would have waved him away.

She steps out into the corridor where the lights have been dimmed and the droopy moustached guard is snoozing on the sofa, his newspaper crumpled on the floor next to his empty cup. She closes the door softly so as not to wake him either and takes a few steps up the corridor before answering.

'Hey!' she whispers.

'Hey. You OK? Everything OK over there?'

'Yeah. All quiet, why?'

'I was just going through the witness statements and a lot of the people in the house-share where Slade was killed are medical workers and I started thinking about Mike Murphy's death bed, you know the drip and everything, and how it looked like it had been set up by someone who knew what they were doing. I was just thinking we should run a check on everyone working in that building you're in, make sure everyone is properly vetted. I tried calling your duty guard, but it went straight to voicemail.'

Laughton ups her pace, a sudden anxiousness banishing all trace of tiredness. She turns the corner and feels a flood of relief when she sees the guard at the far end of the corridor, still sitting in his chair next to Gracie's room.

'He's in position,' she says, 'I'm looking at him right now. The signal's not great in here, maybe it's that. I'll pass on the message.'

'Thanks.'

She passes the nurses' station where the duty nurse is also asleep, his head lying on his folded arms, his chair pushed back and jammed against a filing cabinet.

'Listen,' Tannahill says. 'When we catch this guy, I was wondering whether you'd think about maybe staying on to consult on other cases. I mean we've got a huge backlog, and there's some really interesting cases in there that would really benefit from your insight.'

If he'd asked her that morning she would have hung up on him, but now the thought of carrying on, and getting extra income – and working with Tannahill – seemed much more appealing.

'Maybe,' she says. 'Let me just get past these next few days then let's talk again.'

She draws closer to the guard and sees that he too is asleep, his head tipped back against the wall, his empty cup on the floor by his feet.

So much for black coffee and two sugars.

She steps past him, looks through the window into Gracie's room and stops dead.

The skinny figure in the green orderly's tunic is standing

with his back to her, his hand resting on the drinks trolley as he stares down at the sleeping form of Gracie.

'Try and get some rest,' Tannahill says, and in the quiet of the midnight hospital his voice is loud enough to make the man turn around, and white noise and terror flood Laughton's mind when she sees what is standing by her daughter's bed.

The child's unicorn mask is too small for his face but the eyeholes have been cut larger and his pale eyes now stare at her through them.

He's. Here.

Laughton whispers staring at the monster returned from her childhood.

'What!?'

He's here! she repeats, her mind screaming, her body frozen to the spot, a rabbit in the headlamps of those ragged-edged eyes.

He takes a step towards her and she backs away, not from fear but because Gracie is in the room with him and she needs him to follow her, she needs to get him away from her daughter.

The thought jolts a memory loose and she is back in the terraced house in Acton she grew up in, her mum standing in the hallway looking at the distorted shape of a man through the pebbled glass of their front door, watching as he pulls something white over his face that turns him from a man into something else.

Go upstairs, her mother had said, pushing her in front, keeping herself between her daughter and whatever that was outside their door.

Upstairs they had squeezed into the large airing cupboard at the end of the hallway, closed the door and listened to the sounds of him entering the house, moving around downstairs, opening doors, breaking things.

When he comes upstairs, her mother had whispered, *he'll go in my bedroom first. We need to wait until he's in the en-suite bathroom, then we run. I'll count to three, and on three we run. We run and we keep on running. OK?*

And then he was coming.

Up the stairs.

The slow creak of each step heralding his approach and stretching time tight until it was almost too much to bear. She could see out into the hallway through a gap in the louvre doors as they hid in the cupboard, wrapped in the trapped heat and the smell of laundry, the sound of their own breathing seeming way too loud in the tight space.

And then he was there at the top of the stairs, his face turning in their direction. That mask and those hideous eyes, eyes that could see anything, could even penetrate the door and see where she was hiding.

But then he had turned away and entered her mum and dad's room, just as her mother had said he would, and her mum had started counting, gripping her hand tight, whispering each number as she gauged the right time to run.

One . . .

two . . .

But Laughton couldn't stand it. She had to get away.

She had burst from the cupboard too soon, the door banging loudly as she rushed for the stairs. And her mother, not ready to run, had stumbled to catch up and Laughton had almost made it to the stairs when he appeared and grabbed her arm, the knife rising up, ready to strike.

Then something had knocked him backwards, breaking his grip, and he had fallen on to the floor of the bedroom, Laughton's mother on top of him, beating at his face with her bare hands.

RUN! she had screamed, and Laughton had run, down the stairs, out into the street, her mother's words repeating over and over in her head.

We run and we keep on running.
We run and we keep on running.
We run and we keep on running.

It was only later, when the police had come and the questions had started, that she realized her mother had not been behind her as she ran from the house.

She had told her to count to three.

Three was the safe number.

But Laughton had gone on two, when the monster was still too close, when her mother wasn't ready – and she had died because of it.

It had been her fault her mother was killed, not her father's. All this time she had blamed him for not being there, and for bringing the monster to their door, but she was a monster too, because she was weak, because she was a bad daughter. And now her own daughter was going to die, because she was a bad mother too.

The man in the unicorn mask opens the door to Gracie's room and steps out into the corridor.

Laughton continues to move away, stumbling backwards, weak in the face of this thing from her nightmares but knowing one thing, that she must draw him away from Gracie.

She can hear Tannahill's voice frantically calling her name on her phone but he's too far away, and there's no one here to help her. The nurse is asleep. The guard is asleep, both of them are. Drugged by whatever the man in the mask had given them.

And he has a knife in his hand now. A black-and-green zombie knife like the one that killed Kate Miller.

. . . First he had to kill you, that was the price of entry . . .

That was what Tannahill had said earlier.

. . . Then he could kill Gracie, that was his reward . . .

He has to kill her first, Laughton realizes, that was the deal. So if she can just stay alive, then Gracie will be safe.

But in this same moment of realization her back hits a wall and she has nowhere left to go.

He takes another step, his eyes shining like glass in the ragged holes of the mask, and raises the knife higher, ready to strike.

Then something hits him hard in the side, sending him sprawling across the floor.

Laughton looks down in frozen shock at the tangle of limbs and struggling bodies.

Then her father looks up and says the same word her mother said to her more than a decade and a half earlier.

RUN!!

66

Laughton runs.

She runs past the struggling bodies right into Gracie's room.
She looks for a lock but there isn't one.

She looks for something to jam against the door and drags
the drinks trolley over but it's too light to stop anyone coming
through that door.

She looks around for a weapon, something heavy, something
she can hit or gouge with, but this is a hospital and there's
nothing like that by design.

She ducks her head into the bathroom. There's nothing to
use as a weapon in there either, but there is a lock on the
door.

She jumps to the side of Gracie's bed and lightly slaps her
on the cheek.

'Honey, wake up. Please wake up.'

She presses the alarm button on the bedhead and a red
light comes on above the door. Somewhere outside down the
corridor the distant beep sounds, but it's coming from where
the night nurse is sleeping his drugged sleep.

No one is coming.

'Honey, please wake up.'

Gracie moans and stirs, her eyes rolling half open before

closing again. She's too deeply sedated. Dragging her off the bed and into the relative safety of the bathroom will take too long.

Outside in the corridor, Laughton hears a cry of pain and recognizes her father's voice in it.

She looks down at Gracie, the same age now she was when this happened to her. She remembers what her mother did to make sure she lived. She never thought she was as strong as her mother but right now, in this moment, she knows she is. She will do anything to save her daughter, anything.

Another cry out in the hallway makes her head snap round.

Her mother had fought for her and her father is fighting for her now.

That's what you do when you're a parent. When the wolf comes for your cubs, you fight him.

She looks at the drinks trolley again, not heavy enough for defence, but better as a weapon. She grabs it, yanks open the door and charges into the corridor, letting out a howl that comes from somewhere deep and elemental.

Her father is on the floor, his hospital gown twisted and wet with blood as he kicks weakly at his attacker, who remains standing over him but is now looking at Laughton, the glassy eyes wide with surprise behind the mask.

She grabs the hot water urn from the trolley and hurls it at him, sending near scalding water arcing through the air and burning herself in the process. The monster ducks but not in time and the urn hits him hard on the shoulder, throwing a jolt of water over him that makes him stagger backwards and squeal.

Laughton swings the trolley round, running at him hard and letting go at the last moment so the sharp metal edge of it hits him full in the side, sending him sprawling to the ground before spinning away down the corridor. His mask slips as he falls and she sees the face beneath as he scrambles to put it back. Pale. Unremarkable. Ordinary.

This is no monster.

She hurries over to her father, slipping in spilt water as she drops down by his side.

'You OK?'

He is holding his side, gritting his teeth in pain, bleeding vivid red on to his white hospital gown. He looks up and the pain in his eyes softens for the flicker of a moment, then his gaze shifts, as if fixing on something beyond her.

Laughton twists round and sees the man in the mask lurching towards her. He is limping from where the trolley struck him, the eyes full of hate, his hand rising up again, the knife pointing at her now.

She stands and backs away across the wet floor, away from her father and past the door to Gracie's room with the red light above it that now turns everything scarlet in the dimly lit corridor.

She continues to walk backwards, drawing the shuffling thing in the mask after her.

In almost two decades of obsessing about this moment, dreading it, waking from nightmares where it endlessly played out, the emotion that always coloured everything was fear. Fear of it happening again. Fear of the monster in the mask coming again and this time catching her.

Run and don't stop running, her mother had said.

And she had been running, running her entire life – away from home, away from her past, all that running – and yet here she was and the monster had still caught up with her. She feels the hard lino become soft carpet beneath her feet.

She has been running for long enough. Time to stop.

She plants her back foot on the ground, focuses on the thing limping closer and starts counting in her head.

. . . One . . .

Her eyes meet the ones in the ragged eyeholes and she gauges his height. He is tall, much taller than she had imagined him

380

to be. But this wasn't him. She had seen his face. This wasn't a monster, it wasn't even McVey, it was just a pathetic man hiding behind a mask.

. . . Two . . .

She bends her knees slightly, almost as if cowering, and he smiles behind the mask, enjoying what he sees as a sign of fear and defeat. He raises the knife ready to stab down hard and finally offer this sacrifice to his dead and twisted god. He takes another step. One more and he will be able to reach her.

. . . Three . . .

Laughton straightens her legs and launches upwards, twisting as she rises, her left leg lashing out, catching the edge of the slashing knife but driving on through to connect with the mask and keep on going, shattering plastic and crunching bone.

His body slackens instantly and he staggers backwards, arms flailing weakly as he tries to regain balance.

Laughton lands in a controlled crouch and springs forward again, leading with her right leg this time, her left leaking blood where the blade caught it. She aims at the mask again, just as she has practised so many times. She drives her foot forward, connecting with his head, which snaps back with nowhere near the resistance of the heavy leather bag. His body crumples and he falls backwards, landing so hard on the floor that his head bounces and the knife falls from his limp hand.

Laughton is already on him, the red light in the corridor now indistinguishable from the cloud of red mist in her head. She looks down at his face, framed by the shattered mask, his eyes rolled back on a slack face, blood pouring from a cut in his lip and a nose that looks like ground beef. Behind her, three hospital security guards run down the corridor, finally answering the earlier alarm.

She raises her right foot ready to stamp down on his

head but strong arms grab her from behind and pull her away.

'It's OK,' someone says. 'You're safe now. You're OK.'

And for the first time in her adult life, Laughton feels that she actually is.

67

News of what went down at the Chelsea and Westminster Hospital comes too late to catch the morning print editions but social media, as usual, is all over it and by the time people are listening to the morning news over their sleepy cups of coffee, Commissioner John Rees has gone from zero to hero.

The various interested parties – Celia Barnes, Shonagh O'Brien, the ladies of the Highgate Book Club WhatsApp group – all scroll through their newsfeeds and turn up the volume on their radios to suck up the details of the breaking news, breathing a collective sigh of relief that the killer is in custody, order has been restored, and they are safe in their little worlds once more.

The Home Secretary Charles Nixon makes a rare appearance on the *Today* programme to confirm that a hospital orderly responsible for the murders of care home mogul Mark Murphy, his wife, and a tabloid journalist, gained access to the private wing of the Chelsea and Westminster but had been stopped from killing Laughton and Gracie Rees, Commissioner Rees's daughter and granddaughter, by Commissioner Rees himself, who, despite collapsing at a press conference because of a serious heart condition, had realized something was wrong, heroically tackled the killer but sustained severe injuries and suffered a heart attack in the process and is now in intensive care.

Nixon also deftly performs the unique politician's trick of throwing Rees under the bus while at the same time naming it in his honour by adding that his earlier collapse at the press conference and passionate and uncharacteristic comments had been down to the strong painkillers he'd been taking as he bravely tried to continue doing his job until a suitable replacement could be found. Further to this, Nixon names Deputy Commissioner Andy Bevan as the new Commissioner of the Met who will be holding a conference later that day to officially accept the position and announce an immediate increase to the existing police budget of £450 million to tackle crime in general and knife crime in particular.

Nixon ends by thanking Commissioner John Rees for his long service, and expresses his sincerest hope that he may quickly recover from his injuries and enjoy a long and peaceful retirement.

68

John Rees wakes slowly, rising up through what feels like a warm sea. Sounds leak in as he comes to, muffled sounds of low voices, murmurs and whispers, distant and indistinct, and he is aware of his own breathing, the effort of it, as though something heavy is pressing down on his chest. Then he feels another pressure, light but firm on his hand, like someone has taken hold of it and is pulling him up and out of the warm ocean.

He opens his eyes and a shape comes slowly into focus, then a face he recognizes – and he smiles.

'Grace!' he croaks, his throat dry and raw.

The face slides away, and he panics for a moment, then he hears water pour from a jug, and a hand reaches behind his head and lifts it slightly. He feels the coolness of the water on his lips, drinks and looks up at her, blinking to try and force her face into focus, desperate to see it again after so long. The glass is removed and he whispers his wife's name again, 'Grace', as he starts to remember now – the man in the mask, the knife in his hand, the fear in his daughter's face.

He had told her to run but can't remember if she did. He had grabbed him, held him as long as he could with one single

385

thought sharp in his mind even as the knife had stabbed into him again and again.

Not this time, he had vowed, blocking out the pain and clinging to this one thought as tightly as he'd grappled with the man in the hideous mask.

Not this time.

The figure by his bed leans over him again, pressing a tissue to the damp edge of his mouth, and he looks up at her – his Grace, long dead but here again, which means he must be dead too and that's fine with him, just as long as she got away. As long as Laughton lived he would pay any price, even his own life.

He smiles at his wife as her face comes finally into sharp focus, and then he cries with regret and relief. Regret that it's not his wife standing over his bed, but relief that Laughton did get away, because it is she who is tipping the water glass to his lips, she who is dabbing the edge of his mouth with a tissue.

Laughton sits in a chair in the doorway between two adjoining rooms.

After her father came back from the emergency surgery she'd asked if he could be put in the same room as Gracie so she could sit by both their beds at once. They'd told her that was not possible for various protocol and infection-control reasons, but they could put him in the next room as long as she promised to keep the door between them closed. She had promised, then jammed the door open with the chair the moment they left and now sits on the threshold between the two rooms, neither in nor out of either, looking right at her father, then left at her sleeping daughter, then back again, on and on in a constant vigil.

Once her father had woken briefly. She had given him some water and he had called her by her mother's name then cried before slipping back down into sleep again.

From time to time Laughton gets up to stretch her aching body, walking stiffly around both rooms like an attack dog patrolling a perimeter. The thick bandage on her leg restricts her movement a little and the stitches throb in time with her heartbeat now the painkillers are wearing off. One of the nurses told her she had almost killed the man who had done this to her. She has thought about that a lot.

Gracie has still not woken. She remains in the chemically induced coma that is helping her heal. Laughton longs for her to wake, but she is frightened of it too. When she wakes she will have to tell her what happened and talk about why she is here. And though she is afraid of that conversation she is more scared of the lack of talk that resulted in her daughter ending up here in this bed. So when Gracie wakes they will talk, painful though it will be.

They will talk and, this time, Laughton will listen.

But until then she will watch over her. She will watch over her daughter and she will watch over her father and do whatever she can to make sure no further harm comes to either of them.

On the evening following the attack Tannahill appears, bringing her laptop from home, a file box and some cartons of Chinese food that chase away the smell of disinfectant like a garlicky dragon.

They eat their meal in the open door between the two rooms, using the file box as a table, Laughton sitting in Gracie's room and Tannahill in her father's, talking about everything and nothing. It feels nice, almost normal, though Laughton never stops glancing over at the two people in the beds.

When the meal is finished, Tannahill clears all the rubbish into the bags he brought the food in then looks at Laughton with a serious expression on his face. 'I need to ask you something,' he says. 'You don't have to answer if you don't want, but I have to ask.'

Laughton nods, anxious about what it is he's about to say.

'How come you're called Laughton?'

She laughs with relief and points at her father. 'His fault,' she says. 'Have you ever seen the film *Night of the Hunter*?' Tannahill shakes his head. 'It's an old black-and-white movie with Robert Mitchum and Shelley Winters. Mitchum plays a psycho who disguises himself as a preacher to try and con a widow out of some money. He's got these tattoos on the fingers of each hand – HATE on the left hand and LOVE on the right – and he does this speech where the right hand is getting beaten by left but then ends up triumphant, proving that love always conquers hate, or something like that. It's my dad's favourite film. You should watch it, it's pretty good. It's got murders in it, you'll like it.

'Anyway it was the first film my dad ever watched with me, by which I mean he got up in the middle of the night when I was newborn to give my mum a break and watched it while I slept or grizzled in his arms. Apparently, they couldn't decide what to call me. The director of the film was a guy called Charles Laughton. My dad liked the name, so . . .' She smiles. 'That's the story.'

Tannahill smiles. 'It's a good story.' He glances over at the sleeping form of John Rees. 'You're not a normal family, that's for sure.'

Laughton follows his gaze. 'Is there any such thing?'

Tannahill turns to her, the serious expression back on his face. 'So how does all this leave things between you two?'

'I don't know. I would say time will tell, but I'm not sure how much time we've got. I keep watching him to make sure he's still breathing, so I guess that tells you something.'

Tannahill nods, then he drums his fingers on the lid of the file box. 'This is all the personal stuff from your father's office. There's a few things in there you might find interesting. I've also emailed you the latest updates to the case file, in case you wanted something to read. That's got murders in it too.'

Laughton smiles, then Tannahill leans in and kisses her, just a soft kiss on the side of her mouth but it passes through her body like an electric charge.

'Goodnight, Laughton Rees,' he says, then he heads for the door, the take-away bag dangling from his hand. He opens the door to leave, then pauses and turns back.

'If you want to call me to talk about anything, anything at all, then call. Doesn't matter what time it is, OK? Just call.'

Then he nods and steps out of the room, and Laughton watches the door close slowly behind him.

69

Tannahill's visit had been a wonderful distraction but it left Laughton feeling confused and restless, not because of the kiss – that was the most welcome and least complicated part of the whole evening – but because of what he had brought with him.

She stares at the file box for a while, thinking about how such a large career as her father's has somehow ended up fitting inside something so compact. When she eventually lifts the lid off and looks inside, she is even more surprised by its meagre contents: just a few photos, a thin, faded blue folder and an old laptop and charger that looks like it should have been retired long before its owner.

She picks up the first framed photo of a police officer Laughton does not recognize. A handwritten note on the back identifies him as Commander Peter Fairweather and there's a flicker of recognition like she's heard the name before but it's from so long ago that she can't pin it to anything concrete. The second photograph is of her, aged about six, sitting in the back garden of their house in Acton on her mother's lap. Both of them are frozen in laughter. Laughton stares at the photograph for a long time, imagining it sitting on her father's desk and realizing that, while she has spent her life going out of her way to avoid any mention or sight of him, he had made just as sure he'd seen her face every single day.

Inside the faded blue folder is more evidence of how he had stayed present in her life without her ever knowing. There's a copy of the admission form enrolling her on the rehab programme that was the beginning of her pulling herself out of her nose-dive. Her father's unfussy, distinctive signature fills the section for sponsors with a handwritten note next to it asking that his involvement be kept strictly confidential. The same signature is also on the next document, a scholarship form showing how he had acted as guarantor to ensure she got the bursary that would pay her way through university. If she'd dropped out, he would have had to pay everything back. She had never known that. Also in the folder are copies of each of her degree certificates as well as the cover page of her doctoral thesis. There's also a copy of her admission letter to London Metropolitan University, which the Dean had obviously forwarded to her father asking if he objected to her being hired as a lecturer. A single, handwritten line shows that he had not.

Laughton carefully places everything back inside the folder, wiping a tear away with the back of her hand. She had always viewed her father as cold and uncaring, an absent parent, when in fact he'd always been there for her. Always.

She pulls out the laptop next but the battery is dead, so she plugs it in to charge and settles into her chair between the two rooms, looking across at her father as he sleeps then back at her daughter in the next room.

Her family.

Broken but still hers.

Then, with no hope of sleep, she does what she always did to calm her teeming brain, she opens her own laptop, clicks on the updated link to the case file and sinks into the details of a case, focusing on all the new evidence that will be used to convict Adam Evans. But even as her mind seeks out the comforting connections that should tie everything together into a neat and comforting package it also finds a loose thread, one that refuses to be tucked away. And when she tugs at it, and follows where it goes, the whole neat picture starts to unravel until something else is revealed underneath, something with no loose threads. And when her father wakes again, sometime in the wee small hours when everyone else is asleep except her and the now-armed guard stationed outside her door, she has a question for him.

'Why would Adam Evans send Slade an email telling him where to find him *before* his work was done?'

John Rees looks up at his daughter, so like Grace now that he still finds it almost too painful to look at her.

He swallows drily. 'He made a mistake,' he says, his mouth like cotton wool from all the morphine. 'They always do. Eventually.'

Laughton shakes her head gently and gazes down at him with a look of cold curiosity that makes him feel uneasy. 'If they always made mistakes then we would always catch them, wouldn't we? But we don't. Last year the solve rate for murders in the capital was sixty-eight per cent.'

Rees shrugs. 'Sometimes we make mistakes too.'

Laughton continues to regard him with such an intense scrutiny he feels like she must be able to see inside his head.

'But he didn't make a mistake,' she says softly. 'Not to begin with. The first two murders were meticulously planned and carried out. In fact the killer was so confident he had left nothing behind that would help us catch him, he sent pictures to a journalist so he could write about it. So if he was so careful and precise those first two times, why tell the journalist where to find him then end up killing him in what looks like panic? Why would he panic if he knew he was coming? And he *would* have known he was coming *if* he'd sent the email.'

Rees shrugs, his eyes never leaving hers. 'Maybe the email was scheduled to be sent later but something went wrong. He did make other mistakes: he left a fingerprint on your book at the first murder scene and another on the newspapers at the second.'

'Yes, he did, didn't he, a fingerprint at each location, just enough to place him at each scene and help convict. You know, when they searched Adam Evans's cell, they didn't find any technology at all, no phone, no laptop. He was so low-tech he wrote his journal in an old, school exercise book with a pencil, and yet somehow he managed to send untraceable emails and photos from an old laptop apparently acquired at a liquidation auction of SunnySet assets.'

She pauses for a moment then reaches down below the level of the bed and holds something up for him to see. 'A laptop exactly like this in fact.'

Rees stares at the battered old Compaq, the screen glowing in the dim room, showing the sunflower logo of the company that had once owned it and the series of folders arranged in a line:

1. THE HOUSE
2. THE BOOK
3. THE MEDALS
4. THE KEYS
5. THE LION AND THE UNICORN

He had taken the laptop out of his bottom drawer and put it in the box when he was clearing his desk before the press conference. He had planned on dropping it in the Thames on his way home afterwards.

Everyone makes mistakes.

He looks back into his daughter's eyes and for the flicker of a moment considers denying ever having seen the laptop before. But time is too short, and the very last thing he wants to do is waste what he has left lying to the daughter who's only just started talking to him again. So he looks down at the bed instead because he can't bear to look into her earnest eyes – her mother's eyes – and say what he's about to say.

'They never tell you what justice actually looks like.' He speaks softly, his voice low, making sure no one else can overhear. 'Not when they're signing you up. Oh they toss the word around enough – the politicians, the press – *we are the party of law and order, we are the party of justice* – but there's no justice you can give to the parents of a child killed by a drink driver who gets five years and is out in three. There's no justice for the three-year-old who will never walk or speak again because his mother's boyfriend took him by the ankles and smashed his head against a wall to stop him from crying.' He takes a breath and blows it out slowly as he rides a wave of pain.

'You do your best of course, though you quickly realize your best is never, ever going to be good enough. You tell yourself that you don't make the laws, that you're there simply to uphold them, and you keep on going in the face of all this tragedy and injustice because what alternative is there? You just keep going . . . even when it happens to you.

'So when McVey took my life away from me I kept on going. And then when you slipped away from me, I kept on going then too. But I never stopped thinking about how one day I might put things right, and find a way to see proper justice served.

'So I kept an eye on McVey and everyone else who had helped destroy my life: the junior barrister who'd poisoned our case and helped set McVey free; the journalist she leaked his name to. I used to fantasize about bringing them to justice, proper justice, an eye for an eye, a life for a life. It was a form of therapy for me. But then the lawyer disappeared and McVey died, and it seemed justice had evaded me once again.'

A cough rasps from inside him and he clutches his chest as his whole body shudders in the effort of stopping it turning into a full-blown fit.

'Can I have some water, please?'

Laughton gently lifts his head to let him drink and he savours the feel of her hand.

'I watched you too during all this time,' he says, lying back down and looking up into her eyes, 'so lost and so unreachable. I thought you were lost for good at one point, around the time you fell pregnant, but it was Gracie who brought you back to the world. She gave you a reason to live again. And I felt such pride in who you then became and your success, all the more impressive considering where you had started. But I could also see how you were still locked away inside yourself, still imprisoned by the crime that had defined you. I hoped there would come a time when you might start living in the present again, instead of endlessly focusing on the crimes of the past. I hoped there might be time enough for us too, that we might one day build a bridge across the chasm that separated us too. Then nine months ago I discovered I was dying and suddenly there was no time left.

'At around the same time as I got my death sentence, McVey died too. It was a relief in some ways, one thing on my bucket list I no longer had to deal with. But through all my years of watching him I'd become aware of a man who worked as a volunteer at Broadmoor and had spent an unusual amount of time with McVey.'

'Adam Evans,' Laughton murmurs.

Rees nods. 'I did a deep background check and found all the child psych reports you will no doubt have read in the file labelled THE LION AND THE UNICORN. I'm sure I don't need to tell you the link between childhood cruelty to animals and adult psychopathy, so even though he'd been treated and his files had been sealed because he was a minor, you can understand how alarm bells sounded with me when I discovered

McVey's new best friend had been caught torturing and beheading cats when he was eight years old.

'So I arranged for an acquaintance, a career housebreaker who owed me a favour, to follow him and find out more about what he was like now. He broke into the place he was staying and discovered the journals, McVey's and his. The former proved what I had known all along: McVey was the Masked Monster. Evans's journal was filled with detailed fantasies of how he intended to revive McVey's legend and carry on his work, starting with the death of the little girl who'd got away.' He looks up at Laughton. 'You.'

Rees takes a careful breath, the rattle of a cough threatening the edges of it but never quite taking hold, then continues.

'I knew arresting him would do no good – any half-decent lawyer would have him back on the streets within hours because he'd only written down his fantasies about killing you, he hadn't actually done anything yet. I thought about taking him out myself, just as I'd always thought about killing McVey if I had a chance. But sometimes the universe, so chaotic and cruel most of the time, provides exactly what you need at the exact time that you need it.

'An ex-colleague of mine who now works for a security company had just installed a high-end alarm system in a house in Highgate and recognized the owner. He sent me a photo and I recognized her too. She had a new name, a new look, even a new husband. I recognized him too and realized that here was my chance not only to visit real justice on all these people who deserved it, but also to make sure Adam Evans no longer posed any threat to you after I was gone.'

He looks up at Laughton. 'That was always my main object-ive, to make sure you were safe and well. But I also saw how all of this might help you finally escape from the shadow of your past. I'd read your books and followed your work on cold cases, I knew how good you were. I also knew the reason you steered clear of live cases was because you had once been part of one and had been scarred by that experience. But I felt sure that once you had experienced the electric charge of a live investigation as an adult, using your skills, you would realize this was the job you were born to do and would never go back to your half-lived life in the dusty halls of academia. All you needed was a crime you couldn't ignore. So I provided one, and after I killed Kathryn Warren I left your book at the crime scene to draw you into the case.'

He reaches for her hand and takes it in his.

'I never meant for you to find out it was me who did any of this, and I never meant for you or Gracie to end up in harm's way. I sent Slade to Evans's address to end it. I wanted him to find the journals, alert the police and finally write the true story of who Adrian McVey was. But Slade was killed, my health let me down, and in the end all I did was put you in harm's way again.'

He closes his eyes and rides a wave of pain that is half physical and half emotional.

'I'm sorry,' he says, gripping her hand hard as tears drip down his face. 'I love you more than anything, more than my own life. But all I ever seem to do is let you down. And now there's no time. No time left to put things right.'

A high-pitched alarm sounds and her hand is crushed in his as his back arches and pain engulfs him.

Laughton squeezes back, ignoring her own pain. She looks up at the machine making the noise and sees a single green line flatlining across the screen.

'Dad,' she says, slapping the side of his face with her free hand to try and rouse him. 'Hang on, Dad.'

Behind her the door bursts open and the crash team push her aside. They go to work, shouting out his vital signs, unbuttoning the front of his hospital gown and prepping the paddles of a defibrillator.

One of the team shouts 'CLEAR' and everyone steps back.

Her father's body jerks on the bed and the line on the screen jumps too, then it settles and flatlines again.

The team close in again and the whine of the defibrillator rises beneath their urgent dialogue as it charges up again.

Laughton watches on helplessly, trying to keep a clear line of sight on her father's face through the crush of bodies as though losing sight of him for one moment might mean losing him forever.

70

John Rees does not die that night.

The crash team manage to restart his heart on their third attempt then wheel him away at speed to the ICU, leaving Laughton staring at the space where his bed had been in a room that feels suddenly empty and uncomfortably quiet, like she's in the eye of a hurricane that is still turning all around her.

Laughton glances at the ancient laptop lying open on the ground next to the box file, its screen casting a dull, malevolent glow across the box and the clean floor. She checks the time on her phone. It's late, or early, depending on how you looked at it.

If you want to call me to talk about anything, call.

Tannahill had said.

Doesn't matter what time it is. Just call.

She calls him and he answers on the first ring.

'Hey,' he says.

'My father had another heart attack,' she says.

'Jesus. Is he OK?'

'I don't know. They took him away.'

'You want me to come over?'

'I opened the box,' she says. Tannahill says nothing. 'I found the laptop. I was talking to him about it all when he . . . when his heart . . . I think maybe . . .'

'I'm coming over,' Tannahill says, 'don't talk to anyone else about any of this until I'm there, OK?'

'You knew,' she says, a statement not a question. 'You said I could call you anytime because you knew I'd open the box. You knew I'd open it and figure out the same things you did.'

A long pause stretches out, filled only by the soft hiss of air piping in through the ceiling vents.

'So what do you want to do?' Tannahill says, his voice low and neutral.

His question takes Laughton by surprise because the answer is obvious, they should put the laptop into evidence and she should write up a statement detailing how her father confessed to the murders of Mike Murphy and Kathryn Warren, that's what they should do. But as the silence lengthens and she doesn't say any of this, other answers start to form.

It is Tannahill who finally breaks the silence. 'At the moment,' he says, his voice still low, 'all the evidence, the *official* evidence, unequivocally points to Adam Evans being the killer. His fingerprints are at every murder scene and we know Adam Evans *is* a killer because he murdered Brian Slade and clearly intended to kill you and Gracie, so he's going away for life anyway. Now maybe if he hadn't killed Slade his defence team *might* have questioned how one single fingerprint conveniently showed up at both Mike Murphy and Kathryn Warren's murder scenes. *Maybe* they also would have suggested that someone with enough forensic know-how could have collected Adam Evans's prints from a discarded Coke can or something then planted them at the scene – an ex-cop maybe, or even a serving one. But that's a very serious accusation and they'd need way more than just conjecture before they made it. They'd need solid evidence that someone else was involved, something concrete, something that unequivocally ties the murder victims to a new suspect.'

Laughton's eyes drop to the laptop lying open on the floor.

'As it stands,' Tannahill continues, his voice so low it's now almost a whisper, 'you and I are the only two people who know about the laptop, apart from your father. And your father is . . . well your father is dying.'

Laughton waits for him to say something else but he lets the silence finish his thought and she realizes what he's doing. He's outlining the story already written but allowing her to decide how it ends.

'Why kill Mark Murphy?' she asks, holding up the one loose thread still untied in her mind. 'I can understand his hatred for Kathryn Warren, but killing him makes no sense.'

'That man in the photograph,' Tannahill murmurs, 'the one in the commander's uniform. He was an old friend of your father's – career copper, no family, helped your dad a lot after your mother died and you . . . well when you were no longer around. Anyway, he retired a few years back then developed an aggressive form of Alzheimer's, went downhill very quickly. He died in one of Mark Murphy's care homes.'

Laughton nods and closes her eyes. Normally when the last piece of a puzzle drops into place on a case she's been obsessing about she feels a rare and momentary sense of peace. But there is no peace here. She has spent most of her life hoping for an opportunity to ruin her father, and now here it is. All she has to do is her job, put the evidence she has on record and let justice do its thing.

Justice.

Would that be justice?

She recalls the pain of the last conversation with her father, the confession of a dying man telling her what he'd done and why he'd done it. She looks down at the folder containing the evidence of her father's undiminished love for her, a ghost parent looking out for her the only way he could because it was the only way she would let him. She had always believed she'd done everything on her own, prided herself on it even.

Now she realizes he had been there all the time, watching over her, looking after her the best he could, like she tried to do for Gracie. He even killed for her, like any parent would do, given the right or wrong circumstances, like she would have done for Gracie, like she would have killed Adam Evans if someone hadn't dragged her off him.

'So what do you want to do?' Tannahill asks.

Laughton stares at the empty space where her father had so recently been. 'I don't know,' she says. 'I really don't know.'

71

No time left to put things right.

Those were the last words her father ever said to her, and Laughton thought about them a lot in the next few days.

She thought about it as she sat by Gracie's bedside, watching her condition steadily worsen until the doctor sat her down and told her the therapy wasn't working, and that her daughter's liver was failing, and started outlining all the possible things they might do to save her, and how long she might have left if they couldn't find a donor. But even as the doctor calmly outlined the unimaginable horror of possibly losing her only child Laughton remembered something else her father had said in their last conversation.

Sometimes the universe, so chaotic and cruel most of the time, provides exactly what you need at the exact time that you need it.

Every serving Metropolitan Police officer is automatically signed up to an organ donor scheme when they join up. Some officers opt out. Most don't.

Her father had not.

He had his fourth and final heart attack in the ICU the day Laughton was told Gracie needed a transplant and died having never regained consciousness, or been aware of the media storm that erupted when it was revealed that he had killed Kathryn Warren and Mark Murphy, and all the reasons why.

It was only a partial transplant in the end, a part of John Rees's tissue-matched liver grafted on to Gracie's so the healthy cells could stimulate the damaged ones and eventually grow into something new and whole.

And as she sat by her daughter's bedside and ignored all calls from the media for interviews about her vigilante father, who was increasingly being seen as a hero by many, she remembered an obscure fact she had learned once from a pathologist in an autopsy who was showing her the ravaged liver of a recently deceased alcoholic.

The liver is the only organ in the body that can regenerate itself, he had said, but *sometimes things get so damaged they forget how to heal.*

She thought about this often in the days and weeks of Gracie's recovery where her teenage superpowers seemed to take her in less than a month from death's door to complaining about the fact that she would never be able to wear a crop-top again because of her transplant scar. She thought of it too as they talked and talked, Laughton reminding herself that her job was to listen, not leap in to try and fix or control everything. And as this simple act of love seemed to slowly dissolve whatever darkness had calcified around Gracie and so nearly dragged her down, she thought that maybe the heart was another organ that could regenerate itself, and that in ways more powerful than just the physical it could also relearn the art of how to heal itself, even one that had been as badly damaged as hers.

And when Gracie was finally well enough to leave, Tannahill sneaked them out of a service entrance to avoid the waiting press and they went straight to the large apartment overlooking the Thames that her father had left to them both in his will, and together they went through each cupboard and drawer, and studied each object they found, carefully assembling then nurturing the memory of a man neither of them had ever really known, and slowly sinking new roots in their new life together that shared more than just a history with him.

Laughton stands now filling the kettle at the sink in her new kitchen, in her new life. Somewhere behind her Gracie is singing along to something, her headphones rendering her deaf and making her sound awful and wonderful at the same time.

Laughton reaches for her phone then realizes she left it charging by her bed and sets the kettle to boil anyway, staring out at the river for a moment, feeling peaceful, and safe. Then she takes the tin of fresh tea from a cupboard, a teaspoon from a drawer, and ladles leaves into the pot, thinking of nothing in particular as she does it.

One . . .

        . . . Two . . .

    . . .

Acknowledgements

There are always so many people to thank by the time I finish each new book that I would need another book just to do them all justice, but here goes.

For this one I owe a huge debt to Constable Peter Fairweather (ret) who I went to school with, was always much better at maths than me, and went on to have distinguished careers in both the Navy and the Cambridgeshire Police Force, the latter of which came in very useful when I needed to make my various officers of the law sound and behave like they knew what they were doing. In this regard I also want to thank Detective Sergeant Heather Rook, formerly of the Metropolitan Police, who also gently pointed out the bits I'd made up, particularly with regards to how they do things in London. Needless to say, any mistakes that remain are mine and mine alone.

For various medical matters I am also indebted to Jonathan Hyde, FRCS. MD. Consultant Cardiac Surgeon at the Royal Sussex County Hospital who gave me the kind of invaluable medical advice you should only ever need when writing a thriller. Every crime writer should be so lucky to have their own Doctor Hyde – even though he hasn't technically been a 'Dr' since 1993!

On the publishing side I am, as ever, encouraged, protected, supported (and sometimes told off) by the legends that are Julia Wisdom at HarperCollins, David Highfill at Morrow, Mark Lucas at the Soho Agency, and Alice Saunders – who has long ago become way more of a friend than an agent, but is still the best agent I could have ever hoped for.

As always I must thank my family – Kathryn, Roxy, Stan, and Betsy – for being awesome and funny and for all the love and support they give me, even though I don't really do a proper job, lie around the house all day, and chunter away to myself like a weirdo. Also I owe a lot to Woody and Stevie who stare at me from around 4 o'clock each day until I give in, grab their leads, and take them up onto the Sussex Downs to chase rabbits and foxes. Without them I'd probably never see the light of day and would be even more translucent than I already am.

For all the other hundreds of people who helped turn an idea into the thing you are currently reading, they know who they are, and now you do too because they are listed in a rollcall of honour at the end of this book. Thank you. For everything.

A huge and heartfelt thank you also goes out to all the booksellers, bloggers, librarians and champions of story everywhere who keep their own love of literature burning bright and spend their lives trying to kindle similar flames in others.

And finally, I want to thank you, dear reader. I've said it before and it still holds true – without you I'm just a crazy person, sitting alone in a room, muttering to himself all day long. Just ask my family if you don't believe me.

Simon Toyne
Brighton – Sept 2021

HarperCollins*Publishers*

HarperFiction would like to thank the following staff and contributors for their involvement in making this book a reality.

Editorial
Julia Wisdom
Angel Belsey
Kathryn Cheshire
Lizz Burrell

Sales
Harriet Williams
Alice Gomer

Audio
Fionnuala Barrett
Ciara Briggs

Design
Claire Ward

Production
Sophie Waeland

Operations
Melissa Okusanya
Hannah Stamp

Publicity
Maud Davies

Marketing
Olivia French

If you enjoyed *Dark Objects*, then don't miss out on
Laughton Rees and DI Tannahill Khan's next case in...

THE CLEARING

Coming 20th July 2023

1

Maddie!

Adele violently shakes out another black bin liner.

Where the hell was Maddie?!

She scans the campsite, looking for her sister through the bone-coloured bell tents and artfully rusted camper vans, staggering closer wearing last night's clothes and a blank expression. But all she sees are a few casualties from the Midsummer's Eve revelries lying on the ground where they'd passed out the night before, smoke from dying fires drifting across them like gun-smoke from a lost battle.

It's a mess, it was always going to be a mess, and it all needs cleaning up before eleven when the council refuse lorry arrives. That's why she'd asked her older and supposedly wiser sister to help this morning, why she'd allowed her to crash on her floor in exchange for a promise that she would help with the post Midsummer's Eve clear up. And yet here she very much was not.

Adele wrenches the lid off one of the bins, her long brown hair scraped back and already sticking to her skin with the rising heat of the day, her thin, wiry body nut brown from having to work outside all summer. She recoils at the stench that billows out along with a squadron of angry flies then violently twists the top of the bag into a knot, imagining it's Maddie's neck.

I'll be there – Maddie had said. *I won't stay out long but I promised to meet someone.*

Adele lifts the heavy, stinking bag out of the bin and dumps it on the ground ready to be picked up by the honey-wagon, an old, repurposed electric milk float Maddie should be driving but obviously isn't because she's not here. She fits a new liner into the bin and lets the lid fall with a loud bang.

Movement catches her eye in a dark pool of shadow beneath a sycamore tree as a man wearing a Cinderman costume of charcoal blackened sacking lifts his head, roused by the sound of the banging bin.

'Morning!' Adele calls to him, loud and bright.

He winces as if the word is made of sharp metal, then looks up, eyes screwed tight against the brightness, trying to remember how he ended up under this tree. He looks so wretched with bits of twig and leaves in the greasy tangle of his hair that Adele pulls the bottle of water from her belt and tosses it over.

'Drink!' she commands.

He reaches to pick it up, spots a puddle of puke on the grass nearby with flies lined up along the edge of it and turns away, blowing his cheeks out as if he's about to add to it. He unscrews the cap and takes a tiny sip of water before lying slowly back down on the ground, hugging the bottle to his chest.

Adele yanks another bin liner from her belt and marches past him, heading to the next overflowing bin that needs emptying, scanning the campsite for Maddie again as she works the phone from her pocket.

No missed calls.

No texts.

She taps the screen to unlock it but it won't respond to her fingers inside the rubber glove so she shakes her hand violently until the glove flies off, finds the last number she dialled and calls it again, her fingers leaving steamy fingerprints on the screen. She holds the phone to her ear and screws her nose up against the foul smell of rubber and rotting garbage coming from her hand.

Hey, leave me a message and I'll call you back.

Maddie's smiling, childish sounding voice cuts in without it ringing, which shows that her phone is still switched off.

Adele disconnects without leaving a message because she's left several already and scrolls through her contacts instead, looking for the names of people who might have been with Maddie last night, or might still be with her, or might at least know where she got to. She spots a contact for Ronan, one of Maddie's ex-boyfriends and taps the contact to call him. Again, voicemail cuts in without it even ringing, because of course, all of Maddie's loser friends will still be sleeping off their hangovers this morning.

'*Yo, this is me, do the thing after the thing.*'

Adele clenches her jaw, waits for the tone then forces her voice to be light.

Hey, this is Adele, Maddie's sister. If you're with her, could you get her to give me a call, please? Thanks. Tell her I'm not mad, I'm just checking in.

She *is* mad of course and getting madder with every stinking bag she has to deal with, but inflicting her mood on Maddie's friends isn't going to accomplish anything. She scrolls through her contacts looking for more friends, ex-boyfriends, possible current boyfriends, though Maddie stays pretty tight-lipped about her love life. She says Adele is too judgy, which is true because who wouldn't be judgy about the guys Maddie tends to go for? Laid back, amiable losers are still losers.

She calls a couple more numbers, leaves a couple more messages then snatches the glove back up off the ground, works her hand back into it and scans the campsite one last time.

'*Where the fuck are you Maddie?!*'

2

She wakes to dark beyond blackness and the heavy smell of earth.

She is on her back, arms by her sides, legs stretched out, staring straight up at – nothing. She studies the black, blinking slowly a few times to check that her eyes are actually open, but it looks the same either way.

She raises her hand in front of her face, moves it a little, touches her palm to her nose to prove it is there then reaches up slowly and carefully into the blackness, both wanting and not wanting to touch something. She stretches up until she can reach no further then moves her arm in a slow and widening circle, feeling the faint chill rinse of cold air across her skin but touching nothing but darkness.

She lets her arm fall back down to her side, feeling in her pocket for her phone so she might use its light to see with, but the pocket is empty.

She takes deep breaths, flooding her lungs with damp smelling air and tries to remember where she is. She remembers walking through the forest but then nothing. She was there and now she is here, wherever 'here' is.

She spreads her fingers and starts feeling around at her sides for her missing phone then widens her search, her palms skimming across the cold ground, reaching further and further until something brushes across the back of her right hand and she yanks it away. The sound of her gasp pushes back the dead silence and makes her realize that there are no other sounds here: no scratch of animals, no rustle of leaves, nothing.

She listens hard, studying the thundering quiet, listening out for the dry click of legs, or the patter of dislodged earth that might suggest that whatever her hand touched is alive and crawling closer.

She hears the thud of her own heartbeat and the whisper of blood in her ears but nothing more, so carefully, slowly, she reaches out again, feeling ahead with her fingers for whatever is there, tensing against the moment of its rediscovery.

She finds it again and freezes but forces herself to keep her hand where it is, stretched out in the dark with the unseen thing touching the back of it. She keeps as still as she can, ready to snatch it away at the first sign the thing is alive but whatever it is, it remains perfectly still.

She takes a deep breath then slowly turns her hand, trembling slightly with the effort of reaching out until her fingers close around something cold, and thin, and fibrous. She tests it, squeezing it lightly and rubbing it between her fingertips. There are small hairs growing out of it and she almost drops it in revulsion but then a thought surfaces and she takes a firmer hold instead and gives it a hard, sharp tug. She feels it tighten in her hand and dirt patters down from where the thing is anchored in the earth.

She feels her away further up and along it, her fingers mapping the twisting fibres growing steadily thicker the higher she goes. The hairs grow thicker too, branching out from the main tendril and tickling the back of her hand until the whole gnarly thing disappears abruptly into a wall of crumbling earth and she knows in an instant what it is, and where she is, and fear takes flight in her chest.

The thing she is holding in her hand is a root. A growing root. the root of something big.

She was walking through the forest and she's still there.

But she is no longer *in* the forest.

She is under it.